AUSTIN S. BELANGER

The Long Run to Redemption

First edition

Editing by Hillary Crawford
Cover art by Wandering Jayne Creatives
Cover art by Naiha Raza
Illustration by Naiha Raza

This book was professionally typeset on Reedsy.
Find out more at reedsy.com

I dedicate this one to my mom. I love you.

"You're under no obligation to be the same person you were 5 minutes ago."

— ALAN WATTS

Contents

Chapter 1

O cean spray misted over his weathered face as the salty brine woke the older man's senses. The elder warrior leaned back against the mast and watched a red sun slowly rise behind the thin gray line where it always seemed to hide. Canvas tarps hanging over open hatches flapped wildly in the strong breeze, and it seemed from every direction that random voices called out to others throughout the vessel. The bustle of working men adjusting sails, battening hatches, and tying off ropes, was heard in every corner. This was a common occurrence every morning since this voyage began.

Sipping tea, Orus quietly watched the morning dance. It had evolved into a well-choreographed production. Each crew member found purpose and learned their place, through many mistakes and trials over many miles of open water. Nearly a month had passed since they had last found land. The murmurs had begun. It seemed to Orus that murmurs never ceased, no matter the locale or situation.

The ship climbed over swells as the crew turned her into the waves. Something had caught a lookout's eye, and the duty pilot was directing the ship toward that anomaly. The King watched as the stern slowly bobbed up and down, one minute showing the gray horizon, and the next the clouded sky. His indifference was apparent. Orus looked up, noticing the peaceful morning sky had slowly changed from dull gray to a brighter shade of pink, and then to blazing red. Nothing good came from red skies, and Orus knew it well. Still, he and his men had weathered countless storms, and he knew that this one would be no different.

"Hodan is in the middle of a storm at any given moment," Orus said to no one in particular, sipping his lukewarm tea.

A random sailor answered his King. "I am sorry, Your Majesty, but did you say something?"

"No, nothing, son, carry on," Orus sighed.

"Yes, Your Majesty," the younger man replied, bowing. Then he ran to the ropes to assist another with the sails.

With the wind now picking up, the volume and frequency of the shouts on the main deck increased proportionally. More men joined in the morning workforce, leaning into their assigned tasks. Orus stared at the undulating horizon, mulling over his past and remembering the many sins and indiscretions that lay therein.

"It is the lot of old men to contemplate their legacy," Orus said into his mug. "I guess that I am no different, Runnir," he breathed deeply, muttering, "All that can be expected of me is that I concentrate on now and seek to do the will of the Gods, eh Gunnir?"

Laying his head back on the mast, he listened to the crashing waves. Finally, the King of Hodan closed his eyes, his mind wandering into the past.

* * *

"Puryn! They are not men! They are monsters! They are the same fiends who ripped the sons and daughters of Hodan and Yslandeth from the bosoms of their mothers!"

Orus was livid, and everyone in the capitol would know of his displeasure if he had his way.

"Brother, but these are not those people! They have turned from Haeldrun to the Goddess! You don't mean what you say. You cannot expect me to allow for the slaughter of innocents who live according to the same principles and beliefs that I do—that you do!"

Puryn pleaded with his friend. This meeting was the third one with Orus in the past three weeks. Each time, the conversation became more contentious. The King could sympathize with his Hodan brother. Still, the Yslan would not stand for killing Haya's followers, even if they were Galdruhn, who claimed to be the reformed Todessen claimed by Goddess Haya.

"So, you would reward these turncoats with safety and asylum? If they would turn on their people … If they would turn on their God … Do you not think you are just a convenient, safe space for these vermin? Do you not realize that when a better offer comes along, they will discard you for their own selfish interests?" Orus paced with his hands on his hips.

"I have to believe that the Goddess knows what she is doing. The outward change to their runes is a sign from Haya herself. Adasser confirms it, and she speaks to the Goddess almost daily. So she, if anyone, would know, brother."

Puryn was gesturing emphatically with his hands, trying to drive his point home to his obstinate, debating partner. Still, the younger King of Yslan could see that he was getting nowhere with the older Hodan King.

Orus scoffed, slamming a cup of mead onto a table near him. "The Goddess speaks to her? A god spoke through Kairoth! Haeldrun spoke through his High Priest. So, to whom should I listen? Adasser? Kairoth? Rest assured that I will certainly never listen to a Toad scum, even if he is a Priest."

Puryn sighed. "You don't mean that, brother. We have fought shoulder to shoulder for the Goddess. She knows your heart. I have no idea for whom Kairoth speaks. Think about what you ask me to do and search your heart. Do you feel as if it is an honorable and righteous deed?"

Orus was beside himself. "Was it righteous when they landed in Suden and then proceeded to kill so many that we loved, brother? Where were the Galdruhn then? There were none, because they were busy winning their war—until they were not! Then they conveniently converted to avoid execution! I am not buying their conversion or change of heart! They are as guilty as the scum in the underground Temples. They bear the sin of that entire invasion force. Here we stand, arguing their fate. There should be no discussion. They are murderers and savages. They should die for their past atrocities!"

Puryn looked off momentarily, recalling a tree line on another battlefield before the Great War. Shame and regret filled his throat. The Champion of Yslandeth recalled his own atrocities at the Battle of Torith. There, his Elfish Draj, aided by the Yslandeth Elites of Sir Ontak, slaughtered thousands of men and Dwarves, before the enemy eventually surrendered to the alliance. Their faces haunted the King of Yslandeth's dreams. He would see them on occasion, even when awake. He could not endorse the slaughter of hundreds of new faces, especially when they posed no real threat to his people or his kingdom. They simply pled for mercy, and Yslan would see it given.

Puryn took a chance. "Orus, what about Scribat Ternut Sangras? Were Hodan's attacks there, under Jabar, justified? Why should we not demand the extermination of Hodan for the crimes of their past?"

Puryn knew he was treading on dangerous ground.

"How dare you compare Jabar to the Offlanders. Jabar sought to rule the world, yes, but not to maim, kill, and destroy all that was in it. I saw to it that the mad dog was put down. I nearly lost my life in the process! Yet you, of all people, would equate the debauchery of what this dung has committed to a single battle in Hodan's glorious history?"

Puryn knew he had hit a nerve. Orus's face was flush. The Hodan King was now sweating and cursing under his breath as he stared at his brother-in-arms. Puryn was ashamed.

"Brother, I'm sorry. I didn't mean to equate ..."

"Save it," Orus interrupted, frowning with an oddly hurt expression. "I see what you think of my people. I see who we are in your eyes, Puryn. We are your rabid dog on a leash. We are here to do your bidding, and if we don't, then you pull the collar tight? Hodan will not be ruled. We will make our own way. I will find a way to restore the glory of my line!"

"Orus, wait," Puryn pleaded.

The Hodan King stood and turned to leave. Two Yslandeth regulars met him at the King's door.

"Puryn, if you value these two fools, you will tell them to step aside."

Orus glowered at the two men, who took a half-step backward, hands on their sword hilts.

The guards looked at their King expectantly, hoping to avoid the encounter.

Puryn waved his hand. "Let him pass."

Orus snarled. "Lucky for you, your King knows me very well." He lowered his eyes an entire six inches, coming face to face with the two in front of him. "Oh, and thank you for allowing me to leave, Your Majesty," Orus mocked. "Hodan will not be ruled, Yslandeth. We do not answer to you!"

* * *

Returning to the moment at hand, Orus scowled. His tea was now empty, and there was no porter in sight. Tying his tankard off to his belt with a leather lanyard, he breathed in deeply, leaning against the planks of the chamber room behind him. He could hear a few of his officers eating breakfast while discussing the collection of water and repairs that needed to happen soon.

The old Hodan King stood, his knees creaking a bit. He stretched and looked at the warship he now commanded. He spied his other ships to the port and starboard of his position. All of them were in perfect alignment. It was a beautiful formation, capable of untold destruction and death. Hodan sailed to find its glory.

Of the many events that had laid the foundation for this day, the one Orus hated the most was the sting of betrayal dealt by one he still looked at as his brother. His memories flooded back in a rush while surveying the threatening clouds off to the west on the horizon.

* * *

Orus returned to Hodan. The impasse with Puryn seemed insurmountable. The old King would not wait to see how that situation would develop. The people of Hodan were already murmuring about the Kingdom of Hodan's status. As always, the people complained. The crowd bemoaned the feeling that Hodan had become a vassal state to Yslandeth and that Orus was Puryn's servant, vice his equal. Orus could not argue the point. He felt the same was true, but that was about to change.

Faylea sat in her regal robes. She was not accustomed to wearing a dress and complained loudly to her father. Orus rolled his eyes and smiled. She would never change. She was older now, on the trailing edge of child-bearing age. The old King quietly lamented the end of his line as he looked at his beloved daughter. If only she had been given a chance to find her love, instead of living a life of war and sacrifice.

"Oh, stop fidgeting, girl," the older man said to his child.

"Easy for you to say, Da! You are not wearing this confounded under-dress and garters. They are incredibly uncomfortable. I cannot see why women continue to wear these things." Faylea sat with an unceremonious thump on her chair.

"Kairoth will return, My Lady," the King bantered. "He knows a good thing when he sees it. Half of him is of good Hodan stock. The other half we will forgive him for." Orus smiled.

"Da, I hope he returns, but it has been so long!" Faylea frowned, with her forehead wrinkled in a worried look. "I do not like your plans either."

"I have to do this, my daughter."

The King looked out the chamber window at the fields. The harvest was coming. Peace was won. Peace was not a time for Hodan.

"Why, Father? The people love you." Faylea stood and approached her father, putting her hand on his shoulder. "If Puryn does not see your worth, your people do."

"You know our people, Faylea," Orus responded somberly. "Love is not a thing we do well."

The King turned toward his daughter, abruptly kissing her on the forehead. She could see his eyes were red.

"I will go with you! I always go with you, Da! It will be just like old times!" the Princess smiled, trying to console her father.

"No, my dearest, not this time." Orus held her hands.

"I don't know how to do this, Father," Faylea pleaded.

"You will figure it out. You always do. You are smart, strong, and you love your kingdom." Orus looked into her eyes.

Faylea frowned. Her eyes teared up. She could not keep the warrior façade up.

"I see your mother in your eyes. She stares back at me. I will honor her memory, and I will honor Hodan." Orus straightened his posture, and with that, his resolve returned. His face turned to stone, except for a tiny crack in his own façade as he looked at the tears rolling down the cheeks of the Princess.

"Please don't go, Da."

"I must. To honor Hodan, but more importantly, to protect you."

Orus looked around the room. He gathered a few things. He carried a satchel, some rations, and his weapons. Then, turning from her face, he set off to his room to put on his armor.

"Please be careful in Sudenyag, Father," Faylea sniffled. "You know that many still hold grudges there, even if we did save their skins on so many occasions. Ungrateful, Toads."

"There she is! I knew she was still there! Even with a silky dress on, the warrior Princess still survives!" Orus laughed. "Famlin is there. Harun is there. They assure me of my safety, and no one in Suden dares to challenge those two."

"If you say so," Faylea smirked.

"I must go. I must see about all this talk of the new ships. I hear the Dwarves equipped some with the Thunder Ballista that Palgur used at the citadel. It would be an excellent development if I were able to get my hands on a few of those."

Orus smiled like a champion of old. Faylea looked at the weathered face of the warrior before her. She knew he could not live forever. She knew that he thought of that fact every day. This plan was not only about Hodan and about her safety. It was about his legacy. The legacy of Orus, the Lion. She knew it had to be.

Orus would not be second to anyone, not even the Champion of the Golden Queen.

"I love you, Da," Faylea mumbled as Orus exited the chamber door.

* * *

The voice of a lookout cried out from a crow's nest above, waking Orus from his daydream. "Smoke on the horizon!"

Orus perked up for the moment. Something was on fire. That was different and had piqued the old warrior's interest. The King stood and made his way to the ship's bow, which was now pointed directly at a small, dark, jagged line that rose on the edge of their visibility.

"What is it?" Orus bellowed up to the man in the crow's nest.

"No telling at this time, Your Majesty. I only know that something burns, and birds have begun to fly overhead. Land is close. Someone is fighting. I would wager on that!" The younger man emphasized the last statement with a bit of excitement.

"Damn, whelps," Orus mumbled quietly. "Be careful what you wish for."

The smoke appeared more evident as the ships traveled closer. The lookout was correct. Something was on fire.

"You, there! Keep me abreast of what is happening out there. Send a messenger when we know more! I will be in my chambers, putting on my armor!" Orus bellowed loudly to the crow's nest. "All warriors not manning the lines … to arms!"

A loud shout of affirmation was heard.

"Signalman! Sound the horns and signal the fleet that we approach something unknown. Call the all-ready!" Orus pointed at the man at which he shouted.

The younger man bowed and began blowing a large signal horn. Soon, four ships were returning the signal. "Orders received." The ships adjusted to battle positions.

Orus looked at the weaponry around him. He marveled for a moment at the sheer number of men aboard the large warship he commanded. He remembered days of riding his horse with the legions on the ground, marching into battle in large squares. Ironically, Sudenyag, the weakest nation of the Ert, provided Orus the means to sail around the world. Harun and the Suden had made the already feared Hodan legions exponentially more powerful.

* * *

The Hodan King and his porter arrived in Sudenyag within a few days. Orus had taken it slow. He had no reason to rush. The Ert was peaceful everywhere he went. There was no need for a warrior now. Constables and sheriffs appointed by the baronies handled disputes, and the rule of law had finally begun to take hold. The old warrior felt like a relic of a bygone era, but this only steeled his resolve. As he neared the Port of Valent, his determination was renewed. Even in Sudenyag, the roads were safe, well, as safe as they had ever been.

"Your Majesty, would you like to stop for a meal?" the porter asked politely.

"No, Kepir, I am fine. We should get to the meeting." Orus looked at his man.

Kepir nodded and smiled, handing his King a wineskin full of mead. "At least take this, My King."

Orus took the skin and took a long drink, nodding. Then, he handed the skin back to his trusted man.

"Just around that bend and down the road a mile or two. I can smell the sea already. I am not sure if I like the smell of Sudenyag," Orus remarked.

Kepir laughed.

* * *

A messenger ran to Orus's chambers, his shoes clopping loudly on the wooden deck. The sound disturbed the ruler's reminiscence. Orus heard him coming and shook his head with a sigh.

"Here we go again, Runnir. May you and your brother be by my side today if we are to do battle." Orus sheathed his sword after checking the blade.

There was loud knocking. "Your Majesty, I have word."

"Enter!" Orus bellowed.

A young man entered with a scroll. "For His Majesty."

"Thank you, son. Well, spit it out. What is going on, now?" the King asked impatiently.

"Our man reports that he sees eight to ten ships engaging a coastal fortress or city." The young man looked at his King with excitement.

Orus rolled his eyes. The lad looked as if he was ready to open his gift at Winterfest.

"Go on, what else?" Orus deadpanned, ignoring the glee of his duty watchman.

"The lookout says they are ships with a red standard. Our man cannot tell if they fly an eagle or hawk on the field. They do not appear to be Todessen, but we cannot tell who they are at this point." The younger man bowed with the end of his report.

"Excellent news," Orus droned. "Sound the alert and make sure that our men are ready. Also, tell the gunners to ready the Thunder Ballista, just in case."

"Yes, Your Majesty."

The sound of boots on wood subsided as the young man bellowed out an echo of his King's commands.

"Oh, eternal brothers, hear my prayer. Give us strength and luck in battle. May we be on the right side of this fight." Orus raised his head from his prayer, slid on his helmet, and strapped the chin strap tight.

10

The King's polished, blackened armor reflected the rays of reddened sunlight as he stepped out onto the deck. The white lion on Orus's breastplate shown red from the sun in the sky above. It seemed to the King that the warring brothers were shouting for the blood of those who would stand in opposition to their champion.

As Orus waited for more information. He watched as his men efficiently executed their duties. Smiling, he remembered times, in the not-so-distant past, when this scene would have resembled a carnival fool's show, but now that seemed so long ago.

* * *

Harun greeted Orus warmly. The two Kings bantered and poked at each other as old friends do. Orus slept in the newly constructed palace of King Harun. It was little more than a nice building, refurbished to be a respectable dwelling place for a leader. Orus was not complaining. It was clean, the food and drink were excellent, and the ladies were fair.

"Orus, these ships are incredible. We have figured out how to maneuver the beasts and have a fairly good grasp of how the sails work together. The Dwarves even managed to sink a derelict in the harbor with the smaller version of the Thunder Ballista that they have created!" Harun was proud of their accomplishments.

"That is excellent news. How soon before you can teach a core of my men how to use these vessels?" Orus got straight to the point.

Harun was a bit nervous, but maintained a visage of confidence. "We could begin as soon as they arrive!" Harun smiled, clapping his hands, and asking for more wine and mead. "But what do you need ships for? Hodan is landlocked!"

Harun chuckled at his joke, but Orus was deadly silent. The Suden King read Orus's demeanor, and he felt an aura of defeat and sadness emanating from his confident guest.

"Harun, I plan to leave this place," Orus said plainly.

"Leave what place, Orus? The Ert?" Harun questioned.

"Yes, I will be plain with you, old friend." Orus took another swig from his mug. It was immediately topped off by a steward. "I plan to sail off and find the Todessen. There must be more of those scum. I will cut them all down, one by one."

Harun wore a concerned look. "Are you sure this is the way? What does Puryn have to say about this?"

Orus smiled sarcastically. "I don't know. You should ask him. I only speak for myself. I will not suffer the enemy to live within my borders, nor will I allow them to regroup for another attack. I will find them and kill them all."

Harun stated plainly, "We only have ten ships repaired or built by our own hands."

Orus smiled. "That is perfect. I only desire five. I will pay handsomely for them."

Harun responded, "Let me ponder this offer, my friend. First, we must make sure that they are ready to venture off into the unknown! They will need full storerooms and many kegs for water storage. I need to talk to my people. If we send you off, we must give you the best chance to survive."

Orus knew Harun was stalling, but he also knew he could not force him to give up his ships without starting a war. He decided to let things play out.

"As you say, Harun. Please, take the time to ensure our safety. It is appreciated. I will retire for the evening, then return to Hodan to ensure that I arrange for payment, should you agree to reasonable terms." Orus and Harun stood, shook hands, and then Orus took his leave.

"Come, Kepir, we shall turn in for the night," Orus called to his servant.

"As you wish, Your Majesty," the man replied, moving very close to the King as they walked. "They plot against you, My King. I heard whispering about the worry of what Yslandeth will say. Therefore, I fear that they may not comply with your wishes."

"Thank you, Kepir," Orus replied. "But if Puryn wants me out of the way, he will agree to this offer. It is a perfect solution."

As they arrived at the chamber, Kepir opened the door, checking the security of the room. When he was satisfied that the area was secure, he called his King into the accommodations. After preparing the evening amenities, the porter went off to the tavern to perform his second job—surveillance.

* * *

As time passed, the small Hodan armada of five vessels made its way to within clear view of the battle before them. Orus looked through his spyglass at the conflict, returning to the moment at hand. The warrior tried to gather as much information as possible to determine who they should aid or attack. He then weighed his options, deciding whether to engage either side, or sail on and avoid the confrontation altogether. The King knew that avoidance was a fool's choice. His men were armor-clad and ready to fight. It had been a long time coming. Over the past eighteen months at sea, the Hodan force had found many small islands, befriending most of their inhabitants. There, they resupplied and continued in their mission to find the true enemy of the Light. The Todessen were out there somewhere, and Orus was determined to find them. At this point, Orus knew he owed his men something for their vigilant endurance and loyalty. They had lived through so much hardship and sacrifice, and yet, no Offlanders were dead to show for it all.

The King looked closely through his glass. "Are those Elves on those ships?"

"It appears so, Your Majesty," a Lieutenant responded while standing at attention.

"First Elves we've seen off of the Ert, and they're attacking people from the sea. The world is a strange place, Farhman."

The Lieutenant nodded. "Your orders, Sir?"

13

"Can we see who they are bombarding? And what are they using to cause that fire?" Orus questioned.

"From what Captain Kren reports," the Lieutenant's face twisted in a bit of disgust, "when he maneuvered out of formation and crossed closer to the battle, his men reported seeing the Elves battling what appears to be a Dwarfish sea town. Our ships were fired upon by the Elves, but thankfully, they were out of range."

Orus grunted with annoyance. "I will speak to Kren later. We shall assume the Elves to be hostile, if they fired upon us. Move our ships into a defensive posture and see what these Elves do. If they appear to be shifting their attack to our vessels, kill them all. Employ the Thunder Ballista, if necessary."

The Lieutenant growled. "Aye, Your Majesty."

"Oh, and Lieutenant, if the Elves want to talk, let's try that first." Orus raised an eyebrow.

"As you wish, My King."

Orus pursed his lips, looking around at his five ships, reckoning it to be the best money ever spent by the Kingdom of Hodan. Then, smiling, he remembered how easily he procured them.

* * *

Kepir adeptly collected his information. On the journey home to Hodan, the spy related the plans and concerns of Suden to his King. It seemed to him that Sudenyag also did not want to anger the King of Yslandeth. The night that Kepir warned his King about Suden's reluctance, the spy had learned that a rider was dispatched to Empyr to seek permission or guidance on dealing with the offer to sell Hodan ships. A Hodan with warships was a terrifying notion to Sudenyag. Still, they knew that a war might erupt if they did not comply with a trade request of this magnitude. Both kingdoms were allied, after all.

Kepir contacted the guild in Sudenyag. There, the specialist contracted with a trusted ally within the southern kingdom. A message arrived at Warrior's Crossing from the Port of Valent within the week. It was the tale that Kepir knew his King would want to hear.

Kepir knocked. The spy waited to be called in.

"Who is it?" Orus bellowed.

"It is I, Sire," the spy responded.

"Oh, enter! What do you have for me?" Orus said greedily.

"Your Majesty, my sources tell me that Sudenyag asked Yslandeth for permission to sell Hodan the ships. The King of Yslandeth, as you predicted, agreed, stating that the '*Hodan warring in other climes and places is better than Hodan fighting the kingdoms of the Ert.*'" The spy paused for a response.

Orus was relieved, but hurt behind the mask of confidence and resolve.

"So, how much will they take?" Orus asked plainly.

"From what I read, five tons of gold would probably seal the transaction, My King."

"We have plenty of gold. Five tons is a pittance. Are you sure?" Orus thought for a second. "Oh, of course it is. Puryn wants me gone so badly that he would almost give me the ships on which to sail away on."

The King frowned.

"I suppose you may be correct, Sire," the spy responded, frowning at the statement.

"So be it, my trusted man. I want to leave, and my brother provides the means of my departure. Why the long face!?" Orus smiled sarcastically.

"The kingdom will miss your wise rule, My King. So many love you here." Kepir was genuinely saddened.

"They will forget with time. All Hodan Kings fade away into obscurity, except the ones who bring the kingdom glory." Orus waved him off.

"I have one thing to ask of you, My King, if I may?" Kepir begged.

"What is your request, friend?" Orus smiled.

"May I depart with you?"

"I would have it no other way, Kepir." Orus hugged his specialist, who returned the embrace. "Now, let's go buy our ride into the lore of our people."

* * *

Orus was annoyed. His attention turned to the racket of several officers complaining loudly in the command office. The past faded from the King's attention, as he looked with irritation at the scene unfolding before him.

"What is Kren doing now?" the King scowled. "Follow that fool, but not too closely."

Orus looked in horror as the Hodan Ship *Annihilator* pulled out of his left flank and started to outpace the advance of the armada. The other four responded to the horn signals to follow suit. They locked into a line and approached the smaller and less equipped Elfish vessels, which had stopped bombarding the shoreline to assess who was coming up behind them.

The ship to the left of the Elfish formation fired first, hitting the *Annihilator*'s starboard side, setting it ablaze.

"Curse that fool. If he survives, I will give him ten lashes personally!" Orus shouted.

"Prepare boarding parties! Prepared the Ballista! Stand ready!" Farhman ordered.

Horns sounded, and bells rang. Suddenly, there was an earsplitting explosion as Kren returned fire. The five smaller Thunder Ballistae boomed their report, broadsiding the Elfish ship at close range. The smoldering Hodan ship continued moving laterally away from the rest of the Elfish vessels. The enemy was now turning to meet Kren's attack.

"Looks like they have that fire somewhat under control, Sire," Farhman said with relief. "And that fool gave twice as good as he got."

Orus stifled a smile. "That idiot is good for something."

Farhman laughed loudly. "Look, the Elfish ship is listing. She is sinking. They are abandoning ship."

"There are more of them than there are of us, Farhman, and that idiot

Kren has the *Annihilator* on fire," Orus scolded. "Form us up, three ships broadside on theirs. Blow two more out of the water and see if they run."

Orus pondered how long it had been since he had taken to the sea. In all that time, they had never been in a sea battle. Today was a first. As they readied to fully engage, the King remembered their day of departure from Sudenyag.

* * *

When Hodan finally set sail for places unknown, Faylea, Puryn, Adasser, Basric, and Harun stood by to see him off. The Hodan, dressed in full battle attire, smartly marched five legions of their Elites into the Port of Valent. After a couple of weeks of offshore training, they were as ready as anyone felt Hodan's new navy could be.

Orus went as far as hiring teams of Dwarfish engineers to maintain the ship's guns and manufacture more Thunder powder and projectiles as materials became available. Unfortunately, it was not easy to find his engineers, because Dwarves are none too fond of the water. Still, Hodan found those willing to adventure with them, and after the ships were filled with stores and armament, Orus looked out over the Ert one last time.

Faylea displayed no weakness as she wore the crown of Hodan on her head. "I love you, Father. May you find what you seek. May we meet again in Aeternum, when our purpose is done here on the Ert."

Puryn and Adasser awkwardly hugged Orus, who reciprocated, but the damage was irreparable to their alliance, and both Kings knew that there was no way forward from their differing viewpoints.

"Live long, Puryn, Adasser, Harun, and Basric. May we meet again here, or at the feast in Aeternum. May your days be happy and secure. I will go forth to find my victory. I will find the Todessen. They will pay for their treachery. What I do, secures all that I love here. I only hope that the Gods see fit to honor my sacrifice and forgive my past indiscretions." Orus looked at Puryn, who nodded.

"Be blessed, my brother. May the Gods protect you always." Puryn bowed.

Orus nodded and then turned. "Load up! Captains, on me! We leave within the hour!"

* * *

Orus snapped his head to his starboard side, waking to the present danger. The Elves had set another Hodan ship on fire, to Orus's displeasure. This time the ship, the *Retribution*, was caught by a catapult shot full of some sort of oil that lit the ship ablaze upon impact. The Hodan crew worked furiously to contain the blaze as their ship came about broadside of their enemy, responding as Kren had done earlier.

An earsplitting explosion and the smell of Thunder powder filled the air. Orus smiled as he watched the main mast of the Elfish ship splinter and fall over into the sea. The Elfish ship began to take on water and tipped, listing to its starboard side. Elves were manning small lifeboats, but the Hodan were shooting them with crossbows from the ship's railing, as a Hodan fire party quickly contained the *Retribution*'s flames with seawater.

"These Elfish ships are not built for the impact of a Thunder Ballista," Orus smiled.

"Apparently not, Your Majesty," Lieutenant Farhman chuckled.

As they enjoyed the scene evolving before them, another volley reported from the port side of the ship. The Hodan warship, *Wrath*, had just opened its gun ports and crippled a third Elfish naval vessel. There were immediate horns from the Elfish side as their boats regrouped and began to flee southward, away from both the seaport they were attacking and Hodan's naval forces.

"Sound the 'stand-down' call. I do not want that idiot, Kren, pursuing those Elves. There will be another day for that."

"As you wish, Sire," Farhman barked as he called for the signal to regroup.

"Not a bad day on the battlefield, Lieutenant. Hodan did well. I expect casualty and damage reports as soon as possible. I will be in my chambers. The legions remain on alert until further notice." Orus nodded and turned to find some mead.

Kepir appeared from nowhere with a wine skin, handing it to his King. Orus smiled and patted his friend on the back, passing it to Farhman, and then ordered him to drink.

"As you command, Sire," the Lieutenant barked as Orus walked away.

Farhman carried out his King's commands.

Chapter 2

Admiral Dein of the Vynwrathian Navy watched helplessly from a distance through his spyglass.

"Report!" the Commander bellowed to the Elves around him.

A well-armored sailor ran to his commanding officer, bowing. "Sir, they appear to be Todani ships, but it makes no sense! Why do they attack us, and with what did they attack?"

"I asked you for the report, Lieutenant, and you come to me with the questions?" The Commander shifted his weight nervously with his hands on his hips. "Go find out who they are and what THAT is! Now!"

"Yes, Sir!" the sailor responded, running off to his signalman.

The Vyn were concerned, and the Elfish Commander worried about the morale of his crew. A black ship, remarkably similar to the ones piloted by the Todessen to the north, had just engaged one of his vessels. All that was known about the vessel was that it spewed fire, and then there was a thunderous explosion. Then all present watched as their comrades sank into the sea. It was a short engagement.

The Lieutenant returned. "Sir, I have ordered two of our warships to venture closer to their lines and attempt to communicate with the Todessen. Perhaps they do not realize that we are on their side?"

"Lieutenant, we all knew that this truce only created a shaky alliance designed for us to borrow time. Perhaps today is the day the Todani decide that they no longer need our assistance with the Dwarves."

The Commander scowled. As he did, there were two more loud claps of rolling thunder. Snapping up his spyglass, the Admiral looked over the horizon with an immediate expression of horror. One of his ships had foolishly fired a firepot at the Todani vessel before it. The Todessen replied with the same weaponry, this time sinking both ships. The Elf watched as one mast fell over into the sea. He could see blurry armored individuals on the black ships manning their railings. Then he realized that the Todani were killing his sailors as they swam in the sea.

"They are as ruthless as ever. It must be the Todessen, Valen. Sound the retreat! We must return to our homeland and warn Her Majesty in Vynwratha. The Todessen are our enemies again! They no doubt intend to finish the job they started on the Rynn all those years ago." Dein looked at his man. "They will seek to take Vynwratha as a southern base if we let them. That must not happen. We have already lost too much."

"My Lord, why does the Goddess hate our people? First, the Dwarves take our lands for those abominations, and now the Todessen seek to steal what little we have carved out for ourselves?" Valen looked down at his boots. "We will not let them take our homes again. Not while an Elf still breathes in that forest."

"Agreed, son. Sound the horns! We retreat to regroup and fight another day. If they wish to fight in our lands, we will show them how." Dein turned to signal for the retreat to be sounded.

The horns blew. The Elfish ships disengaged from the tall black ships on the horizon. Dein wondered how many more the Todessen possessed, and how many were equipped with the new weapon. He watched with apprehension as his smaller, faster ships quickly pulled away from the more massive black vessels. Still, his fears were for naught, as oddly, the Todessen held fast their position and allowed their enemy passage to the south.

As he spied through the glass, Dein was confused. "What are they doing?"

* * *

Orus looked through his glass. The enemy ships continued to run, sailing southward. From his porthole, he saw it. A runner reported that all fires on the Hodan ships were extinguished, and that the vessels in question had minimal damage. Orus had lost close to fifty men in the exchange with the Elves, most to fire and arrows, and a few who fell later to various injuries. His Generals conservatively estimated the enemy dead as ten times that.

"Farhman, make sure to bury the dead at sea. There are to be no pyres on the ships. Make sure to reiterate that fact to that idiot, Kren. If anyone tries it, it will be that one." Orus scowled and stood up from his stool.

"As you wish, Your Majesty." Farhman nodded. "One more thing, Sire."

"What is it, man?" Orus responded, buckling his boots.

"We have fished five of them out of the sea. The Elves are our prisoners below deck in the brig." Farhman looked at his King with interest, awaiting his reply.

"Let me guess. Kren?" Orus sighed.

"Yes, Sire, but this may be a good thing. We need intelligence on who and what is going on here. Who better to tell us than the enemy?" Farhman smiled broadly.

"Well, we just killed five hundred of their comrades. So I do not think that they will be accommodating." Orus chuckled.

"They're Elves, Sire. They will break. They always do. Elves are weak." Farhman smirked.

"You have never met a Draj, have you, son?" Orus chuckled again. "They can be the most stubborn horse's asses that you will ever meet. Do not be so sure of how easily they will comply with your demands. Housewives and children … those you can scare, but a Draj—or something like one—that is not a proposition I take lightly. They will kill you if you give them a chance. You had better beware of that fact, or you will pay the ultimate price. Elves are not to be taken lightly. Ask Sudenyag. Ask the Dwarves. Ask Jabir."

"Yes, Sire, but that was in the Age of Puryn. They don't have him on their side here." Farhman's eyes widened at the slip.

"Relax, son. His name is not taboo. He was and is a great warrior and leader. He saved so many," Orus admitted.

"So did you, Sire!" Farhman replied emphatically. "You were there also.

You saw the end coming and did not run. I have not forgotten, nor have the other five thousand here with you."

"Be that as it may, my boy, who is to say that there is not an Elfish 'Puryn' here to save them? Would that not be real irony!? We must send in a landing party to assess the situation on the ground. Send Kren and his boys, since they are so eager to stir the nest!" Orus laughed loudly.

"True, Sire. Puryn should have been an Elf." Farhman bowed to his King. Then, turning to the Duty Officer, the Lieutenant ordered, "Send word to Captain Kren that he is to land north of the Dwarfish settlement and ascertain the situation on land. Tell him he is on a reconnaissance mission, and not to raze and plunder!"

Orus nodded, remembering how Kren could be.

"Come, Sire, let us go speak to our captives. Maybe they will talk, maybe not. We shall see." Farhman offered with a devious smirk.

"Let us try to 'talk' then." Orus put his hand on the Lieutenant's shoulder, remembering how Farhman could be.

They walked to the ladder well to go down to the brig.

* * *

In a cage, a senior captive spoke to his fellow prisoners in a dialect of Elfish of which no Hodan was familiar. He called them all around, and they huddled together in the center of the large cell secured with riveted, banded steel bars.

"All right, brothers, these people have us captive. We are Vyn. We will not talk. Understood?" The Elf looked up and scowled at his Hodan guard. The Hodan showed no visible response.

"But, Lai, they are not Todessen. Who in the Underworld are these scum?" A younger Elf responded angrily.

"I don't know. I have no idea who these invaders are, or from where they come. I only know that they went to war with Vynwratha the moment they sank one of our ships." The leader was angry, but admittedly worried. He looked at his men with great concern.

"They are humans. Humans are weak. Don't let them play games with you. Pain is temporary. Honor is eternal, my brothers." The leader stuck his hand out into the center of the huddle. His gesture met with four half-hearted hands over his.

"I never liked Todessen. The Dwarves were bastards for their betrayal, but the Todani are our masters, not our allies." The younger man made a point.

"They are our ally until our Queen deems them to be something else," the leader stated plainly.

All five nodded as the door to the brig was unlocked from the outside, and several well-dressed human men entered the room.

"One of them is their leader. Be strong, brothers," Lai ordered.

Orus entered with his entourage. Several officers flanked his left and right. All of them were dressed in their armor, having just finished routing the forces that fled southward. The five captives looked at them stoically from within the cage. Orus looked at Farhman.

"Weak, eh? They don't look afraid or amused in any way." Orus turned to his guards. "Pull one out. The one they are surrounding. I will bet he is the senior man."

"Sir, if you need the senior man, I am he." Lai stepped in front of his men confidently.

"Guard, bring that Elf to me," Orus commanded.

"Yes, Sire," the guard replied, complying with the King's order.

The heavy door was unlocked and creaked loudly as the guard opened it. The Elves stood at the ready as the Hodan entered the cage. The encounter ended peacefully as the Elf left quietly. The only confrontation was a stare-down between four Elves and four Hodan guards. The guards locked the door securely behind them, leading the prisoner to their King.

"Sit, Sir," Orus commanded, gesturing to a padded velvet chair.

The Elf sat. "I will not betray my people. You should just throw me overboard now." Lai leaned forward, menacingly at Orus.

Orus did not flinch, replying stoically, "Who are your people, so I may know what to call my adversary?"

"We are warriors from the Kingdom of Vynwratha." Lai squinted angrily. "We are at war with the Dwarves you protect. How do you sail Todani ships, if you are not allied with the Todessen?"

"Is this my interrogation or yours, son?" The older Hodan King chuckled.

"Your ships are their ships. Whatever you used against my comrades is a new weapon from the mind of Haeldrun himself!" Lai's eyes betrayed him. He was worried about his future, and Orus could tell.

"It was not Haeldrun, but our engineers who created these weapons. We are not Todessen. We are quite human, Elf," Orus responded.

"Where do you hail from, outsider? Are you scouts for a new Scourge, come to steal our homeland from us once again?" Lai was frowning with a look of defeat on his face. However, Orus was intrigued by his statement.

"We do not seek to steal anyone's home from under them. We only seek to kill Todessen wherever they may be." The King's face went blank. There was a hatred there that Lai could almost feel radiating from this man's eyes.

"You are not Todessen?! We must warn my brothers who flee south! They will think you are, just as we assumed. Your ships—they are Todani! The Admiral will undoubtedly report that the Todani are at war with us again, and the Queen may attack them without real provocation!" Lai closed his eyes, knowing that he had said too much.

"So, there are 'Todani' here on this continent? Excellent news." Orus's eyes blackened, as if the light around them dimmed. "I will see every one of them dead."

The Elf laughed at Orus's statement, receiving a backhand from the guard to his right. The gauntlet opened a small gash on the prisoner's ear. It bled freely. After the initial shock of being hit without warning, the stoic face returned to the Elfish warrior.

Lai looked at the Hodan guard with disgust. The Hodan guard dared him to disrespect the King again.

"What I was trying to say is that there are many Todani in the north! How will you defeat their horde with only five ships? I estimate four or five thousand men against a million in the north?"

Lai looked at Orus, as if he should know this information.

"As I said, Elf, we are not from this place. We have no idea what we are walking into. If your forces had not so rudely tried to sink my ships, perhaps we could have sat at a table somewhere and spoke civilly. But now, we are at war until further notice. Millions, you say?" Orus looked to the skies as if asking why.

"Well, you wanted Todessen, Your Majesty. I think that you have found the mother lode." Farhman raised his eyebrows, smirking.

"You shut it," Orus replied to Farhman. Then, turning to the prisoner, the King replied, "Tell me what the lay of the land is here, and perhaps our kingdoms will find a way to a truce, sooner than later."

Lai thought for a moment. Then, the Hodan guard nudged the Elf with a baton, urging him to reply to the King's question.

"I will tell you how things stand on the Rynn, but you must warn my people not to retaliate against the Todani. They will lick their wounds and regroup in Vynwratha, awaiting the Scourge to come to them. That is what we always do. It is our best strategy. Fighting them in our forests always works in our favor." Lai smiled for the first time since the conversation began.

Orus could tell he had pride in his men and his kingdom. The Hodan King smiled at the Elf's expression.

"Tell us. We do not have to be enemies. Perhaps, we started on the wrong foot." Orus extended his hand.

The Elf shook hands, much like the Draj on the Ert. Orus closed his eyes for a moment and thought of Puryn. Then, waking from his momentary daydream, he focused on the Elf before him.

"My name is Lai, Sergeant in Her Majesties Marauders, 1st Battalion. These are my men. We were thrown from the deck of our ship when your weapons disabled her. I swam to my men, and we regrouped. Your men shot our defenseless warriors in the water. In a way, it was merciful, as many were dragged down by their armor and drowned. We only survived, because we are scouts and wore only leather and gambesons." Lai looked weary as he thought of the dead.

"Go on, Sergeant," Orus prodded gently.

"Our nation of Vynwratha was not always our home. We lived in the southwestern shoreland now owned by the Galda Risi, after the Dwarves gave our decimated homeland to them." The Elf became visibly angry.

"Go on. We need to know what's going on, before we can determine who to ally with," Orus said as a matter of fact.

Lai nodded. "The Todessen came about one-hundred years ago, invading from the northeast. They engaged Degran-Eras, the home of the human settlements. But, unfortunately, due to infighting, a lack of preparedness, and overwhelming numbers, the humans were almost driven to extinction by the Dark army."

Orus had a look of understanding on his face. Lai looked at him curiously. He wondered about this man. *What experience with the Todani did he have?*

"Scribes, are you writing this down?" Orus asked seriously.

"We are, Your Majesty," one replied. "Humans were almost driven to extinction."

Lai nodded, and continued. "The Todani pushed around the eastern border to the southern sea, capturing all of the human lands and enslaving the survivors. On the western coast of the Rynn, the Todessen were slowed by the mountains and forests to the north of Dornat Al Fer, the Kingdom of the Dwarves. The invaders pushed south to the southwestern-most point, exterminating my people in the forests and plains. We were decimated, but returned the gesture ten times over as we killed thousands before our survivors were forced to board our remaining ships, crossing the sea southward where we found a large island. There, we rebuilt our kingdom, naming it Vynwratha in Elfish, or 'blood wrath' in the human tongue."

Orus replied, "The Toads didn't follow you to your new home and kill you there?"

Lai responded, "We are pretty stealthy, and we hid in the thick forests. After a prolonged covert war run by our rebels and dissidents, they pulled out and returned to the main continent. The Dwarves, as much as we hate them, are a formidable force. The forces of Dornat Al Fer arrived late to the war."

"Of course they did. They're Dwarves. They arrived late when it was our turn also." Orus muttered under his breath. "Please, continue."

"After a prolonged war that lasted almost ten years, the Dwarves successfully liberated everything south of Haeldrun Ir, the Todani Kingdom on the northwestern corner of our continent." Lai stopped and waited for questions.

"So, if the Dwarves decimated the armies that killed your people, why do your people hate them so?" Orus shook his head in disbelief.

"It's not that their prowess was not appreciated in liberating our lands. It's what they did with them after the liberation." Lai's mood shifted to disgust. "The Dwarves owned the Rynn south of the border with the Todani. They gave the lands on the southeastern coastline of the Rynn back to the timid human survivors. They allowed the Orcs and Goblins to keep a small kingdom they established, located slightly south and west of the human territories within the marshlands. They call it Ynus-Grag. The Dwarves only did this as a condition of peace with the invader Orc King."

"So, the Orcs and Goblins are your objections?" Orus asked.

"No, the final atrocity of the Dwarves is what they did with our beloved forests." Lai frowned and swallowed hard. "They reallocated our lands. They kept them and did what they pleased, reasoning that Elves no longer needed them, having established the lands of Vynwratha. Then Dornat Al Fer gave our ancestral lands to them."

"Who?" Orus asked with great concern. "Who inhabits your land?"

"You attacked us as we assaulted the port that leads into our ancestral lands, Sir. You helped our enemies keep us from our rightful place on the mainland." Lai collected his emotions, swallowing hard. "King Hamrik, of Dornat Al Fer, gave our lands to the Galdrissen."

Orus wrinkled his brow inquisitively. "Who are the Galdrissen?"

"The so-called redeemed," Lai spat. "About thirty or so years ago, the Todani ships left with many of their warriors—Todessen, Orc, and Goblin. They sailed westward, as if they were bored and looking for something else to kill. When they left, some ran south, claiming to have turned to the

Goddess, showing their runes as proof of conversion. Naturally, the Elves did not accept them. The Todani are such liars! Who can believe their lies anymore?"

Orus closed his eyes and inhaled deeply, then responded, "Are you telling me that the Dwarves pushed the Todessen back, then made a truce with them, allowing them to regroup and leave, thirty or so years ago?"

"Yes, Sir. That is what I'm telling you." Lai was like a stone as he watched the Hodan King's snarling face.

"Are you also telling me that the Dwarves gave your lands to the Galdruhn?" Orus corrected his statement, looking at a scribe's notes. "The Galdrissen, as you called them? Toads who turned to the Goddess and received gold runes to prove their new innocence?"

"Yes, My Lord. Have you met the Galdrissen elsewhere?" Lai's eyes widened as he sat upright.

"Where do you think those Toad ships went when they left your shores, son?" Orus stood and removed his armor and shirt, showing scores of scars on his body. "Most of these are a result of the Toad army. We called them Offlanders, and now I know from where they came. Are they still here? What an excellent development."

"But there are millions, Sir," Lai asserted.

"We beat them once. We can beat them again, especially if we can sort this mess out with the Dwarves. I am no fan of the Todani 'converted.' I share your distrust of them, but if we watch them closely and convince the Elfish Queen and Dwarfish King to sit down and talk, how many would our army have?" Orus sat eye-to-eye with the now smiling Elf.

"I like your ideas, human, but my Queen hates the Dwarves more than the Todani, I fear. It is a matter of pride and honor now that we retake lands, even though many have nothing to return to." Lai dropped his voice to a murmur, whispering to Orus. "Our new kingdom is all that we truly need. The Queen wants her pound of flesh, but I fear she gets us killed for a fool's errand. Between the Todani and the Dwarves, we simply do not have the forces to defeat either adversary."

"Perhaps we can work out an agreement before things get worse, my new friend?" Orus asked.

"It is not my choice, but I would not be opposed to it," the Elf answered.

"Guards, give them better food and water," Orus commanded.

The Elfish Sergeant stood and bowed respectfully to the Hodan King as he left. He was led back to the cell, where the others eagerly waited for his report.

After the guard had moved out of earshot, the Sergeant began. "The big one is named Orus. He is their King. They have fought the Todessen, and I think they beat them."

"How can you tell, brother?" one soldier asked.

"For one, they are not slaves. Two, they have Todani ships! But, three, when I spoke of the Galdrissen, their King was disgusted, as if he knew what I was speaking of."

"What shall we do now, Sergeant?" the group asked.

"They are discussing their options, but I feel as if they will sail south to Vynwratha to speak to our Queen and try to work on peace with the Dwarves. A slim chance, if any, but their King Orus believes we can combine our forces and push the Todani into the sea."

"If only that would come to pass, but then we have to deal with the Galdrissen. What then?" a soldier replied.

Lai replied, "I am not sure, but we shall travel that road when it presents itself."

* * *

"You were attacked by Todani ships? Impossible! We have been faithful allies to those sons of Dwarfish whores!" the Queen shrieked as much in horror as in anger.

"Your Majesty," the bowing Admiral pleaded, "we did not see them coming until it was too late, because they were the Todani black ships we are used to seeing. They became aggressive, and one of my younger, foolish leaders opened fire."

The Queen leered at the bowing Elf. He cringed, awaiting her response to his revelation.

"So, one of your fools fired on a Todani ship, and you are wondering if they are at war with us? If they had fired on our ships without provocation, would you not call for war with them? Fools! I hope you executed that officer on the spot!" The Queen was livid.

"The ship was lost, as was the man responsible, Queen Lourama. He has paid the ultimate price for his stupidity." The Admiral remained kneeling.

"Rise, Dein. You may be in charge and responsible for this mess. Still, you cannot personally control the actions of every man under your command. I will not ask for your blade. I will not require you to perform Kits-Da." The Queen raised her hand.

Admiral Dein removed the razor-sharp short sword from his throat and stood, sheathing the blade expertly.

"Your Majesty, we must prepare for invasion. If they have more of the weapons like they used near the Port of the Redeemed...," Dein asserted.

"Agreed, Admiral. We must reposition our fleet out of the range of those weapons. How many ships remain, War Advisor?" Queen Lourama looked at an older Elf in golden robes.

"Forty fully operational light warships, My Queen." The older Elf bowed.

"Then set five of them in the northern port harbor. Rig the boats with the fire." The Queen looked at Dein. "If they pull into our ports uninvited, I do not wish any of them to leave."

Dein nodded. "Let us make this so! Rangers in the hills. The insurgency is reborn, My Queen. The King would be proud. Long may his memory live!"

There was an echo of the sentiment. King Cyrkris had died defending the mainland. His death left the rule of Vynwratha to his love, Queen Lourama. Nevertheless, the Elves held his name in reverence whenever they speak it.

"He watches us, Dein. We must not fail, or his sacrifice and the sacrifices of all the ancient heroes are for nothing! We must defend our home against all that would try to take it from us. Never again!" The Queen stood proudly from her throne. "Never again!"

There was a shout of, "Never again!" Elves of all ages cheered with resolve and went out to all locales on Vynwratha, warning the local villages, towns, and garrisons to prepare to defend their homeland once again.

* * *

Kren brought his ship to within one-hundred yards of the shore. Then, teams of men began disembarking in groups of twenty-five. Next, eight small raiding vessels, powered by Hodan warrior-oarsmen, moved two-hundred men per trip to the waiting beach. Finally, the Hodan forces set up a defensive position as they waited for their comrades to join them on land.

Kren boarded the last ship.

"Lieutenant," the Captain ordered, "have the ship positioned out of enemy range, but close enough to deploy the Thunder Ballista if our legions require support. Then, we will make our way southward toward the seaport and determine the situation. Our signalman will send you the proper lantern codes at sundown. Understood?"

"Yes, Sir!" the officer responded, saluting his Captain. "I will have a man in the crow's nest around the clock, watching the situation."

"Very well! Luck in battle!" Kren saluted back.

"Luck in battle, Sir!"

* * *

Jaruz stood with his men on the walls of the Port of the Redeemed. The day had seen a strange turn of events. It had started with their sworn enemies, the Vyn Elfish Navy bombarding the port and the town, proper. King

Hamrik, of Dornat Al Fer, had deployed a battalion of Dwarfish soldiers and siege weapons to the port to stymie any attacks the Elves could muster from the sea. Over the past six months, after the tentative treaty with the Todessen to the north, the Elves had been encouraged to attempt to land to the south of the Galdrissen homeland. The Elves had met with mixed success, but if a Commander looked at the damage the Elves were inflicting on the numerically and technologically superior forces of the Dwarfish nation, any warrior would be impressed with the effective use of their troops and the resolve of the smaller country.

"So, what are they waiting for?" Admiral Jaruz growled impatiently. "Are they anchored out there?"

"No idea, Sir. We cannot see the ships clearly, and the two shots we loosed from the trebuchet landed well short of their position. I am sure they know that they are out of weapons range," the Lieutenant replied seriously.

"Is that your expert opinion, Lieutenant? Whatever would I do without you?" The Admiral was jerking the other man's chain, which had the desired effect.

"I just mean…," Tavro tried in defense.

"Stop before you embarrass yourself again, Tavro. Please, be silent." The Admiral was stifling a chuckle when the Lieutenant saw his Commander's demeanor. The junior officer relaxed, realizing the ruse.

"That is not funny, Sir," Tavro said, trying to stifle a smile.

"It is a bit funny, boy," the Commander said, grinning. "Seriously, why did the Todani attack the Elves if they are allied with them, and then stop without finishing the task? They even let them run without chasing them down. That is not the way of the Todani. Something does not make sense."

"And the weapon, Sir. What in the Underworld was that? They blasted three ships within minutes. It was not even a fair fight!" Tavro seemed a bit disappointed.

"Are you disappointed that the Elves didn't beat them, or are you disappointed that the Todani let them live? Either way, they are here to kill us all and take what is ours."

Jaruz stared out over the ocean through his spyglass. Four ships had not moved in hours, but one was missing, and he had a hunch it was north of his position.

"It is possible they are waiting for reinforcements. Is this an advance party? Maybe the extreme violence of the attack depleted their ammunition?"

Tavro was making sense, but Jaruz felt unsure. A ship was missing, and he had no idea how many warriors could live on such a vessel.

Jaruz looked at the Lieutenant. "Good points, all of the way around, Lieutenant, but we will never know from our vantage point. Time to shore up the defenses, tend to the wounded, and evacuate the Galdrissen inland. Send a response force north of the port, just in case."

"Yes, Sir. The men will reinforce our walls, but I sent several hundred north yesterday to deter possible Todani movements in the forest. The last report was that another border incursion of a significant Todani force was coming toward us from the Haeldrun Ir. We have no more men to spare at the moment, Sir! The well has run dry." Tavro turned to his men. "Let's go, warriors of Dornat Al Fer! We must shore up our positions. They may come from the sea at any moment!"

The men cheered once and went to their tasks. The port had been battered for years by Elfish attacks, but it had never fallen. Jaruz was concerned about the visible Todani ships outside of the range of his weapons. Still, he was very worried by the one he could not see. This enemy was an unknown. The new invaders might succeed if he was not smart with the resources at his command.

"Tavro, send a messenger to our warriors in the north to warn them of Todani reinforcements from the sea. I believe a ship sailed north from the original five. I cannot see it offshore. They need to know that another large reinforcement of the enemy may be on the way."

The Admiral resolved to make the port as nasty a fight as possible for any invading force. He drew up a defense plan and then found a meal. Finally, he laid down in a dark corner for a short nap.

* * *

Kren looked around at the beach before him. It was rocky, with rough sand and sharp rocks to contend with. He was glad that the shore quickly gave way to scrubland that soon turned into forest. The conifer trees told of a temperate climate with rain enough to support vegetation, and at times, cold enough to be an environmental concern. Thankfully, the weather was fair, and the days were not too warm or cold. The Captain walked to where his men were forming up into their ranks.

"Lieutenant, gather your Sergeants and let us get off of this open terrain and into the forest," Kren ordered. "Send scouts to determine the easiest route of travel."

"Yes, Sir," the young Hodan Lieutenant replied, snapping to attention.

Shortly afterward, two camouflaged specialists departed swiftly across the open fields and into the forest. They returned an hour later with a report.

"So, what of the terrain, scouts?" Kren asked impatiently.

"Sir, the forest is vast, but about a quarter-mile east of here, there is a well-traveled road that runs north and south. There is evidence of major foot traffic, and carts and horses. They appeared to be moving southward toward our objective." The scout paused, awaiting questions.

"Did you see anyone on the road or near it?" the Captain questioned.

"We found a body that was attached to this, Sir. Unfortunately, there were many more around this one."

The specialist opened a burlap sack and dumped out the head of one very dead Todessen soldier. The trophy was fresh. The victim had died recently. Kren's eyes opened widely.

"Excellent, gentlemen!" Kren grinned maliciously. "Lieutenant, ready the legion for combat. We hunt for Todessen!"

"But, Sir, aren't we on a reconnaissance mission? Won't His Majesty be angry if we engage the enemy without our full forces?" the Lieutenant questioned.

"We can't wait! His Majesty would attack immediately. We must set the beachhead for the rest of our brothers to make landfall. We can't risk the Toads attacking them as they disembark! Let us prepare!" Kren raised his gauntlet into the air.

The Lieutenant bowed and gave the orders. Hodan marched as one up the slope and into the forest. Once they arrived at the road, they could see evidence of a battle that had occurred very recently. The signs were apparent that the Dwarves were the Todessen adversaries in this fight. Their dead also littered the forest.

Kren nodded somberly and sent hand signals to his legion. "Move quietly … Be on your guard."

Hodan trod lightly toward the south, weapons drawn. The sounds of clashing metal could be heard in the distance. So many of Hodan's new warriors had never whetted their blades with the blood of an actual adversary. Kren knew that it was time.

* * *

Jaruz could see the smoke from within the forest to the north. He knew the Todessen would raid from time to time, but he wondered if the usual fare was attacking his men, or perhaps it was this new enemy. One thing was sure, the medical personnel were transporting many injured to the port. It seemed that the Dwarves were not faring well in this battle. Perhaps, the Elves, Todessen, and a new unknown enemy were just too much to handle this time around.

Realizing that he may lose his position to the enemy, and knowing what that meant to the people he was charged with protecting, Jaruz frowned.

"Tavro, order the immediate evacuation of all Galda Risi. I mean it. All of them. Now!" Jaruz growled with a hint of worry. "They can't be here when the Todani arrive."

"Sir, they will never reach us!" Tavro said confidently.

"There are ships just outside the harbor. Possible reinforcements may have landed north of us to aid the raiding Todani forces. Now, the steady stream of wounded to our location. These signs tell of a different story, son. Form a defensive party, and get the Galda Risi out of this place before the murderers from the north overrun us. Dornat Al Fer underestimated their resolve this time. We will do our best to hold, but we cannot risk the lives of the innocent."

Tavro saw the paleness of his Commander's face. "Yes, Sir, as you command."

Chapter 3

It was the early morning. Orus sat on the main deck of his ship, looking out at the shoreline. It was impossible from his vantage point to make out anything except the main port, the town buildings, and the rising smoke of civilization on fire. Shaking his head, he could see there was also fire and smoke in the forests north of the port. He knew it had to be Kren. He would skin that man alive if he had managed to sabotage a possible friendship by killing Dwarves without reason. Sipping tea, the old King scratched at his beard and wondered what the port's defensive forces were up to while he sat, contemplating his next move. He also closed his eyes and tried to imagine what Kren was up to.

"Well, first, they are shoring up the defense and making it as difficult as possible for us to disembark and land. Then, they're probably consolidating inventory and ammunition. They have also sent a rider to the Dwarves for reinforcements, most likely." King Orus was muttering to himself as a crewman looked on. This was a common occurrence lately. The King spoke to himself all the time.

The crewman looked away quickly and went back to swabbing the deck.

Orus sighed. "Elves at war with Dwarves. It seems like the natural order of things has been restored, or ne'er left this place. Pity ... together, they would have routed the Todessen and reclaimed their lands. Still, the Dwarves did betray the Elves, and I surely cannot blame them for their anger."

Orus looked down at two ivory tokens. They were carved figurines, both of women. One had the letter "L" carved into its base, and the other an "F." Standing, he kissed them both and put them back in their leather pouch. Then, dumping the remainder of his now cold tea overboard, he said quietly, "Well, ladies, it's time for me to get to work. Time to talk to those Dwarves, if Kren does not sabotage me first. I hope they understand a white flag. I don't want to kill them before I have a chance to at least talk to them."

* * *

The guard on the wall rubbed his eyes and rechecked the spyglass. He was not hallucinating. Four black ships on the horizon were indeed moving toward his location. He blew the alert horns with enthusiasm.

Dwarfish forces scrambled from their sleeping quarters and tents. They ran to their assigned positions, concerned with the advancing navy. All defenders checked their weapons, tightened their armor bindings, and donned their helms. Although they were as ready as they could be, the forces sent to the north had not returned, and the Dwarves were worried. Their Dwarfish courier would not reach Dornat Al Fer for two days, and then the reinforcements would take even longer to return. The defenders knew they were all that stood between the Todessen and those they were assigned to protect.

Overnight, most of the Galda Risi had fled inland toward the nearest garrison under Dwarfish guard. It was not an easy task, but the people were used to moving at a moment's notice. Years of oppression and hate made their very existence a reason and rallying cry for war. The Galda Risi lived very simple lives. It was easy to move with the shifting breeze when all you owned could be slung over your shoulder in a burlap sack. These people were strong in spirit, but poor in material wealth. They wished for better, but knew those days were far from being.

* * *

"Why are you still here, My Lady," Jaruz asked, looking at the peaceful face of the Priestess.

"I am here to serve the Gods, my protector," the elder Galda Risi woman replied.

"Then be with your people. They will need you now, more than ever, if the Todani come for us all." Jaruz never flinched, saying the words as if he fully expected that the next few days could be their last. He had come to terms with the inevitable eventuality that evil would regroup, and that they would have to fight it again or die.

"They have Ta' Ryn. She will serve them well. I am here for you, Dwarf. You doubt. Do not doubt. The one above does not sleep. She sees her children's plight. She knows your fears and will send a deliverer or provide one from your ranks." The elder smiled gently, her face lighting up momentarily, then the light was gone.

The Dwarf looked at her sincerely. "I know, but our Goddess has a penchant for the dramatic. How many must die so the rest may live in peace?"

"Oh, to be a Goddess and know the ways of her thoughts," the Galda Risi woman replied, smiling. "I am here to heal those in need if you need me, Sir."

"Thank you, High Priestess." Jaruz scowled at the sound of the horns. "Here we go, Haya. Please, be with us today."

* * *

Kren and his men spread out in the dense forest. They hid in the heavy underbrush and bushes, moving as silently as a legion in plate and chain could move. The battle they discovered raged on before them. The riotous noise covered the Hodan advance. From his vantage point, Kren could see a small detachment of Dwarves in plate mail, who had formed square in the middle a vastly larger enemy force. Kren's eyes were large as goose eggs. They were Todessen. They had to be. All the stories about them were alive, right before his eyes.

"Form on the edge of the field. We will begin the killing, Lieutenant. I am sure that His Majesty will not be disappointed in us. Perhaps we can rescue those valiant fellows in the center of the maelstrom!" Kren was smiling, much to the Lieutenant's dismay.

"As you command, Sir!"

* * *

"We can't hold them off forever, Sir!" a Sergeant remarked to his Lieutenant.

"We have no choice! Hold your ground, or die and take as many with you as the Gods allow!"

The Todessen lines hit the Dwarfish shield wall with relentless fury. As Dwarves on the line fell, others immediately stepped in to fill the gaps in the shield wall, but it was now a matter of attrition. Their enemy was exhaustion, as much as the Todani.

Looking through his enemy, the Dwarfish Commander squinted, pointing at another arriving adversary. There was a bright reflection of the sun on metal through the flying dust. It was clearly visible in the large clearing that had become the killing ground. The Lieutenant struggled to see, but he could only make out the vague shape of gold and silver breastplates against a dark background of the shade of the trees.

A loud horn was heard over the din. Then the reply of three others in unison. The Dwarves kept defending out of desperation, but their hearts sank as it was now evident that another army had entered the battlefield.

"Great Gods, now what? Who is that?" the Sergeant shouted back to his Lieutenant.

"I do not know, but I surely hope that they are not Todani reinforcements!"

Shouts of, "Stand Fast! Hold the line!" were heard throughout the ranks of beaten and weary Dwarves.

One benefit of the new arrivals was that the distraction split the Todani attention, causing the Scourge Commander to reconsider his position on the field. He regrouped, letting up on their assault against the Dwarves, turning to meet and determine who the new arrivals were.

Half of the Todessen forces turned toward the Hodan, splitting the focus of the attack.

"Well, whoever they are, thank the Gods that the Todani don't seem to know them either! This is our chance, boys! Regroup, hold the line, and let's deal with the rabble they have left us with! The odds have vastly improved! Let's at least make a good dent, just in case the Todani decide to change their minds and come back this way. Worst case, the new shieldmen are reinforcements, and we are done for anyways! Send as many to Haeldrun as you are able!" The Commander laughed and let loose a war cry.

His men returned the gesture.

* * *

Kren heard the loud, determined war cry of the hopeless Dwarves and smiled at their defiance. He also noted that half of the Todessen were making their way toward his forces with purpose.

"Greetings, Toads. I am Kren of Hodan. These are the glorious legionnaires of my homeland. King Orus sends his regards!" Kren scowled.

The Hodan war cry echoed so loudly in the forest that the Todessen stopped and formed ranks as a precautionary measure.

The Todani leader was puzzled. "Are those … humans? Impossible! Charge! Run them down and spill their bellies on this ground!"

The Todani locked shields and charged the Hodan shield wall.

42

"Prepare to repel!" Kren bellowed, and his shield wall expertly moved, locking their shields together.

* * *

Since the reallocation of Todani forces, the Dwarfish fortunes had improved. They had succeeded in holding their own. The Dwarfish legions were so effective that they began to turn the tide of battle after a short time, routing the remaining Todani and sending the survivors scurrying northward toward the mountains. Too tired to pursue, the Dwarves shored up their weary lines and watched helplessly from across the field as the majority of the Todani forces had begun their attack on the unknown newcomers.

The first wave went as the Dwarves had envisioned. The Todani attackers proficiently dispatched the first rank of newcomers. Then, the scourge attempted to continue their momentum to divide, conquer, and demoralize the ranks of their foes. It appeared to be a textbook attack with expected results, but their new enemy did not flinch. Instead, the warriors reset their shield wall, shifted, and returned the favor tenfold by maneuvering through the disorganized, over-extended lines of attacking Todani.

The golden shields of the new army moved in unison, and blades whirred in circular arcs, mowing down entire ranks of Todani as the charging Scourge tried to exploit what they thought were gaps in their lines. Whenever Haeldrun's spawn attempted to exploit a breach, it closed, devouring whatever had entered it.

"They're doing that on purpose?" the Sergeant gasped, looking at his Lieutenant.

"It appears so, but who are they, and how are they such a deadly unit? How do we not know who they are?"

"Sir? Are those warriors ... HUMAN?" The younger Dwarf squinted as he watched the helmet knocked off a defeated Hodan warrior.

"Human? How? When did they learn to fight such as these? Degran-Eras is full of cowards, fishermen, shepherds, and slaves! Never in one-hundred years have humans fielded such an army! Regardless of who they are, they appear to be friendly, or at least to have similar motivations in mind. I think perhaps they may have bitten off a bit more than they can chew. We will assist! Form the remaining men and attack from the rear!" the Lieutenant bellowed.

There was a cheer, followed by the clanking of steel, as several hundred Dwarves formed ranks and marched smartly toward the rear of the occupied Todessen forces.

* * *

Kren was concerned. His forces were outnumbered, and even though they were inflicting heavy casualties on the Todessen lines, Hodan had lost close to one-hundred of their own. A victory where Hodan won, but their legions were destroyed, was no victory at all. The Captain looked for a way to change the odds. He needed a way to tactically retreat, or at least channel the enemy into a smaller area to limit his opponent's maneuverability. Kren backed his Hodan into the trees. He silently wished for Yslan's High Priestess, Adasser, to send the forest in to do the dirty work, but he knew that Puryn's lady was nowhere nearby and that help was not coming. Hodan hunkered down and prepared for the worst, that is, until the legion Commander heard a cheer through the din of battle and witnessed the decimated, but still very determined Dwarfish legion attacking the enemy from the rear.

The tree line limited the movement of both armies. Still, it allowed Hodan to remain static, creating the opportunity for a solid shield wall against irregular and erratic Todani attacks. Now, the number of attacks was divided on two fronts. Seeing a new immovable ally on the other side of their sworn enemy, the Todani, the Dwarves pushed the Black Army up against the unyielding Hodan shield wall.

The Dwarves were magnificent and the Hodan steadfast. The Todessen were trapped. Both armies ground their common enemy to a bloody pulp over the next hour.

When the carnage was complete and the dust had cleared, two opposing shield walls remained, one-hundred feet apart, facing each other over a heap of dead Todani, and both were ready for anything.

"Well, at least they are not advancing on us," the Dwarfish Commander said to his remaining men. "Someone tie a white handkerchief on a stick and let us go talk to our potential new friends."

At the sight of the white flag, the Hodan horns called for a hold and allowed the Dwarfish delegation to approach. Kren and his contingent marched smartly to the center of the two armies, where three well-armored Dwarves waited.

"Well, Haya help them if they attack us," Kren said plainly, to no one in particular.

His guards grunted in unison at the remark.

* * *

The Dwarfish Commander stood across from a much taller adversary. The new warriors spoke the common tongue of Etah, but some words were not quite right, and there was an odd accent to everything they said. Their helmets still covered their faces, and their armor covered everything else. They really did look human, but it made no sense at all. Humans were slaves, not warriors. In one-hundred years, a human warrior had not been seen on the Rynn.

"I am Tamariz, Commander of His Majesty's 23rd Legion. Who do we have the pleasure of working with this day?"

The Dwarf had removed his helmet. He was middle-aged, had a ruddy, muscular, coarsely bearded face. He did not look like a Dwarf who one would be wise to pick a fight with. Kren loosened his chinstrap and removed his helmet.

Those present from the Dwarfish delegation gasped at the sight. He WAS human!

"I am Captain Kren, of His Majesty's, 5th Hodan Legion. Well met."

There was an awkward silence, and then Tamariz spoke again "You … you are human? From where do your people hail?"

Not fearing any tactical disclosure, Kren responded. "We come from far away. A land called Hodan, located far across the sea. We are a great warrior nation. Our warriors are feared whenever they enter any battlefield. Hodan will never retreat. We will not leave the field before death takes us."

"Well met, Kren. Would you like to meet the rest of our friends?" The Dwarf smiled and nodded south toward the port town. "The Port of the Redeemed is our garrison. Admiral Jaruz would love to make your acquaintance, I am sure."

A murmur of disbelief among the Dwarfish ranks could be faintly heard. "Human warriors!?"

Kren thought quietly and then accepted the offer. "I think we shall, friend. My King has sent me on a mission to discover the nature of this place. Of course, we did not intend upon war, but killing Todessen is always a welcome event!"

"Excellent! If you agree, we shall leave at first light. It is the end of the day, and my warriors are exhausted, as I am sure that yours are also." The Dwarf bowed with respect.

Kren bowed slightly, returning the gesture. "A wise idea, Sir. We shall set our watch and gather wood for fires. Sleep well."

The Dwarf bowed, smiling, and returned to his men who cheered at his report.

Kren did the same, to the same result.

Watches were posted. Fires were kindled and rations distributed. Hodan and the Dwarves rested among the Todani dead. They kept a safe distance from each other, each trying to feel out what the other side was thinking.

* * *

Orus advanced his ships beyond what his officers estimated were the enemy's siege weapon range. As expected, the ships were met with a momentary barrage of projectiles, all of which fell harmlessly into the sea.

"I don't think they are in a talking mood, Your Majesty," Lieutenant Farhman stated as a matter of fact and with a dash of snark.

"I don't suppose that they would be after watching our ships obliterate an enemy they are obviously concerned with. Besides, they think were Toads." Orus smiled. "Let them be afraid."

"Yes, Sir!" Farhman saluted.

"Oh, and fire one broadside at the city walls. Exploding shot. Send a message that we will not be intimidated by Dwarves."

Farhman bowed, smiling, and carried out the order.

* * *

Jaruz stood on the wall directing the fire of his siege weapons with his officers. The weapons could not reach the ships in the sea before them, but the Dwarfish Admiral felt as if their show of force would perhaps make a point to the Todessen who were advancing. The Port of the Redeemed would not be quickly taken. Jaruz calculated that the show of force would give the impression that he had many more Dwarves to defend his post than the actual number he had. Maybe the Todessen would leave, or at least hold and allow his reinforcements to come from Dornat Al Fer. Unfortunately, the Dwarfish armies from the north had not returned. Jaruz feared they were dead.

He smiled smugly. "That should give their Commander pause."

As the Commander of the Dwarves nodded with confidence, one of the

Todessen ships turned broadside. A look of horror washed over the Dwarf's face as he witnessed five-gun ports open on the side of the black boat and five silver tubes protrude from them.

"Ceasefire and take cover now!!!" Jaruz bellowed, but it was too late for that.

As he heard the echo of his command, making its way down the lines, the relative calm was shattered by the explosions of a weapon he had never seen up close or in action.

* * *

Orus watched without emotion as his ship fired on the port's defensive wall. The smaller projectiles filled with Thunder powder and shrapnel hit their marks with deadly accuracy. The Hodan King could see figures running in disarray through his spyglass, as fire and death arrived at their location. Orus swallowed hard, but remained stoic.

"Aim at that same location." Then, Orus commanded coldly, "Fire the big one."

"The big one, Sir?" Farhman's eyes widened like a Hodan whelp that was being allowed to fight with live weapons for the first time. He had never fired the big one.

"Yes, do it now. Send the message that one doesn't want to fight Hodan." Orus scowled. "They shot first. We will show them the folly of their ways."

"As you wish, Sire." The Lieutenant gave the command.

The deck of the ship cleared, except for the siege weapons team. No one was sure of what the Ballista would actually do if it didn't blow the ship itself to smithereens. This device was expressly made for land warfare, according to the Dwarves at Dornat Al Ar. Still, Orus saw potential if affixed to a ship. So the King watched as his men readied, aimed, and then lit the charges.

An immense explosion left Orus with a loud ringing in his ears. His ship was now rocking vigorously from the recoil of the immense gun, but it had worked. The Hodan ship, *Vindicator,* was still in the water and ready to do more damage.

The King raised his spyglass and surveyed the damage.

"Holy Mother of the Gods," the King shouted. "Hoist the white flags and run our ships parallel to their weapons range limit."

* * *

Jaruz was knocked from his position as an immense explosion sent an eighty-pound metal projectile through his stone defensive wall as if the wall were made of parchment. Stunned and disoriented, the Admiral forced himself to regain composure and focus, assessing the damage to his lines. It was extensive in the direct location of the Todani attack. Any Dwarf in the area of impact was dead or on their way to Aeternum. Coughing, the older Dwarf stood up, staggering.

"Regroup! Regroup! Take defensive positions within the breach in the wall. Stand your ground, warriors!"

Dwarfish forces swarmed to the breach, taking cover on the sides where the wall still stood, but none felt too confident of the protection afforded by the stones. They braced for a second assault. It had not come. Many began looking at each other as if questioning what the Todani plan may be.

Jaruz raised his spyglass and surveyed the seas as his enemy moved again. However, there was one difference in their advance this time. The ships all flew with large white flags that were clearly visible.

"What does this mean, Sir?" Tavro asked, limping to where his Commander stood, puzzling over the tactics he saw unfold before him.

"I don't know, Tavro, but I think they mean to come into the harbor and dock. If they do that again, we are defeated. Our walls are useless against that thing." Jaruz shuddered.

"Why do they fly a white flag, when they know that they could surely crush us? Are they mocking us?" Tavro was angry.

"Maybe they're looking to see if we will surrender?" the Admiral offered. "But that is not the Todani way. Regardless, they come under a white flag after thoroughly routing our outer defenses. I don't see how we keep them at bay."

"Perhaps when they get on the ground, if they are still hostile, we can make a good run of it?" Tavro stood proudly.

"Agreed, son. Reposition everything we have at the docks. Tell them to keep cover and to stay as hidden as possible. Then, when the Todani decide to betray the parlay, we kill as many of them as possible. Gods help us."

* * *

Orus's men lined the railings of his ships. The front ranks all carried crossbows at the ready, fingers on the trigger. The ship gun ports were open, and the Thunder Ballista shone brightly in the morning sun, as the ships entered the harbor to silence. The Hodan King knew the Dwarves had not evaporated; the adversary had repositioned his troops, but the Hodan saw no movement anywhere.

"Anything yet, Farhman?" Orus asked.

"Nothing major, Sire. Just some minor units were caught taking cover behind buildings on what appears to be the main road." Farhman pointed in the direction of the reported troops.

"How many?" Orus asked, emotionless.

"Approximately one-hundred, maybe one-fifty, Your Majesty," Farhman replied.

"Continue to the docks. No one fires unless fired upon. We are under a flag of truce." Orus glared at his First Officer. "No one had better goad these people into combat, or I will flay that man."

"Understood. I will pass the word, Your Majesty."

The Lieutenant gulped at the facial expression of his King. He had not yet been born when Puryn and Orus took the field against the Offlanders all those years ago. As a boy, Farhman had heard the stories of how even hardened Hodan warriors who opposed the King would lose their resolve when Orus set his jaw and leaned into a task. No one stood up to Orus, the Lion. Now, plainly he saw why. The man was a god to the Hodan and the Ert. He had earned that distinction, not only when dealing out brutality on the enemy, but also when leading his people with swift and unwavering justice. He was more than just a man to many. He was Hodan's chosen.

The ships made their way to the docks. The facility was abandoned, and the Hodan Elites quickly disembarked over the side of their vessels by rope ladders. The next rank covered those landing in wave after wave. Finally, the men moored the ships and set up defensive positions. The gun ports remained open and in plain sight, by design.

* * *

"They've landed, Sir!" Tavro reported with horror.

"Yes, they have, boy." The Admiral looked through his spyglass.

"Why are you smiling, Sir?" Tavro was puzzled. "They outnumber us ten to one and have the backing of that terrible weapon."

"Well, son, they aren't advancing. They simply set up a perimeter and seem to be waiting on us." Jaruz stood up, putting himself in plain sight.

"Get down, Sir!" Tavro said in horror, pulling on his Commander's cloak.

Jaruz laughed. "Hiding will not serve our cause, my young friend. Besides, look at them. They are humans. They are not Todani!"

"But humans are nothing but slaves and cowards!" Tavro spat.

"Be careful about the history that you preach, fool. The humans fought the Todani with the Elves while we gathered our forces for almost ten years. The humans may be a shadow of their once-great kingdom, and the Elves, our adversaries, but neither are cowards." Jaruz looked at Tavro with an eyebrow raised.

"Yes, Sir," the young Lieutenant replied, gazing downward.

"Bah, let us go meet our new neighbors, Tavro. Aren't you curious as to who in the Underworld they are?"

"I suppose I should find out who the people I am at war with are … so I know how to address them in an official capacity," Tavro smirked.

Jaruz smiled, sighing apathetically as the two made their way out of a small market building and down the main street.

* * *

Ma 'Dryna patched up the wounded and prayed for the departed as she saw the large black ships enter the port. She was alarmed. Closing her eyes, she whispered a prayer to the Goddess as tears began streaming down her cheeks.

"Goddess, have mercy. The Dwarves do not deserve to die by their hands. I must go to him."

The Priestess ran faster than any Elf, her physical prowess hidden by her light flowing robes. She caught up to Jaruz and Tavro as they made their way to meet certain death.

"My Lady, why are you here?" Jaruz stated, betraying his concern.

"You cannot go there alone, Sir," the woman stated, frowning. "You will die."

"All Dwarves die, but few truly earn their gold along the journey." Jaruz quoted a Dwarfish text Ma 'Dryna knew very well.

"Do not seek after glory, for it is hollow and reeks of death," the Galda Risi woman replied.

Softly, she grabbed the Admiral's hand. Tavro looked away in a vain attempt to give the two their privacy.

"Speaking the words of the new revelation, again? Who wrote those words? They are new." The Dwarf smiled at her.

"My Lord, they were written in the book this morning." She smiled and openly hugged the Dwarf, who was slightly shorter than she. "A prophet or perhaps the first. His name was Kairoth, but the God has not revealed HIS name yet. I fear he is shy?"

"Shy Gods? Brazen humans in Todani ships? I do not want to ask what is next." The Admiral looked at the Priestess and smiled. She kissed the Dwarf, then frowned.

"Do not die, Dwarf. This is not how our story is supposed to end."

"Please, go back to the wounded. They need you, My Lady," the Dwarf responded.

"I will if you promise to return!" the Galda Risi pleaded.

"I will do my best." The Dwarf pulled her close and hugged her.

Tavro looked at his Commander and nodded silently. They both trudged to an uncertain future.

* * *

A makeshift gilded throne was placed on the port. Orus sat upon the chair with a crown on his head. He was in full armor, and his sword was unsheathed and laid across his lap. He was alerted to the arrival of two Dwarves who came to the port via the main road in the town. Naturally, the Hodan King was intrigued.

"Bring them here. Treat them respectfully," Orus commanded.

"Yes, Sire!" the Duty Commander bellowed, passing the orders to the line of men before him.

Soon, six Hodan Elites brought two unarmed Dwarves, hands bound to their King. Orus shook his head. The word respectfully must have been lost on his men. Still, he maintained his bearing and did not indicate that he was displeased with their treatment.

The King rose, and Hodan Elites surrounded him, forming a perfect circle of shields. Each warrior's blade protruded from the gap between warriors. They moved with their King without effort, maintaining their defensive formation while walking forward, backward, or sideways as if they were one organism. Orus knew that they would fight that way also. The visual display of skill and training was not lost on Dwarves, who watched with concern.

Orus spoke. "Who are you. Why are you here? Why did your forces fire upon my vessels?"

Jaruz spoke. "We are His Majesty's defense forces. We have been deployed to defend the Port of the Redeemed against Todani and Elfish aggression. However, it seems we need to add humans."

One of Orus's guards looked at his King, angered at what he thought was a disrespectful response. Orus shook his head, waving the young Hodan guard off. Then, the warrior resumed a stoic stance.

"Perhaps you should." Orus moved closer to the Dwarves. "We have captured several Elves from the sea battle yesterday. They tell us an interesting tale."

"I would suppose our enemies would tell any tale to save their skins. But, unfortunately, they tend to be ruthless, and their honor is suspect at times," Tavro responded sarcastically.

This time, the guard had none of it and backhanded the Dwarf, opening a small cut on his lower lip. Jaruz looked at Orus, raising his eyebrows.

"Enough," Orus said, glaring at the Hodan guard, who recovered his bearing and stood tall. "Let them tell their side of the tale."

"What are we accused of, Sir?" the Admiral asked, already knowing the answer.

"The Elf said that you stole his ancestral lands and gave them to the Todessen redeemed. I say 'redeemed' with a bit of skepticism and disdain. I am not too fond of cowards and turncoats." Orus was not holding back. He hated the Galdruhn on the Ert and made sure this Dwarf saw it plainly.

"That is a simplified version of the truth, My Lord," the Dwarf responded. "It's 'their' skewed view of events."

"So, tell me yours! You seem to think your side's oppression of the Elves is somehow justified. Weren't they your allies when you stabbed them in the back?" Orus crossed his arms, glaring at the more diminutive warrior before him.

The Hodan King stared intently at the Dwarfish Admiral. He tried to get a feel for who the Dwarf was, but all he could gather was defiance and resolve. The Dwarves would be a worthy adversary if this one was any indication of the rest. If there were as many as the Elf claimed, the Hodan were in for a fight.

"Well, it is true that they were our allies. We were both fighting the same enemy." The Admiral searched for the right words. "We were already on the same side, by default."

"Go on." Orus looked impatiently at the Dwarf.

"At the beginning of the war, the Todani came on hundreds of ships invading Degran-Eras, the human kingdom. It was by far the largest kingdom, but they were never truly united, and warred as much among themselves as with the invaders. These Elves are very warlike. They are consumed with combat. Even their monarchy rests on who can kill the King. It's barbaric." The Dwarf shook his head in disgust.

Orus stifled a smile. He was beginning to like the Elves of this part of the world. "Go on. Get to the point."

"Well, warlike and looking for a fight, the Elves with pretty substantial numbers jumped into the fray with the larger, but disorganized human forces. But, because of treachery, treason, and bad tactical decisions, the humans were defeated. So too were most of the Elf forces." Jaruz paused for effect. "When I say defeated, and I'm talking about the Todani. You realize, I mean they were slaughtered."

"I am fully aware of the nature of the Todessen, Dwarf." Orus scowled as he remembered the fall of Hodan.

"The Elves, losing the majority of their forces, retreated to their homeland, only to be greeted weeks later by a second Todani offensive from the northwest. We Dwarves, at that point, had sat out long enough and entered the war, stopping the advance of the Todani army in the mountains. We invaded occupied Degran-Eras and began pushing the Todessen northward until we could do no more. The landmass we reclaimed was too much to control." Jaruz looked at Orus, who was processing the new information.

"So, you pushed them back, and you stopped short of the goal? Do they still live north of here? How many days ride if they attack?" Orus looked annoyed, and the Dwarf picked up on it.

"I didn't see you out there," Jaruz replied angrily.

Orus held up his hand, stopping a Hodan elite from hitting the Dwarf in his mouth with a spear shaft.

"For your information, you little fool, I was not here killing those swine, because they left this place after regrouping due to your kingdom's incompetence, am I correct? According to the Elf, hundreds of ships sailed westward to places unknown." Orus was becoming angry with the banter.

"Yes, they did leave like that. It took them over seventy years to regroup. Still, our people were so stout in our defense of the lands that we made peace with the Orcs and Goblins to the southeast, reestablished the port here, and rid the southern lands of the Scourge." Jaruz looked at the ground for a moment, then solemnly looked up at Orus with remorse. "Are you saying they went to where you hail from and that you killed them there?"

"Aye, they nearly wiped my entire continent clean of any life." Orus frowned.

"I am sorry we were unable to kill them all. We ran out of Dwarves and materie[AB1] l. Men cowered and became slaves to the northern kingdom, because their heroes were laid to waste. No one dared to resist. We made peace with the Goblins and Orcs, because they split from the Todessen and wished to settle in peace. They ended up in the southeastern corner of the Rynn."

"The Rynn? I heard this name before." Orus said.

"Yes, our continent is named the Rynn. The Todani Kingdom established in former Degran-Eras is called Haeldrun Ir."

"What of the Elf city that stood here and is now a Galdruhn den?" Orus spat.

"The Elves, during a major battle almost one-hundred years ago, withdrew to small ships after being driven out of their homes by the Todani. They left their kingdom and landed in an uninhabited place twice as large and with twice as many riches as their homeland! They vowed to return, but did not do so for almost twenty more years. The land was fallow and the buildings in ruins. Then the Galda Risi appeared. They were rebels of the Todani religion. They resisted the leadership and fled oppression and murder from the north into the mountains right above the lands that the Elves no longer occupied." The Dwarf was almost begging in his tone. He could see Orus's expression and needed him to understand the Dwarven position concerning the event. He was unsure if the Hodan King was listening to anything he said.

"So, the land was empty for twenty years? Did the Elves ever express their desire to resettle?" Orus inquired.

"They only protested when the Galda Risi occupied the empty lands and had reclaimed the ruined territory. Then the Elves wanted the land back. After the new inhabitants had spent almost ten years reclaiming it ... it's their Queen Lourama. She lost her King to the Todani in a viciously contested battle north of those lands. He is still a hero, spoken of in reverence among the southern Elves ... Almost a God in their eyes. Their Queen hates the Galda Risi as if they killed her man personally, when most who live there now were not yet even born! It's a matter of hate, not nationalism or need. She wants them dead, and the occupation of these poverty-stricken lands is her excuse. She is consumed." Jaruz looked at Orus intently. He saw that he was making a dent in his demeanor.

There was a commotion at the front lines of the Hodan defensive. The guards encircled the two in front of their King within a ring of Hodan blades. Jaruz closed his eyes and waited for death. He could hear the rapid breathing of Tavro, who was praying.

* * *

The Hodan warriors tightened up as a small platoon-sized group of individuals walked in a loose group toward Orus's lines. The shields interlocked, blades were out, and all men were at the ready. Archers nocked their arrows and awaited orders. Orders were being shouted back and forth between units.

The Hodan Duty Commander shouted toward those advancing. "HALT! All who go there, stop where you are, or die! Hodan, forward MARCH!"

The legion moved as one as they had done a thousand times before. They enveloped the advancing group like a machine and held them in a tight circle of blades and arrow points. Shaking in fear, one of the shrouded figures dropped her hood, and the rest did as she had done. Before the King's men were fifty or so men, women, and children. They all bore the tell-tale runes, and when they smiled nervously, the pointed teeth of their lineage stood out in contrast to their sullen demeanor. They were not warriors, but instead looked like poor street urchins or farmers. One stood and spoke.

"I am High Priestess, Ma 'Dryna of the Goddess Haya." She knelt, begging. "Please, do not kill my friends or my protectors. They are good people."

The Hodan Commander stoically looked at the Galdruhn woman before him. Instinctively, he saw an enemy, but in his heart, he also saw someone who was terrified and begging for her life.

"Please, Sir, I beg of you, do not murder these innocents!" Jaruz stood. "I offer my life in her place. Kill me instead. They have done nothing to you. I fired on your ships. I am at fault."

Orus looked at the man's face. It was clear as day. He loved this woman. She loved him also. At first, the thought sickened the King, but then he remembered his daughter Faylea, and ultimately his memories drifted to Hodan when he was young … to[AB2] [h3] a time when he met and fell in love with a young Hodan woman named Lyndia. Her loss still haunted his dreams, and he could see the same look of dread on this Dwarf's face as he contemplated life without the Priestess who stood just out of reach on the road ahead of him.

The Commander looked at Orus for guidance. He sighed in relief as the King gave a stand-down signal.

"What is this? A trick? You try my patience, Dwarf," the King said, pushing through his guards and grabbing the Admiral by the front of his aventail.

"She never listens to me. I told her to leave with the others. She would not leave, because of me. I guess you have figured us out. Will you kill us?" The Admiral looked at Orus defiantly, so much so that Orus smiled and almost laughed.

"What do you take me for, Dwarf? A barbarian? I will not kill you. I will not kill them, but if you fire on my men again, I cannot guarantee that they won't use your corpse for target practice." Orus released the Dwarf and called his guard to bring the captives to his location.

The Dwarf bowed respectfully. "I am in your debt, human. I will not forget this kindness. I suggest a truce between us. Perhaps if we get to know each other, all of us, we can come to some sort of agreement or arrangement."

The two captives were led to the larger group, where the Dwarf began yelling at the Galdruhn Priestess. She sat there smiling and poking fun at the angry Dwarf, until he grasped her in a hug as if he thought he'd never see her again. She returned the favor, and they held each other for some time. Secretly, in his silence, Orus watched the embrace. The Hodan King felt a twinge of jealousy. He missed his wife and daughter.

Opening the leather case, he looked at the ivory figurines, kissing each one and then putting them securely away.

Somewhere off north of the port town, Farhman swore he heard men singing. Raising his spyglass, he gasped loudly and then handed the instrument to Orus, who pointed it toward the road that ran between the thick northern forest.

"I see Kren has made friends, Farhman. We will need to bring some barrels from the ship." Orus sighed. "Oh, and have the men on duty gather wood for pyres. It looks like we have many to send to Aeternum. Send that man on a scout mission, and he goes to war. He better have a good tale to tell, or I'll have his head."

"Yes, Your Majesty, right away," Farhman replied, passing the word to the working parties.

* * *

A somber celebration broke out in the meager tavern at the Port of the Redeemed. The remaining Galda Risi greeted their new friends and welcomed their protectors. Casks of ale, mead, and wine were tapped. Food was roasted and served. The Galda Risi spared no expense. They had very little, but what they did have, they shared freely with Orus and his men.

Off in the distance, the pyres lit the night sky. Orus frowned, as did Jaruz. The Hodan King could see Galdrissen stopping and bowing near the burning bodies while praying for the dead. He shook his head and scowled. *It's a trick*, he thought. *They are naught but liars and deceivers!*

The Dwarfish Commander, Tamariz, reported all that Kren and his legion had done. Kren reported that the Dwarfish legion fought valiantly. Both warriors had begun to warm up to the idea of a potential cooperative alliance. Orus was impressed with all that Kren had accomplished. The Hodan King was secretly jealous that his Captain had been the first to find the Todessen and not him. Still, the Scourge was finally located, and with them, the Hodan's eternal allies, the Dwarves.

"So, Jaruz, where do we begin in our newly found quest to mend fences and unite the people of the Rynn?" Orus asked, swigging down some mead.

"I am not sure, Sir. This has been a point of contention for decades now. I mean, I understand the Elfish reluctance to forgive and forget, but they abandoned the land, and we had no idea that they would be so angry. I guess we should have thought it through a bit more." The Admiral tore off a piece of bread and chewed on it.

"I am here for one thing. I want to kill Todessen. I want their wailing to reach the Underlord's ears. I want him to show up. I want to cut him down where he stands." Orus poured another drink. "I know, I will never kill Haeldrun himself, but it's a dream I've had after I watched everything I love burn and so many that I cared for die, so needlessly, to the scum that lives in your northern kingdom." Orus scowled. "I see them in these Galda

Risi that you protect. I cannot shake it."

Orus was almost apologetic. That put Jaruz off-guard. The old man had a different side, and he let the Dwarf in on it. The Dwarf Admiral suspected that this was by design.

"I understand. They remind you of those who did you harm, but if you speak to them and get to know them, they are completely different from the heartless scum who live in Haeldrun Ir."

"Be that as it may, Dwarf," Orus sipped some more mead, "how do we get a vengeful Elf Queen to play along with our new military alliance?"

"Before we go declaring alliances, know that I am just an officer who serves at my King's pleasure. I have no authority to sign a treaty with your kingdom. Hodan, is it?" The Dwarf tried to recall.

"Yes, Hodan. I understand your position, but if Dwarf and Hodan can unite, and we can get those damned Elves to play along. Then perhaps, we get the humans to rise and fight!" Orus raised a fist.

"It sounds like a grand plan, and I love your vision, Sir, but many have tried to accomplish this very thing and failed miserably. The petty hatreds of our lands run deep." Jaruz took a long drink of his mead, then continued. "The humans are weakened to the point of being unable to resist in any real way, the Elves hate everyone for some reason, and the Dwarves police the world and hold the Todani at bay."

Orus stared into the fire. "Your people almost squashed them by yourselves. All of us together can accomplish the task."

"I will send a rider to Dornat Al Fer and ask the King for guidance. But, until a formal alliance is formed, I promise no hostilities from my side of the fence." Jaruz extended his hand, and Orus shook it.

"Hodan will stand down and help you protect this place and all of its people," Orus promised.

"Then, may I say as your new friend, welcome to the Rynn, Orus of Hodan, welcome."

Orus raised his glass. "To friendship, alliances, and future endeavors. To our future success in battle."

Chapter 4

Queen Lourama sat on her throne, fidgeting with a bauble on her wrist, as she listened to the report of her military commanders. Vynwratha, assuming the worst, had dispatched twenty-five of its remaining forty warships to Haeldrun Ir in retaliation for the attack on her forces outside of the lands now known as the Port of the Redeemed. That was the official name on the maps, but no Elf would utter such a blasphemy. The *Redeemed* were savages. They were evil-incarnate. They would not be allowed to remain if the Queen had her way. The proper name of the lost lands was Edhelseere. At least to the Elves, it would remain as such until the lands were returned to the Vyn.

The Queen looked up and sighed. "So we sank four of theirs and lost all of ours in the process?"

"Yes, Your Majesty, you are correct." The Admiral stood straighter. "The enemy has sunk twenty-five of our vessels, and we have lost by estimate, ten-thousand warriors during the event."

"How many ships remain, Minister?" the Queen somberly remarked as she turned to an older man in golden robes. He was holding a massive leather-bound ledger.

"Your Majesty, we have seven ships, ready for battle, and five moored in the harbor for other duties." The old man looked up at the Queen seriously.

To Lourama, the old Minister resembled an old sheepdog. His bushy eyebrows and thin beard gave the impression of an unkempt and disorganized man. Still, the Queen knew of no other man who was as obstinate and exacting in his duties.

"Twelve remains of the original fifty." The Queen stared at a statue of her deceased husband. Then, she frowned. "How has it come to this, Admiral?"

"We are not defeated, My Queen," the uniformed man replied. "We sank four of their ships and crippled many others. This is but a rut in the road. The enemy will not dare to invade Vynwratha proper. If it does, the consequences to its army will be devastating. They know this, but I fear that reprisals are a foregone conclusion, and they will occur soon."

"What is your counsel, Generals?" The Queen looked at two lines of perfectly aligned elder Elfish men in dress uniform. They lined either side of the red carpet leading to her throne. They were very stiff and official. The Queen always hated the meetings with these men. They seemed passionless, as if a battle were an everyday job and the losses of their men just the fee of doing business.

A General on the left spoke. "We have conferred, My Queen," he stated officially. "We must bolster our outer defenses and call the Rangers to the Wood."

"The Rangers have not been active in our Wood for almost a century, but I fear that you are correct in your estimation of our current state of affairs. They began this war. We must, no … We WILL finish it. Execute the orders and make it so, gentlemen." The Queen stood.

The entire room shifted to stand taller and with pride. The Queen looked out over the faces, young and old. Her brow wrinkled, and she frowned momentarily. Then, she thought, *I must send these souls off to kill or die once again. What have we done to deserve this treatment by Aeternum?*

Clearing her throat and regaining her resolve, the Queen stated firmly, "Call up the Rangers. Call up the Reserves. All Elves, men, and women of fighting age will stand—men in the Wood, women, and the young within our walls. We must survive. We WILL survive!"

Closing her eyes, Lourama turned sharply and marched out of the throne room to an adjoining side chamber. She could hear the shouts of her men behind her.

"Long live the Queen!" they declared.

"Long live us all," Lourama muttered, wiping away tears that began to flow freely from her eyes while she sat privately contemplating the death that was to come. Memories of the carnage of the last days that her Rangers were in the Wood freely flooded her mind.

A lady-in-waiting carefully approached with a handkerchief. "My Lady," she said, bowing and averting her eyes from the tears of her Queen.

The Queen took the silken cloth from her girl and smiled weakly. "Thank you, my dear."

* * *

Haeldrun Ir did not know what was about to hit them. A small armada of Elfish ships had left Vynwratha a couple of weeks earlier. The Todani patrols thought nothing of the Elfish troop movements. They were allies. The Elves would never dare to betray the Todani trust. They knew better.

The Todani forces at the Port of Wargyrnim knew something was wrong just before the dawn on the day of the Elfish betrayal. As the sun began to crack the horizon, twenty-five Elfish warships came into view on the horizon. The Todani Commander could see that they were advancing toward his almost undefended port with purpose. General Xyr of the Capital Defense Militia felt the hair on the back of his neck stand on end. They were under attack, and the navy was out to sea. It would be up to him. He just hoped he was not wrong. The King would not forgive him if he attacked the Elfish allies without cause. Still, the Elves were unpredictable, and the warrior did not trust them.

"Ensign!" the older warrior bellowed to the Duty Watch. "Sound the alarm. I need these ships manned and ready for battle now! Where is the patrol?"

"The patrol is several hours north of us, Sir!" the Todani officer replied.

"Get with the mages and recall all who are in the area! Do it now! Sound the alarm and muster the remaining troops to the port. Set to repel a landing force of significant size!" Xyr was very animated now as he could barely see the standard of Vynwratha on the sails of the approaching vessels.

"Sir, do you think the Elves attack us? But why?" the younger man questioned.

"They are Elves, Ensign. They hate us, and with cause. We showed them no quarter the last go 'round. I was there." Xyr smiled maliciously.

"Aye, Sir! I will carry out the orders immediately." The Ensign ran over to a messenger and sent the orders.

Large, deep-toned horns began to blow out the call to arms, and bells rang in the city square. Todani men and women stirred from their homes. The warriors quickly set the land defenses as the Todani Navy expertly readied the ships to intercept. Then, as ordered, the mages recalled the vessels on the coastal patrol north and south of the Haeldrun Ir. Within hours, three more Todani warships would join the fight.

General Xyr nodded, thinking, *Now, all we have to do is hold these vermin off until reinforcements arrive.*

Sipping a mead, the General watched as his forces manned their assigned fortifications.

* * *

"Good, they are sleeping," Captain Ulfyris said to his First Mate as he looked out at the black horizon. No lights were visible as the Vyn Navy approached from the sea.

"We hit them hard and leave nothing afloat!" the Lieutenant said in an overly exuberant voice.

"Just hit your targets, Yanas, and keep your head down," the Captain droned.

The Lieutenant feigned offense and then laughed, "Yes, Sir!"

Ulfyris smiled, patting the younger Elf on the shoulder and calling for the signal to be sent for the attack. The Elves used bull's-eye lanterns pointed directly at the ships beside them to conceal their messages from the enemy who may be watching. For the most part, it worked well, but any light in the darkness was detectable by an observant sentry, and the Captain knew that all too well.

The Elfish ships moved into an attack formation. Ulfyris knew that any Todessen who saw them in the formation they were holding would know that something was afoot. Still, he needed to maintain positive control over the forces under his purview. Command and communication were almost impossible with this many ships attacking at once. Sailing toward the port, the Captain spied through his glass, seeing activity that concerned him. It was dark, but the Elf could tell the ships in the harbor were on the move with his superior vision.

"Hmm, did we do something to tip off the Todani, or are they just moving their ships to send them out on patrol," the Vyn Commander pondered.

"Sir, ships are all in position, and all weapons are at the ready. Our landing teams stand by." Yanas saluted.

Ulfyris was concerned, never putting the spyglass down. "Advise all ships that the Todessen appear to be readying to repel. I cannot tell for certain what is going on, but the ships in the harbor are repositioning."

"Surely, they cannot know!" Yanas said in shock.

"I am not sure, boy! I just see what they are doing, and it screams to me of a defensive maneuver. Tell the ship Commanders that we are going in, but expect them to be ready for us. We knew when we received these orders that it would be no summer's walk in the forest." Ulfyris wore a pained look. "Tell them all that I wish them luck in battle. Kill every Todani scum in sight. Burn it all to the ground if the opportunity arises. Give no quarter."

"Yes, Sir!" the younger Elf responded, saluting and then running to his signalman.

"Gods help us. It was a grand scheme and a big gamble when we had the surprise. If they are ready for us, this will end in a massacre." Ulfyris bowed his head. "Goddess, help us!" he prayed.

CHAPTER 4

* * *

General Xyr was satisfied that he had enough Todessen Militia in place to repel the Elfish attack on the shore. The Todessen were numerically superior, but the reputation of the Elves of Vynwratha preceded them. They had acquitted themselves well in every battle fought against them on the Ert. Of course, the Elves had not always won, but the attacker was always sorry that they had stirred that hornet's nest.

The first volleys began as the Vyn Navy set the outer edge of the port on fire. Small landing boats could be seen rowing from the first five boats. The Todessen General's mood shifted south quickly.

Grabbing the nearest Todessen warrior by his neck, he pulled the man in front of him with a jerk. "Tell the Commander on the pier to meet their advance as they come down the boardwalk. Do it now!"

The warrior grunted and lit off, running at an unnatural rate of speed toward the pier's defense forces.

"Ensign Gryl, send a messenger to the Royal Guard. Inform His Majesty that we are repelling an invasion by the Elves of Vynwratha. Tell him we may need reinforcements and that I have recalled our patrolling ships. Do it now!" the General growled sternly.

"Yes, General!" The younger officer nodded and sent the rider.

Xyr paced as he witnessed the prowess of Vynwratha. The landing forces set the line to defend as their brothers landed in waves. The Vyn had landed within thirty minutes. The actual assault began minutes later as Vyn Raiders made their way down the boardwalk. The outposts of Todessen defenders were engulfed by thousands of disciplined warrior Elves who dispatched them all as if they were a bump in the road.

Xyr was worried. These Elves were motivated, but by what? "Sergeants! Reinforce our forces on the boardwalk."

The General gestured with hand signals to his men ahead of him, receiving the responses of, "Affirmative" and "Acknowledged." The Todessen adjusted to the threat as it evolved. Eventually, the Elfish advance was stopped at the entrance to the main port facility. The ships in the harbor had begun to respond to the Elfish incursion. Catapults and Ballistae began to rain down on the Vyn from the larger, black ships as sailors on either side maneuvered their vessels into position. Soon, an all-out battle was being fought within the harbor. The Elves had brought too many ships, and the area was too congested. No boat could maneuver effectively.

Xyr lowered his head as three Todani ships burst into flames. After an hour or two of enemy bombardment, one large Todessen ship developed a large crack in its side and began taking on water. It listed to the starboard side and eventually sunk. To the General's ire, he could see the Elves picking off Todessen in lifeboats and those swimming toward the shore.

"Ensign, tell the Todani Captains to ram those damned Elves. Sink them at all costs. They may as well take the bastards with them if we are fated to die this day." Xyr showed no emotion. He commanded loudly and with anger, but his face did not change— not a scowl for the loss of his men, no tears. He had his duty to his King and the Underlord. Fealty is what transcended all else.

"Aye, Sir. Perhaps you should retire to a more defendable position," the Ensign suggested.

"Perhaps you should shut the hole beneath your nose and do as you are told," the General snarled.

* * *

Captain Ulfyris watched eagerly through his spyglass as his Raiders made easy work of the initial Todessen defensive positions. Still, his encouragement waned as the push was stopped cold at the main port. His men were in a static fight against superior numbers. It did not look good for the Vyn.

"Lieutenant, tell the ships near the port to rain down on the Todessen forces holding us from advancing!" The Captain raised his spyglass again.

"Yes, Sir." The Lieutenant passed the orders.

The fury of the Vyn Navy began demolishing not only the position where their men were in peril, but it also began burning down the entire port facility. Every building from the sea to the port was now in flames. Half of the Todessen defense force was destroyed, and the Elves were advancing again, albeit slower than before.

"Destroy their ships and kill them at will. We are in a fight for our lives now, my friend." Ulfyris took a deep breath and exhaled, looking around with concern.

"Cheer up, Sir! We are winning." Yanas smiled.

"Never underestimate your opponent. To do so is to forfeit your life," the Captain responded.

Yanas subdued his happiness and acknowledged the quote from the Elfish Book of Wisdom.

Two more Todani ships were ablaze and taking on water. The battle was four hours old now. The Elves saw success, but Todessen's reinforcements were overdue. Nevertheless, the Vyn Commander intended to do as much damage as possible before that eventuality presented itself.

"Keep up the pressure. Sink those damn ships!" Ulfyris demanded.

* * *

Xyr's orders finally reached the ship's Commanders. Two of the much larger black ships dropped their sails and turned toward their nearest opponents. They were gathering as much as much speed as possible. Todessen warriors rowed furiously to get the momentum up to attack their Elfish foes. The Elves had miscalculated and boxed in their own ships. Too many vessels clogged the lanes. Vynwratha was unable to maneuver effectively. The first enemy impact drove the metal bow of the Todessen ship through the much lighter Elfish vessel's hull, crushing in it in a single blow. The ship's oarsmen furiously paddled to reposition their vessel as the first Elfish warship sank. Elves filled the water as the Todessen returned the gesture and began killing those retreating to the shore.

"Good, kill those ornery little bastards!" Xyr raised a fist in elation.

Yet another Todani charge struck another Elfish ship. Again, the result was the same.

"Get them! Sink them all!" Xyr was invigorated.

The port was ablaze. The Elfish Navy was in disarray. The Todessen had resorted to ramming vessels at will to inflict damage. Soon, Elfish warship Captains began to maneuver without coordination, which was disastrous. It was bad enough that the Todessen were sinking their ships, but several unsanctioned Elfish ship maneuvers also resulted in collisions that disabled more Vyn vessels, destroying an additional two.

"The fools flee and, in their cowardice, kill each other in an attempt to save their skins." Xyr smiled in disgust. "You will pay for this aggression, Elves."

"NO QUARTER!" A random Commander bellowed out to the Todessen ground forces.

A roar of NO QUARTER!" echoed back from the troops.

* * *

Captain Ulfyris could see the push had once again slowed. The navy was in disarray, and much to his displeasure, it had just been reported by his sentries that three more Todani ships were joining the fight from the sea behind them. The naval battle was lost. The Commander changed tactics.

"Tell all warriors to abandon ships and head to the beachhead that our landing forces established. We will make their defense a costly one. Every Elf is a foot soldier. NO QUARTER!"

The Ensign passed the order. Two ships took it upon themselves to run interference for the remaining ten that offloaded their warriors with the proficiency of a Dwarven machine. The additional five-thousand warriors allowed the Elves to obliterate the Todessen defensive foothold. Soon, the port was taken, but the city proper was now filling with Todessen civilians who would not flee. Instead, they armed themselves with whatever they had on hand. Todani stood in the streets, lining them like a gauntlet. Ulfyris looked down the cobbled roads and knew it was an impossible task to take the city. As he contemplated this development, the Vyn invaders overran their enemy's command post. A Todessen General and his guard were being held prisoner. Captain Ulfyris made his way to the location of the prisoners as the Vyn Raiders set the defensive perimeter as best that they could. Ships in the harbor were still a concern, but the Vyn Navy was still afloat for the moment and harassing the Todessen as best as could be expected.

A well-armored Todessen stood proudly as the Elfish Captain approached. He spat in the Elf's general direction, receiving an Elfish gauntlet to the mouth as recompense. The older Todessen warrior grinned at the Elf who struck him. His bloodied lip was torn. Blood coated the Todessen man's pointed teeth. The Elf squinted and readied to hit him again.

"Hold your hand, son," the Vyn Captain commanded. The Elf stood at the ready, lowering his fist.

"Who are you, Elf?" Xyr asked with disdain. "You traitors attack your allies while they sleep now, eh?"

"It is your people who attacked us as we fought for Edhelseere, while under the agreement we struck with your King. This attack is retaliation for three sunken ships and hundreds of lost souls." Ulfyris leered at the Todessen, but in the back of his mind, he wondered why his enemy was unaware of his own people's betrayal of the Elves.

"I know nothing of what you speak, Elf." The Todani General sighed. "Your lies will not save you when our King arrives. He is due."

Ulfyris knew Xyr spoke the truth. Todessen reinforcements were overdue, and the Elf knew that none were coming to aid him.

"What is your name, Sir?" the Elfish Commander asked officially.

"Xyr, the Bloodthirsty, General of His Majesty's defensive forces," the Todessen declared defiantly.

"Xyr? I remember hearing that name. Aren't you the petty murdering rapist who plagued the lands of Edhelseere during the Great War?" Ulfyris wished his Queen was present to witness the capture of this war criminal.

"I had my way with a few Elves, as did all of the Todessen as we wiped you from your lands. Pathetic, weak, insignificant little Elves." Xyr chuckled.

Ulfyris drew his blade. He expertly drove it into the Todessen General's throat without warning or hesitation, twisting the knife as he withdrew it. The Todessen guards with the General turned to respond, but they were restrained by their Elfish captors. Xyr clutched the wound as blood sprayed everywhere. Ulfyris stood in the spray, and then he kicked out the knee of the Todessen man, sending him to the ground. The exchange was over within seconds. The Captain stood, covered in black Todessen blood.

Looking over at the Sergeant, Ulfyris droned, "Did I not order NO QUARTER, Sergeant?"

The Sergeant's eyes opened wide for a second, then a smile crossed his lips. "Yes, you did, Sir! Men, execute the prisoners, now!"

The Todessen warriors turned and tried to fight back, but they were dispatched without difficulty, being that the odds were five Elves to one Todessen. Ulfyris wiped the blood from his face with a dirty rag as the horns of the enemy made their report. The King's men had arrived. The end was near. The Todessen were not known for taking prisoners unless they wanted slaves, and warriors made terrible servants. The Todani knew that living warriors posed a threat no matter where they stood.

"Prepare, men," the Captain somberly said. "The end has arrived. Make your peace with the Gods. There is no escape. It is better to die than to have them take you alive. So make your last moments count. Take as many as you can with you to the afterlife!"

"Long live the Vyn! For the Queen! In memory of Edhelseere! For the memory of King Cyrkris!" Lieutenant Yanas bellowed.

A loud battle cry and a cheer rose from the men. They formed a shield wall and awaited their fate.

* * *

The King's Royal Guard arrived, three legions strong, and entered the port area from three roads. One was to the front of the Elves, and one to each flank. Ulfyris knew their fate was sealed unless they were taken prisoner. That was a slim possibility.

"Hold the line, men. Form SQUARE!" the Captain bellowed.

Several hundred remaining souls moved to form a perfect square, two Elves deep around their Commander, who watched the enemy from within their protection. All Vyn were ready to kill as many of the enemy as they could before their end.

"Yanas," the Captain mumbled, "come here."

"What do you need, Sir?" the Lieutenant whispered into his Commander's ear.

"Take this, put it on, and escape south to warn the Queen of the incoming reprisals that are sure to follow. There is no time. Move silently, under cover, and complete this task."

"But, Sir, what about you?" the younger Elf asked plainly.

"What about me? I have served honorably and lived my life. So many have died under my command. Today is my turn."

The Todessen enemy bellowed out orders in a guttural language to the troops they commanded. After that, there was a shift in the Todani formations, and then they started marching confidently toward the outnumbered Elves.

"Go! Tell the Queen of our heroism. Encourage her! Ensure that we did not die in vain. Make your report. GO!" Ulfyris whispered emphatically. "GO NOW!"

Yanas looked at his Commander with a pained expression. His Commander smiled weakly back at him. Nodding, the young Lieutenant waited for his chance. The Todessen made it easy. The melee began within a minute or two, and the Elves were pushed into a corner near a side alley. The Lieutenant ran to a darkened doorway as the Elfish Raiders held their line valiantly. He slipped into a building. He was not alone.

"Mother! An Elf! Can we kill it?" a young Todessen boy of about ten years hissed.

"I will call your father. He will deal with this one," the mother replied.

Yanas, seeing no alternative, pulled a small dagger from his belt, throwing it in one motion. It hit its intended target. The Todessen woman fell, clutching the dagger that now protruded from her throat. The artery was severed, and blood freely sprayed as she removed the knife and stood. Gurgling, knife in hand, the woman took two steps toward the Elf before succumbing to her injuries. Yanas was shaken that even the Todessen civilians were so determined to kill an intruder. Even though death knocked, they ignored the reaper and advanced on their prey. He did not have long to think about the event, as he was knocked to the floor from his blindside by a smaller attacker. It was the boy.

Rage filled the Todessen child at the death of his mother. His hot anger oozed from every pore as he pounced on the unaware Elf and then proceeded to drive his victim's head into the edge of a table. Stunned and bleeding, the Elf was brought back to consciousness as he felt the distinct feeling of an animal biting him. The Todessen child had bitten him with his pointed teeth, missing the intended target of the Elf's jugular, and instead, chomping down on his shoulder near the neck. Yanas yelped in pain and began to fight back.

The Elfish warrior struck his attacker firmly in the side of his head, detaching the biting youth from his shoulder. When the boy returned angrier and more violent than ever, the Elf delivered a snap kick to the aggressor's leg, dislocating the young one's knee. Yanas bent down to retrieve his dagger from the Todessen woman. He frowned as he noticed the boy roll over and continue his assault. There was no way around it.

The Elf kicked the Todessen boy in the face. The advancing Todessen was disoriented for the moment. Still, Yanas could tell that he would soon gather his faculties and continue the assault. The Elf could hear the battle raging down the street and knew his time was growing short if he intended to escape. Lunging expertly, the Elfish Ranger stabbed the boy in the same spot he had struck the mother. Yanas sat on the boy and watched his angry face turn to one of fear as his life ebbed away. Sobbing, the Elf stood and changed his clothes into those of an average Todessen warrior. Looking around for a father that both of his victims hoped would rescue them, he saw no one. The scout left the home, hood over his head, and made his way down the street to hide in a hole under a nearby building until a lull in the mayhem appeared.

* * *

The Elves were defeated. Captain Ulfyris was battered and bloodied, but still stood sword and shield in hand with a handful of Elfish survivors. Of the ten-thousand who attacked the Todessen, only six seemingly survived.

Surveying the damage to the port, Ulfyris nodded at the pile of ashes and mound of Todessen bodies that he left in his wake. "Not a bad day's work," the Elf thought silently.

A Todessen warrior in elaborate armor and dress walked forward with two guards in tow. They were Orcs. The leader nodded, and the Orcs executed the five Elves with Ulfyris, leaving him to face his fate alone. The Elf frowned and then sneered at the Todessen leader.

"Still treating prisoners of war like dogs, I see, Todani scum," Ulfyris said in a biting tone.

"Still stabbing your allies in the back, I see, Elf scum," the Todessen man replied calmly.

"Your ships sank three of ours without provocation near the Port of the Redeemed not even a month ago." Ulfyris looked for a shred of acknowledgment in the opponent's face. There was none.

"What are you yammering on about, Elf? We had no such encounter with the Elves at the port. You are mistaken," the Todessen countered.

The enemy drew closer. He was aware the Elf was still armed, but arrogantly sauntered up as if he were the conquering hero of the day. Xyr lay dead, and Ulfyris assumed that this rat intended to take the glory and credit for the victory. The Elf did not like this man in the least bit.

"Large black ships with incredible weapons, so I'm told. Sank three of ours in minutes? No inkling of what I speak? How convenient for you!" Ulfyris goaded.

"We WERE allies, Elf. The Todessen do not need to surprise attack your weak vessels. Look what ten did against twenty-five of yours. Relinquish your blade, Sir," the Todessen said calmly, holding out his hand with expectation.

The Elf handed over the blade and stood ready, expecting anything. The Todessen responded to the gesture by stepping forward in one motion and running the Elf through his abdomen with the Captain's own sword. Ulfyris yelped in pain, then stood proudly to return the favor. He removed a hidden dagger from his belt and, in one rote motion, stabbed the cocky Todessen in the neck. As the Elf's life began to fade, black blood sprayed on him from his enemy's wound. The Vyn Captain pulled himself close to the Todessen Commander.

"See you in the Underworld, you pig's ass. Maybe you can show me around when we get there." Ulfyris's grip loosened as he fell over. The Todessen Commander fell, dead, on top of the body of the Elf.

Several of the Todessen in the ranks were not pleased, but some of the officers laughed.

"Serves that fool right for walking up to an Elfish Ranger without regarding who his enemy is. Look at the destruction that this small army of vermin created."

"Agreed. Never trifle with your enemy. A dead enemy is a good enemy," another officer responded.

* * *

Within a week, Yanas made his way down the western coast. He avoided settlements and Todessen patrols, hiding as Elves do within nature. The Elf crossed the mountains into Dwarven-held territories within three or four more days. He skirted the Port of the Redeemed borders and intended to make his way south to a safe house where he could get on a boat back to his homeland of Vynwratha. Instead, his plans were cut short by a roving patrol of Dwarves, a day's ride from the southern shore.

"This one's an Elf, Sir, not a Todani," the patrol leader reported to his Officer of the Day.

"Then why in the Underworld is he dressed that way? Fool. We may be at war, but Elves and Dwarves can talk. We give no quarter to Todani. He is lucky. Take him to the capitol and have him questioned. Maybe he can tell us what has the Todani in such an uproar." The Lieutenant returned his man's salute.

The guard locked the cage. A silent Elf sat defiantly in his prison on a horse-drawn cart. He was already formulating plans of escape, and the Dwarves were fully aware of his intentions. They doubled the watch on their new captive and rode to Dornat Al Fer.

Yanas looked at his surroundings. Then, roughly determining where he was, he continued to scheme.

"These pitiful fools. They will not hold me." The scout quietly looked at a small sack hidden on his person; the tools were all there. He had what he needed.

* * *

At midnight, Yanas continued his travels southward. The Dwarves had no idea he was missing until dawn. When they did realize their blunder, the Elf was miles away in the southern forests. It would be impossible to catch him now. The Dwarfish Patrol Commander decided to forget about the incident and told his men to do so as well.

No use worrying his leadership over one rogue Elf.

Chapter 5

The invasion was repelled, but the Todessen King was still not pleased. King Lyax scowled while reading a parchment that detailed the past day's events. His High Commander stood silently at attention, awaiting his orders. Standing stoically, General Sulfga listened carefully as the King read his victory to him as if it were a condemnation of his ability to command.

"So, General," the King said, concluding his beratement, "the weakling Elves mounted a marginally successful attack on our only naval port."

"It was not successful, Sire. They were soundly defeated, and ne'er one breathes to tell of the battle," the General respectfully retorted.

"Unsuccessful?" The King rose from his seat. Several guards around him perked up to see what the monarch's next move would be. One never knew what the angry Todessen ruler would do from moment to moment.

The General looked at his King as if questioning why he was angry.

"You fool! The Elves burned our ENTIRE port! We have no sea access from the mainland without it!" The King grimaced, as if in pain. "The bastards, in their tactical miscalculation, even proceeded to bring more ships into the harbor than was wise, only to have that folly also rewarded." The King motioned for a mug of ale.

"But they were destroyed, My King. How were they rewarded?" General Sulfga was confused by the King's displeasure at the destruction of the enemy ships. He did not understand why he was not celebrated, but instead criticized.

"Truly, your men did a fine job of sinking the Elf navy. This is undisputed, but WHERE they did it is a problem." The King sipped from his mug, expecting his hint to bring a revelation to the General before him. Instead, Lyax decided at that moment that Sulfga was a great warrior. However, an intellectual, he was not.

Sulfga stood silent. His look of confusion said it all.

The King bellowed, "Their ships and ours now reside at the bottom of our shallow harbor. No large vessel, especially our warships and supply galleons, can access the now almost non-existent piers that your glorious victory has left us with. The Vyn have effectively rendered the Port of Wargyrnim useless for the foreseeable future."

Sulfga gazed downward. He had not realized how badly the battle had crippled the Todessen military.

"What are your orders, Your Majesty?" the General asked, hoping to change the subject.

The King's eyes were wide, and he shook his head in apathy. He handed his empty mug to a porter. "Sulfga, inform our mages that they are to communicate with the fleet that is at sea. Have them send ships from the eastern sea to Vynwratha. Send five with full troop compliments. Land wherever they can to load them. Use the human ports. If the sheep in Degran-Eras object, kill them as a reminder of who is in charge there."

"Yes, Sire. Immediately," the General bowed.

"Dismissed. Do not fail me again, or I will have your head, and your replacement will hand it to me. Understood?" The Todessen King smiled menacingly at his Commander.

"Understood completely, Sire," Sulfga replied, leaving for the mage's guild.

∗ ∗ ∗

Orus had been in the Port of the Redeemed for almost a month when his men reported a large contingent of Elfish ships traveling northward.

The warrior was concerned when he was told that over twenty warships sailed toward his current location, bearing the red standard of the Vyn. The Hodan King had ensured that two of his own vessels were patrolling just outside the port entrance. At the same time, one stood at the ready, immediately within the harbor mouth. The remaining two stood down in the port, allowing rest for his men.

As the Hodan prepared for a massive assault by the Elves, they worried about their future. They were relieved when that small armada of enemy ships did not turn toward their position, but instead continued to sail northward toward Todessen territory.

Jaruz looked through a large spyglass at the ships on his horizon. "I wonder where those lads are off to? Haeldrun Ir, or a landing up the coast to try a land assault against us?"

Orus looked through his glass. "I would wager either is possible, but they look like they are determined to push northward. Do you have spies, ahem, I mean, scouts to the north?"

"I have a few human slaves who I have recruited to report back to my field officers," the Dwarf smirked. "I will see what they have to tell us. If the Elves do sail to the land of the Todessen, we will know in about five days."

"I see," Orus replied, putting his spyglass in a hardened leather case. "I will have my reserves readied for the alternative of an enemy attack from the north."

"Much appreciated, my friend," the older Dwarf replied as he left to ready his own.

* * *

The Elf scouts knew someone stalked them, but they could not find a trace of their observer. Quietly, they hid in plain sight, bows drawn, walking with purpose among the trees. Unbeknownst to them, all that is in nature is not always truly a static part of life.

Kepir was dressed in his suit. It was comprised of a net made of coarse hemp rope, strips of leather, and sinew. Adorning his garb were the flowers, leaves, grasses, and dirt of the surrounding environment. The human specialist crouched silently behind an Elf, who was completely unaware he was there.

The Elf made hand signals to someone. Kepir calmly observed the horizon, picking out movement fifty yards from his target's position. Then, as silently as any Elf, the human crept up behind his quarry, stabbing him with a dart that was coated with a concoction designed to induce sleep. Covering the victim's mouth, he waited until he was still. No one seemed to come to the spy's aid. They either kept their positions hidden due to a higher mission, or had not seen their man fall. Kepir searched the Elf for information and left the immediate area.

The mountains south of the Todessen were usually a solitary place. Kepir had been alone, wandering the vast wilderness area for three weeks when the Elves arrived. His interest in them was piqued. Typically, no Dwarves would come north for fear of accidentally crossing the border and starting a war. In turn, no Todessen ventured south for the same reason, unless they were a raiding party. The Wood was an excellent buffer zone between the two rivals. The Elves, however, consider the woods to be their natural home and are most dangerous among the trees. Kepir was interested in what was going on, as the Elfish military presence had begun to increase over the past three weeks. The Hodan scout began to suspect that all was not well between Elf and Todessen.

Orus had quietly dispatched his man to get the true lay of the land. These new Dwarfish friends were a fantastic new bonus, but the King was wary of trusting anyone in this new locale. The specialist was the Hodan King's friend and most trusted man. The skilled spy looked at the papers he had pilfered from the Elf scout. The language was not exactly what he was used to reading, but he could decipher word of an attack that he guessed was scheduled within days. Taking out a sharpened charcoal stick and a rolled parchment, the human jotted down the specifics he could glean.

Then he snuck back to the still sleeping Elf scout and put the papers back in his satchel to avoid detection over missing documents. The spy expertly covered his tracks.

Looking southward, the human slowly and methodically slithered his way through the trees to the tall grass. He waited until nightfall. Kepir traveled to the spot where he stashed his supplies, finding them still well-hidden in a small hole and covered with soil and branches. He removed his field suit in the dark and dressed in clothing he had stolen from a wash line in the local area. There were a few humans living here and there within the Dwarfish lands, but they were few and far between. The clothes fit, but were a bit tight. The spy adjusted as best he could, throwing a cloak over him and covering his head with a hood.

Within a few miles, the Hodan happened upon a small caravan of traveling human merchants. He spent some coin at the cantina they erected in a tent and flirted with a few local women, including Dwarves, for good measure. He was very popular. Saying his goodbyes and leaving a generous tip to the bar wench, he pretended to travel south toward the Port of the Redeemed, only to pull off of the road a couple of miles later. He hid in the woods and covered himself with the brush for camouflage.

Later that night, Kepir returned to the merchant camp, incapacitated a watchman with the same concoction he used on the Elf scout, and quietly stole a horse. He walked it peacefully away from camp until out of sight and hearing, and then rode at a trot for a few miles to avoid suspicion. After a couple of miles, the specialist pushed his newfound steed to a gallop and entered the borders of the Galdrissen port by sunrise.

"Halt, who are you?" A sentry challenged him on the main road to the town. Five Dwarves in plate with spears and swords backed him up.

"Good morning, gentlemen," the rider said, removing his hood. "I am Kepir, of Hodan. I am King Orus's man. I bring word for him from the north."

After Kepir produced the favor of Hodan to the guards, the Dwarves confirmed his identity, taking him to Orus and Jaruz, who sat eating breakfast and talking politely.

"Your Majesty and Admiral Jaruz, greetings!" Kepir said enthusiastically.

Orus was happy to see his man, but sarcastically rolled his eyes. "How can you be so happy this early in the morning, Kepir?"

"I have news, Sirs. The Elves are attacking the Todessen for some reason. A major force should march through here within a few days if it has not somehow already come. I am not sure how I could have missed them if they have already passed through." Kepir waited for a response.

"Elves attacking the Todessen?" Jaruz squinted.

"Of course, my friend. They think we are the Todessen, because of our ships. We attacked them. They will retaliate in kind against the real Todessen, thinking they are getting payback." Orus chuckled.

Jaruz's eyes widened in concern. "They can never win. Lourama is a foolish Queen."

"Why the long face, friend?" Orus responded.

"Well, if they attack the Todessen, they will be crushed," Jaruz responded.

"Good?" Orus questioned the objection to the enemy's destruction.

"If they are destroyed at that battle, the Todani will not be satisfied," Jaruz continued. "The Scourge will send an attack force of thousands to Vynwratha. They will seek to seize the kingdom from that fool Lourama. If we seek to ally with the Elves, to forge a peace that can stand against the Todani, we cannot let them fall. When our time comes, we will need them in the trees."

"I see your point," Orus said, rubbing his face with both hands. "We should counter that threat."

"How do you propose to counter thousands of motivated Todani warriors?" Jaruz snorted.

"I will sail my five ships and five legions to Vynwratha. I will talk to the Queen and try to work out the alliance. If the Toads show up, I will fight them. You are invited to attend with the 'glory of Dornat Al Fer' in tow, if your King so wishes." Orus smirked confidently.

"These Todani are nothing to trifle with, Orus," the Dwarf said, as a matter of fact. "Be wary and be ready."

"I always am," Orus replied and then turned to Kepir. "Get yourself clean.

Get out of those rags. Eat some real food and rest, for tomorrow we sail, my friend."

"As you command, My King. Be well," Kepir replied, bowing to both men.

* * *

Orus could see five large black warships on the horizon. Their white sails were blazoned with black runes around the edge and a large black gauntlet in the center. They were the Todessen from the north. As expected, they were making a beeline toward an Elfish port to his west and the opposite side of the hills where the Hodan Navy hid. Orus thought about attacking, but then reconsidered, deciding to wait until the Todessen were fully committed to their assault on the beach fortress. Then, when they were not looking, he would hit them with everything he had from behind.

"Kepir! Tell Captain Naldira to unload her legion on this shore. Their orders are to travel to where the Toads are to the southwest, engage, and destroy them all. Tell Captains Ilmat and Barian to do the same. Naldira's 2nd Legion has the command. The 3rd and 4th legions will follow their lead."

Kepir nodded solemnly.

Orus was his old self. The seasoned warrior was determined and moved with purpose, looking out over the starboard side of his command ship. There, he saw a broad open grassy plain, inland of a soft sand beach which was suitable for the landing. "Tell them that is the place. Tell them to make it happen now. Go! There is no time!"

Kepir smiled at Orus, who looked and him with a bit of annoyance. The King raised his eyebrows, then waived him off. "Get out of here."

Kepir met with the signalman. They sent flag signals to each ship left and right of the command ship. Soon, small boats, loaded with men and equipment, rowed from each vessel and made return trips until the three legions were on the beach.

Orus nodded in approval to Kepir, who had returned to his King's side as usual. The Hodan ruler looked back over the mountains and could see the Todessen had entered the harbor and were bombarding the coastal defenses with catapults and Ballista. Fire was raining down on the Elfish walled port. Todessen ships began unloading their warriors onto the beach. What was not lost on the King was how efficient the operation was. They could have been Hodan troops if he did not know better.

"Signal the attack. Let's go, Kepir! Get the word out to line it up! We go to the Elves … again." Orus was sarcastic, laughing at his own joke. He was happier than he had been in a long time.

Kepir smiled at his King's jubilance. "Luck in battle, My King."

"Luck in battle, my trusted friend," Orus responded, checking his blade.

* * *

The Elfish shore town of Tadvynmir was little more than a fortified port and stronghold with a small town of Elves that had sprung up around the emplacement. The name meant "Death from the Sea." It was named such by the Queen of the Elves when the place was used as the primary invasion point of Vynwratha by the Todessen in the Great War. It had served for over one-hundred years as a deterrent to Dwarf, human, or Todessen attacks. It was not only where death came from the sea, but it became the main port from where the Elves dealt death back. At present, most of the Elfish ships were out to sea or at the bottom of a Todessen harbor. Ten ships remained in port. Three were in the process of responding to the Todessen advance, when the black ships entered the Elfish waters.

The Elves were not faring well, but had slowed the Todessen advance. The Todessen had a new problem. The fortress they sought to breach had begun its bombardment of their positions with catapult and trebuchet. The Todessen numbers were in the thousands. Now, fire and explosive rounds did their jobs, but the Elves knew they were in trouble.

"How many have they got, Deras?" an older Elf in silver mail asked, stringing an Elfish longbow.

"Five-thousand, perhaps, maybe more, brother," the Elf responded, looking over the fortifications.

"Well, we had better hope the Queen is paying attention then!" The Elf strapped on his helmet and grabbed a quiver. "We had better slow their advance, because if they get siege weapons off of those ships, we are done for!"

"Understood, Relas. Be careful, brother! Do not die. I would miss you." Deras wore a sad look and hugged his friend.

"Always! I will never stick my neck out unnecessarily. Light the red beacon if anything of major importance happens. I will watch for it." Relas ran out of the room, dressing as he went.

Deras limped to his station. He was maimed as a child when the Todessen came to Vynwratha the first time. Now a young Elfish man, he knew he was not a Vyn warrior, but he could be their eyes from the towers. Raising his spyglass, he surveyed the situation about him. He noticed something very peculiar in the distance. An unknown army was making its way through the wood. He had not noticed them before, because every Elf on two feet was engaged elsewhere with the Todessen.

The new army came out of the wood and into plain view. To Deras, it almost seemed as if they dared him to notice them. They wore chain and plate, carried sword and shield, and entire divisions of their forces were armed with crossbow. Each army had a similar gold lion's head standard, but each lion was on a different colored field. Red, yellow, and blue were the colors of their fields, and it seemed that yellow and blue took their cues from the red. Chills ran down his spine as they moved expertly into position. The lines appeared to be humans, and they were marching without delay toward the surrounded Elvish forces. The professional band attacked the Todessen without mercy when they arrived, decimating the Black Army's rearguard.

Deras had seen enough. He struck the flint on steel and lit the oily rag on his torch. Taking it to a small furnace, he tossed the torch in, and the contents immediately began to burn. The magic on the kindling and the fuel for the fire gave off a distinctive bright red hue as the light emanated in every direction out of a large circular window above the fireplace. Now he waited for someone to notice so he could pass the news.

* * *

Naldira was commanding the assault. She had her legions right where she wanted them. The Todessen had no idea what had just arrived. Seeing humans, they sneered, ignoring the Hodan. At the same time, they continued dealing with what they thought was the real threat—the Vyn—that is, until the human units began killing Todessen at will. That development brought attention to the enemy lines, which was what Naldira wished. She smiled, growling out orders, and her legions tightened up. The Elves had found an escape route, and thousands ran toward the trees to regroup. The Hodan watched as the Vyn defenders disappeared. The Todessen were looking at the humans in disbelief.

"They do not approve, warriors," the Commander of the 2nd Legion declared. "Show them that we care not for their opinion. CHARGE!"

The Hodan forces charged effectively, killing one in five of the Todessen Commander's men in one engagement. He was losing warriors quickly, and the naval battles seemed to be turning in favor of new ships that had arrived on the scene. At first, the approaching black vessels appeared to be friendly reinforcements. However, when two eventually fired upon a Todessen warship, it was apparent they were imposters. The Todessen ship was sinking before his very eyes. In response, the Todessen Navy had attempted to ram what appeared to be the enemy command ship, but another of the enemy warships cut them off. This human ship absorbed the full impact of the attack, sinking into the Elfish harbor as the imposter's crew attempted to escape by boat. Several Elfish vessels moored in the harbor spontaneously burst into flames, spewing magic and destruction all around. The water was on fire, and another Todessen vessel was seriously damaged, listing to port. The Todessen warrior could not see anything more from his vantage point.

"Regroup, fall back, regroup!" the Black Army's Commander ordered, and the Todessen complied, forming up on the opposite side of the field. There, as he saw the rest of his troops arriving on shore, the Todessen leader estimated that he outnumbered the human contingent four or five to one.

"We have the numbers, Commander. So why do we pause?" a junior Todani Officer complained.

The older, more experienced warrior pointed to the enemy command ship that had begun to bombard the shore. There appeared to be more small boats with men disembarking to join the fight on the beach. The younger warrior's eyes widened, and he fell silent.

The older man nodded, raising an eyebrow at the questioning youth. "We must be smart. I have no idea how many more reinforcements this sheep dung has coming. But rest assured, these weasels will pay for this breach of trust. These atrocities will be met with much suffering in Degran-Eras. The King will see to that!"

The Todessen were in formation and ready to fight. The humans had reformed near the reinforced gates of Tadvynmir and appeared to be allied with the Elves within. The odds of losing this battle were rising by the moment. The Todessen Commander could not hold much longer. The Black Army charged the gates as one. The Elves watched from their walls in horror, killing as many of Haeldrun Ir's as they could with their Elfish bows.

* * *

Orus landed on the beach. Kren had saved his hide, and he was not about to waste the sacrifice. Angrily, the King of Hodan remembered Captain Kren piloting the *Annihilator* into the path of an oncoming battering ram of a Todessen warship. If he had not, the *Vindicator* would be at the bottom of the bay, and the King knew he would probably be there with it. Kepir had reported that some had made it from the wreckage of the *Annihilator*, and Orus found himself hoping Kren was among the living.

"Kepir, we must maneuver to a position to aid the other three legions. We must avenge the 5th," the Hodan King ordered.

Kepir simply saluted and ran toward where the legions had formed. Naldira had chosen an excellent place to make her stand. Still, there was no escape, unless the Elves opened their gates if the fighting became untenable.

Orus frowned. He realized the pain of losing an entire unit in one blow. The loss of the 5th Legion began to sink into his bones as he waited to join the lines. Then, remembering Puryn's loss of the 1st Yslan Legion at Cinnog, he somberly nodded, realizing what his brother-in-arms felt that day. Orus was thankful that some might have survived to be a thorn in the Todani's side.

Kepir returned. "Captain Naldira is ready for your arrival, Sir."

A thunderous shout of unity filled the air as he reported in, and the Todessen charged across the field, pinning the 2nd, 3rd, and 4th Legions against the fort behind them. The Elves were not opening the doors. The Hodan were in trouble, and Orus knew it.

"Kepir, tell the flagman to signal a barrage offset on the beach. Signal danger close. Signal caution." Orus grabbed his man's shoulders, looking him in the eye to ensure that he understood completely. "Do not let my warriors die … by the Todessen or by our own gunners. Understood?"

"Completely, Your Majesty," the specialist replied, and he left to comply with his King's wishes.

Soon, the report of staggered Thunder Ballista fire could be heard from the port harbor. Three Todessen ships were sunk, and the remaining two ran northwest toward home. The Hodan Navy did not pursue them, but instead began taking turns ensuring a constant barrage of exploding shot landed upon the beach just far enough away from the fighting to injure and kill some of the Todessen in the rear. It was not as effective as it was raining down death, but the Todani looked worried. There was no safe retreat from the rain of Elfish arrows and wall of Human blades. The Scourge was trapped.

The 1st Hodan Legion charged into the flank of the already engaged Todessen army. The newly arrived forces had their way for a bit, before the Todessen Commander noticed the fresh mayhem on his right flank. He ordered a wall of shields to form up on the right, and soon another battle of attrition was created. This time, however, the Todessen were on the receiving end. The Hodan efficiency at land warfare, the Elfish bowmen accuracy, and the exploding shot coming from the sea, combined with yet another fresh human legion arriving on the scene, was too much to handle, even for the most seasoned Todani Elite. The Todani made a hasty retreat to the tree line. Hodan pursued.

* * *

"Your Majesty, our legions return. Damage report: One sunken ship and crew. The 5th Legion is missing in action and presumed perished at sea. The remaining four legions report light to medium casualties. Estimates right now are thirty-six-hundred remaining Hodan Elites, four ships, and enough ballistae ammunition to level any coastal defenses, or perhaps sink a few Toad ships." Kepir rolled up his scroll and stood tall in front of Orus.

Orus was tired, hungry, and bruised. "Oh for the love of Runnir, stop with the formality, you horse's ass, and bring me a skin of mead. We shall toast our victory."

Orus looked at the fortress he had liberated. The Hodan moved their forces out of bow range, just in case, and set up camp on the opposite side of the beach. They hoped that someone would come out to talk. So far, there had been no luck. Occasionally, the sound of battle erupted in the woods, but it was quickly silenced. Orus chuckled, remembering the Draj.

"Those Toads are meeting Elves in the Wood. They must be more stupid than I recall them being," Orus said to Kepir as he was handed a mug of mead.

Kepir raised his mug. "To the crew of the *Annihilator*. To Captain Kren. To the heroes who afforded me the chance to stand here and make this toast."

"To the *Annihilator*," Orus responded, lifting his cup and then drinking.

"Your Majesty, my operatives observing the Elf fortress, state that an Elf on horseback was seen galloping northward up a path into the trees. They figure he is their messenger," Kepir reported.

"Good news. Maybe the person running this place does not have the authority to speak to foreign powers? Perhaps, he or she sends for someone who does." Orus smiled briefly, then drifted off, staring into the fire for a bit. "I was too hard on Kren. I should have treated his initiative with more acceptance. If he were alive, I would give him another ship and another legion."

"Indeed, he was an interesting charge," Kepir said, downing his mead. "I must return to the watch, Sire."

"Agreed. Keep an eye out for the Toads, Kepir. The Elves sound like they might drive them out of the woods and back into our laps, if any survive." Orus chuckled and leaned back, and began napping on a large stone. He gripped his drawn sword, which was laid across his lap. Guards were posted everywhere.

* * *

Kren was not alone in the Wood. He had two hundred and fifty armed survivors of the *Annihilator* with him. They hid much like the Elves did, having learned Puryn's Draj techniques while training on the Ert in the northern alliance. They were not Elite Rangers, but they were far better than the enemy expected. Finding a cave and making it a base of operations, Kren split his forces into fifty-man teams, assigning team leaders to each group. The orders were simple: Ambush and kill any Todessen in the area of operations. Kren rotated his groups; fifty on watch at base camp, one-hundred-fifty resting, while the remaining fifty patrolled, wreaking havoc.

The Todessen did not know how to deal with the new human threat. They were dying in droves. The Scourge lost five foot-soldiers for every human they found and killed. This violence was not lost on the Elves. They hid in the forest, watching and assisting the Hodan covertly, whenever possible. Kren's scouts had detected the Elfish spies, but the Elves were unaware. The human Commander sought to win them over. He was on the right track.

* * *

The Queen was abruptly interrupted by a guard who jogged into the room with another man in tow. "Your Majesty! I request an audience; it is of the utmost importance."

The Queen looked away from her scout, turning her gaze to the unkempt visitor and the annoying guard. "What?" she bellowed. Behind them strode a Ranger scout with his report to give. The Queen sighed and sat on her throne.

"Your Majesty, I am a rider from Tadvynmir. Lord Deras sends greetings and word that the Todessen have invaded our southern shores. They are moving in our forests as I speak this message!"

The Queen dropped her crystal goblet. "WHAT!?"

"There is more, Your Majesty," the rider continued.

"More? Do you seek to kill me with your news? What else could have happened?" The Queen sat on her throne and called for another goblet of wine.

"Humans, Your Majesty, and perhaps the Dwarves?" The rider stopped and cringed, awaiting a shriek.

The Ranger scout awaited his turn, but could contain himself no longer.

"Your Majesty, humans ARE in our Wood, slaughtering our enemies!" The spy was animated and excited at the prospect of the new human allies.

"Fool, the humans are cowardly slaves. They would never raise a hand to their master. They quake in their piss whenever a Todani rides by." The Queen was disgusted by the thought of humans.

"Not THESE humans, Your Majesty. They fought like the humans of old, and then they fought like, we Elves. It was unnerving to watch. They were so magnificent a sight to behold in battle! You should see them in the Wood, My Queen. They hunt like a wolf pack, and the Todani are rabbits. The enemy has no idea what has hit them." The spy was obviously enamored with his newfound friends.

"Where did they come from, boy?" the Queen snarled.

The excited one was smiling happily. He shrugged in response to the dismay of the Queen.

"This is no smiling matter, you fool," the Queen barked.

The spy tried to contain his glee.

The rider from the south continued. "Human warriors of amazing prowess made a landing on our shores east of the fortress. Deras saw them and sent the signal. He said there were thousands of them." The rider was handed a cup of water. He sipped a bit and continued. "The humans rescued our Elfish forces who were surrounded, and then held the Todani at the fortress gates. They sank three Todani warships in our harbor and caused two to flee northward. They even succeeded in pushing the remnant of the Todani forces into the Wood."

"How many, Rider?" the Queen questioned abruptly, calling over a military advisor.

"Five thousand, perhaps, My Queen," the messenger replied. "The humans were encamped on the beach when the Todani returned several times from the forest during the night. We think that they sought to escape ambush and harassment, seemingly attempting to finish the job they had started. But, unfortunately for them, someone in the Wood was killing their soldiers very efficiently, which forced them to attempt to find safety elsewhere. A fight in the dark ensued on the beach, and it looked as if the scum from Haeldrun Ir had achieved the upper hand in the blackness, but then Dwarves arrived in the night as if they knew where these humans would be. Lord Deras estimates that the Dwarves are allied or at least in a truce with the humans, or he has no idea why they would risk two legions of foot soldiers for strangers."

"A worthy observation. Deras has always been a bright lad." The Queen wrote something on parchment and handed it to a General. "The Rangers are in the Wood as of now. Apparently, human Rangers or Elites of some sort are killing the Todani at will within our forests. My scouts tell me that they are exceptionally good at killing. We shall aid them. Rider, return south and take my minister with you. He will act in my absence if an alliance can be forged with these foreigners. Steer clear of the Dwarves. I have no idea of their intentions."

"As you wish, Your Majesty." The rider bowed. He and the diplomat were on the road within minutes.

* * *

Orus was bloodied and wounded. Kepir was favoring a nasty gash to his left side. The legions had suffered another six-hundred dead from the night raids, and Orus was concerned that in his first day of real battle on the Rynn, he had lost forty percent of his men and women, as well as one warship. If the Dwarves had not arrived when they did, the Todessen would have killed them in the dark, and the King knew it.

"Thank you for your assistance, friend," Orus said, grunting and standing. He towered over the shorter warrior, but shook his hand respectfully.

"It is my duty to aid my friends when they are in need, My Lord," the Commander replied.

"Please, set your camp wherever you like, Commander, but be wary of those Elves in that fortress. They are ornery, and they are magnificent shots, too!" Orus sipped a bit of Dwarven ale from a flask, grimacing as he swallowed it. He offered it to his new friend, who accepted.

"I knew I liked you when I met you, human! Not too many men will touch this stuff. It tends to be too much." The Dwarf handed back the flask, half-empty. Orus's eyes widened. *The Dwarves could drink!*

"It's for the pain," Orus lied. Both laughed.

"We shall camp closer to the water. I fear the Elves will come soon. I hope that they wish to talk. One would think that saving their necks might be a cause to rethink old animosities." The Dwarf bowed and left Orus to his thoughts and his Dwarven ale.

* * *

The bellowing of the watch wakened Orus. His head ached from too much drink the night before, and his body ached from the beating it took in battle. He knew he was getting too old for this.

"To arms, to arms! Battle on the edge of the forest! Battle to our north!" the sentry cried loudly.

Within moments, the legions were falling in. Many were strapping down armor and wiping off their blades. All the warriors were beaten and bruised, but none shied away from the line. Every Hodan still fought to be at the front of the battle. Orus stood and hid his pain.

"Make ready, legions! Prepare to repel!" Orus bellowed, as if Runnir or Gunnir himself.

The remaining three thousand warriors set the line, and the bowmen covered the flanks from behind. The Dwarves were almost formed when the enemy arrived.

The Todessen were running at breakneck speed toward the shore. Something swift and deadly pursued them. The Wood was aflutter as leaves, branches, and debris flew freely into the air. The screams of the dying filled the air as the dust of the massive charge made visibility difficult. The Dwarves and Hodan stood together, Hodan at the front, the Dwarves bringing up the rear. They were as ready as they could be. Orus stood proudly with his men, preparing for what was coming, but he was not prepared for what he beheld.

The chanting began with a few individuals in the Wood, but quickly spread to all present there. The Hodan and the Dwarves stood in witness of the full fury of the Vynwrathian Rangers, as fifty-thousand warriors pushed the remnant of the Todessen invaders out of the Wood and back onto the sand. By the time the dust had settled, a line of Elves had stretched along the entire beach, and scarcely one-thousand Todessen remained in front of the Hodan lines.

Orus spoke to the Dwarf. "I hope they have come to talk."

"I, as well, my friend. Those are the Rangers. They don't do much talking," the Dwarf replied.

"I like these Elves more, with each passing day," Orus said to no one in particular.

The Dwarf Commander stepped back with a bit of alarm at the statement.

As the conversation ended and the last remaining Rangers had joined their brethren, one stood and faced his line shouting, "Ela Cyrkris! Zem fyr Vulk Isi!"

The army exploded, echoing their apparent Commander. "Ela Cyrkris! Zem fyr Vulk Isi!"

Orus looked to his new Dwarf friend. "What did they say?"

"It's their war cry. It means, 'Long live Cyrkris, Victory to his people!'" The Dwarf was concerned. "Cyrkris is a revered hero and former King of the Vyn. They usually chant this before destroying the enemy or winning a great battle. I just hope they stop with the Todani!"

The war cry continued for a minute or two straight. It was deafening. Then another inaudible command was made, and a roar of Elfish warriors shook the very ground around Orus. He stood proudly with Hodan, smiling as he watched the Rangers surround and pulverize the remnant of the Todessen invaders.

* * *

The leader of the Vyn stepped forward of his lines toward the Hodan shield wall. Fifty heavily armed and armored individuals flanked him. He surveyed the line without emotion until he spied the Dwarves behind Orus. The Elf spat.

"Who commands this army? Who dares to step on Elfish lands without an invitation?" The Elf Ranger strutted confidently in front of the vastly superior Elfish army. "Who is prepared to die, this day?"

Orus, flanked by Kepir and the Dwarf Commander, stepped forward. Hodan was on alert. They could not win this fight, but they could bleed the sand red with Elfish blood. The reports of the prowess of Hodan did not escape the Elfish Ranger, who postured for a parlay. He watched with apprehension as two black ships adjusted their angle, and doors opened on the sides of each vessel. Within each hatch, a shining metal tube protruded. The Ranger noticed a human with a red flag on a pole above his head. It was very prominently displayed. It was no doubt a signal to the ships. He looked at the tubes on the sides of the vessels and remembered the supposed new weapon of which his scouts spoke earlier. The Elf sucked his teeth absent-mindedly, muttering to a man on his left, who took off running to the army. He disappeared.

"I am Orus, King of Hodan. I have come to offer a truce and alliance with the Elfish people of this land. But, unfortunately, there was a misunderstanding when we first met, resulting in many regrettable events."

"You sank three of our ships and killed thousands of our men, from what I am told," the Ranger stated plainly.

"We did, but in self-defense," Orus retorted.

"Maybe you did, maybe you did not, but that is not for me to decide. The one who speaks for us is coming. She will tell you about your fate. Until then, relax, human! We will not attack you." The Elf laughed condescendingly.

"Commander," Orus called out, "as a gesture of good faith, I wish to return a few men we captured during our unfortunate introduction that first day."

Kepir whistled, and five Elves marched forward to where the Commander stood.

The Commander smiled and declared, "This is a good start, human! We are also generous. We will return to you many more than you returned to us. They live, because they fought valiantly in the Wood to preserve the lives of Elves. Bring them forth!"

Orus smiled, shaking his head as one-hundred or so of the Hodan 5th Legion marched proudly back to the Hodan lines. They were led by none other than Captain Kren. Orus smiled. Kepir joined him.

"Sire, we will have to muster more men if you are to give Captain Kepir another legion," Kepir smiled mischievously, knowing he had struck a nerve with Orus.

"You are now a jester, I see." Orus smirked and laughed. "Seriously, though, you are right!"

* * *

The delegation of the Elves, Hodan, and Dwarves met within the fortress at Tadvynmir. They sat around a polished wooden table, not unlike the works of the Elves of the Ert. Orus always loved a good piece of Elfish woodworking.

The Dwarf was visibly uncomfortable. He was in a den of enemies, and the only ally he had seemingly liked the lot of them. Dwarfish General Macrynna was silent and stiff. The Elves present rolled their eyes, snubbed the shorter warrior in the golden armor, and focused on the massive human warrior in blackened armor.

Queen Lourama sat across from Orus. She had decided she wanted to meet these humans face to face. She left her diplomatic team at home and had traveled south personally. Now, she sat, sizing the man up. She could ascertain from his demeanor that he perhaps felt that he could conquer the world. She sneered at the idea. Humans were no match for Elfish prowess. Still, Lourama remembered the sting of defeat at Edhelseere harbor and the reports of her men concerning the actions of the Hodan on the sea, on the beach, and in the forest. They were not the average stock of humans who resided on the Rynn.

"Who are you, and what do you want, King Orus?" Lourama asked plainly.

"I wish to find, close with, and kill every Todessen soul in the world," Orus said seriously.

The room erupted in laughter. Orus was unmoved.

"Silence!" The Queen raised her hand, and the quiet returned. "How do you propose to do that?"

"The same way my men and women defeated the Todessen in my homeland and now here in yours," Orus said, poking at the Queen's pride.

"You are mistaken, Sir. My Rangers defeated the Todessen while you licked your wounds on the beach out of arrow range." Lourama's tone struck a nerve with Orus.

"Our intervention saved your fortress on the beach. My men rescued the fortress militia that was surrounded by the Scourge. We combined forces and pushed them into the sea and the forest. By many accounts, two-hundred or so of my heroes killed another thousand in the Wood while you finished your needlepoint. You sent out your troops when it was safe to do so. Hodan did not cower when the odds were not in our favor. You only acted when you knew that you would win." Orus leaned forward, daring the Queen to slander his men and women again. He was missing too many souls in his ranks to listen to her insults.

Queen Lourama smiled. "My reports are correct. You people are fearless, and you are the reason, Orus, of Hodan. You have no fear, do you? I have fifty-thousand to your three, and you beat your chest in front of me? The humans of these lands would be on their faces begging for mercy, but not Hodan."

The Queen said Hodan with reverence, and that was not lost on Orus, who smiled. "I hear tales of fearless Elves with many customs akin to our own. I have wondered what an alliance of like-minded kingdoms could foster. I want the Toad army under my boots, Queen Lourama. I would love to see the Elves of this land with me when I do it … and make no mistake … I will do it."

"What of this Dwarven dog? Are you in bed with these thieves? How can I ally with someone who is my enemy?" Lourama sneered at the Dwarf, who kept his bearing and sipped an ale.

"I have heard both renditions of the history between you. I understand the need to save face for both sides, but the threat of the Todessen army is too great to ignore. Put aside your differences. Think of the future. Think of the people who rely on us to defend them from annihilation." Orus sipped from his mug.

"There can be no discussion without the return of our lands," Lourama dictated.

"Well, Dwarf, you heard the Lady. What grand gesture does Dornat Al Fer propose to heal the rift between the people of the Rynn?" Orus raised an eyebrow and was not impressed by the Dwarf's demeanor. This attitude endeared him even further with the Queen of the Vyn. She snorted into her glass and then laughed loudly. Orus chuckled also.

Lourama felt at ease for the first time in forever. Her army had just defeated the enemy without giving quarter, and now a powerful new ally pressured her rival right in front of her. Orus was someone the Queen wished to ally with, but she had to make sure that the Dwarves were kept in check.

"Your Majesties," the Dwarf began, "His Majesty King Hamrik sends greetings and well wishes."

Lourama rolled her eyes and drank more. "I am sure that he does."

The Dwarf continued ignoring the sarcasm. "His demands are a cessation of all raiding by the Elfish forces on Rynn mainland settlements. We, as a gesture, have relocated the Galdrissen to another locale."

"So, you are telling me that you have no need for our ancestral lands? We can reclaim them immediately?" Lourama's demeanor changed, but she did not believe the Dwarf. "Tell him that I want one-hundred talents of silver for the destruction of my ships at Edhelseere, and another fifty tons of gold for the lost time in our lands."

Orus looked at the Dwarf with a bit of worry. The Queen wanted her pound of flesh and more.

"Oh," the Elfish Queen quickly added, "and of course, I want all Elfish citizens and warriors released from your prisons and returned to our mainland immediately. We will reciprocate the prisoner exchange."

"The King of Dwarves has decided, under counsel from his closest advisors, intelligence reports regarding this Hodan race of men, and the increasing incidents of Todessen aggression on the northern borders, that the Port of the Redeemed is not as strategic a location as he once thought. Besides, the people who lived there willingly have left the land to make peace with the Rynn and in search of better security." The Dwarven General sipped his ale and waited for the Elfish Queen's reply with impatience.

"It is not lost on me how much you despise me, Dwarf. But, rest assured, the feeling is mutual," Lourama declared with irritation. "Will Dornat Al Fer relinquish control of our ancestral lands or not? Will your kingdom meet my demands for peace and alliance? Speak plainly, or leave my lands immediately!"

"Your Majesty, please!" Orus interrupted.

"I am sorry, my worthy friend, but the treachery of the Dwarves is legendary. They act only for their own best interests. They fancy themselves the Keepers of the Rynn. That they are! They keep whatever they wish in the guise of protecting our freedoms." The Queen leered at the Dwarf. "What is your answer?"

"The Kingdom of Dornat Al Fer will relinquish control of the lands known to Vynwratha as Edhelseere, on the condition of a lasting peace between our people and a military alliance to stand against future Todessen provocations. I am authorized to negotiate for the King as his agent."

The Dwarf whispered to his adviser. The conversation was short. The advisor nodded and left the room immediately. "We have the payment you demand aboard our command ship. Our King anticipated that you would ask for war reparations and has wisely planned. I will give you what you have requested. Furthermore, I will guarantee the release of your people. We are granting everything you desire. Do we have a deal? What say you, Vynwratha?" The Dwarf finished his ale and set his cup down quietly, trying to mask the look of disgust on his face.

"If you back out on your word again, Dwarves … if you betray us again … I will see Dornat Al Fer in flames! We accept your proposal. We shall cease all military operations against the settlements of the Rynn and reclaim our land of Edhelseere immediately! Our alliance will be an equal partnership. We are not vassals to the Dwarves." The Queen stood.

The Dwarf stood, and some snickered. Orus was not one of them. "I present you with the treaty written by my King's hand. It is signed and binding, should you reciprocate."

"Bring me a quill and some ink, scribe. You have yourself a deal, Dwarf," the Queen said, smiling.

Chapter 6

The Todessen did as was expected and began to persecute the human settlements on the eastern coast of the Rynn in retaliation for the defeat at Vynwratha. They came in the night and burned entire villages to the ground, raping, pillaging, and destroying everything and everyone they met. What they did not destroy, they stole. Those they did not kill were taken as slaves. The actions did not have the exact effect that King Lyax had intended. Much of the human population already feared and respected Todessen rule by proxy. The Dwarves paid lip service to the defense of Degran-Eras, but had left long ago and never returned. The most the humans saw in aid were strongly worded letters of condemnation to the Todani leadership when they invaded Degran lands. The Dwarves were more concerned with the northern buffer zone. They had long ago given up on territories inhabited by humans.

Humanity knew they could not defeat their Todani masters in direct combat; therefore, most bowed whenever called to do so. All the great heroes of old had died fighting the Scourge and had, in turn, brought thousands of the Degran ancestors to early graves with them. Any soul daring to defy orders or caught rebelling against Todani rule faced a swift and violent end. All people who now resided in Degran-Eras were raised by the survivors of the last Great War. Some of the younger generations were raised by the children of those original survivors. It was ingrained over two or three generations of human culture that Degran-Eras avoided conflict at any cost. The people felt it was their best way to survive.

Many looked at the debauchery of the latest attacks with fear and disillusionment, while others looked with a sense of rage. An underground rebellion began to form. Some humans, feeling left with no alternative, packed what little they could carry on their backs and swiftly left their homes and lands. Entire families, young and old, snuck out of their villages and towns, traveling westward and inland, over the mountains toward the nations of the Dwarves. These refugees decided to take their chances within the wilderness, living in hiding, rather than waiting in plain sight to become the targets of amusement for a Todani warlord. Those who fled would not allow their children to be used as the Todani saw fit.

The Todessen, seeing this new development, began patrolling the hills on the borders between Degran-Eras and Dornat Al Fer. Still, to their displeasure, the humans continued to filter westward to freedom. The edge of the land was simply too big to patrol, and the humans knew the area much better than the visiting security forces from Haeldrun Ir. Moreover, if a patrol detected refugees in the field, they had to consider their position concerning the forest border. Worrying about the peace, the Todani forces dared not cross into Dwarfish held lands to recapture their slaves. Soon, the numbers of escapees swelled, gathering in the relative autonomy of the mountain forest. A few small towns and villages began to form, as humans gathered together and built homes and fortifications in the unoccupied Dwarven lands. This did not go unnoticed by Dornat Al Fer.

The Dwarves, seeing the human incursion into their lands, ignored it. They were not a threat. They were simply viewed as refugees seeking asylum and protection. Anything or anyone that angered or made the Todessen look bad was welcomed by King Hamrik of the Dwarves. If the humans began to be a problem, the Dwarves had the means to push them back into Degran-Eras at will, or destroy them where they stood. King Hamrik looked at the pathetic hodge-podge of suffering humans and took pity. Eventually, he sent a peaceful delegation to the human settlements. There, his men found a young man, more of a boy, by the name of Uilam, the Hunter, had assumed a tentative role as leader. Over the months after the battle of Vynwratha, these humans had organized into semi-defendable wood-walled forts. They had gone as far as setting squads of bowmen as watchmen. They were not a terrifying force to any organized militia in the area. Still, they were an excellent deterrent to bandits and wildlife.

A Dwarf delegate sat at a rough-cut wooden table, sipping a surprisingly good ale from a carved wooden cup. The room was full of concerned faces. "Relax, good gentles. We are here to determine the state of things here."

Uilam answered. "We are well, My Lord." The man gestured to the crowd, and the dirty faces in the room all smiled and nodded appropriately. "My people wanted to assure Dornat Al Fer that we only took what we needed from His Majesty's forest."

The human spectators buzzed nervously, but quietly.

"Please, be still, brothers and sisters," Uilam begged of the crowd. The room quieted. "I wanted to admit that we have cleared five large plots of land on the slopes of the mountains. We used the wood to construct fortifications, built homes from fired clay bricks, and planted what seed we gleaned or took with us from Degran-Eras. We only hunt for what we need. In fact, we have captured several wild horses, a few cattle, and turkeys. We shall repay in full for anything we have taken. We promise. I plead for the King's mercy. We had no choice but to take what we needed, or die in our former lands."

The crowd of faces was sullen and afraid, listening intently for what the Dwarf would say in response.

"Understand this, humans," the Dwarf replied gently, "I am not here to conquer you or to send you back over the border. Instead, I am here to check up on you." He smiled.

There was a sigh of relief in the room and a few tears of joy.

Uilam was confused. He figured the Dwarves would be angry and demand that they leave. "We had no choice, My Lord. The Todani are ruthless and unkind. The cruelty of the last retaliation was untenable. We were driven to action. We meant no disrespect to Dornat Al Fer. On the contrary, we knew the Dwarves to be a just and kind nation and fled here to escape certain death."

The Dwarf could see the look of distress and fear under the façade of strength the young leader put forth in public. "Again, I say to you, Sir, you have nothing to fear from the Dwarves." The Dwarf smiled kindly. "I speak the truth; we only came to assist. So long have we wished that we could free you all from the grip of the Todani, but your former nation is in disarray and a no-man's land at best. No disrespect intended, friend."

"None taken! What you say is true. We are kidnapped by the Todani on their whim. They take their captives off for sport, pleasure, or plain slavery. They are wretched scum. They all need to die." The young man's face changed to a determined scowl.

The Dwarf could see why he was the leader. His resolve and intentions were clear. He wanted payback, but the young man did not know how to make it happen.

"Be at ease, my friend," the Dwarf responded calmly. "I bring provisions to assist in your building. When you are ready and on your feet, the King will discuss taxation. Until then, freely prosper and grow here. You are welcome."

There was a subdued cheer in the room as Uilam smiled for the first time during the meeting.

"Thank you so much, My Lord. Our people are in your debt. It has been a long time since we were shown any kindness." Uilam replied.

The Dwarf stood, smiling, and shook the human's hand.

"Then, let this be the first day of many good days to come, my new friend."

* * *

The Dwarves rode off on horseback out of the steep forest hillside and into a clearing several miles away. There they met up with the rest of their band. The encampment was not a large one by any measure, but it was a considerable force. Two Dwarfish legions and three Hodan legions were encamped. Organized patrols from both armies patrolled their respective sections of the perimeter. The delegation was challenged by the watch and allowed to pass.

Kepir met the Dwarves at the Hodan command tent. "How may I be of service, my esteemed comrades in arms?"

"We seek to speak to your King, My Lord," a younger Dwarf said, bowing.

"One moment while I see if His Majesty is prepared for visitors," Kepir replied politely, bowing and then entering the tent.

Orus was poring over maps and devising strategies for invading the north. Kepir saw him and waited to be addressed. He stood at attention.

"At ease, my friend," the King said softly. "What is it?"

"Dwarf delegation. Three of them. Outside. They seem very eager to tell you some new news. Do I let them in or tell them that you are indisposed?" Kepir said the last sentence with a snobbish tone, eliciting a snicker from the King.

Rolling up his personal maps and tucking them in a large scroll case, Orus replied, "No, let us see what they have to say. They haven't failed us yet, Kepir."

"As you wish, Your Majesty," the specialist replied softly, bowing respectfully and exiting the tent.

The Dwarves stood expectantly. "Is he available?"

"He is. He wishes to speak with you all immediately. Right this way," Kepir replied, pulling the tent's front flap aside.

The Dwarves entered the moderately lit tent. They could see a modest, portable war table with several chairs around it, a few chests of varying sizes, a surprisingly small bed with armor and weapons stand nearby. Clothing was hung on hooks built into the two center tent poles. Orus sat on a padded seat by the table, drinking out of a tankard.

"Kepir, would you mind fetching three cups for these gentlemen?" Orus asked.

"At once, Your Majesty," the specialist answered immediately, leaving the tent.

The Dwarves each sat at the table at Orus's request. Kepir returned with three cups and a fresh pitcher of mead and a smaller pitcher of Dwarven ale. The junior men accepted the human mead out of respect, but the senior diplomat poured himself a Dwarven ale immediately.

"Much obliged, Your Majesty," the senior man said, raising his cup. "It is tough to come by in the field. To King Orus! To Hodan!" the top Dwarf declared.

Orus raised his glass, then sipped his mead. "Enough formalities, friends. Why have you come to visit? It's not for the ale, I'm sure!"

"No, but the ale was an unexpected happiness! I come to talk to you about the humans of Degran-Eras, Sir," the Dwarf replied.

The messenger set his cup down. Orus noticed that he had barely drunk any. None of them had. They were polite, but this was a business visit, no doubt. Orus was interested.

"What about them. Cowards and weaklings, the Elves said? What say you, Dwarf?" Orus betrayed his skepticism.

"They are simply a tribe without a true leader. They are people without a hero. They are without hope." The Dwarf sighed and looked at Orus's hardened face. He was unsure of how much Orus was listening.

"I wish to offer you an opportunity, Sir." The Dwarf paused for effect.

Orus rolled his eyes. "Spit it out. Enough posturing. What do you want?" Orus was becoming impatient.

Kepir poured the King another mead and then gently grasped his King's shoulder. The King nodded and took a deep breath.

"Thank you, Kepir," the Hodan said plainly to his man. "Now, what are we talking about here? What opportunity?"

"I have been told that Hodan wishes to engage the Todessen. Everyone on the Rynn knows that it is impossible to accomplish as it stands. You, yourself, have stated publicly that you wished that you had ten more legions." The Dwarf paused again.

Orus raised his eyebrows. "Are you suggesting the humans of Degran-Eras would join my ranks?" The King laughed. "If they are as useless as you say, why would I want the dead weight, and if I did take them, it would take years to train them to fight like the Hodan Elites do. Our men and women begin training in childhood. These are grown men with habits to break and known cowards ..."

"You are correct in your assessment, as usual, my ally," the Dwarf responded. "But King Hamrik and Queen Lourama have become concerned with the increasing bold-faced aggression of the Todani in the north and especially in the east. Even the Orcs and Goblins have begun to arm in the southeast at Ynus-Grag. That has not occurred in over fifty-five years."

"You should watch your 'allies' to the southeast. Better make sure that a small army of Orcs and Goblins does not decide to reunite with their kindred of Haeldrun Ir, or you'll pay a heavy price," Orus stated with disgust.

"Your distrust is well-earned, from what you have told us, Orus," the Dwarf retorted. "But be reassured that we have investigated the situation, and they are only setting up a defense against incursions into their lands. They don't want to be caught up in the fray, so it seems."

"That's a first. An Orc or Goblin who seeks to avoid conflict?" Orus laughed loudly. He unceremoniously wiped his mouth with his sleeve. "So humans from the east are our new secret weapon. How many?"

"As it stands, we estimate maybe fifty to one-hundred ..."

Orus cut off the Dwarf. "One-hundred? What good is that? I have thirty times that number now, and I cannot move against the Scourge. I need thousands, not one-hundred!" Orus motioned for another mead.

"Another factor is that humans have seemingly had enough. The reason we brought the Hodan here was to witness this change firsthand. A few miles east of here, two-thousand or so humans have set up a settlement of five fortresses in the mountains. They were far from grand emplacements, but quite nicely done for what they had to work with. These are the refugees who fled the most recent atrocities by the Todani. They suffered the brunt of the Todani retribution for our victory at Vynwratha. The displaced are led by a young man named Uilam. At first, we thought him to be an anomaly. However, my scouts report that the men of Degran-Eras say their countrymen are disorganized and afraid, but becoming more radical by the day. Nevertheless, they are ready to fight back."

"So, train a few up? Take my boys and this rabble into Degran-Eras-south and do what? Attack a Todessen stronghold?" Orus cocked his head to the side with a puzzled expression. "Are you mad?"

"Our intelligence states that the Todani only station one- to two-thousand at Whaleford, the large human town, to the southernmost border with Ynus-Grag. They do not station more, because every time that they do, the Orcs and Goblins move large numbers of troops and weapons to the southern border. They are afraid to fight the Orcs and Goblins!" The Dwarf smirked and sipped his ale.

"They should be afraid. One Orc is equal to three men, and those Goblins are wiry little sons of whores, but on average, I would count two men for every one of them." Orus sipped his mead and thought hard. "IF, and I am only running this out as an idea, we were to take three legions of Hodan and a compliment of the Degran into Whaleford and capture it, how would we hold it?"

"Hold it? We could assist in that, but it would be a bloodbath." The Dwarf smiled widely. "If our reports are accurate, and your forces decimate the Todani as we estimate that you will, the city has ten-thousand souls living in it … maybe more. Perhaps, a thousand or two of fighting age! We suggest that you escape back to the mountains and establish a base of operations in the forest. The Dwarfish legions will deploy to our southeastern borders to ensure the bloodshed does not extend to our neutral lands."

Orus chuckled. "I always thought the Elves were the devious ones. Not here. You Dwarves have that title, hands down! So, how do I meet the young lad who has captured the fancy of the refugees?"

"I thought you would never ask," the Dwarf said, quickly finishing his ale. "I can arrange to take you there in the morning, if you like?"

"I would like that. My man, Kepir, will be attending with me," Orus stated as a matter of fact.

"Of course, Your Majesty. These humans are not the warriors you are. They will not refuse an official visit." The Dwarf stood and bowed. "Until tomorrow, then?"

Orus nodded. "Tomorrow. Early."

The Dwarf bowed again. "As you wish, King Orus. I am eager to see how the people of the settlement react to human heroes. This will be very interesting."

"Interesting? I surely hope so. I hope they don't piss themselves," Orus answered as the Dwarves exited his tent.

Once they were alone, Orus asked, "What do you think, Kepir?"

"I think that it is worth the look, Sire. We can evaluate the operation's viability once we see what we are working with. I do not trust the Dwarves to cover our escape from Degran-Eras, though. It would look too convenient to the Todani." Kepir stood straight.

"I agree, my friend," Orus said, tearing off a piece of bread and munching on it. "Despite the Dwarfish posturing and calculating, they may be the deterrent we need, nonetheless. With the numbers of people we could glean, we could rebuild Hodan here if we can mold them. That would be a legacy worthy of a God in Hodan lore."

"Agreed, My King," Kepir said, watching as Orus left the tent. Then, he muttered to himself, "As if standing toe-to-toe with the end of all things and surviving is not good enough for such a remembrance. Our people can be so foolish at times."

Kepir poured himself a cup of mead, raised it silently in a salute to his King, and then downed it.

* * *

Orus and the Dwarfish delegation left the camp and headed east on a well-traveled road. The ruts from wagons and carts clearly defined two routes of travel. Orus knew that a Dwarfish town was in the area, but he was not sure of the region's geography. So he relied on the Dwarves to guide his way, as Kepir took copious notes and drew out the route. Another war map was in the making.

After about two hours of riding, the mountains stood out plainly against the horizon. They had served as a natural buffer against the Todani attacks for a century. Now, they were the home of a newly established human garrison town. Orus could see the rise of chimney smoke within the trees.

After a short trip up into the forested hillside, he and his party arrived at the main gate to a ramshackle but sturdy, walled town. A guard, who was little more than an older boy, checked to see who approached and then banged on a metal triangle with a rod, raising the feeble guard patrol to the door. They opened the gate and allowed the party to enter.

Orus looked around. There were many large halls, presumably to house those who fled aggression. Orus also noticed water storage, food storage, and defensive towers at the corners of the walls. Each building had murder holes cut into it. The Hodan King smiled and nodded. At least they were trying to defend themselves. That was a start.

A young man dressed in little more than rags and animal skins approached the horse-drawn carts of the Dwarfish delegation. He stopped and addressed the Dwarves.

"Greetings, friends! What can we do for our most appreciated hosts?" the man asked seriously with a bow.

"We come bringing supplies to augment your stores and to introduce you to our friend and ally, King Orus of Hodan. He is human, but from a faraway, foreign land." The Dwarf gestured toward the Hodan, who sat stoically, sizing up the youth.

Orus grunted, nodding. "Hello."

The young man bowed. "Greetings, Your Majesty. I am Uilam, son of Yerd. My father was a Constable for many years before being murdered by the Todani for attempting to save my mother and sister from the horror of being raped and murdered by the same savages from Haeldrun Ir." The young man, realizing that he had said too much, added, "I do not know why I felt the need to tell you of my lineage, but there it is." The young man's face was red with anger and embarrassment. Orus smiled, seeing it plainly.

"I knew another man who was the son of a Constable. He was and remains a great man in my lands." Orus paused. "But that is another place, and that was another time. We are here now. What do you say that we get an ale and discuss the future, lad?" The old man hopped spryly from his seat in the wagon. Kepir followed in tow.

"Go with him, lad. I feel the tides may be turning if his plans come to be. Listen to him closely." The Dwarf smiled. "I will deliver this to your quartermaster, My Young Lord."

Uilam blushed at being called a Lord. "I am no Lord, My Lord. I am only a servant to my people."

Perhaps not yet, son, but soon, the Dwarf thought, smiling. Nodding, he drove the wagons to the storehouse.

* * *

Orus looked at Uilam. He was no older than seventeen years of age. He was not an exceptionally large young man. He did not seem imposing in any way, but from his speech, the Hodan could tell that his heart was different from the others. Orus thought about the years gone by. He remembered his own upbringing. His father was a ranch hand, and his mother wove fabrics and sewed. They were also deceptively humble and meek people.

The young man cleared a table in the small tavern that was more of a hut than a building. The Hodan smiled, thinking of his father's old saying, *there must always be a tavern where warriors gather for war.*

"Please sit, Sir," the boy-man said, motioning to a seat near the table. Orus could see he was wide-eyed and nervous.

Orus sat. The boy spoke to a girl, who brought out a bowl of fresh venison stew and a tankard of ale. Orus did a double-take as the hair on the girl's head fell just the right way, reminding him of Faylea. Looking the second time, his heart ached at the realization that it was not her.

The food was warm and tasty. The ale was better. Orus silently ate, looking at the boy across from him. Memories flooded from the back of his mind to a time on the border of Erynseere. Those days were miserably cold, wet, and muddy. The Hodan were eating their horses, and famine was rampant. A young lad with golden hair, on a white horse, rode in from the north and saved Hodan from certain starvation.

Orus wondered, "Uilam, is it? Are you ready to die?"

113

Uilam stopped staring and responded, "What is that, Your Majesty?"

Orus set his utensils down and wiped his beard with a burlap napkin that was provided. Then, he leaned forward with the most serious of faces. "Are you willing to die and take untold souls with you to the afterlife?"

Uilam swallowed hard. "I don't understand why you would ask me this, Sir."

"I only ask, because the Dwarves tell me you have retribution on your mind. You do realize that conflict, war, strife, whatever we call it, is just wanton killing? You know this?" Orus sipped from his tankard, and the girl came over sheepishly to refill it.

"Of course, there is a chance of death when the stakes are this high, Your Majesty," the boy replied diplomatically, dancing around the answer.

Orus's demeanor changed to one of annoyance. He slammed his wooden mug down forcefully, sitting up abruptly. "That is NOT what I asked you, boy! Are you committed to the fight, or will you cower and run at first sight of blood? Have any of your villagers spilled a drop of blood in combat? Anyone? Even an elder?"

The boy looked down, ashamed. "No, Sir."

"Do not be ashamed, son. War is not all that they tell you it is. Sometimes a hero avoids conflict to save lives vice fighting and losing them. If you cannot win, it is not wrong to bide your time. Your people are maligned by other races as 'cowards' when I hear you all fought valiantly to rid the Rynn of the Scourge. No one came to your aid when the defeat happened, except those damned Elves. No one has the right to condemn your people. They cowered on bended knees just as you did. The only difference is your people did it to preserve themselves … to avoid a fight that would eradicate all of you from the face of the world. The others knelt out of fear, while possessing the means to fight back. That is the true meaning of cowardice and a lack of honor."

Uilam was shaking. Tears now fell freely from his eyes as he heard Orus's words. The boy seemingly aged five years as he gulped down a mead, then wiped his eyes. "You, Sir, are the first man in forever to command their respect. You are the only person alive who has ever said those things aloud

... to me, or any other of Degran-Eras. I wish to win back the honor of my people. I wish to free my kingdom. I wish to raise an army, and yes, as much as it pains me to admit it, I am ready to die and take many with me to achieve these goals." The young man sat straight in his chair.

"How many can you muster, Uilam, son of Yerd? I hear one-hundred?" Orus sat back, smiling at the young man across from him.

"I can guarantee twice that, Sir, but so many more are trapped in Whaleford. We could get at least ten times that number if we could manage to drive the Todani from that town and show those who sit upon the fence that it can be done." Uilam's eyes were fixed on something on the wall. He was earnest and unwavering in his speech.

Orus followed his gaze to a sword hanging on the wall to the table's left. Above the blade were an amulet and a small makeshift plaque. The elder King stood and walked over to the display and read the inscription.

"The Sword of Neirmynd, the brave.
Last Hero of Degran-Eras
Destroyer of Todani
Restorer of our hope
Liberator of the slaves.
Bringer of hope."

Orus turned to Uilam. "What happened to the man who wielded this blade?"

"He died while repelling the last push of the Todani in the last Great War. The Dwarves kept promising support, but they came too late to save the remaining warriors. The legend has it, they held a million Todani at the Jackrabbit Canyon three days ride north of here. The Todani utterly wiped out our last army, and then proceeded to pillage us at will, until the Dwarves finally arrived and decided to push them somewhat back. Still, to this day, the Dwarves only come to our aid when it is in their best interest."

"In my experience, the Dwarves are very good at that sort of thing," Orus said in a subdued tone, returning to the table. "Back to our plans. Do you want your people to join the Hodan legions? My plan is to attack the southeast of Degran-Eras, and then to take as many humans to your fortresses as possible."

"If we do this, the Todani will come. It will be an overt act of war. We cannot stop them," Uilam said plainly.

"I have friends in Vynwratha who may choose to aid us in the forests, as well as an offer from the Dwarves to deploy their legions on the borderland to keep the attacks on the Degran-Eras side of the border." Orus crossed his arms.

Uilam smiled. "When can we start? How do we start? As you have pointed out, we plainly do not possess the training to fight."

"But you do have the will to learn and to fight when it is time. I can and will work with this group if you are willing. There is no turning back once you join Hodan. You will be considered Hodan for life. You will be our people, no longer your own. Will your people accept this?"

"We are nothing as it stands. If we become Hodan, we become strong. I will convince them. I am praying for victory and soon!" Uilam exuberantly exclaimed.

"Youth," Orus snorted, "be careful what you wish for, son! Go talk to your people. We will do a demonstration for the refugees if they need to see it for themselves. I will bring a legion with me tomorrow when I visit. Maybe the Dwarves would like to do some training with staves in the fields in the morning."

"Many of my people, young and old, would be interested in seeing that!" Uilam left the hut. "Thank you, Your Majesty."

Orus nodded. He wondered why the boy was thanking him. The boy had no idea of what being a Hodan meant. He would soon find out.

* * *

The Dwarves smugly accepted the invitation to engage the Hodan on the field before the humans they sought to enlist. These Dwarfish Commanders were not present at the assault on Vynwratha. They laughed privately at

Orus and his men. Kepir had advised his King as much. Orus sought to show the humans from Degran-Eras the prowess of Hodan, but he also sought to establish a reputation with these haughty Dwarves. Time would tell if this would be the day.

Up the mountain, two legions of Dwarves marched with an army of Hodan Elites behind. The Dwarves were singing songs about the glory of the Dwarfish race, warriors, and kingdom. Orus had his men listen carefully.

"Listen to them brag, my Hodan brothers! These Dwarves would boast of being our equals, if not our betters. Remember that on the field today. Staves or not. We must defend the honor of Hodan! A few Dwarves need a lesson in humility and the pecking order around here."

"HODAN! HODAN! HODAN!" the legion chanted in response to their King's words.

The small fields below the forest were filled with warriors, neatly packed into rows and squares. As Orus arrived, he could see thousands of human men, women, and children lining the forest edge. They all came to see the new human heroes. The children cheered as Orus turned his legion moved toward the tree line, saluting Uilam in front of his people. It was by design to let all present know who Orus was dealing with personally. Uilam saluted the Hodan back.

The legion roared as one: "Long live Degran-Eras, kingdom of the heroes!"

The people watched in wonder at the words of the Hodan.

A very well-dressed military officer marched smartly to the center of the field. Orus and a lower-ranking Dwarfish legion Commander joined him in the center of the area. The two shook hands, and the officer informed both warriors of the rules of combat. The rules basically stated anything was fair, but both sides were required to protect the lives of their opponents. No one was to intentionally kill or maim the other side's warriors. This was training, after all—a demonstration of the prowess of the alliance to prospective recruits. No one was to die unnecessarily.

Both men nodded, turning to their respective sides. A horn signaled the start of combat. The people near the woods waited eagerly to see what would happen next.

Hodan formed square and marched forward smartly, shields locked and staves in position. The Dwarves did similarly, advancing to within ten yards of the Hodan lines. Both sides engaged in a stare-down for several minutes when the Dwarves decided to strike first.

A column formed at the rear of the Dwarfish unit. The formation was two ranks wide and twenty men deep. The Dwarfish legion opened as practiced a thousand times before. The column of twos charged at a single point of the Hodan lines.

"Set to repel!" Orus bellowed, and his lines immediately hardened. "Welcome to my world, Dwarves. Meet my children," Orus said with a strangely dark tone.

The Dwarves managed to push Hodan's middle back a rank at a width of four shieldmen wide, but the breach was there only momentarily as the reserve filled in the hole, and the rest of the wall stepped back to shore up the defenses. Then Hodan responded forcefully.

"Hammer and anvil now!" Orus bellowed out to the response of his Sergeants, echoing the call.

Immediately, the entire legion formed a wedge and charged forward into the Dwarfish shield wall. Teams flanked left and right in an attempt to outmaneuver the now retreating Dwarves. The effect pushed the Dwarves backward thirty yards and had them in disarray for several minutes, as the Hodan inflicted destruction in their ranks.

"Regroup!" Orus bellowed out, and the remaining forces of Hodan reformed into the perfect square once again.

* * *

Off to the side, the smug Dwarf General wrung his hands. He would not have his men routed by the likes of humans.

"Lieutenant, send in the 2nd Legion," the General snarled.

"But, Sir, they are armed with live steel. That is not a safe idea," the young officer complained.

"I do not care, Lieutenant," the older Dwarf said, growling out his orders. "Tell our boys to keep their weapons sheathed."

"But, Sir …" The Lieutenant shook his head and went off to give the orders.

The 2nd Legion marched out to the Hodan left flank.

* * *

Kepir was in the trees with his scout platoon. Unknown to anyone, he and two-hundred other specialists were in the forest in their customary suits, watching the whole mock battle unfold when they witnessed the Dwarfish treachery.

"Ah, so we are going to play it that way, are we? Silly Dwarves. You will pay for that dishonorable move," Kepir muttered.

The Hodan scout gestured subtly to a bush nearby that gestured back. Suddenly, as if by magic, hundreds of shrubs began moving swiftly and silently toward the battlefield. No one saw them coming.

* * *

Orus saw the marching second Dwarf legion. "Well, apparently they think we are worth two Dwarfish legions, men," Orus declared loud enough for the Dwarves to hear. "A pity they miscalculated. A truer estimation would be closer to four or five. Shore up the lines and prepare for attacks from the left flank, Sergeants!"

A reply of affirmation met the King's ears as the second Dwarfish legion plowed into Hodan's lines without care. They confidently felt their numbers would save them, but Hodan had begun to assert itself. The days of the northern alliance training became valuable now. Hodan fought as only Hodan could, but then automatically, as rehearsed and practiced, the lines alternated, allowing gaps to pull Dwarves through. The second and third ranks *murdered* the Dwarves in the rear, then turned to the next batch. The Dwarves had never seen anything like it.

Orus was winning the battle, but losing the war by attrition. He went on the offensive, calling a play out of Puryn's book. In the voice of Runnir and Gunnir, Orus bellowed, "Hodan shift, Draj offense number ONE!!"

Again, the remaining Sergeants responded affirmatively, and the Hodan began a shield pulse with a wave of whirling wooden blades. The shift in tactics and style caused the second legion of Dwarves to back up and regroup, having lost three-quarters of their fighters within moments of engaging what now was essentially a Draj shield wall.

Orus grinned maliciously. "Thank you, Puryn." Then he shouted, "That was a gift from my brother back on the Ert."

The Dwarves were in disarray. Orus attacked the weaker group on his left flank. The Hodan began routing them at will when the 1st Legion, now at fifty-percent, began to advance from Hodan's rear. Kepir had seen enough. He gestured to a patch of dry grass in the meadow, and the field came alive from the back of the Dwarfish 1st Legion.

The people, watching near the wood, gasped in surprise. So did the Dwarfish Commanders on the side of the battle.

"Kill them all!" Kepir shouted, then reconsidered his order. "JUST A FIGURE OF SPEECH, my comrades!"

A crash of two-hundred specialists hit the rear of the Dwarfish 1st Legion. Within minutes, the Dwarfish advantage began to wane. The Hodan specialists were so capable that the Dwarves surrendered, conceding the fight. The 2nd Legion was decimated by Orus, and Kepir had whittled the 1st Legion down to two-hundred or so souls. Humans stood around a gaggle of Dwarves who now sat on the dry ground with their hands up. Dust swirled in the spring breeze, but the scene was clear. One human legion had *killed* nearly two-thousand Dwarves, even though the Hodan were outnumbered two to one. The Hodan had *lost* thirty-percent of their men in the battle.

The tree line erupted in a happy cheer of elation as two-thousand souls watched the first human heroes in one-hundred years emerge from a battle victorious. Many humans, Hodan and from Degran-Eras, laughed as Orus removed his helmet and walked over toward the Dwarves. The Hodan King bowed sarcastically, and then performed a vulgar gesture in salute. The protests of the Dwarfish General elicited more laughs from the spectators.

Orus looked at the trees. He called his men to fall in. After a quick accounting of personnel, it was determined that no Hodan or Dwarf was seriously injured. The only thing that would take time to heal was the pride of Dornat Al Fer. The Hodan King marched his legion proudly to where Uilam stood speechless.

"Well, son," Orus said sarcastically, "Do you think we can win now?"

"Yes, Your Majesty. Yes, I believe that we can," Uilam said, smiling with a fist in the air.

Uilam shook the hand of the Hodan King, as both looked left and right. Every human was kneeling, faces to the ground, in front of Orus and their leader.

"Please, tell them to rise. They should kneel to no one. No one, ever again!" Orus said emphatically.

"We will be Hodan, My King," the young man said, "or I will leave this rabble and follow you myself."

"Thank you, boy," Orus responded, smiling. "Your loyalty is accepted and appreciated, but do not forget, we need Whaleford and its men to stand with us."

"When we liberate that town, I have no doubt that they will flock to you, Your Majesty," Uilam stated, awed by the person of Orus.

The Hodan King smiled, looking at all of the people who now encircled the area around his legion. His memories flashed to the cold mud of Hodan after the Great War of the People. He saw the same desperation in the faces of these people.

"Long live Orus, King of Hodan! Long live Hodan, land of our deliverers!" Uilam shouted.

The crowd loudly echoed the sentiment.

Orus looked at Uilam as the shouting subsided. "Have your men ready tomorrow. We will move our forces over to these woods. We will train and form plans to get the men from Whaleford. We will take every soul we can bear to this place … man, woman, child, young and old—all of them. This will take a bit of time, but we will begin to train soon. I must address logistics with the Dwarves, and then I will send a rider to my Elfish friends. In the meantime, we will build defenses of our own here, and we will reinforce the ones that your people have already created. Time is short. We must be prepared for a war that is coming soon. Make no mistake, it is already in Degran-Eras. You, of all people, know that to be true."

Uilam nodded once. He was standing proudly. That made Orus smile.

"Kepir!" Orus bellowed.

A bush responded, "Yes, Sire!"

"Dismiss the legion and have them set up camp within the woods," Orus said, grinning at the bush. "And nice job today, my friend. They never saw you coming!"

"That's the point, Sire!" Kepir replied, his coal-blackened face looking back at Orus from under his leaves. He was grinning mischievously.

The specialist bowed, then turned to execute his orders. Several Degran children looked up at the mobile bush as if they had seen a ghost.

Kepir turned toward them abruptly, raising his hands above his head. "Boo!" he said to the giggling response of younglings.

Chapter 7

The concession of Edhelseere was a blow to the prestige of Hamrick. The King was not an utterly vain Dwarf, but he did not like to look like a fool when politics and military prowess were in question. The Dwarves had kept the balance of peace for almost one-hundred years by making sure the Todessen were concerned with what would happen if they ventured south to challenge the vast Dwarfish Empire that existed on the other side of the mountain ranges. Hamrik knew that to keep the peace, respect, if not fear, would need to be maintained. Admiral Jaruz, former Commander of the forces at the Port of the Redeemed, now the Elfish lands of Edhelseere, had injured the reputation of the Dwarfish troops in the lands controlled by Dornat Al Fer. His military defeat to humans was a black eye, even if the Hodan were now their allies.

Ma 'Dryna smiled at the Dwarf who was carrying in a load of firewood. He was older and respected by the refugees—a former warrior who was not afraid to get dirty with the rest of the laborers. She watched him while quietly working a drop spindle.

"Jaruz, my love, put the wood down and come sit by me," the Galdrissen woman begged. "Come, drink some water. You must not work yourself into an early grave."

The Dwarf looked over to where he heard someone calling out to him. He saw his love sitting on the stump of a cut tree. She was wearing ragged, dirty robes, but her face showed the same happiness and light it always did. He walked to where she was. Ma 'Dryna handed him a water skin. Jaruz took a long drink and then handed the skin back to her.

"Thank you, My Lady," the Dwarf said, bowing ceremoniously.

The Galdrissen woman giggled and then forcefully pulled the man to her, kissing him.

The Dwarf smiled and then laughed out loud. "You never have to wonder what a Galda Risi woman wants. She just reaches out and grabs ahold."

Ma 'Dryna smiled, looking into her man's eyes. "And I will never let go. I am glad that you are here with me."

"Aye, me also," the Dwarf replied, kissing her on her forehead. "Now, let me get back to work, woman! There are fortifications to fortify and homes to build. This place will not build itself."

Ma 'Dryna reluctantly released her captive. "And I am sure that you, alone, will build it all. You damned fool! Enjoy your time while you have time left!"

"Yes, yes, of course, my dear," the Dwarf said sarcastically, receiving a glare from his lady. Laughing, he picked up a hatchet and left for the woods.

* * *

Orus rode southward over the plains with a contingent of fifty Hodan men and fifty initiates from Degran-Eras. The King traveled to the southern borderlands to investigate a disturbing report from Kepir concerning his Dwarfish friend and ally, Jaruz. It was a cloudy day. The humidity was high, and cumulous clouds floated inland from the sea, breaking up the flawless periwinkle sky. Rain was not out of the question.

"Kepir, how much longer until we reach the new settlement?" Orus asked, shifting in his saddle.

The specialist adjusted expertly in his own saddle, reaching backward into a leather saddlebag. He retrieved a small, rolled leather map. After looking at it and then looking around to get his bearings, he responded, "Another hour or so, Your Majesty."

"Excellent. Let us move over into the shade by those trees." Orus motioned to the east at a small glen of trees that were growing on the side of the foothills to the mountains farther east.

"Yes, Your Majesty," the specialist replied.

"Break for food and drink," the King added.

Kepir nodded and passed the orders. The unit marched to the shade of the trees, checking the perimeter for threats, and then posted four guards while the rest of the foot soldiers ate.

Orus sat alone, brooding. Kepir knew he was angry with the Dwarves, but he also knew the King was a practical man. He needed their army and their logistics to go the distance and achieve the goal of removing the Todessen from the Rynn. The specialist approached his King bearing a skin of mead, a couple of loaves of fresh bread, and a block of cheese, which he cut in half with his dagger.

"Your refreshments, My Lord," Kepir said as if he were a butler.

Orus snorted and shook his head. "Sit down, you ass!"

Kepir smiled and accepted the skin back after Orus had taken a long pull off it. "Are you all right, Your Majesty?"

"I am still baffled by what that King Hamrik thinks he is doing. He throws away the services of a good man, as if they are worthless! How many Jaruzes does the fool think he has?" Orus took the skin back, drinking more mead.

"Well, Sire, the King is trying to save face, and unfortunately, that means destroying the good name of an honorable man. It is despicable, but politics often is."

"True," Orus replied, swallowing, "but to banish him from his capitol and send him out here to this gods-forsaken place ... with those people? What kind of a heartless bastard does such a thing?"

"A Dwarfish one?" Kepir answered, shrugging. "But perhaps it was a reward, but a secret one?"

"How could any of that be considered a reward? Have you been in the sun too long today?" Orus quipped.

"Think about it, Sire. The Dwarf loves a Galdruhn. She is in the encampment he left the capitol to move to. Perhaps, the Galdruhn are not as well-accepted as Jaruz made it out to seem. Maybe they are Hamrik's dirty secret. He could hate them as much as you and say they are 'valued subjects,' just to put on a façade of tolerance and support?"

Orus nodded. "Maybe. I have already gleaned from our many interactions with these short fellows that they fancy themselves better than everyone else. They look down on humans and tolerate the Elves as a 'necessary evil.' They are not truly the friends of anyone but themselves."

Kepir nodded back. "Aye, Sire. They are some self-serving little bastards. Whatever is in their best interest is what they will do. They seek to maintain the status quo when the Todessen are driven from the lands. I fear that the Elves may have something to say about that."

"To the Underworld with all of that, Kepir. They will need to consider the Hodan also. When Degran-Eras is joined to our people, we will be another threat, especially if the Elves choose to remain our true allies. So far, so good, but that is no indication of future success!" Orus chuckled, pondering the absurdity of the alliances he was a part of.

Kepir nodded, standing. "Sire, I will gather the men and tell them to get ready to move on, if that is your desire."

"As always, you read me without fail. Make it so, my trusted friend."

Orus stood and put away the rest of the food and equipment. He mounted his horse and awaited the gaggle of initiates to form into a professional band once again.

* * *

An hour or so later, Orus could see the rough outline of a city being built. The palisade walls were only partially up, but they were progressing nicely. The Hodan King also noticed a taller structure in the center of the fort. The large tower was designed to house civilians and provide for archery coverage three-hundred-sixty degrees around the fortress. All around, in random locations, one-room, wattle, and daub homes dotted the countryside outside of the walls. Their roofs were thatch or wood.

Each small homestead had a personal crop plot. In the center of it all was a massive community plot. As the King watched, he could see crowds tending to the plants. Many from the community were pulling weeds, fertilizing, and ensuring the irrigation troughs were bringing the water to needed locations.

"It almost looks like Hodan, Kepir," Orus said, drifting off in memory for a moment.

"Aye, Sire, but these are not humans growing beets," Kepir reminded the King.

"Still, I have never seen Todessen grow anything, my friend," Orus said, looking around.

"Truly, the Todessen are not known to bring life to the world, unless it is useful in destroying something else!" Kepir smirked.

* * *

Jaruz heard the horns. He was in the forest felling trees for use on the palisade walls when he listened to the call to arms. Panicked, the Dwarf dropped everything that he was doing and began running toward the Galdrissen settlement.

The Dwarf shouted the those around him. "Come on, boys, let's go! They need us at home, now!"

The Galdrissen men ran after their Dwarfish leader, overtaking him in short order. All of them could see a large army advancing on the city walls.

"What does it mean, Jaruz?" one man asked to the Dwarf as they ran toward the oncoming militia.

"I do not know, my friend!" Jaruz said, panting. "We must meet them and find out."

The leader and his twenty reached the gates as the army passed the community crops.

"Arm up!" Jaruz commanded. "DRYNA! Take the children into the cave!"

Off in the distance, Jaruz heard his lady reply in confusion. "What is happening, my love?"

"No questions! Do it now and quickly!" Jaruz commanded.

Hearing the worry in his voice, the Priestess and her acolytes shooed all the women and children into a cave nearby the settlement. It was behind the tower and went directly back into a natural stone cliff-face that the Dwarf had decided to use as one side of the city walls. The town was up against the mountain foothills. He would use the terrain as best that he could.

The natural fortress under the mountain was a perfect hiding place, and the Dwarf was accustomed to making underground accommodations livable. The narrow passageway was hewn to allow two to enter at a time, and after one-hundred or so feet in, the cave widened into an ample, open, circular space of around seven-hundred-fifty measures in diameter. The passageway was cut in ninety-degree angles every so often to allow for better security. The townsfolk were very familiar with it. The small cavern had, in fact, been their home until the town on the surface began to rise.

* * *

"Kepir, it appears we have roused our hosts. Please hoist a white flag and let them know that we mean them no harm." Orus looked at the gathering rabble at the hole in the gate. He knew the townsfolk were assembling to attempt to mount a defense. No doubt this was the Dwarf's doing.

Kepir tied a white handkerchief to a spearhead and held it high in the sky.

It was met by another white flag on the other side of the field. The Hodan approached cautiously until Jaruz began waving at Orus. Orus smiled, knowing his friend was still at it, even if it was in an unofficial capacity.

* * *

"I am sorry, gentlemen, but we are a poor shire, and we have no mead for you!" Jaruz said in jest.

Orus laughed. "That is fine, but we don't want to drink your ale either!"

The King dismounted and walked over to the shorter man. They shook hands. The Hodan legionnaires and trainees set up a defensible position just outside of the city walls, to the relief of everyone within.

Jaruz invited his friend to a table near the growing central tower. The two sat and talked for some time, eating and drinking, even though the ale *was not to Orus's liking.*

* * *

The Hodan King was pleasantly numb by nightfall. Dwarfish ale had that effect on most humans. The lights of the fires danced on the faces of the half-erected structures. Jaruz had long since gone to bed, leaving his friend by the fire to enjoy the coolness of the evening. The Hodan unit was still in place just outside the wall. Orus looked over at them and nodded in approval as he spotted the watches vigilantly patrolling the area. Leaning back in his rickety chair, something else also caught his eye.

Off behind the tower, the warrior looked at a patch of tree branches that seemed out of place. Even stranger to him was that every now and then, a flicker of light seemed to play from behind the brush, as if there was something more to the pile. Sipping from his cup, Orus sat up straight and snapped sober at what he saw. It appeared to be a hewn opening, leading directly into the face of a cliff, and covered by brush. Shaking his head, the King squinted as if he could not believe his eyes.

Looking around, Orus could see no one in his direct vicinity. The King grabbed his shield and walked silently in disbelief to where the cut brush lay. His breath began to quicken, as did his pulse as he neared the opening. The dancing lights were now clearly visible, and the warrior could now hear the murmuring of voices and scuffling sounds from deep within what appeared to be a familiar, but unwelcome sight.

It seemed to the Hodan that he had happened upon a Todessen temple entrance, just like the ones that Kairoth, Puryn, and he had purged from the face of the Ert. Suddenly, breaking the still of the evening, a female voice shrieked loudly from within the hidden chamber. To the drunken King, the scream called out in abject horror. The Hodan had seen enough.

Without thinking, Orus burst into the passageway, brush flying this way and that. His sword was drawn, and he was moving with purpose down the corridor behind his shield. There was a bright light at the end of the line. That is where the screaming was coming from. Thinking the worst, the old warrior charged.

Roaring angrily, Orus bellowed as he turned into the lighted room. The change to bright light impaired his vision temporarily, but as he squinted, the King could still make out a robed figure on top of what appeared to be a screaming and resisting young woman. Charging, the King met the attacker with a shield bash and the hilt of his weapon. The blow sent the figure airborne ten measures from the impact.

A more petite humanoid figure hit the ground with a thud. Scrambling, the attacker kneeled and bent over, holding his face while sobbing. The female was now shrieking uncontrollably, running away from the towering Hodan warrior, as several other terrified faces appeared on the edge of the firelight where all this had just taken place.

Orus shouted, "What is going on here? What is this place? Show yourself!" The King pointed his sword at the kneeling assailant.

The figure turned to face him. It was a young teenaged Galdrissen boy. Tears were streaming from his eyes, and he was bleeding from a nasty gash where his sharp teeth had penetrated his upper lip from the blow that Orus had dealt him with his hilt. The girl, still screaming, ran toward the boy, removing her scarf and applying pressure to the wound. She was frantic.

Orus was confused. *Where was the temple? Where was the altar? Where were the sacrificed souls in the vats full of dead?* Slowly, as he calmed, it occurred to him that this was not a Todessen temple, but instead a reserve shelter for civilians. Looking around him, the King could see the terrified faces of children everywhere. Their ages ranged from five to sixteen years of age.

"Oh," the King said, looking at the damage he had done. He was in a shock, "I ... I thought..."

"He was just playing, Sir! Why did you have to hurt him so?" the young girl sobbed.

Another boy shouted, "I will fetch the healer, Ega. Stay with him." The girl nodded, never taking her eyes off Orus. Her fearful face shamed the warrior.

The Hodan was numb. He did not know if it was the shock of attacking children, or the ale he had consumed earlier. *They aren't people,* he thought. *It is nothing to worry about.*

The girl looked at the giant King with tears in her eyes. "Why does everyone hate us so?"

Swallowing hard, he saw the eyes of his own daughter in the face of the crying Galdrissen girl. It cut him to the heart.

Orus was ashamed. He tried to reinforce his resolve. *They are not people, you fool. They are demons,* he reassured himself. Still, his heart was broken at the scene he had created. He sat on a rock to the side as the healers entered the cave.

Ma 'Dryna asked angrily, "What happened here?"

"We were playing, and Ega pulled Torg's hair, so he tackled her and was wrestling with her. He had pinned her down and was tickling her. Next ..." The girl stopped, looking up at Orus, afraid to finish the tale.

"It is all right, young one," Orus interjected. "I caused this, Milady."

"Why?" Ma 'Dryna asked in exasperation.

"It was a huge misunderstanding, Milady. I thought something bad was happening, and I sought to stop it. I had no idea of what this place was." Orus looked at the floor and sighed in shame. It was not lost on the Galdrissen woman.

"What did you think this was ... a temple to the Underlord?" the Priestess asked sarcastically.

"Actually ...," Orus replied, "Yes."

"What?! Why?" Ma 'Dryna shouted at the King. "Oh, of course, we Galdrissen are liars and demons. I forgot!" The Priestess was livid.

Orus absent-mindedly looked around and realized that he still had his sword in his hand. Quickly sheathing it, he stepped forward to where the Priestess was working on the boy's wounds. She had expertly sewn them closed.

"With any luck, he will not scar badly," the Priestess said, hugging the lad who cowered at the presence of Orus. "Haven't you done enough, My Lord?"

"I have." Orus said solemnly. "I thought the worst, and in my rush to judgment, I almost killed a child." Orus closed his eyes and saw his daughter's face again. She was a young a girl. Stammering, the King responded, "I only wish to say that I am sorry, young one."

Ma 'Dryna looked at the human in wonder. No one ever apologized to the Galdrissen, not even Dwarves who claimed to be their friends. *Who is this human?* she thought silently.

"Wait, Orus," the Priestess said, softening her tone. "I appreciate that you came to rescue lives, but know this, we are not lying when we tell you that Haya is our Goddess by choice. We are not Todani."

Orus nodded silently, leaving the underground chamber. The children of the Galdrissen looked up in terror and awe of the giant who walked before them.

Once back outside, the King found Kepir and drank another skin of mead before he fell asleep.

* * *

Orus sat at a table in the bright sunlight. It was relatively early, somewhere around the second hour of the morning, when he found himself eating porridge and drinking hot tea across from Jaruz, who was asking questions like a machine.

"So, you charged into our underground safehouse and bashed in a boy's face last night? What is wrong with you?" Jaruz chided.

Orus scowled at the condemnation, bowing his head. He had a bad hangover and was still dealing with the guilt of what he had done the night before. The Dwarf's commentary was not helping his mood.

The King responded, "Listen here, little man, I have fought many wars. I have been through many battles. I have seen the end coming and stood on the Arondayre with Haya's Chosen. I have defeated the Todessen, only to find them recover underground in lairs that much resemble the cave you have fashioned for your loved ones." Orus sipped his tea. "I saw atrocities that were unimaginable in those caves, and when I heard the scream of that Todani girl, I thought …"

"You thought what!? And no, she is not a Todani … for the last time. What do I have to do to get you to understand that fact?" Jaruz scowled.

"I know, I know. I saw it plainly last night. They were not the foul beasts who live to our north. They were simply children playing. But Jaruz, if you had seen the temples in Cinnog and Sudenyag, you would understand what I thought I saw. I am sorry, it was an honest mistake." Orus looked up sincerely. He was genuinely sorry. This was a new look for the human, and it was immediately seen by Jaruz, who was taken aback.

"It must have been truly horrible for you to be affected so, my friend," Jaruz replied sympathetically.

"It really was, Jaruz, truly abominable," Orus replied.

"You do not have to worry about that now, friend. The only enemy we have is north of us. Let us remember that in all of our dealings as friends and allies." Jaruz weakly smiled and offered his hand to Orus.

Shaking the Dwarf's hand, Orus promised, "I will make it up to that boy and to all of you … on my honor, I will. Here, please, donate this to the children of this place. Please, tell your lady that I am sorry for the harm I caused."

Jaruz took a small coin purse from Orus. It contained an average person's wages for a year and then some.

The Dwarf responded, "My lady will forgive you if she hasn't already, my friend. The forgiveness of those who thought themselves unforgivable is never-ending. You would be surprised at their capacity to pardon our transgressions."

"If what you say is true, my friend, then maybe I can learn a thing or two from a Galdrissen about forgiveness and redemption." Orus smiled awkwardly.

Chapter 8

Orus found Kepir in the gaggle of initiates. He was teaching a class on wilderness survival. The King stood back and watched his friend expertly show the Degran recruits how to set snares and traps for small wildlife. After a short class on hunting techniques, Kepir segued seamlessly into a lesson on how to adapt the hunting traps to booby traps. Orus smiled, impressed with his specialist's ability to teach and with the material he was presenting. The young men in armor around him were glued to his instruction. Orus waited for his second in command to finish his lecture.

"Kepir, when you have a moment," Orus stated softly, gesturing with a head nod.

"Yes, Your Majesty," the specialist replied. "I will be right there."

The specialist finished his demonstration, called the unit to attention, and then dismissed them, ordering the squad leaders to form their men for inspection. Kepir turned smartly and approached his King.

"How can I be of service, Sire?" The specialist greeted the King, bowing.

"After you are done with the daily routine, we need to take these boys into the woods for some forest time," Orus replied seriously.

"Sire, one tactical note to add, if I may?" Kepir waited for acknowledgment from his King.

"What is it?" Orus questioned.

"We are operating awfully close to the Orcish borderlands. They are very skittish when it comes to troop build-ups. The Toads, er, I mean, the Galdrissen, have already piqued their interest, and my scouts tell me that they are building up troops at their northern border, as we had feared that they would." Kepir paused for commentary from the King, but there was none, so he continued. "The Toad … damn it … Galdrissen … are moving closer and closer to their border. Something is bound to happen, Sire."

Orus's brow furrowed. Kepir looked at the older man's weathered face and handed him a water skin. The King accepted it and took a long drink from it. He was still a bit hungover from the prior evening.

"I will warn Jaruz to watch the south, but I'm sure that Dwarf has already thought of that. Still, the Orcs had better watch themselves, or after we deal with them, they will have a serious Dwarf problem inside their borders. Hamrik will not take too kindly to an invasion from the Scourge. If they break the peace, we might just get to see the full fury of this huge Dwarfish army they keep yammering on about."

"The Todessen … the real ones," Kepir stressed, "have sent out scouting parties into the southeast border of Ynus-Grag from Degran-Eras. They incurred into Orcish lands and were repelled, but not without killing many Orcs during their withdrawal. The Todessen brought humans along for the mission."

"Do we know if the humans were there voluntarily or were they forced?" Orus asked with concern.

"From what I have been told by my spies in Whaleford, the Todessen are grabbing young men, putting them in ragged armor, and then leaving them to deal with the Orcs after they rile the brood and then tactically withdraw." Kepir sighed.

"It sounds as if the Toads are trying to make the Orcs believe that the humans are working with them. Then the Orcs can finally finish the job at Whaleford that they cannot do overtly … and in the process, they may be able to start trouble here in the Dwarfish Kingdom." Orus scowled.

"Orcs are not intellectuals, Sire. This plan will work. The Orcs have been looking for a reason to attack the humans for decades, from what I gather from the Dwarves. This could end badly if we are not careful." Kepir stood tall, awaiting orders.

"Send a rider north to the main camp and bring our legions here. I will tell Jaruz what you have spoken. He will understand. I hope he gets the opportunity to build his wall before those animals to the south come here seeking to pull it down." Orus nodded to Kepir, replying, "Time to prepare, my friend. Orcs it is."

"As you wish, My King." Kepir turned to an attending squire repeating the King's orders.

The young man wrote everything down on a small parchment, securing the message in a small pouch on his belt. He ran to the nearest horseman. Within moments, the messenger was off riding at a breakneck pace northward. Orus watched him go and turned to find Jaruz.

"Gentlemen, stack your equipment near the wall. Come with me. We need to find a Dwarf who is in charge and help with securing this place. Now!" Orus looked at his recruits, who stood tall.

"Aye, Sire!" they bellowed as one, hurrying to set their gear at the ready near the wall.

* * *

Jaruz frowned. He looked up at Orus, and the King could see the fear in his eyes. The Dwarf paced, calling for the local militia leaders.

"Orus, this is terrible news. We have people foraging all over these lands. We are trying to prepare for winter. It is not a new thing on the Rynn. These damned Orcs are always so paranoid and distrusting. They look for enemies where none exist." Jaruz was shaking his head.

"My friend, I thought you should know. We need to prepare. The Toads are working some sort of evil plan to lure the Orcs into open combat. The Dwarves will eventually arrive and crush that incursion, but in the meantime, we are all we have to defend these lands. I have called my legions. The rider is sent."

"Thank you, my friend. We will need anyone available, if they come in force." Jaruz looked around in defeat.

137

A young Galdrissen man and several others arrived where Jaruz and Orus spoke. One addressed the Dwarf. "Constable Jaruz, we have assembled."

"My apologies, Orus, but I must now prepare the meager defenses to meet the onslaught," the Dwarf sarcastically said. "A handful of guardsmen and a weary band of foragers is all we have."

"Understood, my friend, but I also wish to help you there in some capacity. I would like to offer the services of my recruits. They are hardworking young men and know how to build fortifications. Use them as you will. Where can we help?" Orus smiled.

Jaruz smiled back. "Thank you again, friend. Would you please ask that engineer over there what type of lumber and the sizes he needs?" The Dwarf pointed at another Dwarf with a funny hat on. "We have axes and saws, but no bodies. If your men could get us the poles necessary and we combine forces, perhaps we can raise that wall within the week?"

"Consider it done, Jaruz." Orus turned to his squad leaders who stood behind him. "You heard the man, get over there and find out what that Dwarf needs to build this wall, then get to it. Go!"

The men stood tall, turned smartly, and sprinted to the Dwarf, who was looking at a scroll with an odd-looking measurement device. After a short discussion, the Dwarf showed Orus's men what he needed. The young leaders organized the recruit unit, which then went about filling the list of needs.

The Dwarf smiled at the human enthusiasm and effective teamwork.

Privately the engineer marveled. "This wall will be built within three days if these men have any say in it."

* * *

Jaruz looked around with concern. She was nowhere to be found. Ma 'Dryna could be so obstinate! The Dwarf looked in the cave with no success.

"Watchman!" the leader called out.

"Yes, Jaruz, what is it?" the older Galdrissen man replied, leaning on his staff.

Jaruz sighed at the sight. "Have you seen the High Priestess today?"

"She took a band of young ones into the southern forests to forage around daybreak, Sir," the old man replied.

Jaruz was more concerned now. "Thank you, my friend."

The old man tipped his cap and went back to looking out over the construction of the main front gate. Humans were stacking up trees and stripping them of branches faster than the Dwarf builders could use them. It was a happy dilemma from what the watchmen saw, as the engineers smiled and cheered with every load the young humans brought to bear. It was getting into the late afternoon, and there was no word from the foraging parties that were out. This was not uncommon, but the threat of Orc invasion had Jaruz imagining the worst.

* * *

It was late afternoon when the Hodan legions arrived on site. Kren and his one-hundred survivors had joined Kepir's ranks as covert troops. Orus smiled at his wayward Captain, who stood at attention.

"Good evening, Your Majesty!" Kren bellowed.

"Easy, Captain," Orus smirked. "You will scare the enemy away before we have a chance to kill them!"

"I will calm myself, Sire, but it is difficult to do so before we are to meet actual Orcs on the battlefield. Most of us have never seen a real, live, Orc, Sire!" Kren was chomping at the bit.

Orus sighed, realizing how young his men were. Many had never seen a member of the Scourge before they left the Ert for the seas, but most had fought battles against human foes in Cinnog or Sudenyag. Orus patted him on his spaulders and walked down the lines as the legions prepared to march southward.

"Be careful what you wish for, son," the King said, looking him in the eye. "Get with Kepir and get your men in proper stealth gear."

Kren replied too loudly. "Yes, Sire!"

Kepir suppressed a smile at his King's displeasure, while Orus looked at his trusted friend with *Why me?* written all over his face.

Kren and his one-hundred shed their metal armor and replaced it with light leather. They built their grass suits under the tutelage of Kepir. "You will be under my command, Kren. I will give the orders while in the field. Do you understand?"

"Yes, Sir!" the former ship Commander replied thoughtfully. "I have no animosity. I was a decent ship's Captain, but covert operative ... I am only average. But then again, my men were glorious in the Vyn forest!"

"That they were, Kren. That is why you will be my second, but I must teach you the finer details of stalking your prey. You have a good foundation and good instincts, but you still have your rough edges, because you are inexperienced. We will fix that." Kepir smiled and tried to put Kren at ease.

"I will endeavor to make you proud, Sir," the young man replied.

"I am already proud of you and of Hodan. To please me, all you must do is learn, survive, and kill the enemy with grave proficiency." Kepir held out his hand to Kren. The younger man shook his Commander's hand and then returned to standing tall.

"I must make my suit, Sir." Kren smiled.

"I will show you, son," Kepir said calmly, pulling up the net and inserting grass.

Orus watched the exchange, nodding. Kren was becoming an asset. He always had heart, but lacked common sense. Kepir would teach him and hone his new apprentice into a devastating weapon for Hodan. Orus could not wait to see the result of these efforts.

* * *

It was late. Hodan was camped outside of the hole that remained in the palisade wall. It was much closer to completion, but not close enough to allow for a proper gate to be built. Jaruz knew that the wall would be a reality within days, but he did not know if they had days to complete it. There were many missing Galdrissen still outside of the fortifications.

The foraging parties had all checked in except for three parties consisting of thirty Galdrissen who went southward into the wilderness. One of the parties was led by Ma 'Dryna, and Jaruz was worried. The Dwarf approached the Hodan sentries and asked for an audience with their King. After several moments, the guards let the Dwarf approach the command tent. He could see no other tents erected. Hodan was in the field, readying for war. Thousands slept in perfect squares on bedrolls. The hair on Jaruz's neck stood up as he thought of a nation filled with men and women of war such as these.

Orus opened the flap to the small wall tent. "Come inside, Sir," the King said gravely.

"Orus, I …," the Dwarf stammered, trying to suppress his emotions unsuccessfully. He looked at the dirt floor.

"She's out there, isn't she?" Orus asked seriously.

"Yes, she is, and twenty nine other souls, mostly young ones," the Dwarf said sadly.

"She is wise, my friend," Orus replied gently, offering the Dwarf a seat and a mug of mead. "She will guide them, and the Goddess will protect her."

"I am not sure if the Goddess cares for the Galdrissen, Orus. They always seem to suffer for no other reason but existing. I cannot live without her. She is all I have. I would ask to go with your legions to find her and stop this Orc aggression." Jaruz sipped his mead and looked up at Orus with a face the King had seen many times in the mirror.

The Hodan warrior smiled. "But who will protect this place if we fail?"

"If we fail, you know as well as I do that no one can protect this place until my kingdom arrives. We are all dead if Hodan falls." Jaruz sipped the mead again.

"One of my recruits is a man named Uilam from the human settlements in the forest. I will leave him in charge of the defenses with his men. He is green, but he is the best I have if I take all my assets south with me. Will you trust a young human to defend your fortress, Dwarf?" Orus smiled sarcastically.

"I have one concern, and she is still out there, friend. Your human will have to do," Jaruz replied.

"Then I will inform the lad of his burden of command." Orus shook his head and chuckled. "And you, Sir, need to get your gear and a good night's rest. We march in the morning."

"Thank you, my friend and ally. Long live Hodan," Jaruz said, downing his mead. "I will be here at first light."

"See you then." Orus smiled as the Dwarf left. Once Jaruz was out of sight, the smile left Orus. "Kepir, did you hear that? Civilians, and one who I promised to repay for my misdeeds. Inform Uilam of his tasks and then set off with your band to find the best tactical location that you can. I need your men to be just like they were a while ago at that demonstration. We will shred this enemy until it begs for mercy. I must rescue a Toad ..., er, I mean, a Galdrissen woman from Orcs. The irony."

"As you command, My King." Kepir disappeared into the darkness, never truly revealing himself. A shadow swiftly moved to execute its orders.

* * *

It was still dark. Orus stirred. There was noise in the town behind him. He rolled off his cot and slipped on a pair of sandals exiting the tent, half-dressed, but with sword and shield in hand. Kepir was there standing in the field, looking at what the matter was when Orus joined him.

"What in the Underworld is going on over there, Kepir?" the King asked, sheathing his sword.

Kepir replied proudly. "Uilam and his fifty recruits are shoring up the

142

defenses and setting up traps for the enemy."

Orus looked at Kepir with surprise. "Apparently, he was paying attention to your classes, teacher."

"My best pupil, Sire. I left the others with him, because the lad needed someone to command. I figured that you would not want the fresh meat mixed in with the regulars … too many unknown variables with untrained fighters." Kepir waited for the King's response.

Nodding, Orus replied, "A wise decision, as always, my friend. They would have been fodder, or worse yet, gotten a bunch of my legionnaires killed. Soon, they will be ready, but not today. However, this display of industry encourages me greatly. Our efforts are not lost on these people. They may become real Hodan yet."

Kepir gestured toward the opening in the fortress wall. "Your Majesty, Jaruz, comes."

"He is one who honors his word, Kepir. That is why I like him. It is a desirable trait among brothers and allies."

"He has a tiny horse, or is that a pony, Your Majesty?" Kepir snorted.

Swallowing his smile, Orus cleared his throat. "Do not insult our guests, damn it!"

"I would never dream of doing such a thing, Sire," Kepir said with a laugh.

* * *

"Sergeant! Sergeant!" A voice cried.

A young warrior was running toward Uilam, who snapped back to reality. He had forgotten again that he was the Sergeant now.

"Yes, brother, what is it?" the young leader replied seriously.

"We have the materials, and the Dwarf engineer is helping us to set up the obstacles that you ordered, Sir."

The soldier was barely old enough to be considered a man. "I am not a Sir; I am a Sergeant. Do not address me as an officer!" Uilam scolded him looking around.

"Sorry, Uilam," the boy responded.

"It is fine, Edmund. What is the status of the civilians?" Uilam ran his fingers nervously through his hair.

"We have relocated them to the cave as ordered, Sir ... er, Sergeant. The Dwarves are constructing doors made of reinforced stone, but we are short on metal." Edmund frowned at his report.

"It is not your doing, friend. We are in a hard spot, but we must do our duty," Uilam replied.

"Sir," Edmund replied, suddenly looking as if he were five years younger. "I'm afraid."

"I'll let you in on a little secret, friend. I, too, am terrified," Uilam said, frowning. "But we must not fail. We must prove that human beings are not cowards. Courage is simply deciding to do what is right while letting the fear wash over you. We must conquer not only our enemies, but also our fears. We must prove our honor! We must re-establish the place in history that our ancestors fought bravely for, even if this world thinks us cowards now."

Edmund looked down in shame. "I am sorry, Uilam. I will do better."

"You are doing fine, Ed. We are all doing our best. Soon, the real test will arrive." Uilam patted the younger boy on the shoulder as they turned back to his task.

The duo passed a Dwarf who heard the exchange between them. The engineer bowed and put his hand over his heart in a salute. Edmund looked at the Dwarf in confusion for honor shown, but Uilam swallowed hard and returned the salute, rising to return to the tasks that remained. The Dwarf watched closely as the young leader left to check on the Galdrissen villagers and their cave defenses.

Smiling, the old Dwarf nodded solemnly, muttering, "Humans. You never know what to expect from them."

* * *

Hodan had been on the march for several hours. It was midday, and the sun was high in the sky. It burned like coal in a Dwarven forge. The temperature had risen to an uncomfortable level, and the humidity from the sea winds was making it worse. Orus called for a halt, and the legions formed into squares, eating their rations, as water was distributed as best as could be done from the wagons. Jaruz watched the humans. They looked as if they went about their duties as if nothing were amiss.

"How do you do this?" Jaruz questioned with awe. "How are you not affected by anything, Hodan?"

"Oh, rest assured, we notice our environment and the obstacles to our objective, but no man who wears the standard of Hodan wants to be the one who dishonors himself by failing in his mission or falling out on the march to battle," Orus replied confidently.

"So, they just endure it for appearances?" Jaruz retorted, smiling.

"No. I would not expect you to understand our culture, Dwarf. I will put it to you another way. If your legions marched on the Todessen today, would a Dwarf wish to be the one who could not hold his shield to defend his brother on the shield wall? Would a Dwarf cower or run when superior numbers appear on the field? If your lands were threatened, would not death be preferable to surrender?" Orus spoke as if these things were self-evident.

"Orus, we are proud, but I fear that we would give up the land and pull back to regroup for another day. Would you sacrifice the lives of your men in an unwinnable fight?" Jaruz was puzzled.

"How does one know the fight is unwinnable unless one fights it to find out?" Orus responded, mentally revisiting the day he stood in the face of doom on the Arondayre with his brother, Puryn. "That is right out of the Hodan Book of Wisdom. We all learn it from the day we can speak. My mother taught it to me, as hers did to her. I was a whelp when my father died fighting the Yslandeth hordes in some foreign locale, the location of which I am not exactly certain." Orus looked over his men. "I want to establish the honor of my line. I wish to be redeemed for allowing Hodan to become a second-rate power in the world I left. There are many things I seek redemption for."

Orus sipped some water from a skin and then checked his blade. The Dwarf did likewise.

"I think you are too hard on yourself, Orus." Jaruz said, handing the water skin back to the King. "Your men tell me a different story than you do. You are a god to them."

"I am certain that even the gods have things they wish to forget," Orus responded, changing the subject. "We need to get these people moving and now."

"I will let Kepir know," Jaruz said, leaving the sunshade they sat under.

* * *

Deep ruts were cut across the road leading to the entrance to the village. They were designed to hobble horses and slow war wagons as well as to siege weapons. Pickets and spiked obstacles were set into the ground to channel any enemy force into one narrow avenue of approach. In that avenue were pits filled with kindling, tar, and oil. Everywhere else, snares and traps were set to hinder the enemy approach to the central defensive objective—the cave.

Uilam surveyed the mayhem he sought to inflict upon the Orcs if they ever made it to his position. He was not satisfied that his contingent of inexperienced warriors would be effective in a head-to-head encounter with a large Orc assault force. The young leader reasoned that if he could hinder their movement, his archers in elevated positions could kill or maim as many of the attackers as possible before the final defenders in the cave passageway were forced to intervene. It was as good a strategy as could be.

"Edmund, tell the men to get into position. Give them provisions. Tell them to use Kepir's hiding techniques to cover their positions to the best of their abilities. If we are lucky, maybe the enemy will think that no one is here and just continue by. If not, we will have the element of surprise to use against them."

"Yes, Sergeant," the young man replied.

Everyone was in place; the traps were set. Now, they waited.

* * *

The legions had halted and formed skirmisher lines on the flanks of one massive shield wall. Orus was near the rear of the procession and could not clearly see what the matter was. He wondered why his forces now held their ground. Scanning the horizon, he saw no Orcs to speak of. Looking closer, through his spyglass, the King could make out his scouts rapidly advancing on a person who ran toward Hodan's lines. It was not the enemy. It was one person in dark robes, and the figure ran with purpose toward the shield wall.

"Who in the Underworld is that?" Orus asked to no one in particular.

A squire rode up and replied. "A civilian is making their way to the lines northward from Ynus-Grag. The forward patrols state we are within two miles of the Orcish border, Sire."

"Tell them to bring that person to me. Tell my Captains to set the line and be prepared for anything."

"At once, Sire!" the young man said, turning his horse and galloping to the front lines.

Raising his spyglass again, the Hodan King could see a horseman grab the person running toward the lines and pull them up over the saddle. The person was lying flat and hanging on, but could not sit up from what Orus could tell. Someone had been running for a long time.

* * *

Edmund was calling to the gatherers. The last of the Galdrissen and Dwarves went into the cave fortress carrying water and provisions for several days. The defenses were set. The warriors were in place. He climbed a wooden ladder and looked over the wall from a small ledge, noticing movement in the hamlet outside of the fortifications. The intruders were not clearly visible until one of the huts burst into flames. The young man saw twenty or so Todessen in the fields, setting them afire and advancing on the unfinished wall.

"Goddess, please, hear my prayer. Please, forgive me for my cowardice. Forgive me for my fear. I ask that you bless us all. If we are to die this evening, I only hope that it will be a good and honorable death. May our sacrifices save the lives of many of your people."

Tears now streamed down the young man's face as he lifted a metal rod and began striking a metal triangle furiously. "To arms! To arms!!" Edmund shouted. "The enemy is here! The Todessen come!!"

Inside the cave, the warriors hid and prepared for battle, each one wide-eyed at the word of the Todessen invasion. The archers stayed hidden on the walls as they watched the enemy attempt to skirt the spikes and obstacles. Those who did were caught in mantraps and were filled with many arrows. The first two or three teams were probing the defenses. Edmund could see another thirty or so forming in the main field near the outer hamlet.

"Kill them all or die trying! Goddess, please, hear my prayers. If not, then if the warring brothers are not too busy, please, help us!" Edmund pled.

The young sentry pulled his sword and slid down a pole near the ladder. Grabbing his shield, he called out to his fellow foot soldiers and a few local militia men present in the courtyard. The archers were readying in their elevated positions. Uilam appeared at the cave entrance.

"Honor and glory, brothers!" the new Sergeant called out loudly to his men.

Edmund responded, saluting Uilam as a Hodan Elite would, "Honor and glory! May they never reach your position."

Edmund looked different to Uilam. His demeanor had suddenly changed.

He was resolute and prepared. Uilam knew he would have to be.

"Slay them all, brother," Uilam replied.

"As you command, Sergeant!" Edmund replied, turning to his men. "Form it up and prepare to repel, gentlemen!"

* * *

Orus stood silently looking at the young Galdrissen girl, who was gulping down water from a skin in front of him. He recognized her from Jaruz's village. The Dwarf was trying to calm her and get her to talk.

"Ega, please, tell us where they are, girl!" Jaruz pled.

"She fought them viciously to defend us all." Ega gasped for air after drinking for too long.

"Dryna? She fought the Orcs?" Jaruz was hysterical. "Is she all right?"

"I do not know, Sir," the girl sobbed. "They surrounded her and beat her pretty badly."

Jaruz was in shock. He staggered, dejected and numb, unable to speak. Orus put his hand on his friend's shoulder, sitting him down and steadying him on a field stool. The King approached the young girl.

"She was alive when you last saw her?" Orus responded optimistically.

"Yes, Sir, but she was hurt, as were many of the older gatherers who tried to assist her. We are not as big as they, nor do we have any weapons or training in fighting. Why would they do this, My Lord?" The girl was shaking as a healer brought her a wool blanket and some rations for comfort.

"Because they are filth, and that is what they do. Orcs and Goblins cannot be trusted. They are part of the Scourge that almost wiped my people from our lands," Orus snarled. "They will pay for this."

"There are too many, King Orus," the girl said in defeat. "How will you defeat so many?"

"We are Hodan, and we fight smarter than the average Orc. You shall see, young one. You will see your people again, hopefully still standing above the green." Orus gently brushed the Galdrissen girl's hair from her face. "You will not fear for your life from the likes of them."

Jaruz was stopped in his tracks at the Orus's gesture. He swallowed hard. "We must find her, brother. We must find them all. I want many Orc heads on poles outside of my fortress. They will think about this day forever, if I have my way."

"You will not be the first Dwarf to become a Hodan! You speak like us already, friend!" Orus smiled and helped him up.

"Let us go get our people, Orus," Jaruz said, regaining his composure. The fear and sadness on his face were replaced by a wave of burning anger.

The Galdrissen girl smiled through her tears. She had never seen anyone committed to saving the Galdrissen. Now, two great warriors stood ready to decimate her enemies with their great army. The girl laid prostrate in reverence before both of her saviors.

"Thank you both for your compassion and honor," Ega said to the two who stood above her.

Jaruz was horrified instantly, but Orus stopped him from embarrassing the girl.

Bending down, the old Hodan gently touched the girl's hair, remembering Faylea. "Rise, young one, and never bow to another as a slave. You are worthy of much more."

Orus helped the girl up. She did not know how to reply to the giant before her. She looked at Jaruz, who stood stunned. His mouth was open in shock at the action of the Hodan King.

Orus, sensing the confusion, replied to both of their faces. "Do not believe the rumors that Hodan is a nation of berserker warriors. We are warriors, philosophers, artists, and yes, we can even learn from past mistakes."

Ega reached out and hugged the Hodan man around the waist. Her head reached his solar plexus. He towered over her. When the King's guard began to react to the display of affection, Orus waved them off and let the girl be. He returned the hug gently.

"We must prepare to get the others, young one. I must go," Orus said, smiling at the girl's tear-stained face.

"Please, be safe, hero," Ega replied. "I am sorry for the horrible things I said when we first met in the cave."

"I am sorry for my horrible actions, My Lady. Hopefully, today I can redeem myself for many misdeeds and prejudices. Let us go, Jaruz. Physicians, attend to this lady's needs."

Orus and Jaruz left the sunshade and found the unit Captains.

"Any more out there, Captains?" Orus bellowed with authority.

"None found yet, Sire," the men replied one by one.

"Then we proceed southward at a slow march. Conserve the energy of the men. There are twenty-nine more. We will find them alive, or bring their bodies back to the fortress for proper burial. Understood?"

The leaders replied as one. "Yes, Sire!"

* * *

The Todessen had hit the emplacements with fury. The probing units had discovered a couple of viable avenues of approach into the fortress. As they made their way into the killing pocket that Uilam had designed, parts of the unit began destroying the spiked emplacements and going around them. From the outside of the fortress walls and under cover of darkness, Todessen specialists scaled the walls and engaged the hidden Hodan archers. They were dealt with eventually, but not before the Todessen had executed most of the men in the emplacements. The traps needed fire from above to be effective. The Todessen were in the killing pocket, but Uilam had no way to ignite the oil without exposing his men.

"We need to hold them at the courtyard exit as best that we can, Edmund," Uilam barked out as he directed his few remaining men forward to form a shield wall at the mouth of the spike channel.

"We need to set those bastards on fire, Sir!" Edmund growled.

"Edmund, do as I order! Get them to the shield wall, now!" Uilam barked angrily.

"I've got this one, brother," Edmund said, looking at Uilam with a blue glow to his eyes.

"Wait for me, brother!" Uilam replied with his own eyes aglow.

Uilam charged with sword and shield in front of Edmund, who grabbed a lit torch from a sconce and followed his Sergeant closely behind. The pair ran to the channel full of oil and pitch, then Edmund pounced, throwing his torch toward the kindling. As they did this, several Todessen saw them coming and ran to counter.

"Out of the way, vermin," Uilam roared in a voice much too large for his modest frame.

Edmund's torch landed at the edge of the channel, just out of range of the goal. Looking at Uilam, he said, "I will drink with you at the hero's table in Aeternum, brother."

The recruit charged, knocking one Todessen off his feet and grabbing his torch from the ground. Uilam could see two arrows appear as if from thin air into the back of his friend. They were long black shafts with large feather fletching. Still, Edmund crawled furiously toward the fuel source. He was now dragging two Todessen on his back while one kicked furiously at his side, but the warrior continued slowly forward as if his opponent did not exist. Uilam could see his shield wall barely holding the majority of the invasion force in the desired location. He charged at one of the Todessen on his friend.

"Honor and glory! Degran-Eras! Fight!" the sergeant encouraged.

Two Todessen were knocked from Edmund by Uilam's charge. The Sergeant stabbed one enemy through his back and then turned to decapitate another as it spun to face him. Two more were now on Edmund's back, and one had begun to twist an arrow shaft, stopping the advance of the determined warrior. Edmund was crying out in pain. Uilam was not pleased.

"Get off of my friend, you dishonorable pigs," the blood-soaked human demanded.

"Finish him," one Todessen said to the other. "I have this fool."

Edmund was on the ground, moaning in pain, torch still in hand, as one of his assailants got off of him, grabbing a sword from the ground beside him. The torchbearer was now groggy and exhausted from fighting. His sight blurred by pain. Edmund saw his friend square up against a sizeable Todessen warrior. The enemy looked, from the weary warrior's vantage point, to be a head taller than Uilam.

"Come get me, vermin," Uilam said confidently. However, he was anything but.

"I will eat your heart tonight, boy," the Todessen warrior said, advancing on the human.

"Edmund, the shield wall holds, brother. I will see you in Aeternum if that is the will of the Goddess, but we still breathe, and you have not reached your objective! Go! Carry on until we no longer draw breath, and our heart no longer beats within our chests."

Edmund laughed. A puzzled look covered the face of the Todessen, holding him down from the back. The boy quickly rolled to his left, putting the Todessen attacker behind him. Uilam's eyes were as wide as goose eggs as he saw Edmund grab the head of one arrow that stuck through the front of his gambeson and jerk it entirely through his chest. Before the Todessen was able to see what was happening, the beaten warrior rolled over again, jamming the arrowhead into the exposed throat of his attacker. The Todessen squealed, grabbing his throat. He gurgled momentarily and then ceased to move. Uilam quickly severed the head from the other surprised Todessen, who had turned to aid his fellow invader and forgotten the warrior behind him.

The two young men smiled at each other. They were both a gory mess of entrails, blood, and flesh ... their own and their enemy's. They looked as if they had both just crawled out of the catacombs of the Underworld. Uilam limped over to his friend and offered him a hand. Carrying him and the still-burning torch, Edmund finally reached his objective and dropped the flame into the trench.

Instantly, the oil ignited, and flames quickly traveled down the channel to where the Todessen lay in the belly of a Dwarven fire trap. Uilam lifted his heavy head and, through swollen eyes, saw the enemy trying to retreat.

"NOW!" the leader of the Hodan recruits yelled.

A Dwarf chopped a rope, releasing a spiked tree trunk that swung over the exit path, skewering several trying to flee. Others crawled like insects trying to avoid the flames, but most were consumed where they stood. The fire burned hot with a Dwarfish concoction mixed into the oil. Very few escaped, but those who did, ran for the field where Uilam figured more Todessen awaited.

"You did it, Edmund. You saved us, my friend," Uilam said. He was greeted with silence.

The leader looked over at his friend, who was barely breathing and unconscious, but through all the gore, he wore a subtle smile. Uilam wept.

"Healers! Healers, now! Bring a stretcher! Save Edmund! Save this man!!! He is why we live!" Uilam shouted frantically.

The young leader was pleading more than ordering, and his men could see it plainly. The Todessen were repelled for the moment. No counterattack seemed imminent. Several warriors grabbed Edmund by his shoulder armor and boots and took him into the cave. There were healers there, but none of them, looking at the carnage, believed he could be saved. Still, they would not give up on him.

Uilam stood alone in the darkness, tears streaming down his face, as well as sweat and blood. He had survived his first real battle against the Scourge, but the win felt hollow, as he looked at the twisted corpses of his men in every corner of the fortress. He had scarcely fifteen left, including the barely alive Edmund. If this was a victory, he was afraid to "win" again tomorrow.

Uilam looked out at the field and saw movement. It was much less than before, but he knew it was them.

"Everyone outside. Get in the cave and reinforce our warriors in the passage. We will make our stand there! Move!" Uilam collected himself and entered the cave.

The stench of burning hair and flesh filled the hair.

* * *

Orus and his forces breached the border early the following day. The Orcs were dug in. They were not pleased with the human response to their expedition into Dwarfish Lands. Several units began to stir. They were organized and moving with purpose to where Orus had set his own pickets. The Hodan archers were behind the cavalry that roamed the left and right flanks of the two legion-wide shield wall that was five ranks deep.

Looking out over the numbers, Orus squinted and said a quick prayer. Then he said out loud, to no one in particular, "Kepir, I hope you picked this place."

"Your orders, My King?" a legion Commander asked.

"Wait for the enemy to engage. Use the Draj shield wall on them for the first and second waves. When they try to adjust, we use our archers and switch to Hodan tactics. We will split them in the middle and kill the weaker flank first, then swing around to the other side. I am hoping that my specialists are here, but I have no idea. They are, after all, supposed to be invisible." Orus smiled. "They come. Let us greet them appropriately."

The Commander blew a horn. He let out a succession of tones that signaled the King's orders. Each Commander on the field had a bugler who responded with a song that signified "understood." The legions adjusted and prepared to engage. It would be a minute or two until combat as the Orcs charged across the open field.

* * *

"What do these humans want with these Todessen? Are they truly the allies of the evil ones?" an Orc leader asked his Commander.

"I do not know, Lieutenant." The Commander looked at the gleaming armor on the field and wondered who these humans were. "But they are here. They must be dealt with. Engage and destroy the invaders."

"As you command, Sir," the Orc replied.

The Orc units, dressed chiefly in cobbled together armor pieces and roughly made leather tunics, grabbed wooden door-sized shields and set their lines. When the humans did not advance, the Commander of the Orcish forces was emboldened.

"They are well-dressed, Lieutenant," the ranking Orc sneered, "but they still fear us and do not advance to contact. They are weak, and they are cowards. Kill them all. Take slaves if you are able."

"Yes, Sir!" the Junior Officer responded, calling for the charge.

The Orc Commander sat in the rear of the onslaught of Orcs with a spyglass, watching the whole affair. He saw the enemy shift its lines in response to his charge. Wondering what they were up to, he readied a second wave just in case.

"Second!" the Senior Commander bellowed.

An even younger Orc responded, "Yes, Sir!"

"Ready your forces, just in case these humans surprise me."

"As you wish, Sir."

* * *

The first wave of Orcs struck the Hodan lines with a fury. The Hodan pulsed like Draj, cutting them down with ease. Although Orus could see that he was losing men, the losses were not nearly as bad as he had anticipated. Shocked, the enemy retreated and regrouped. The Hodan stayed put and called for the line shift. The Orcs were puzzled that the humans did not pursue.

Emboldened by what they saw as fear, the Orcs charged anew, but again, the Hodan lines deterred their advance. Expecting the same shield wall pulse to greet them, the Orcs repeated their first maneuver. Instead, the Hodan stepped back, allowing the Orcs on the front line to fall on their faces. The Hodan legion dispatched the first rank of Orcs as the attackers lay face-down in front of them. The fallen of both armies made it more difficult for the second and third waves of Orc marauders to effectively push against the Hodan lines. Orcs died in droves, taking a few of the Hodan with them.

Orus was covered in black blood and entrails, standing beside Jaruz, who looked very similar. The Hodan King could see the second unit forming in the back of the field. Hodan had not lost too many, but the battle was taking its toll. The King did not want to get into a war of attrition with this enemy. Looking around intently, the old warrior hoped to catch a glimpse of Kepir and his men, but he saw nothing.

"They have more than we do, brother," Orus said to Jaruz, pointing his sword behind the decimated first Orc unit that held the center of the field.

"I see that. What should we do?" Jaruz asked in exasperation.

"Well, my friend, I have a secret weapon, but I am not sure where they are," Orus said, sighing.

"Well, I hope they show up soon, for our sakes!" Jaruz panted, attempting to catch his breath.

* * *

Kepir made hand signals to his men. They were on the outskirts of a larger Orcish village. He and his specialists could see many Orcish women and children in their huts and on the surrounding roads. They appeared fearful and kept looking toward the racket that Kepir knew was Orus and the Orc forces locking horns directly to the north. The Master moved in closer to a hut, setting an incendiary device beside it. Rolling out a long fuse back to his original position, he again covered up, appearing to be a scrub bush once again. Kepir lit the end, watching as it hissed quietly toward its target.

Within seconds, there was a loud pop, and bright white sparks lit the area. The display ignited several huts and crude supply wagons in the area. Orcs began streaming out of their homes, bellowing. Orcish mothers clutched their children as they noticed the trees and bushes of the surrounding countryside began to stir and stand up. Then the fields looked, to their confused observers, as if they were walking toward the village. Soon, each of the specialists was clearly visible. They were armed with crossbow, short swords, and various throwing weapons. The fires raged, sending black smoke into the sky as the circle of Hodan closed tighter around the several hundred Orc villagers.

Inside the circle of Hodan, Orcish matrons growled angrily in a show of brute force. One mother and several older children attempted to defend their collective, but when they were cut down from all angles by bolts, the remaining Orcs cowered, huddling together, with their children in the center and the adults surrounding them. The children whimpered in fear within the circle.

"Well done, gentlemen. Secure the perimeter. My guard with me. We will meet with the prisoners." Kepir made hand gestures, and the lines went about complying with his wishes automatically.

Five guards and Kepir approached the gaggle of frightened Orc families. None dared to try anything with the specialists after witnessing the quick execution of the last Orc to attempt resistance.

"Who is the village chieftain of this place?" Kepir demanded.

An older, almost toothless female Orc stepped forward as many hands tried to hold her back.

"I am she," the Orc said in a raspy, deep voice.

"I am Kepir of Hodan, Commander of the forces that have captured your people. I am here by order of my King."

"I am Yotum, Priestess of the Brothers," she responded. "Why do you come here? Why do your people threaten our peaceful lands?"

"Well, I could ask the same thing, but I doubt that either of us knows the real answer to any of these questions, except that we are here to rescue some of our people who your forces have captured, well over the border, and deep into the Dwarfish held territories." Kepir was very official in his account.

The specialist showed no compassion to the dozens of fearful faces that met his gaze. It was a skill he was well-versed in. Subterfuge and psychological manipulation of the enemy was a helpful tool. They did not need to know that he was not, in actuality, a savage murderer. In fact, he knew that the enemy outnumbered his men, so Kepir needed them to think that he was every bit as ruthless as they believed. Only then would they fear him and comply with his demands. In other scenarios, he played the friend while secretly plotting against the target. He was an assassin by trade and loyal to very few in this world. Orus was one of those few, and his King was in trouble if he did not get this right.

"The Todessen are evil, My Lord," the Orcish woman responded. "They seek to invade us from the seaport with you humans as their allies. They got too close to our borders for our liking."

"Still, they are our people. They were in our lands. Your people assaulted them and kidnapped them. That is an overt act of war." Kepir stated facts and stuck to them.

"But we have nothing to fear from weak humans," the old Orc said sarcastically. "They're weaklings and cowards." She laughed out loud.

"Yet we hold the field against your 'valiant' warriors, who assaulted women and children picking berries and gathering nuts? That is not ..." Kepir's words scalded the pride of the Orc.

She interrupted. "They are Todessen. They are evil. You fools will pay the price for allying with them."

Kepir responded. "They are Galdrissen. They have turned to Haya, and she is the mother of your Gods. Perhaps you should rethink how you treat followers of the light. And when did Orcs turn from Haeldrun?"

"When we saw what He was all about. We bled the fields in His name, and He left us to rot when we lost. We were on our own when the Dwarves came for revenge. We held them as best we could and made it too expensive for them to try to eradicate us." The Orc snorted angrily. "The Underlord despises us for losing the war, but does nothing to help His creations win. We realized that this land had plenty for all and that we wanted to live. So, our original religious leaders decided that a good compromise would be the warring brothers, Runnir and Gunnir, vice going fully toward 'peace' and 'love,' since that is not truly our nature. It worked out in our favor."

"All personal grievances aside, you have aligned with the light, as we have. Why do we fight each other?" Kepir asked rhetorically.

"Because light or no, hatreds and old prejudices are hard to end. We fear that everyone will one day come for our heads, because Orcs ... and Goblins ... are known to have been evil and ruthless in the past. We just want to live in peace, but the Dwarves do not trust us, the Todessen hate us, and now humans seek to invade us." The Priestess sat sadly on the ground.

"We did not seek this incursion, My Lady," Kepir reassured. "We only came here to retrieve our people. Where are they?"

"In a cage within the largest hut at the center of our village. Thankfully, you did not burn it to the ground like the others, or I'm sure that we would be blamed for their deaths also."

Yotum stood and motioned for the human warrior to follow. The five guards accompanied Kepir.

"They are here," the Orc pointed.

There, in a dilapidated iron-barred cage, Kepir counted twenty-nine Galdrissen. The human ordered, "Let them out, now!"

An Orcish boy brought a large ring of keys to the Priestess, who inserted one in a rusty lock and turned until the door opened.

"Come out, friends. We have come to save you," Kepir announced loudly.

He could see that many of the captives were severely battered, but most were able to walk unaided. Still, some required assistance from the others. The Galdrissen were led outside of the Orc village to a group of Hodan specialists tasked with their protection. Ma 'Dryna smiled at Kepir as she herded the children to freedom. The Priestess limped to where the human protectors were standing.

"Did Ega survive, Lord Kepir?" Dryna asked hoarsely, remembering the attack.

Kepir smiled. "Yes, My Lady. She told us where to find you. Jaruz is here to fetch you personally. He insisted."

Ma 'Dryna smiled, thanking the Goddess. "We must mend fences if we are to be at peace, warrior."

"This will require a conversation between the leaders. I fear the Todessen are playing the three kingdoms against one another. I just hope the Elves have not fallen prey to their schemes." Kepir bowed and returned to the lines. The Orcs were sitting silently in the mud, awaiting their fates.

"Kren!" Kepir shouted.

"Yes, Sir!" the new specialist leader responded.

"Sneak your way His Majesty and let him know what has happened here. Advise him to call for a parlay. We have hostages if need be."

"At once, Sir!"

"And Kren," Kepir added, "make a noise, out of arm's reach to let His Majesty know that you are there, or the old man will remove your head from your shoulders … maybe with his bare hands."

"Thanks for the advice, Sir!" Kepir smiled, running into the grassy field.

He disappeared to the gasp of several watching Orcish children.

* * *

A healer had prayed over the human's wounds and bound them the best she was able. Uilam walked with a slight limp, but was still in the fight. Edmund was unconscious, and his breathing was shallow. The arrows were out of him, and the bleeding was stemmed, but the young man had lost too much blood, and his skin was pale and clammy. A Galdrissen girl changed his bandages regularly, packing Edmund's wounds with fresh herbs. She wore a frown as if she expected her patient's last breath to occur at any moment.

"Shore up the barriers and the hatches with whatever we can find. The bastards know that we are in here, and they keep trying to knock the doors down." Uilam was talking to the remaining ten battle-worn warriors he had left.

None of them responded to their leader's words.

"Listen up, gentlemen! Edmund and the rest risked their lives to save all of ours! Without their bravery, we would have been overrun! Do NOT let their sacrifices be in vain. Edmund is clinging to life. We should honor him appropriately."

Uilam saw five of the men nod and stand up, but the other five did not. "Hey, you five. What is your problem? We have come this far. There is only one way out of this mess, and that is right through the middle of them. They come, and you can sit here and cower in your own piss, or you can pick up your swords and fight for our lives. What will it be? They will show us no quarter after burning half of their warriors alive in that pit."

"Who made you the leader?" one boy responded.

"Actually, the King did," Uilam responded angrily. "So, shut it and get up now."

"He's not my King. He is not YOUR King! He is a King from another land. What does he care about us?" the boy sulked.

"Have you learned nothing from him? He has shown us the path to greatness! We must restore the honor of our people, boy! Get up! Fight!" Uilam was little more than seventeen years of age. This was not lost on a Todessen girl, who snickered when he called the other warrior a boy.

Uilam rolled his eyes. "So, your plan is to cower here and hide behind the girls? Do you expect us to fight alone to protect you?"

The boy became indignant. "I am no girl! I will show you, you bastard!"

"Fine, show me!" Uilam laughed. "Just get up and fight!"

The last reluctant boy stood, joining the other four who welcomed him, patting him on the back.

"Fight two by two. Switch out when you are tired. It is our only tactic. We are too few. If injured beyond the ability to fight, crawl back here for attention. The next man fills in the hole immediately. Do we understand?" Uilam looked around at all the nodding faces.

"Let's do this, men," a younger boy challenged.

The ten entered the passageway and could hear the invaders beating on the hatch with a ram. It would be a fight in minutes. Some prayed, some drank a bit of water, and chewed on hardtack. Uilam stared at the barrier wall and waited.

* * *

Kren had arrived shortly before the Orcs gathered with their second great army. Orus sighed in relief with the report of the specialist, as he knew the second verse of this song would bring much more destruction than the introduction had. Kren advised his King that he now had the upper hand with Kepir's hostages. Jaruz was overjoyed to hear that the Galdrissen prisoners had been rescued and that the specialists were secretly moving them back into friendly territory. The Hodan and the Dwarf had the enemy where they wanted them.

Orus called for a white flag. He sent a rider to call for a parlay. The Orcs laughed at the rider, expecting him to ask for terms of surrender. They were horrified when they received the report of covert Hodan forces sneaking behind their lines and capturing a settlement just south of their position. The Orc Commander grudgingly accepted the parlay and rode out to meet Orus, who was waiting patiently on horseback in the middle of the field.

"What is the meaning of this, human?" the Orc Commander bellowed.

"Greetings, Orc, my name is Orus, of Hodan. I come to get my people you stole. I have them and, as a bonus, a whole village of your own women and children. Whatever shall I do with them?" Orus stared menacingly at the Orc, who backed down a notch.

"What is it you want, human?" the Orc Commander asked calmly. "You have no use for our kind. Release our kin."

"I need assurances that this will be the last time we meet on the field for a LONG time, Orc," Orus demanded. "The settlements to the north are not in your lands. Stay within your borders."

"It is your people who need to stay within your own borders. Whaleford and the Todessen raid our eastern borders daily," the Orc said with disdain.

"It is my understanding, from my men in the field, that the Todessen scum are dressing up innocent human civilians and invading your nation with them in tow. Then they leave them to be slaughtered by your armies, making it look like Degran-Eras is your enemy. They are playing us against one another so they can divide our forces and defeat us."

The Orc had a concerned look on his face. He had seen with his own eyes that the humans found within Ynus-Grag were no more than fodder for the Orcish blades. He wondered about what the human before him spoke. If Degran-Eras did have armies such as this man possessed on this field, the Orcs were doomed.

"How can I believe you?" the Orc asked, almost begging for a reason to consider the possibility.

"How about a gesture of good faith. I withdraw my people from around the village south of here. I will return your people to you, as unharmed as I can. Four or five died when they charged my lines from what my man tells me. I am sorry that occurred, but it is the price of war. Innocents are not immune to arrows and blades. My men tell me that your people roughed ours up quite badly." Orus had a face of stone. He had dealt with Orcs before.

"I agree to this gesture and pledge a truce for the time being. I must review what you tell me, human. If you are correct, then we all have a common foe in the Todessen … as if that was ever a question. I wonder if the Dwarves will ever accept us as equals … or the humans for that matter." The Orc Commander bowed.

"Humans, Dwarves, Elves, Orcs, and Goblins would make a formidable alliance against the instigators from the north. We will pull our forces back, collecting our dead as we go. We will leave the Orc dead alone in respect." Orus bowed back.

"We agree, human. A truce is in effect." The Orc growled out orders, and the armies of the south began to withdraw.

Kren shot an arrow that burned a bright red. It streaked across the sky toward the Dwarfish lands. Off in the distance, Hodan horns replied with the tune for "acknowledged." Kren smiled at Orus, who grinned back.

"Good job, Kren! Now, let us depart this land before they change their minds!" Orus looked over the field. He had lost another two or three hundred souls. His legions were dwindling, and he had not even faced a severe Todessen threat. He needed the humans from Degran-Eras now more than ever.

For now, Hodan had won a hard victory, the Galdrissen were rescued, and a truce was struck with an enemy not known for diplomacy. Despite losing more men, Orus considered it a tactical victory, but not without its price. The Hodan leader looked out over the killing fields as his dead were gathered on carts. The high cost of glory burned within the King's saddened heart, and his smile was quickly extinguished.

* * *

It had been two days. Uilam was bleeding. He was down to eight men, including himself. The Todessen were attacking in waves, two by two, and the young warrior knew that if he could not figure out something soon, everyone he was entrusted with was doomed to die at the end of the sword. The Todessen hated the Galdrissen the most of any people of the Rynn. To them, the Galdrissen were the worst of traitors and heretics. Shedding their blood was considered an honor to Haeldrun. A bounty was paid for the heads of those who were hunted down. Uilam knew he and his few remaining men were all that stood between the killers outside and the victims within. He could see the look of sorrow and fear on the faces of those who were counting on them. Some of the young Galdrissen girls had picked up swords and were looking at the bloodied blades with fear. They had no idea what they were going to do, and Uilam could see it plainly.

Edmund was still alive, against all odds. Uilam smiled and saluted the timid hero, returning to the passageway. The Todessen had not struck in an hour. They were due. Somewhere up ahead, one of his boys began calling out.

"Movement ahead of point three, Sir!" The boy shouted in a hoarse, exhausted voice.

Uilam responded, "All warriors to point three, now! Reinforce our men!"

The remaining five warriors limped their ways back to the battle. Uilam felt doom spread over him as he heard unintelligible screams of Todessen and growling coming toward their position.

"Stand fast, boys!" Uilam said calmly, awaiting the end. "We kill them all, or die trying. Take as many as you can with you!"

The racket became louder as it seemed a more significant force approached their location. In the darkened, smoky passageway, it was almost impossible to see.

"Form shields two wide, three deep. Two rest!" Uilam ordered, and the remaining few complied.

Then the shouting stopped, and the growling ceased. The sound of boots on stone and clattering armor was heard forward of point three. Everything was a blur of adrenaline, blood, and stinging sweat as a Todessen warrior charged toward the shields as if his life depended on it. The Todani hit the weary shield wall like a battering ram sending the spent boys sprawling all over the passageway. Uilam stood and braced for impact when something odd occurred.

"Come back here, you son of a whore!" a quite human voice bellowed, as a mailed hand reached out of the dust and smoke, jerking the fleeing Todessen by his gorget to the floor.

Uilam saw his chance. He pounced on the fallen foe, pounding the invader into a bloody ragged pulp with both his sword and shield edge. Exhausted, he leaned on his side on top of the shield, trying to focus his blurry gaze on where the voice had come from. There, walking through the smoke, was a Hodan legionnaire who smiled from ear to ear. He was nodding and helped Uilam to his feet.

"Sire, they live!" the more prominent man shouted to his men in the passageway, who then relayed the message outside the cave to Orus and Kepir, who smiled in relief.

Jaruz was beside himself with joy and wept as he hugged his tired and beaten love, Dryna. "They live, my love. Now rest!" he ordered.

Dryna smiled as she finally breathed a sigh of relief, drifting out of consciousness. Jaruz immediately panicked, thinking the worst, but then relaxed as he watched her chest rise and fall regularly. She was very much alive, but snoring gently and completely exhausted.

"Take her to my chambers and give her my bed for as long as she needs," Jaruz ordered.

The older Galdrissen healers smiled and nodded, doing as they were told.

The people exited the mouth of the cave. One by one, they gathered in a large group, praising the Goddess for their protectors and deliverers. Orus sat proudly on his horse, watching his man from Degran-Eras and five remaining warriors lean on each other as they emerged from the cave and into the bright sunlight. The old King remembered many similar scenes in his life. He smiled as he did.

Kepir met with Uilam immediately. The boy could barely see out of his two swollen eyes and had a broken nose. He also had multiple lacerations and significant bruises. His men looked the same. The Dwarfish engineer with the funny hat limped over on a makeshift crutch to the Hodan King.

"Your Majesty, if I may ..." The Dwarf waited politely.

"You may, Sir," the King responded politely.

"That young man, and the one they are carrying out on that stretcher ..." The Dwarf engineer pointed at Edmund. "... They are the reasons we live. The others were part of it, but these were the heart and soul of the effort. They were recklessly brave and incredibly resilient. I just thought you should know of their prowess in battle and devotion to duty. They were prepared to die in order to protect those people. Degran-Eras and Hodan were well represented these past few days."

"Good to know, my good Sir. Thank you for your report. I have heard your words, and I will consider them when making future leadership choices," Orus responded, dismounting. "I must attend to this. I apologize."

The Dwarf bowed respectfully.

"Kren, Kepir, I need damage reports. Casualty reports ... the usual." Orus was not in the mood, but he needed the intelligence.

"At once, Sire," Kepir replied, nodding to Kren, who acknowledged him and then sprinted off.

Orus raised his eyebrows, lowering his gaze at his friend. Kepir knew he was asking about Kren. He just smiled and gave Orus a thumbs-up.

Orus smiled broadly, nodding, and stated smugly, "I knew he was good for something!"

* * *

It had been three days since the Todessen attacks. Uilam was limping along better than the day before. Edmund was still in and out of consciousness, but alive. Five other Degran warriors followed their leader everywhere he went. It made Uilam uncomfortable that they had such a devotion to him now, even after so many had died, but they knew what he and Edmund had sacrificed for them. Uilam had survived, but Edmund was not out of the woods yet.

The young hero leaned on a makeshift crutch, but still wore his sword openly. All his men were armed and on crutches. Kepir stifled his chuckle, looking at Orus. The King strode over to where the six young men stood in a rough formation of invalids.

"Good morning, gentlemen!" Orus greeted warmly.

"Good morning, Sire!" the six replied unanimously.

"This was a great victory for Degran-Eras and for Hodan! You should be proud of your accomplishments." Orus stood and clapped. Others in the area clapped also.

Uilam was not impressed. He was flattered, but he looked over the scorched courtyard. He remembered where every man fell, lying motionless in his own blood. The young warrior's eyes were not lost on Orus, who frowned as a knot formed in his throat.

"It is not your fault that they are gone, young one. It is the enemy's fault," Orus said to Uilam.

"I was in command, Sire. Forty-three of my friends and comrades are gone because of my decisions," Uilam lamented.

"They died so others could live," Orus replied gently, looking with understanding into the face of his newly battle-christened warrior. The old King remembered the Arondayre and sighed.

"Sire, if you were here and the real Hodan were guarding these gates, I doubt forty-three would have perished," Uilam said sadly.

"Son, here are the numbers." Orus held a scroll in his hand. He opened it. Uilam awaited his condemnation.

"Be it known to all warriors and citizens present that Uilam, son of Yerd, led fifty Hodan initiates against the great Scourge of our generation. Hodan scouts confirm the deaths of forty-three initiates, who died of wounds sustained while holding their assigned positions. These fifty souls with minimal training held a force of not less than three-hundred trained Todessen Raiders. Estimates from the Vyn scouts who engaged them in the northern and eastern forests state that thousands had attempted to pass over the mountains for some unknown reason. The Elves killed many, but estimate that upwards of FIVE-hundred may or may not have made it to this very stronghold." Orus paused for effect.

There were gasps from the gallery listening.

"So, from three- to five-hundred trained enemies assaulted fifty Hodan trainees. Forty-three gave their lives, and we collected two-hundred-fifty-six enemy dead from this fortress alone! By my math, those are numbers I expect from trained legions, not squires and trainees. Your men killed six for every one of ours who fell, Uilam. That is incredible, even for Hodan."

"Your Majesty, why does it hurt so badly? And I don't mean my body." Uilam looked up with reddened eyes.

Orus put his hand on the young man's shoulder and replied, "Because losing your warriors should never be trivial. Losing those who are brave and loyal should hurt as if your heart has been ripped from your body … as if your soul is burned with fire, because those you command are not just your men; they are your brothers, son. They are your family, and the love of family is above all things. Even though we are of different mothers, we are all Hodan. After today, I consider you one of Hodan. I will honor all of your men in the manner befitting a Hodan Elite."

"Thank you, Sire. I would be honored as well as the families of those that fell in battle," Uilam replied.

"Each family will be cared for by the crown, son. It is the least that we can do. Every family will get a year's wages for a legionnaire to help recover. I know it doesn't replace the person, but some will be without a son to aid in providing for the family, now ..." Orus trailed off and could see Uilam's lip quivering.

"Thank you, Sire," Uilam replied with a shaky voice.

"It gets easier with experience, son, but it never completely leaves you." Orus patted the boy on his shoulder, knowingly. "Kepir, make sure he is taken care of. Let them heal before you train them any further, understood?"

"Yes, Sire," the specialist said sincerely. "I remember my first battle, son. I understand. Let us get a mead and talk."

Kepir walked the six to the tent serving as a tavern and ordered up several rounds. Every time one of the warriors tried to pay, they were told by the barkeep, "your money is no good," or "it's on the house."

Each man drank his fill. As beaten and saddened as they were, they were still grateful to be alive.

Uilam hoped Edmund would heal to join his band again.

He had much to talk about with his friend.

Chapter 9

Orus slept soundly on a feather mattress within the first actual room he had inhabited since leaving Hodan. Jaruz and the Galdruhn would have it no other way. When Orus protested and attempted to join his men in the field, the women of the Galdruhn pleaded with the warrior King to accept their gesture. Jaruz ribbed the old warrior, stating that refusal would be akin to a slap in the face to the old, stubborn, Galdrissen. Orus reluctantly complied, but voiced his objection to their generosity. Still, he was thankful for the comfort of a real bed. It had been almost two years since he had slept in one.

Sitting up and rubbing the sleep from his eyes, the old man poured water into a wash bowl on a nightstand beside him. He stood and began scrubbing diligently, noticing that his beard was longer than usual, and the hair that was once soft and silky had become dry, coarse, and tangled. Looking in the mirror, Orus also realized that the gray now outshined the black hair on his head and face. Time was catching up with him. He could feel it in his bones, quite literally.

Disrobing, he washed the places critical for civilized interaction with people. He did not want to smell like a barnyard animal. The King dressed in a clean tunic and trousers, lacing his boots on his feet. Looking up for some oil for the leather, he saw the makeshift shrine he had created the night prior. Two ivory figurines stood affixed to the table in candle wax. The candles around them had long burned out and were hardened pools on the rough-cut table. He stared at the two for a time.

Rising from his stool, he walked over and carefully broke each figure

171

free from the table, kissing them and cradling them in his hands. He prayed momentarily for his wife and then asked the Goddess to protect his daughter. Sighing, he put them in their leather pouch that had come to hang around his neck.

"I wonder how she is," Orus said to no one there.

"She is well, Orus," a voice gently replied.

Startled, the old King turned expertly, drawing his sword from the scabbard that hung at the ready on his bedpost.

"Who is there? Kepir, is that you?" Orus's demeanor immediately transitioned to a warrior from pining parent.

From behind the warrior, the voice replied, "A friend, King. I am not Kepir, but that man is never far from your side. You should value him as a son."

"I do value him, intruder. If you have harmed him, I will send you to Haeldrun, personally," Orus growled.

"Ah, how I love the Hodan," the voice said happily, chuckling.

Orus spun about, looking around wildly. "What magic is this, coward? Face me like a man!"

"Oh, but I am not a man, King of Hodan. Quite the opposite!" the voice said in a slightly condescending tone.

"Enough banter, who are you!?" the King demanded loudly.

There was a stirring of the guard outside of the King's lodgings, followed by a loud knocking.

"Sire! Are you all right!?" a young warrior bellowed.

The King opened the door. "I seem to have an intruder in here somewhere, but I can't find him! He is using magic of some sort!"

The sentry burst in loudly, annoying the King a bit. The guard immediately began tossing the room upside down. When he was done, he was puzzled. He found no one.

"No intruder found, Sire!" The guard squinted, as if trying to find an excuse for his King. "Perhaps, he escaped?"

"No doubt you frightened him off, son," Orus replied, sheathing his sword and smiling. "Thank you, you are dismissed."

The guard bowed and exited the mess he had created. Orus looked about and sighed.

"Can't find good help these days," the voice said to a visibly aggravated Orus.

"Now, that is downright infuriating. You hide so well that my men think me mad, and now you make jokes," Orus scowled.

"Ah, my first friend once told me of your demeanor, Orus! Your daughter is much like you—and I think that is a good thing!" the voice snickered from out of view.

"I warn you, intruder, speak of Faylea again, and I will have your head on a stick by nightfall." Orus's eyes seemed to glow angrily.

"Hmm," the voice said smugly, "All right, what about Puryn? How about Kairoth?"

There was a hint of a taunt in the words that was not lost on the Hodan King.

"When I see your face, perhaps I will remove your tongue for speaking their names," Orus responded.

"Then you are the sort of man I need," said a dark-cloaked figure who seemingly appeared in the chair beside the washbasin.

Orus turned to engage his adversary, "Finally, you show yourself."

"Ah, this is where you will kill me, I suppose." The man's head was covered by a hood, but he raised his fiery eyes to meet Orus's.

The King stopped and evaluated his opponent. He was a mage of some sort, and from watching the battles in Sudenyag unfold, he knew that they were not to be trifled with. In one motion, the warrior re-drew his sword and was on his opponent in a second. Even at an advanced fighting age, Orus, the Lion, was still godlike in armor. He gasped, looking around feverishly, as his sword stroke met thin air and the adversary was nowhere to be seen.

"Damn you! Fight with honor! Where are you?" Orus demanded angrily.

"Behind you, you oaf!" the voice replied. "Are we going to do this all day, or are you going to talk to me like a rational human being?"

Orus turned and swung again. Darkness surrounded the warrior, and he was disoriented for a split second, but that was all his opponent needed to escape once again.

"Remember when you said that Hodan were not just horse's asses and warriors, but philosophers and intellectuals? I distinctly remember you suggested this thing to a person or two. I am beginning to wonder, Orus, are you really? Kairoth is most definitely more than brawn. Faylea is a strong-minded, intelligent leader. They raise your namesake in that tradition!" The enemy face was obscured by shadow, but Orus could see his smile.

"Who in the Underworld are you? How could you know such things!? My namesake? There is no namesake! I am the last of my line. My name will die with me. I had no sons." Orus stuck his sword in the floor in front of him. It stood just in reach as he grabbed the stool and sat down.

"Are we going to talk, King? Or should I try another hero? My brothers look to the new generation for entertainment, but not me. I love a good redemption story, old man. Are you that man, or should I seek another?"

The voice sat on the chair beside the washbasin.

"Talk," Orus said, squinting skeptically at the eyes under the hood.

The voice smiled. He knew the King did not fear him, and that was good for his cause.

"I wish to help you in your quest to redeem your honor and wash away the sins you feel that you have committed, Orus. How can I convince you that I am the one who can accomplish those things with you?"

"Only Haya or one of the Gods can free me of my guilt, stranger. No mage nor Priest in their robes can wipe away my stain." Orus raised his eyebrows. "If you are so omniscient, tell me what you know of Kairoth and my daughter. This should be good. You know of them and guess about children, but you do not know of what you speak. Faylea was past child-bearing age when I left, and Kairoth had not returned to her. I fear that she has been removed from the throne and possibly dead. Hodan is not a place for those who cannot defend what they have taken." Orus scowled and then, frowning, crossed his arms across his chest.

The adversary across the room could see that the King had absent-mindedly clutched the leather pouch holding the two ivory figurines he looked at every day.

"Fine, Orus. I will tell you of what you left behind, if you promise to go forward with me to the future! What you have done is done. You cannot change the past, my friend. You are no more guilty of sins or crimes than the ones who give no care to what they destroy on the path to their own selfish ambitions. You killed Jabir to save your people, then you saved your people with your own blood." The voice waited for a response.

"That statement proves nothing. The men speak of my 'deeds' on that day as if it were a holy day in need of remembrance. It is common knowledge. You could have heard that from anyone sitting around a fire. It shows me nothing, but that you are observant or have a good intelligence gatherer. You have your own Kepir, no doubt?"

Orus chuckled, reaching for a bottle of mead. Pouring himself one, he blew the dust out of another cup and offered it to the figure sitting across from him. The adversary bowed his head slightly, accepting the tankard.

Raising the cup, the hooded voice toasted. "To proving myself to a stubborn old goat."

Orus chuckled. "To old goats and secretive intruders."

"Fine, Orus. How about I tell you of what has transpired after the end of your service on the Ert?" The figure crossed his legs confidently, sipping from his cup.

"Tell me," Orus said with skepticism.

"Puryn called upon you to deal with the treachery of the Edenyag King. You negotiated his surrender with the Elder races, but you wanted to burn them to the ground over a past slight. After Puryn joined you in Empyr, you executed the two vile evildoers? Correct so far?"

"Still, common knowledge, stranger. Not convinced." Orus poured another tankard for both.

"You found a Temple in Suden that was overrun with Todessen and undead. The Northern Alliance fought hard to enter it. Many were lost. Kairoth and his friends held off a demonic Dragon at the gates to the pit you sought to enter. There, the boy's former love perished, saving his life."

The voice seemed a bit saddened as he recalled the events. Orus noticed

175

the tone in his voice and was intrigued.

"Still common knowledge, friend," Orus sighed.

"Is it common knowledge what happened to Kairoth *after* they entered the Temple of the Underlord?" The face smiled again.

"Perhaps, but many things happened after that. Give me details and not generalities. Give me insight into what happened that day, and perhaps I will believe you. You only tell me what everyone in Hodan already knows." The Hodan King sat back in mild disgust.

"Kairoth and Faylea became close. You thought of him as a suitable heir, even if he was half-Yslan. He showed his love for her many times, killing anyone who would harm a hair on her head. A Suden fool met his doom that night. Hassim was King within days." The face smiled again.

Orus was silent. He knew his companion was right. Kairoth was the man for Faylea.

The voice continued. "After entering the main sanctuary to Haeldrun, Adasser was taken by Haya, and Nyzur, the High Priest of Haeldrun, was possessed by the Dark Lord. Kairoth also spoke for someone new! You were both impressed and terrified by your choice of son-in-law."

Orus thought back to the conversation between three Gods in the Temple of the Underlord in Sudenyag. He shuddered at the thought of the Underlord being present on the Ert, but remembered Kairoth scolding both Gods and sending them back to their domains. Everyone was surprised and puzzled at the new voice that Kairoth channeled.

"That is when he became a Priest, or monk…," Orus stammered.

"That's when the boy promised to return to your girl. He had to see the Galdrissen to their new home. Then he had a quest to complete for training and enlightenment." The voice smiled, snorting at Orus's new look of apprehension.

"Kairoth went north, spreading the new message of his new god, gaining followers and power. He delivered the Galdrissen with a couple of worshippers of Haya. One was named Valtyr, a priest, and another a follower of the Elfish disciplines, Reynir, I believe. Kairoth disappeared into the monastery in Empyr for a bit, then off to Torith, and finally he left to find his ultimate teacher."

The voice was becoming more serious. The red eyes had changed to blue while the speaker waited for a response from the Hodan.

"The boy never returned after he left her. Then I left her, because of the inevitability of a challenge to my reign. I did not wish to lose and put her life in danger. I left not only for the honor of Hodan and my anger at Puryn, but also to protect her from my own inevitable failure. Time claims every warrior. Even legends eventually fade. This is a cowardice that cannot be forgiven, stranger." Orus looked at his boots.

"It is not cowardice to know your limitations and to sacrifice for those you love, old man. I will tell you the rest now, if you wish." The voice now sounded sympathetic. The blue eyes now looked at the old man, who frowned and swallowed hard. Somehow, the ivory figurines had found their way out of the bag and into the old King's hands. He was looking at them with misty eyes.

"Are you a Denir who followed me here to torment me? If not, then tell me plainly if my beloved still lives." Orus choked on his words, but then composed himself almost immediately.

The hooded head cocked to the side, seeing how the Hodan man's resolve immediately returned to him. He nodded, smiling.

"Orus, I am not your enemy—quite the opposite. I will tell you." The voice sat up, leaning forward as if to tell a secret. "Kairoth went to Hodan, stopping off for a few months at a ranch of an old man. That man was one of Hodan's finest specialists. Ei'Nyorn was his name, and he is my friend. There, the lad learned his last lessons and sealed his fate!"

"What do you mean, sealed his fate?" Orus asked with concern.

"I mean, I gave him every chance to flee, but he kept on coming back for more! The boy is intolerable at times, but he has a heart of gold. He is now the single deadliest warrior on the Ert, second only perhaps to my mother's champion, Puryn—or perhaps—you." The eyes below the hood widened in fake surprise, as if he let a secret slip.

"What are you saying?" Orus asked wide-eyed.

The face beneath the hood smiled widely as Orus began to comprehend the gravity of the conversation he was engaged in.

"Well, after the boy finished with Ei'nyorn, he found out that some fool had challenged Faylea to a duel. It does not fare well for anyone who challenges the well-being of one that the young the man cares for." The smile grew wider below the hood.

"Go on!" Orus demanded, sitting up with his mouth gaped open.

"Kairoth married Faylea before her duel was to take place—an hour before actually. I do like the drama, don't you?" The voice chuckled.

"Get on with it," Orus yelled, irritated.

"As you wish! Kairoth married Faylea, then informed her that he was assuming the lead of Hodan as King, as the law dictates. She was not amused, but then she realized what her love was up to. Finally, my High Priest crushed those who would oppose him and anyone he loves." The voice was deadly serious. The smile was gone.

"YOUR High Priest?" Orus took a long swallow from his mug, emptying it. "Are you saying..."

"I am not finished, human. You wished to know; I will tell you. Faylea was too old for Kairoth. She was past her child-bearing years. I turned back time for her and for Kairoth. She became pregnant and bore him a son, who they named Orus, son of Kairoth, in tribute to you." The voice looked from under his hood at the silent King.

Tears ran from the stoic Hodan's face. He showed no emotion, but still, they came.

"Ah, Orus, you are human after all. The Hodan may be formidable, but you are all mortal. Love is in the heart of every man, if only he looks." The adversary lowered his hood. "How would you like me to appear, Orus?"

As the King watched in quiet awe, the face of his guest changed from that of a small boy to an old, crooked man, and then from a beautiful young woman to an old crone. The look and body shape of the being before him evolved and changed in form, race, and stature, finally resting on a reflection of Orus, the Lion, staring back at the shaken King.

"Who am I in your eyes, Orus?" the reflection asked.

"I believe my son-in-law called you Likedelir, Lord," Orus responded.

"I am Likedelir, Orus. Know that Kairoth, Faylea, and Orus, the junior, thrive and live in peace. The Alliance holds with Yslan, and it appears the light has taken hold of the majority of the lands," Likedelir responded confidently.

"I have never been that religious. Why did you come to me?" Orus asked, puzzled.

"You are a hero, King! I like heroes! I like balance! Most men, if they could accept their darkness, as well as their light, would be incredible in furthering my influence. Alas, most heroes or villains cling to one side or the other." The god paced.

"So, what am I to you then? You are a god who needs no man," Orus responded solemnly.

"True, I could do this all myself, but where is the adventure in that, human!?" the God chided.

"Are we entertainment?" Orus snorted, looking at his wife's figurine. "Where is she?" Orus held up the figure.

"In Aeternum with mother, I fear," Likedelir responded.

"Is that a bad thing?" Orus smiled.

"Too much of anything is a bad thing, Orus. At least, that is how I see things." Likedelir smirked. "May I revisit you, Great King?" the God asked sarcastically.

"I don't think a locked door or any number of sentries could keep you away," Orus responded in kind.

"Orus, I feel that you and I will soon become great friends. You have united so many foes under one common banner—many with petty hatreds now fight against the ones who would skew the balance. You are what Gods like I look for." Likedelir turned to go.

"I don't know what to say, Likedelir. I have never been chosen by a God before," Orus responded.

"Oh, but haven't you been!? I am not sure which of my idiot brothers chose you, and which chose Puryn upon the Arondayre, but you both impressed those dimwits with your deeds—and be it known, that is no small feat—but there is sadly never a shortage of great warriors. There is, however, a shortage of legendary warriors. You are half of that story. You and Puryn on that field. Adasser—well, Puryn's bride is another story altogether. She is an anomaly!

"I will leave you with a book, like I did Kairoth, Orus. It will write our story. The story will end when you wish it to, or when you are dead. I wonder what tale the future will reveal. Your path will appear in Kairoth's book also, King. It is only fair that I make a separate tale and include it in his tome. He is a High Priest, after all, My Champion! Perhaps, I will write down his story for you also—to read by the fire in your old age!" Likedelir winked and faded away, disappearing.

A small leather tome remained on the wax-covered table. Orus picked it up and opened to page one. There, a one-line introduction was written.

"Today, Orus, the Lion, King of Hodan, while searching for redemption, made a friend."

Startled, the King dropped the book on the tabletop.

Looking in the glass on the grooming table, he spied his reflection. His wavy beard had softened, darkening to black with grey highlights, and his facial wrinkles were reduced to crow's feet at the corners of his eyes and mouth. Touching the mirror in disbelief, Orus stood abruptly. He looked at the figurines in his left hand, kissing them both and quickly putting them away. Even his body felt invigorated.

"I will not waste the time you have gifted an old fool, my new god. You will find that once I know a truth, I will not let go of it. I guess today, I will seal my fate also. I knew that boy was a good choice. Please, protect them from all harm."

Orus armored up in silence, thinking he was mad, but knowing that madness had not altered the sand in his hourglass. A God was interested in his comings and goings. He would not disappoint him.

Trying to grasp the enormity of that, the King left the room in search of breakfast. He needed to speak to a High Priestess.

As he crossed the commons at the center of the fortress, he could see the industry of citizens building the fortifications. The gate and its frame were ready to be hung.

Looking out through the gaping hole where the fortress doors would soon be, the Hodan King smiled at what he saw. Ten thousand Vynwrathian Raiders had encamped during the night outside of the villages, surrounding the Galdrissen Keep. Once the sworn enemy of the Galdrissen, Vyn Elves, now stood the watch over the innocents and within the new home of their former adversaries.

A traveler with a bag on a pole caught the eye of the Hodan King. He was walking through the crowd toward the gaping exit. The wanderer gestured toward the Elfish Amy, nodding. He bowed, then waved, fading slowly out of view.

Orus knew it was his new God.

Smiling, the old King felt renewed.

Chapter 10

Ma 'Dryna squinted as she looked at his face. Even his gait had improved. The old man stood straighter and moved with greater ease, as if his armor were suddenly lighter. Something was afoot, but she did not know what. The Hodan King approached her in battle dress with his weapon strapped under his left shoulder. He was, in fact, making a beeline for where she sat, eating a small breakfast with two young Galdrissen girls who had become her acolytes. His face told her that he had something on his mind.

"Girls, go find something to do. I have business, and it approaches quickly," the High Priestess said quietly, muttering to the acolytes who attended her.

The young girls nodded, looking up with concern at the large man who quickly approached their Priestess. They complied with her wishes, melting off into the corners and shadows, but watched intently and waited for the call of their mistress. They were worried. They could see the confusion on their mentor's face, and that was not a typical look.

"Dryna!" Orus called out earnestly. "I must speak to you."

"Yes, Orus, what is the problem!?" the Priestess responded with a concerned look.

Orus sat on a cut stump beside her. He towered over the shorter woman. He clenched his jaw, looking at Ma 'Dryna while trying to gather his thoughts before speaking. After a few awkward moments, he decided he would just tell her the whole story.

"Do you notice anything different about me?" Orus asked, seriously raising his eyebrows.

Dryna swallowed her tea. "You seem well-rested today, My Lord. Perhaps a feather mattress suits you?"

Orus chuckled. "If it were only that simple."

"All joking aside, King Orus," Dryna replied, "what has happened? You have been blessed, it appears! The Goddess rewards your deeds?"

"Not the Goddess," Orus said, looking around nervously, "but another."

Dryna's face turned to one of apprehension. She frowned and swallowed hard, looking at the sword at the side of Orus. "I hope it was not from the opposing side that you received your blessings, Orus. The Underlord gives nothing for free."

Orus saw the expression of the Priestess and smiled, raising his hands. "Relax, Dryna. I have not come to harm you, and no, Haeldrun has not 'blessed' me—if that swine is even capable of something such as that."

Dryna sighed with relief, closing her eyes for a moment. "Who then? The brothers? I have read that Aluia has no interest in warriors."

"May I see that leather tome that you carry around and are afraid to look at?" Orus gestured to a small satchel that Dryna always carried with her, but rarely opened.

"Oh, that book, it's nothing, Orus. You should not worry yourself about that old thing," Dryna dismissed.

Orus reached behind him, pulling a small leather satchel around, producing a small leather tome of his own. It was finely tooled with runes and knotwork. Tiny unidentifiable jewels were embedded in its cover. The book glowed slightly in the shade.

"I have one of my own, given to me by the same god that gave you yours, I suspect," Orus said, opening to page one of the book.

"What does yours say, Orus?" Dryna asked curiously, but with a hint of fear.

Orus was reading and chuckling. "I think I know why you fear to read your own."

"Orus … please, what does it say? I must know if I am mad or if I should accept this new revelation." Dryna was pleading.

"Fine, but you must read yours to me. I have three sections. One is the Book of Kairoth, and strangely enough, the second is called the Book of Orus. I would ask you to guess the name of the third, but I think that you already know that answer." Orus paused, then cleared his throat and began reading from the Book of Orus. "Chapter 1: Today, Orus, the Lion, King of Hodan, while searching for redemption in foreign lands, made a friend. That friend's name was Likedelir, the Conflict, the establisher of balance and preserver of existence. After much doubt and reluctance, the hero skeptically conversed with the God within his bed chambers, doubting every word he was told. In true fashion, conflict ensued! An argument was had to establish the truth of things and to prove the words that were spoken, but in the end, the balance was achieved. After much reasoning and internal turmoil, the Champion accepted his new appointment as the Champion of the Rynn and the Champion of his new God. This book is the story of his journey to redemption and peace. This is the tale of how he becomes an instrument of balance in a world skewed by strife and ruled by conflict."

Dryna was confused. "So, this Likedelir chose you in your bedroom?"

"Yes, he did. I tried to kill him, thinking him a mage and assassin. I quickly learned otherwise. Oh, there is a second chapter in my book. Would you like me to read it to you also?" Orus smirked.

Dryna squinted, as if in pain at the facial expression and responded with reluctance. "Yes, but I will not like what you read, will I?"

"Maybe, perhaps not." Orus shrugged. "Chapter 2: The reluctant Priestess. Orus, the Champion of the Rynn, left his room, rejuvenated and quite literally a younger man. He lit off to find an ally who was once his adversary. Upon finding her, he asked her for her book, but she held onto it tightly, afraid to read the words that her God had written within it."

Dryna scoffed. "It does not say that! Let me see!"

Orus chuckled. "Go ahead and look, Priestess."

Dryna read the words, and a line appeared as she read. "The Priestess scoffed at the invitation of the Champion and demanded that he show her this revelation. She did not believe that Orus was telling the truth."

The Priestess closed the tome abruptly, handing back to the King. Orus was now openly smiling and trying not to laugh. Dryna was pale. She reached to her side and pulled out her satchel. Frowning, she opened the burlap sack and pulled out a finely tooled tome of her own. Opening to page one, she read the words that were written. Orus was surprised to see that Dryna's book had many written pages, as opposed to his one or two. This Priestess knew the truth, but was in denial.

"I have worshipped Haya since the day of atonement. I have spent decades in her service. She has never responded to me or visited me once. I supposed she granted me redemption from the Dark Lord when my runes were changed to gold, Orus, but if so, she has been absent ever since." Tears now streamed down Dryna's face. "Do you mean to tell me that all this time, it was not her who answered, but this new God? A God, who I have spurned and ignored? This god has given me everything, and I have turned my back on him since the beginning?"

"Dryna, you are the Kairoth of the Rynn. I am sure of it. You are this God's High Priestess. He has not claimed another to my knowledge. It is not written in either of our tomes. I would wager that he has not given up on you." Orus was strangely sympathetic in his tone.

Dryna smiled and turned her head slightly. "Did he change your heart? You seem different, King Orus. I mean no disrespect."

"There is none taken, Ma 'Dryna, High Priestess of Likedelir. Take your place. He has chosen you, even if you have not chosen him. I know how that feels!" Orus stooped down to look the Galdrissen woman in the eye.

"He is correct, Dryna. I have not given up on you," a strange, but familiar voice said from just out of view.

Startled and closing her eyes, Dryna responded, "Is that you, My God?"

"If you wish me to be, then yes. If not, I must go to find another. Time is short. The wheels of eternity turn forever, but they do not stop for any man or woman," the voice responded calmly.

"But I have disrespected you and rebelled, Lord. Will you still have me?" the woman responded somberly.

The figure materialized behind his Champion. Placing his hand on Orus's shoulder, he continued. "You have done nothing but question. Question all things, My Priestess. To know the truth and to find the middle of every argument, one must question and listen."

The Priestess sat silently, looking at the God's hooded visage.

"Dryna, you are not worthy, nor am I, but we have been chosen where we are at in life. The future is not written yet." Orus abruptly turned and questioned the God with his hand on his spaulder. "The future is not written, My God, is it?"

"No, Orus, you are correct. We write the story as we go!" Likedelir chuckled and approached the sniffling Galdrissen woman. Gently, he touched her face, raising her gaze to his face. "Open your eyes, woman, and know the truth. See reality for what it is. I will show you, if you wish to know."

Dryna looked at the face before her. He looked as if he were just another human walking from place to place on the Rynn. Nothing stood out concerning his appearance—no fine clothing, no shining armor, no jewels or crown upon his head. Orus had a relaxed look about him.

"What of Haya, My Lord? Will she be angry that I have left her service?" Dryna asked.

"Mother? She does not concern herself with individuals, unless they suit her needs. I concern myself with everyone. In fact, I will let you in on a little secret, My Priestess. Those runes did not change, because Mother was pleased with you. In fact, you were the spawn of evil, and she dismissed your petitions outright. I, however, heard the pleas of your people and changed your runes, removing my father's grip on your souls." Likedelir sighed and continued. "But of course, Mother gets all of the credit and worship."

Orus sarcastically quipped, "I know nothing of how that feels, My God."

Likedelir openly laughed at the statement from his Champion. "Oh, but I think you do! Dryna, I am the God of your people. For everything to survive, I must have them on my side. I will do what is necessary to establish their kingdom on the Rynn. Your kin, upon the Ert, have already accepted my offer and live within the protection of a fierce northern warrior's kingdom.

Ironically, this brought Orus to you."

"How so?" Dryna asked, looking at Orus.

"I am not proud of my past, Ma 'Dryna." Orus shifted in his seat and took a deep breath. "I came here, because that great warrior of whom our God speaks saved your people. The warrior's name is Puryn, and he is my blood brother, but I hated the Todessen so badly that I lumped you all into the same group, calling for your heads. I demanded the execution of all of you as demons and evildoers. Then I came here, because he refused to comply with my demands. I came here to kill the Todani and to kill your people, Dryna."

Dryna gasped and frowned. "I saw it on your face at the port when I first laid eyes on you, King Orus, but what about now? Do you still feel the same as you did back then?"

"No, Dryna. I have seen your faces. I have heard your laughter, witnessed the hugs and kisses given to your small ones. I have seen the joy in everyday life that you all exhibit. I am ashamed of who I was. I am ashamed of what I wished upon your people." Orus looked at the ground in embarrassment.

"You have shown your repentance, King," Dryna said, grabbing Orus's hand. "You attacked the Orcs and Goblins to save my children ... to save me! How can you be the same man you were back then? You are a new creation, yourself. I would wager that if you had runes upon your skin that they too would be golden. Our people love you, Orus, despite your past. You simply did not know us, nor we, you."

"This is the way forward, King," Likedelir said smiling. "Forgiveness, reconciliation, and alliance."

"I will promise to do better, Dryna. You must teach the truth to these young ones and to the old! I am no teacher ... except in death." Orus looked at Likedelir and Dryna, sitting up. "What say you, Priestess? Will you lead us to the truth, or shall another?"

Meekly, Dryna looked at Likedelir and the mountain of a man before her. "I will do my part, but it will be up to you to save my people, Champion."

"She prophesizes already, My Champion!" the God said gleefully. "I am glad that you decided to join us, Dryna. Call upon me anytime, day or

187

night! I must go see what is happening in other places in the world. Please, don't let me interrupt your breakfast any longer."

"Farewell, Lord," Orus said, standing and bowing. Dryna did the same.

"Oh, this again? So be it, bowing it is!" Likedelir smirked.

The two watched the god walk down the street, walking stick in hand. He wove his way through the morning marketplace off toward the large hole in the wall, where a door was finally being hung. As he approached the opening, he faded into the crowd and disappeared out of sight.

Orus and Ma 'Dryna looked at each other apprehensively. They were now in charge of the new religion. They had to figure things out fast.

* * *

Orus stood in front of two and a half legions of Hodan regulars, a unit of a hundred or so of Kepir's specialists, and a gaggle of around fifty civilian conscripts. In front of the conscripts were the boy, Uilam, and his second in command, Edmund, who had recently recovered from his injuries sustained during the Todessen attack on the fortress. Edmund was not entirely himself yet, but Uilam made it his mission to see to it that his friend was returned to total health and status. Orus nodded in approval.

The units shifted to attention and were covered and aligned smartly. Even the civilian team made a respectable effort. Orus took his place at the center. Kepir reported to the King, who saluted back, but was only half-listening to him. Instead, Orus stood in front of several thousand warriors, getting ready to tell them something they probably never thought they would hear come out of his mouth.

"Warriors of Hodan and of the Rynn! I have great tidings to pass to you that have been granted to me by the Gods themselves—one God in particular!" Orus paused for effect.

There was murmuring, then a quick call for quiet by the unit Commanders. Silence returned.

"I have been visited by a god whose name has never been mentioned in any of our tomes of knowledge, yet he has existed since the Universe was born. His name is Likedelir, known in hushed whispers as 'The Conflict.'" Orus paused again. "He is the son of Haya and Haeldrun, just as Runnir, Gunnir, and Aluia are their children, yet he was spurned for refusing to choose a side in the cosmic struggle."

The murmuring started again. Men began looking around and shifting their weight, wondering what their King was going on about. More calls for silence erupted. Silence returned.

"Now, before all of you run off and discuss how your King has lost his mind, as a physical sign of his power and existence, I give you this." Orus removed his helmet.

Kepir's jaw dropped. There was a collective gasp from each formation, as everyone saw King Orus, of Hodan, but he appeared as if he were thirty years younger. Long black curls of hair spilled out to his shoulders. His beard had no hint of gray. The wrinkles that had once adorned his face were now gone. The murmuring was now a dull roar of questions and pointing, as Orus stood his ground quietly and allowed his Commanders to regain control of their units. When silence had returned, Orus continued.

"Hear me, all who stand before me, Likedelir, the God of Balance, has chosen me to be his Champion. His will is that we, as a people, train up the oppressed of these lands. His plan is that we rise up and take back the human lands to the east!"

The response was instantaneous. The raucous cheers of approval were joined by fists pumping in the air. After a few moments, the din subsided, and the order returned.

"Now hear me, warriors, not only has humanity suffered under Todessen aggression, but there also are many races who need their freedoms restored. The Elves have their lands, the Dwarves theirs, even our shaky alliance with the Orcs and Goblins to the south afford them a place to call home, but we forget one people. We always forget one people, because we saw them once as the enemy, but they are not."

The crowd was silent and listening intently to their King as a glow enshrouded his person. A small robed figure walked up beside the king and removed her hood. Ma 'Dryna bowed to the King, and then turned and bowed to the warriors before her.

"Your King speaks true. We are the discarded, and you warriors have bled on this soil to save us from certain death. You protect us though we were despised. As time has passed, I hope that we have shown all of you that who we are is as far from what others claim! We only wish to live and serve the god of balance. I was chosen many years ago, but resisted, because I thought that Haya was our savior, when in fact, it was always him. The silent bringer of justice and equity, Likedelir. You have seen my elders and my children. Many cry out for deliverance from over the mountains. Many are slaves and murdered by the Todani for turning from Haeldrun. Will you save us, heroes? Will you deliver us from this evil?"

Orus roared. "What say you, Hodan? What say you, Rynn?"

There was a pause, and then Kepir turned and bowed to the duo. "I will follow you to the catacombs themselves, my King. I am honored to be in your service, Champion."

Orus bowed back.

Kepir turned to the units before him. "The King asked you a question, Hodan. What do you say?"

As if one voice, they replied with a loud roar of affirmation.

Kepir turned about smartly. "Liberation forces and militia formed. Ready for inspection, My King. What is your order, Sire?"

"Kepir, please break the men up into teams and begin training them in your specialties. They must understand blending with their surroundings and subterfuge. We cannot attack the Toads head-on, brother. Give that Kren a command if you can. He is an asset. We need smaller, more agile, autonomous units that can attack in a coordinated manner." Orus scratched his chin out of habit. "We also need to contact our ships and have them sail around to the ports of the Orcs, but let our green friends know that the navy is coming first. If they see those black ships on the horizon, without warning, they will think Toads, and nothing good will come from that. Also, we will be incorporating liberated people into our ranks, including

Galdrissen who are able and willing to fight."

"Understood, Your Majesty. I am not sure how the Galdrissen will be accepted on the battlefield, but I will pass your orders to the men. I am sure there will be 'incidents' in the beginning, but if we make a few good examples of the men who disobey, we should be able to quell the nonsense and bias in due time." Kepir stood tall.

"I would prefer not to have to kill my own men, brother. Please, impress upon our ranks that these are our allies, not the Todessen. It took me too long to know the difference. War is coming. We need all the shields we can get on the field ... Archers also!" Orus smiled and slapped Kepir on his shoulder. "Carry on, brother. We have work to do."

"Yes, Sire!" Kepir responded, saluting.

Orus returned his salute, and then guided Dryna away from the formation. "He's got this, My Lady."

Dryna smiled and bowed, walking back to the fortress gate.

Orus could hear Kepir barking out orders, and he walked away thinking. Incorporating Elves and Dwarves was one thing, but Orcs, Goblins, and Galdrissen was going to be something else entirely. He wondered how many men were going to be whipped before his legions saw these additions as fellow warriors vice lesser beings. The King wondered if trust would ever be achieved.

"One step at a time, Orus," the King muttered under his breath.

Off in the distance, he could hear Kepir's distinct voice cry out, "Dismissed!"

Chapter 11

The spring turned to summer, and the summer to fall. By the first snows, Kepir had trained five specialist units, each with one-hundred of the best of the Degran enlistees and Kren's survivors. A few transfers were allowed from the legions, but those numbers were already low, and Orus did not wish to deplete them further. Kepir had begun to use his new recruits over the mountains against their intended enemy. Until the heavy snows started, travel and concealment of movement were still very possible. Weekly rotations of three- or four-hundred specialists, skilled in stealth and subterfuge, wore on the Todessen forces occupying Whaleford and territories north of the city. Kepir's corps of rangers quickly became a legend among their enemies. The Todessen referred to them as Dole'kyn or the Hidden Death. Covert attacks from the Hodan began to take on a life of their own, as the few enemies who did survive their encounter told others within the Todessen ranks of the prowess of the new unseen force. Fear was a tool, and Kepir knew how to use it well.

Over a six-month period of withering attacks, the populace of Whaleford began a massive exodus through the foothills to the west and over the mountains. They were emboldened in their actions as they witnessed the Todessen pulling out of the city proper and regrouping in the rural northern areas. Those who escaped quickly joined the new crusade against the Todessen, pledging their loyalty, not to the King of the Dwarves, in whose land they now resided, but instead to Orus, their deliverer. This slight did not go unnoticed by the King in Dornat Al Fer. Quietly, the

King of the Dwarves moved his forces into the surrounding countryside villages within striking distance of the new perceived threat building near the palisade built by Jaruz and his people. The Dwarves were not only concerned by the Todani threat, but they were also becoming wary of this new charismatic leader of the humans and Galdrissen. Orus, of Hodan, had united so many different tribes and peoples on the Rynn that his power now rivaled that of the Dwarfish empire. This did not sit well with the Dwarfish leadership. Upon arriving at the camp, King Hamrik of the Dwarves stared in awe.

There, at the foot of the mountains, was a well-built fortress, surrounded by artfully arranged military camps. The King absent-mindedly muttered numbers as he calculated each camp square as one-hundred warriors. The humans covered the open fields and nearby countryside. Hamrik's brow furrowed as he estimated the combined forces of humans, Galdrissen, and Elfish forces to be about thirty- or forty-thousand souls, and they did not look like an unorganized militia, as he had been briefed by his Generals.

"General Lamyrk understated the situation, Falros." The King looked at his most trusted advisor and diplomat. "This army is anything but a gathering of cowards and weaklings. These humans—they follow him as if he were a god."

Falros surveyed the field and responded. "Truly, Your Majesty, Orus has been no threat to our lands, nor have the other races. Are you certain that the Todani emissary was not twisting the truth to his advantage? It would not be the first time a Todani lied to save his skin."

Hamrik snorted once. "Agreed, but the human presence here is desta-bilizing. It has the Todani up in arms." The King frowned. "Orus is too good at what he does, and it is beginning to affect our ability to control our borders. Look at all of these refugees!"

"Please reconsider, Your Majesty. The humans are gathering themselves, finally, after so many years of subservience. The Elves are at peace with our nation for the first time in many, many years—even the Orcs and Goblins stay within their lands." Falros's eyes pleaded, but he could see his words were falling upon deaf ears.

"I have considered these things, my friend. I must look to the safety of our own people. Orus is upsetting the balance of our world. I must restore the status quo, or risk invasion from the north. All people on the Rynn must look to their own defense." Hamrik shook his head and looked to his man expectantly.

"I will contact King Orus and set the meeting, Your Majesty," Falros said, bowing his head.

"And another thing, Falros—you and many others call him a King, but I am the only rightful King of Dornat Al Fer and the southern lands. I, and I alone! What is Orus the King of, if anything? I will not hear of him being addressed by my court in that manner again." The King turned his horse and angrily rode away.

Falros muttered, looking over the fields full of tents and the small castle fortress before him, "Apparently, he is the King of all of this, My Lord, and of all of these people."

The Dwarf sighed and goaded his horse. "And this man has made three alliances, where we seek to sever ours."

Falros frowned, shaking his head.

* * *

The Dwarfish emissary arrived at the gates of the fortress within minutes. He rode unopposed as all forces within his view were friends. He hoped after this visit that would remain true, but as much as he respected King Hamrik, he had known him for many years and knew that the King could be a vain and patronizing leader. The aristocracy was in charge, and because of that, they were considered better than the average Dwarf. If you were not a Dwarf, you were an inferior race that owed the Dwarves your livelihood and your life. In turn, Hamrik honestly felt the Rynn owed him personally for protecting them from Todani aggression for almost a century. Falros sighed and rode to the central tower. There, the ruling seat was located.

There, he would most likely find Lord Jaruz and his friend, King Orus, of Hodan.

A guard challenged the approaching Dwarf. "Halt, Sir! What is your business?"

"Good afternoon, guard. I am Falros, advisor to King Hamrik of Dornat Al Fer. I require an audience with Lord Jaruz and King Orus if they are available." Falros sat straight in his saddle. He fumbled in a small satchel for a writ from the King of the Dwarves. Finding it, he handed it to the young human with the glaive who stood in his way. The boy looked at the paper as if he was reading it, but from the human's face, the emissary knew the boy had no idea how to read.

"Very well, Sir. Please, stand by," the guard replied.

The young warrior shouted to a nearby boy, who took the writ and ran into the tower, returning within minutes.

The fierce demeanor of the human was not lost on Falros. He wondered if all humans were Hodan now.

"Sir, our Lord, and King Orus are present in the meeting hall and accept your invitation to a meeting with His Majesty, King Hamrik. Please inform His Majesty that a meal will be prepared, and refreshments served. Jaruz and Orus eagerly await his arrival at the evening meal."

"Excellent! Thank you for your assistance, guard," Falros replied, leaving the keep and taking the hand-written invitation back to his King.

* * *

Kepir slid out of the shadows and to his King's side. He could see the old warrior's look of concern as he looked out over a field of thousands of warriors and citizens. Orus knew that Hodan had been reborn in a strange land, of several strange alliances and new friends. Occasionally, the old man could make out an Orc or two making their way through the keep's marketplace. Orus knew the Dwarves saw what he saw, but in a different light. This was not a coalition of peaceful allies fighting a familiar foe in their eyes. This was an occupying army and a threat to the Kingdom of Dornat Al Fer.

"They will call for our withdrawal, My King," the specialist remarked, looking out at the scene.

"As they should," Orus replied. "I was wondering when they would."

"What will we do now, Sire?" the specialist asked calmly. "What are your orders?"

"After this 'meeting of allies,'" the Hodan King snorted, "where the petty Dwarf King orders me to submit, vice negotiates with me as an equal," Orus turned to his trusted man, "we shall mobilize and claim Whaleford as our new home."

"What of the Orcs?" Kepir questioned. "Will they not see it as an aggressive move if we move south?"

"I have conferred with our green friends to the south, and believe it or not, they are for the idea." Orus smiled at Kepir's look of confusion. "It seems the Orc Chieftain would like nothing more than 'friends' on his eastern flank, vice marauding Toads."

"What of Todessen in Whaleford?" Kepir stated plainly, unrolling a map and looking at the eastern shoreline.

"They will leave or die," Orus replied firmly. "We will make life extremely unpleasant for any Toad who wishes to resist our claim to the lands."

"I will prepare our forces. I will give the orders to begin breaking camp and to stand by for further direction," Kepir said, saluting.

The Hodan King stood tall and returned the salute. "Do not make it seem as if we are in a hurry to leave, just in case I have misread this short fellow's intentions."

Kepir turned to go and then remembered why he had entered the room in the first place. "Oh, Your Majesty, the Elf Queen is here also. She arrived during the evening and is encamped with her men outside the fortress walls."

Orus nodded. "Perfect. Inform her of our predicament and invite her to our parlay … quietly."

"Of course, Your Majesty." Kepir nodded and disappeared into the daily crowd of shoppers and laborers.

"Now, if only the Orcs were here," Orus said, sighing.

* * *

Queen Lourama sat sipping a bit of wine. The humans did not make it quite as well as the Elves did, but this was an excellent try. She motioned for more, and a porter brought another decanter to her location. The human delegation consisted of Orus, Kepir, and Uilam. Uilam had solidified himself as a young, trusted leader, and was considered a Chieftain of sorts by both local humans and Galdrissen alike. Orus smiled and rolled his eyes. The young warrior looked more like a boy in his father's armor than a hardened soldier, but the Hodan King knew him well, and he was no longer a child.

Lourama approached Orus raising her glass. "Not bad for a human vintage." The Queen smiled and sat nearby Orus. She was flanked by two handmaidens, who waited for further instructions.

Orus stood briefly. "Good evening, Your Majesty. I am not sure where our short allies are at the moment, but I am glad you are here for this evening's talk."

Jaruz interjected, sitting on the other side of the table from Lourama. "I heard that, you old goat." Both men laughed, and the Queen snorted while sipping a bit of wine.

"Uilam, come here, boy," Orus called.

"At once, Your Majesty." The young man rose and trotted to his King. "How may I be of service, Sire?"

"Come sit with the leadership, boy. You have earned your place among the men and shall ne'er be called a boy again. Do you understand?" Orus rose and extended his hand.

Shaking his King's hand, Uilam responded, "Thank you, Sire."

The young human sat beside Jaruz as the small collection of allies sat and passed the time, waiting for the Dwarfish emissaries who were late … as usual.

"They anger me so," Jaruz scowled, surprising Lourama.

"But they are Dwarves, My Lord. They are your kin!" Lourama goaded.

"They are pompous, self-righteous, tyrants!" Jaruz snarled.

"I like this Dwarf more than the others, Orus," the Elfish Queen snickered.

"They will tell us to swear fealty, or they will claim everything we have achieved here, in a place they have never bothered to inhabit." Jaruz was disgusted, and he was not hiding it.

Kepir nodded. "I agree. This bulwark against Todessen aggression should be enough to secure peace, but the pride of Dornat Al Fer was stung by the loss of Edhelseere and now the eastern regions. That will not go over well. They will not relinquish these lands to the humans, Galdrissen—or even to you, Jaruz."

"That is why we must have a united front should it come to that," Orus offered.

"Agreed," Lourama replied to everyone present. "Our peoples united are a bigger threat to the Dwarves than any one of ours alone. They are more likely to negotiate with a force that could harm them, vice a nation they see as a vassal state."

Orus and the other nodded.

"Then it is agreed. We are all of the same mind? This is our land by right, but if we are unable to retain it peacefully, rather than waste our resources fighting the Dwarves, we should take our new alliance east and reclaim the area known as Whaleford. There is infrastructure there—farmland, a small harbor, fishing, lumber, a quarry for stone, and possibly even veins of metal."

The others sat and thought silently for a moment. Orus looked at each of their faces.

Lourama spoke first. "We shall need to clear that barony. It still reeks of the Scourge. Still, your people secured my homeland after it was lost for many, many years. I will pledge my support in securing one for yours, if these petty little tyrants force our hand. You will have the seas with your ships and the land with this coalition's warriors."

Orus nodded and smiled. The rest grunted in affirmation. One by one, they threw their lot in with the rest.

* * *

The Dwarf delegation entered the small feasting hall amid much fanfare. Horns blew, drums were played. A small procession of elderly Generals preceded the King. They were all dressed in gold and gilded plate mail. Orus pretended to be impressed, rolling his eyes while he looked at Kepir. Kepir just nodded and pursed his lips. Jaruz barely held his contempt in check, and that brought a tiny giggle from the Elfish Queen, who sensed his disgust. She reached across the table and patted the Dwarf on his hand, which brought a smirk to his face.

"Is it that obvious, Your Majesty?" Jaruz winked.

The Queen bit her lip and snickered.

Uilam sat up straight blankly, looking at Orus for direction.

"Oyez, Oyez! All rise! The court of King Hamrick, the benevolent, is now opened within this, his borderland fortress of Redemption! Long live the King!"

There was an echo of, "long live the King," as the last of the Dwarves presented themselves to the allied feasting table. The Dwarves sat at the opposite end of the long wooden surface. Orus sat up straight with his own cohort, guards, and servants present.

Lourama smiled as she noticed the Crown of Hodan atop Orus's head. She was impressed by this human. He never needed to flaunt his position. Everyone knew who he was and rendered honors appropriately. He did not need to remind a soul.

Lourama openly grinned at the look on Hamrick's face as he saw Orus and the alliance delegation. "Oh Hamrick, it is well you have come! The

Orcs wanted to be here, but the Todani have them preoccupied at the moment."

"Ahem." The Dwarfish herald cleared his throat and began reading a proclamation. "To all who hear these words, greetings! Know that King Hamrick, the generous, sends each of you wishes of luck, prosperity, and health! It has come to the notice of Dornat Al Fer that these lands have greatly increased in population, development, and wealth. That is why the King, in his magnificent benevolence, extends a grant of barony to these lands. With this appointment, all those living within the borders of the Barony of Redemption must acknowledge the sovereignty of the Kingdom of Dornat Al Fer and swear fealty to its rightful ruler, Hamrick."

A voice from the gallery spoke out of turn. "What if I've sworn fealty to another, you pompous ass?"

A Dwarfish guard perked up. "Who said that?" He searched the small crowd menacingly.

Orus stood and then spoke to the guard. "Hail and well met, Dwarf warrior! You dare to approach me armed and in my own hall?" Orus drew a sword and laid it across the table. "You had better stand down, or I will put you down, my little friend."

Kepir drew his sword as well, smiling as he noticed that Uilam had his at the ready tip to the floor.

The Dwarf turned angrily and began to respond. "Who do you think you are and …"

"Enough!" Hamrick shouted. "Sit down, General."

The Dwarf bowed sheepishly, sitting down on a bench beside the King, who nodded for the herald to continue.

Nervously, the scribe began reading again. "This is the rightful land of the Dwarves. You are guests in our land, but if you wish to stay, you must swear fealty to the one true King of these lands, King Hamrick. A Lord will be appointed as Baron of this region. You will pay taxes to that man, and he will ensure proper revenues are collected and remitted to the kingdom. All private military operations and militia are commanded to disband and halt all operations within or without the borders of Dornat Al Fer. What say you, Orus, of Hodan, and people of the Rynn?"

There was a general murmur among the people present at the feast. As the word was passed to the eavesdropping commoners outside the hall, a loud, angry mob began shouting obscenities toward Hamrick and his delegation.

Orus chuckled. "I think that you can hear the response to your 'offer,' Hamrick. Did you seriously think that men, women, and children who have scraped this place together from the very ground would just hand it over to you and kiss your boots? Are you that foolish?"

"This is my land, Orus," Hamrick responded, holding his hand up and shushing his warriors. "I have every right."

"I have lived here for several years now. My men have patrolled the mountains with those who escaped Degran-Eras and joined us. Where were you? Who has repelled incursion after incursion of Toad Scourge? You? Hardly! You never even sent the materiel support you promised us! We had to make everything ourselves, down to every bow and spear shaft!" Orus now stood and paced as he spoke.

"We owe you nothing, human," Hamrick responded angrily.

"If it were not for us, you would have Todessen here and maybe even an occupying Orc force. You owe us plenty. All we seek is autonomy and this place as our home." Orus leaned on the table, knuckles down on the tabletop. "What is this small piece of land when you own most of the continent already?"

"It is OUR land, human," the King said as a matter of fact.

"That is debatable, 'oh benevolent one,'" Lourama slurred her speech slightly.

"Oh, what do you mean by that, Elf?" Hamrick sniped back.

"Well, these mountains and some of these plains are actually the lands of Degran-Eras, which your benevolence failed to return to the humans at the end of the war." Lourama leered at the King across from her. "Seems you runts enjoy doing that to those who cannot stand up to you. Now, you come here and try to lord your 'supremacy' over your allies. Pathetic little Dwarf. History will judge you when all is united and peaceful, and the

Dwarves are left behind to hide under their mountain, speaking of prowess and power."

Jaruz's eyes were wide and looking at the Elfish Queen. She winked and sat back down. The Dwarf across from her swallowed hard.

The Dwarves had formed a small circle and were muttering quickly back and forth. There were legal officers and cartographers arguing historical precedence and historical borders. Several looked up at the Elfish Queen, and they could see her nodding. They knew Elves lived a long time, and she knew what she was talking about.

"The spoils of war, good Queen," a legal officer declared.

"As was Edhelseere. Humph. You Dwarves speak of honor and show truly little more than an illusion of it." It was Uilam who spoke.

Orus snorted, spitting out a swallow of mead, and then looked at the young man with wonder.

"Who are you, whelp, to lecture his majesty of honor? You are nothing more than a wet-behind-the-ears human boy!" the herald snarled.

"How many Toads have you defeated, My Lord?" Uilam responded calmly.

Orus openly laughed. "How many indeed, Dwarfish messenger boy? This is one of my human Commanders. He has defeated over three-hundred Todessen specialists with little more than fifty farmhands armed with bows or crude swords, while you sat on your gilded asses and did nothing. Choose your next words wisely, fool. Maybe he has a taste for Dwarf tonight." Orus winked at Uilam, who smiled briefly at the King's praise.

"Enough banter. If you will not submit to the Crown, then we are at odds, Orus. Do you wish war with Dornat Al Fer? We greatly outnumber your forces and have the logistics to crush you." Hamrick sipped from his goblet.

"Hardly," Orus droned. "At Vynwratha, you were soundly defeated and retreated. I have bested your forces on the practice field numerous times, despite cheating by your officers. I have the seas under my control. Your ships are pathetic. I also have forces you cannot see deployed where you know not. Kepir, a demonstration?"

Kepir nodded, then made several hand signals. As if from thin air, twenty

Elite guard specialists materialized around the room. The Dwarves gasped and drew their swords in fear.

"Hold a moment, gentlemen!" Orus shouted. "There is no reason for alarm. It was a demonstration. If we wished you dead, your bodies would be cooling on this stone floor. I suggest you sheath those weapons immediately or suffer the consequences."

"Do it," the King commanded, and his men complied. "Very well, Orus, you leave us minimal choice, but to sever our alliance with your coalition and to declare you a hostile occupation force."

"Good King," Orus replied.

Jaruz spat.

Orus looked at his friend, asking for calm. Jaruz nodded angrily.

"As I was saying … good King, we will not submit ourselves to your claim of rulership over the citizens of Redemption. We shall, however, offer an alternative that may solve all of our problems and avoid war between us."

Hamrick scowled, but nodded. "Go on."

"We ask for one month to gather our people. We will move against Whaleford in Degran-Eras. Once it is secured and we have the land required to move our people eastward, we shall abandon our claim to this land and its fortifications. We shall leave your choice of leadership and inhabitants to you."

The Dwarves conferred for a moment or two. Several legal scholars shrugged and gave the King a favorable opinion of the deal. Hamrick turned to respond.

"One month, Orus, beginning in the morning. No longer," Hamrick barked.

"Oh, I require one more thing from you, your benevolence," Orus mocked.

The Dwarf rolled his eyes, but refrained from a retort. "What is it, human?"

"Leave us a defense force of adequate strength to protect my civilians while I pull my full might out of Redemption and attack Whaleford. If you can do that, we can move faster. Most who will be left behind are the refugees from Edhelseere, the Galdrissen, and those too young or infirm to serve in the King's army." Orus stood, the crown still on his head. "What say you, Dwarf?"

"I will leave adequate forces to protect the fortress and those within. Just remove yourselves from my kingdom with haste, Hodan!"

Hamrick was annoyed. He stood and turned to go. The horns and drums again began, increasing his annoyance.

"Stop it! Stop all of that. Let us depart to our encampment outside of this goat-water locale," Hamrick said as the entourage made their way into the commons.

The King's voice was loud enough that the commoners all around heard the comments and began booing and cursing at the Dwarves as they made their way toward the portcullis. Soon, rotten cabbages and tomatoes started raining down from the darkness around the main road out of the fortress. The darkness hid most of the protesting, but the Dwarves tightly surrounded their King, protecting him from the projectiles.

"This may get ugly, Kepir," Orus said, sheathing his sword.

"I agree, Sire. Uilam, Jaruz, we must prepare." Kepir bowed to the slightly drunken Elfish Queen, who returned the gesture.

"You will have any Elf I can muster, Orus," Lourama said with a severe tone. "These proud Dwarves will betray you before the month is out. I assure you of it."

"Agreed, good Queen. I will escort you to your quarters, unless you wish to return to your tents?" Orus smiled.

"A bed would be much appreciated, my gracious ally." The Elf smiled, standing.

Lourama stumbled a bit, and Orus steadied her, handing her off to her handmaidens. "See the porter, ladies, and he will ensure she is given a good room."

Orus stood alone, contemplating the meeting. He knew these events had to happen, but he wished he had more time to gather his forces. While his men sat around the table drinking, scheming, and planning, the Queen was tucked into bed. Orus sat up and looked out over the Dwarves in the field. There were thousands of tents on the horizon—and this was just a tip of the spear.

* * *

The Dwarfish King threw open his tent flap and called in his advisors. His entourage entered and sat around a small war table. There was a map with wooden pieces designating all the players on the field before them. The advisors chattered away about strategy for a bit.

"Gentlemen," the King spoke. The room quieted. "Please, pray attend to this message from an ambassador of the north."

From the darkness emerged a humanoid figure. He moved gracefully as if he floated above the surface of the ground. His skin was covered in black, vile shapes. His eyes were yellow with red irises and large black pupils. He was of average build, but the Dwarves could see his well-defined physique as he walked into the light. He was most definitely a Todessen warrior scout.

The gathering gasped and drew their weapons.

"It is too late for that, Dwarves. You would be dead if I wished it," the dark figure said, moving into the light a bit more.

"What is the meaning of this, My King?" a General squawked in horror.

"This, my General, is a way to maintain the status quo. We Dwarves maintain our lands and power, and the Kingdom of Haeldrun Ir preserves their own to the north." Hamrick nodded to the Todani visitor, who sat beside the King to the discomfort of the Royal Guard.

"The Todani wish to establish a truce with Dornat Al Fer," the emissary hissed. "Too long have we dealt with border skirmishes. We have repelled Elfish attacks on our naval forces, but now humans and our own traitors launch attacks on Todani occupying forces from the very same Dwarfish lands on which we converse."

The room was silent, thinking of their situation.

"We are besieged on all fronts, my worthy adversaries, because of this pathetic human, Orus and his band of insolent slaves. Our glorious King Lyax has proposed a truce, and we will deal with this pestilence here and in Whaleford. Let the humans invade us. Give them a false sense of security, and then withdraw. Allow the Todani to dispose of your enemies without sullying your own honor!" The Todani warrior laughed. "The enemy of my enemy is my enemy in this case?"

"I am in agreement with this proposal, men," Hamrick said solemnly. "We deal with two problems at one time and reduce this threat to nothing by simply not interfering."

"Let them come to Whaleford, Dwarves," the Todani said with malice. "We shall bleed them well there, and keep them occupied while my men raze this place and all of HIS support to the ground! Then all things return to normal. The status quo is reestablished, and order is restored. Our mages have devised a special welcome for Orus and his men."

Many around the table looked at their King and nervously nodded. The Todessen smiled, showing his pointed teeth. To the Generals present, he looked as if he was ready to use them to rend the flesh of anyone who dared to oppose the plan.

Falros stood silently in the corner of the tent. Sadly, he looked at his King with disgust in his heart. He felt the filth of disgrace. He wished to be back in Dornat Al Fer, where he could soak for hours and look for a way to remove the fetid stench of betrayal from his person.

* * *

"Your Majesty," the messenger said enthusiastically, "I bring news from the south." The Todessen scribe walked confidently before his King.

"You had better have good news, or I will have your hide!" the King hissed.

"King Lyax, the Dwarves are more pompous, conniving, and intolerable than ever! They wish to quell the rising of a human called Orus. This human is the one who has built that southeastern fortress and united the armies that now vex our occupation of the human territories near Whaleford. His Dole'kyn harass our forces freely and have even inspired a significant entrenched underground human resistance. It has become an untenable situation overall." The messenger paused and read from his notes.

"So, what is new?" Lyax sneered, sipping mead from a goblet. "What is there to be cheerful about? Tell us!"

"From what I gather from observation, Your Majesty, the Dwarfish King is not pleased that another who claims the title King lives within his lands. This Orus, of Hodan, wherever that land may be, is claiming a crown, and that act angers Dornat Al Fer above all things." The messenger looked at General Sulfga, who stood beside the King's throne. "He hates this human, so much so that the little deviant is willing to pull back from his own territories and leave human refugees and our own traitors to defend that stronghold ... alone."

The King was not impressed. He glared at his messenger.

"Yes, the humans, Elves, Orcs, and even some Dwarves are encamped around the place. He has a substantial force—and the Dole'kyn is an unseen variable that supports his movements from beyond our sight—but our secrets still await their discovery. I believe that our unleashing of that power will be the undoing of their coalition. With the help of the Underlord, we should be able to seriously injure, if not destroy, this alliance of races in our first major encounter. Our forces would then take the fortress in the Dwarfish lands and effectively extinguish any hopes of retreat. There would be nothing to reinforce this rabble in the future. The humans of Degran-Eras will be demoralized. All will eventually return to normal."

The messenger could see the King's genuine concern by his demeanor. Kepir's units had decimated Todani forces in the southeastern Rynn and succeeded in the unthinkable—spreading fear among the fearless. Lyax looked at his messenger with expectation. He was unsure if the plan would work.

"Yes, Sire," replied the messenger clearing his throat. "Orus plans to assault Whaleford with his full might and establish a human stronghold there. The Dwarves have pledged to guard the rear and the civilians in the fortress while the humans and Elves are away. The betrayal by Dornat Al Fer will be lamented in song for eternity."

The Todani monarch dismissed the statements of his scout, waving a hand. "The Dwarves are not a kingdom we need to trifle with. They are by far the strongest of the lot."

"And still those little fools agreed to betray their own kind to maintain the status quo!" the scout said, smiling.

The King laughed loudly. "Followers of Haya, in a pig's ass! These stout fellows have taken a page right out of our Lord's dark book! Perhaps they will ally with us next!"

"I would not put it past them, Sire," the messenger said, bowing.

"Sulfga, inform our occupation forces of this plan and ready the elites to raze that region to the ground." The King looked at his general.

"At once, Sire!" Sulfga replied.

Chapter 12

Kepir and his men had been covertly operating in the field for over a week. They gathered information as usual—troop strength, weaponry, logistics routes, traps, obstacles, as well as defensive positions. Orus waited impatiently back at Redemption for word from his scouts. The reconnaissance teams knew the King needed information to plan his attack, and that was what Kepir and his men did best. During the gathering of intelligence, however, the Dole'kyn continued with their usual trickery, killing as many Todessen defenders as possible, while observing the layout of the city. A new development was encouraging to the Hodan spies. Scattered reports of a Degran underground began to reach the Commander of the Dole'kyn from his scouts scattered throughout the region. The Todessen were dealing with a whole new threat—the people of Whaleford. Kepir grinned, thinking of the possibilities of an overt uprising of thousands of angry residents.

The mist hung on the land, as the coolness of late autumn was all around. Hodan's second in command silently ate a piece of dried meat, while observing the town from the shadows. Something was off. Kepir's observations began to see beyond the usual Todessen troops moving in and out of town. A vast, crumbling Temple to Haya was in the center of Whaleford. The Commander could see that it was protected by several groups of Todessen soldiers. Raising his spyglass, Kepir looked at the enemy defenders, puzzled. The Todani appeared to be heavily armed and supported by siege weapons. They were also well dug in and appeared to be very disciplined. Reserves were stationed nearby in camps.

"Hmm," Kepir thought, "What have we here?"

Signaling to his team, Kepir moved invisibly toward the Temple. Several operatives from his personal squad accompanied him on the mission. The loud chaos of nearby exploding supply sheds met the team's ears. Kepir's coal-blackened face smiled with mischief in his eyes. Off in the distance, the Todani army was now preoccupied within the din of disorder. Kepir smiled knowingly, wondering which of his teams was responsible.

* * *

After circumnavigating the defense forces at the main entrance, the Hodan specialists slipped silently into the darkened Temple. Anguished wailing could be faintly heard emanating down the dark passageways ahead of them, masking any misstep by Orus's men. Screams of the afflicted randomly cried out and then went eerily silent as quickly as they arose. Kepir knew what was happening. He scowled angrily. Staring intently at his team, he made eye contact with the point man. After several hand signals and a nod from his operative, the unit made its way toward the sounds, which had seemingly stopped for an extended period.

The passage was pitch black. This darkness was so oppressive that it seemed to take on a life of its own. Kepir could smell the familiar odor of human waste, carrion, and rotting flesh. Traveling hundreds of feet, the Hodan invaders traversed a series of switchbacks and ninety-degree tunnels. Finally, after some time in the blackness, the leader saw some light coming from the end of the underground passageway. Signaling, Kepir gathered his men in a small, concealed space.

Using the hand language of his trade, Kepir signaled out, "Here to observe. Do not let them see you. Do not attack. Surviving members report to King immediately."

The other four men nodded silently and then faded back into the darkness, taking up positions of opportunity. Kepir turned and looked again at the opening as a human man began loudly cursing and shouting at his captors, who were dragging him to the center of a subtly lit room. After a moment or two, the human taunts turned to screams and pleading for mercy. Kepir's anger was now thoroughly kindled.

The Dole'kyn slithered invisibly into the sizeable sacrificial chamber. The room stunk of death, but there was also another foul odor that none of the Hodan could place—something Kepir had experienced somewhere in the past, but where the specialist could not put his finger on.

The Hodan scanned the area from their vantage points. In the center of the room were two giant statues with burning red eyes. A few acolytes were stoking coals in furnaces at the bases of the figures to maintain their God's blazing stare. Between the two sculptures was an obsidian altar. A channel connected it to a pool for collecting the blood of living sacrifices. The tribute was stored in a basin at the feet of a more prominent statue, which was a representation of the God Haeldrun.

On the altar, there was a man, his mouth agape and eyes wide open in terror and agony, disemboweled and bleeding. The sanctuary was large, and that made it impossible for the Hodan to see the entire room outside of the circle of various burning objects. The smoke and darkness hid the outer edges, far from their positions. Kepir signaled his men subtly, and they all moved farther in toward the unknown to get a better view of the activities at hand.

As they pushed farther, the strange smell became more substantial. It was unpleasant, and while fighting the urge to wretch, Kepir closed an eye, allowing it to adjust to the dark. His other eye witnessed another hapless victim being led screaming to the altar. Silently, the specialist prayed. He was frowning. This time it was a young girl. Willing himself to focus his determination on his mission, the scout swallowed hard and returned to his survey of the facility. Turning from his distraction, Kepir was startled by something huge. Instinctively, the Hodan leader froze in his tracks, hiding in plain sight. Both of his eyes snapped wide open in fear. His body language signaled his men to pull back and escape. One by one, each did as ordered, swallowing hard in fear at what they saw from across the room—at what their leader now saw face to face.

Inhaling deeply, Kepir muttered a prayer, while looking into an eye that had just opened its eyelids to reveal what he had smelled earlier. The Hodan was staring into the giant iris of a creature of great size and reckoned that it looked almost as large as a nobleman's mirror stand. Standing quite still, he realized the beast could not see him yet. It began sniffing furiously, like a dog that knew its prey was in a hole right before its face. Kepir readied to die.

The eye moved upward into the dark, then lurched forward and closer to the light, revealing a large white, reptilian head. Kepir estimated the maw of the beast was the size of a large tavern beer keg or two. It continued to rise effortlessly and lifted itself out of Kepir's sight, into the darkness above him. The ceiling was exceedingly high, and after the creature had stood up, he could barely make out the shape of a giant thunder lizard Dragon—it was at least an adult, he guessed, but he was no expert in Dragons. Kepir figured the lizard to be forty measures or taller, but had no idea how long it was. Silently, the scout hid in fear.

The Dragon thunderously roared, prompting several of the Todessen guards to rush into the area, along with a solo mage, who appeared annoyed by the sudden outburst. As soon as the Todani showed themselves, they scattered into a predetermined formation, protecting the caster in expectation of an impending attack. Kepir figured the Dragon was not supposed to be awake.

The Dragon searched emphatically in wonder, trying to locate the presence it had detected moments ago, but that smell had moved out of its range, so instead, she turned to greet those who had interrupted her search, entering her prison.

Kepir could see the well-dressed mage behind a glowing arc of energy. Figuring it to be some sort of a shield, the scout noted the field did not completely encircle the mage; it only covered him from the front. The specialist skirted the edges of the light, making his way to his newly designated target. The spy knew, if the Dragon fought these Todessen, it would be preoccupied, but Kepir noted that the mage's appearance and pompous attitude while facing a Dragon seemed to indicate he possessed some significant proficiency. That opponent might give the large, scaly prisoner a run for its coin, and Kepir did not need more mayhem and guards flooding this already too-busy location.

As predicted, the warriors in formation rushed in and began attacking five on one. The mage was muttering an incantation when Kepir finally revealed himself, driving a short sword through the mage from behind. The Hodan blade appeared just below the breastbone, and then the assassin slid his blade expertly at an angle out the side of the mage. There was a gurgle, and then entrails fell from the caster's side into a pile slightly in front of him. Kepir looked up at the Dragon and swallowed hard. The Todessen engaged in battle with the Dragon wondered where their magic support was as the Dragon appeared to smile and ravage them one by one.

"Where did he go?" the Dragon pondered as it absent-mindedly chewed on the corpse of a Todani attacker. Again, it looked for Kepir.

Her question was answered seconds later when three priests and one acolyte met their ends at the efficient hands of a human shadow of death. The Dragon saw him plainly now. Kepir could no longer disappear from her sight.

Trying to hide in vain, Kepir was startled by a voice in his head. It spoke in the language of the Todessen. It sounded angry and taunting. The Hodan looked at the Dragon, hiding behind a nearby stone column, hoping for protection from incoming fire. From his new vantage point, he could see that the Dragon's legs were held by large metal shackles that glowed dimly in the darkness. The scout guessed that they had to be enchanted if they held this being in check.

The voice tried again in Etah. "Who are you, intruder, and why do you help my children and I?"

"Great Dragon, I had no idea you were here," Kepir replied, quickly peeking around the pillar and then pulling back behind.

The Dragon chuckled at his actions, replying, "If not to harm or attempt to enslave us, what would humans want with Dragons?"

Kepir answered, "In days past, My Lady, Dragons saved my people from the end when the champions of my lands had given their all."

The Dragon squinted with skepticism. "Do you speak of the Arondayre? Are you of the Ert?" The Dragon shifted her weight. She was uncomfortable due to sitting in one position for many days on end. Groaning angrily at her predicament, she demanded, "Who do you serve, human?"

"I am a servant of King Orus, of Hodan. What do I call you Dragon, for 'Dragon,' seems so rude. I am called Kepir."

The Dragon snorted, amused at the formality of this human. "Kepir, I am known by my family as Henargya, and I am the last mother of the Copper Clan. Those leathery orbs by the blood bath are my eggs. These fiends are turning them to the darkness. There are two chambers behind me and many others in the hills, hidden in the wilderness mountains of the Dwarves. I doubt those foolish Dwarves even know that the Todani are there!"

Kepir listened and grunted in affirmation.

"The Todani will sacrifice my children to perfect the desecration of our line. The two behind me are half-mad, but they are still my kin. There are several others in this place. I am not sure where. Evil Dragons do not exist naturally—some are unbiased, yes—but never truly evil, until now."

"There are evil Dragons?" Kepir questioned.

"Yes, but they were created from the innocents they stole from our dens. The Todani consider these bastardizations failures or mistakes, and seek to use the blood of captive innocents to raise an army of black-hearts who will do their evil will." The Dragon sat down abruptly, slightly shaking the chamber. Dust floated down from the invisible ceiling, far above.

"I will let Orus know of your predicament and your warning. He will not tolerate this," Kepir solemnly declared, while worrying about the possibility of evil Dragons. The specialist remembered Kairoth at the Temple in Sudenyag and the aerial battle of Maradwynne and the Black Dragon of Haeldrun. He shuddered at the thought of more like that one.

The Dragon smiled. "I know of Orus! Tell him he had better not think of killing my confused children, or he will feel my wrath. I may not be Maradwynne, my mother's sister, but I am formidable, just the same." The

Dragon sniffed the air. "Now go! They come. You are the best hope we have, Master Kepir. Bring mages, for these shackles are impossible to break! The Todani mages have a device—a wand or rod of some sort. It has a glowing blue orb atop it. It will release these bonds. Please, find it and return to us soon."

Kepir nodded. "We will return. Persevere, Henargya. Hodan will come quickly."

Kepir disappeared before the Dragon's eyes. "You are exceptionally good at that trick, human! Elfish magic? Puryn, son of Durn and his Draj, no doubt taught you, but you have taken it even further, it seems, Master Kepir."

"I will return with my King, Dragon. Rest and bide your time as best you can."

"Please, hurry," the Dragon pleaded in a manner most uncharacteristic of an ancient being.

* * *

"A temple to Haeldrun —AGAIN!" Orus roared. "And more Dragons, you say?" Orus closed his eyes and breathed deeply, taking the news in.

"Yes, Your Majesty. The temple is located here." Kepir showed the King his field notes and map.

Orus lowered his voice looking around. "How many guard them? How many mages?"

"A small detachment, but well-disciplined and armed. Perhaps, one-hundred or more Todani, Sire—but there are camps around the Temple that I believe are reserve units," Kepir responded, estimating. "I did dispatch a few Priests and one of their lackeys—oh, and a mage of some proficiency, Sire. I would guess that after the Dole'kyn breached their lines, they may have reinforced the position."

"Well, they already know and fear the Dole'kyn. Let us make them piss in their trousers again. We need to attack the barony and city proper soon, and with full strength. Kill every Toad!" Orus called Kepir over to his war table map. He moved pieces around to show his plan. "What am I missing, my friend?"

Kepir moved another scout unit to the mouth of the Temple. "Sire, we will need reinforcements at the Temple. Perhaps a full unit. One-hundred men to secure the Dragons. I also require a contingent of mages to operate the enchanted devices that house them."

Orus sighed. He had no human mages, but there were two young female Galdrissen who were aspiring adepts. One was Ega, who was a favorite of Ma 'Dryna. He knew the risks, but had no other alternative. Dreading the conversation with the High Priestess, the King looked at his Commander.

"Ega is the only capable mage we have in our service, Kepir. She is like a daughter to Ma 'Dryna. This request will be received like I was asking to marry the girl off to an Orc." Orus looked around to ensure no Orcs were listening in the area and exhaled sharply.

"Is she ready, Sire?" Kepir questioned.

"Do we have any other choice, my friend?" Orus replied.

Kepir shook his head. "I supposed not, Sire. Shall I send word to Ynus-Grag that our navy should soften the beaches before our arrival? It seems that Kren has noted a great number of Toads are camping near the sea to avoid being caught by the Dole'kyn in the city's shadows."

Orus snorted. "They are not stupid—or are they? Tell the naval Commanders to set the beach on fire with the Thunder Ballista and oil."

Kepir bowed. "Honor and glory, My King. Be blessed."

Orus saluted. "Honor and glory. May Likedelir be with our cause."

Chapter 13

The Princess skulked in the darkness, listening to her father's open rebuke of his advisors. As usual, someone or something did not please him. She despised his voice. Her mother had long joined Haeldrun in the Underworld, and since her death all those years ago, her father, the King, spent his time finding new distractions in an attempt to pretend that she had never existed. In addition to the King's antics, he ostracized his daughter and ignored her. The young Todani royal endured long periods of isolation, but she kept her tongue under control, never showing overt ambition, in fear of gaining her father's notice. Being a paranoid and unbalanced leader, King Lyax now spent his days devising ways to ensure his firm grasp on power, and that zeal, at times, even extended to his own children.

Vyqua sat and listened to him rant on. She remembered the siblings she had *lost* along the way. Each child was close to each other—as close as Todani ever were. They protected each other from the reach of their father. That was until they grew up and became rivals to the King, at least in his warped, hateful mind. Her older brothers—Yzo, Wyrn, and Jux—all found untimely ends in *accidents* after questioning their *loving* father's rulings. Vyqua was the youngest child of Queen Aixa and the sole survivor of her father's wrath. The Princess could not prove her beliefs, but she was intelligent and had a cunning mind. She could put the clues together. Each time a member of her family stood up to her father, they would meet a suspicious and untimely end.

Vyqua's hate for her father was sealed after her mother's demise. Her third brother, Jux, had just succumbed to a mysterious illness. Queen Aixa, enraged at the death of her third child, investigated the body with alchemists. She did this in direct violation of orders from the King. The investigators determined that Jux was poisoned. The Queen immediately confronted her husband concerning the incident, demanding blood for the crime. The problem was that the Queen Mother aimed her accusations directly at the King himself. An argument ensued, which escalated to a violent confrontation, much like many Todani disputes do. In the official statement, it was declared that the Queen was distraught with grief and had lost her mind. The report went on further to exonerate the King, stating that he fended off an attempted murder. As usual, Lyax was the victim even though, when the guards on duty entered the royal chambers, they found Lyax stoically over the body of the Queen, who had a dagger in her chest. There was no emotion or terror evident on the face of the victim, just a look of disgust. Shortly after the incident, Vyqua's suspicions were confirmed when every investigator who aided the Queen was found murdered or having committed suicide in their quarters. As usual, no one dared to question Lyax, fearing that they would be his next victim.

Vyqua wanted to see her father fall. She wanted it to be a mighty crash. She would find a way to destroy him and take all that he cared about. He may have feared her brothers and her mother, but he overestimated his remaining daughter's allegiance. He thought of her as a cowed, obedient daughter, but what he did not realize was that she was a coiled serpent waiting for the right time to strike. From what she could hear, a human named Orus and some foolish Dwarves were playing right into her deepest desires.

"The Dwarfish delegation has signed a covert alliance, King Lyax. We have a cessation of hostilities with Dornat Al Fer," the lackey informed.

"So, our foolish neighbors to the south have decided to abandon their grand alliance! What an excellent development." Lyax sounded as if he were a hungry wolf, licking his chops before sinking his teeth into the kill of the day.

"Pull back our troops from the Dwarfish borders and redeploy them to

Degran-Eras. Leave enough that the Dwarves do not get any ideas, but send most of our forces and ships to that hamlet called Whaleford. We end this rebellion and these human delusions of unity with this battle." Lyax leaned back in his throne confidently.

"As you wish, Sire." The lackey bowed and scurried away like a rat.

Lyax laughed haughtily to his remaining advisors. "After we are finished with these humans and Elves, we will deal with the Dwarves straight away."

Vyqua pondered the statements of her father carefully. She knew the Dwarves would never fully trust an alliance between Haeldrun Ir and Dornat Al Fer. Looking around for a bit, she searched her surroundings. As if from thin air, a man appeared in the shadows. She squinted, making sure it was a friend, vice a foe, her hand on her dagger.

"It is I, Princess," a familiar voice said from the shadows. "You have nothing to fear."

"Thank the Underlord, it is you. Father is in a mood tonight. He has been an irrational mess since the harbor attack. I fear he is becoming unhinged. Good," the princess scowled.

"How may I be of service, My Lady?" the eyes in the darkness replied, almost without speaking.

"Please, take this message to the King of the Dwarves. Show him the folly of his ways." Vyqua handed a black, cloth-swaddled hand a small scroll. "My father's arrogance will be his undoing. When he is gone, and I am Queen, you will be rewarded handsomely, my ally."

"There is only one thing that I desire, Princess—that I am by your side. I do not want to rule, just to be by your side." The dark figure bowed and disappeared from her sight.

The Princess faked a smile and nodded in agreement with her ally. She had no intention of honoring that agreement, but this man was the only one willing and capable of aiding her cause, and he was loyal to a fault. Sighing, she felt a twinge of guilt and then shrugged it off.

"Men are stupid," the Princess reasoned silently, justifying her deceitful actions. "I will use their stupidity when it can further my plans."

* * *

Hamrick disrobed and washed in a golden tub. It was not just the color of gold. It was, in fact, made of the metal. Drying his hair and wrapping a long crimson towel around his waist, the King called for his servant boy. It was late, but His Majesty insisted on servants being on hand all hours of the day and night to serve his desires. The Queen was away visiting her sister, and the King was enjoying time to himself in his enormous living quarters under the mountains. There was no answer.

"Steward! Where are you!?" the King bellowed angrily.

His voice echoed slightly off the hewn stone walls, but there was no answer again. Irritated, the Dwarf waddled, barely clothed, out of the bathing area and into the master bedroom. Again, it was an enormous room, with many decorations and baubles. Still, the King looked around in the darkened room; the only light cast was from a few candelabras that were strategically placed around the perimeter of the space. Off in the distance, a figure on the floor caught the King's eye.

"Steward?" the King asked, hurrying to the location of a young Dwarfish lad who was lying face down on the marble flooring. There was no blood, but he was not moving. "Are you all right?"

Before the King could react, a razor-edged blade appeared at his throat. An intruder had him in a shoulder hold, and the Dwarf was unable to break free. His attacker was very skilled in hand-to-hand tactics and extraordinarily strong to boot.

"You should not shout, or I will be forced to sever your head from your body," the figure said in the darkness.

"Who are you? What is it that you want? If you want riches, I can pay!" Hamrick offered quietly.

"If you relax and hear my words, I will let you free unharmed," the voice suggested calmly.

Nodding slowly, Hamrick agreed. The King looked at his steward. "What about the boy? Is he …?"

"He is subdued, not dead. He will survive this encounter, as will you, if you listen and do as I tell you. Can I release you, or should I just kill you now, Dwarf?"

"I agree! I agree! Release me. I will comply," Hamrick agreed, begging for his life.

The attacker released his grip and withdrew his knife. The King stumbled forward, gasping in fear. There, in the darkness, was a Todani assassin dressed in black from head to toe. He moved so silently that the King wondered if he was real or if he might be some sort of magic or perhaps a spirit.

"My Mistress sends you a missive from Haeldrun Ir. She wishes me to hand it to you, allow you to read it, and for me to answer any questions you may have concerning the information she has provided."

"We are allied with the Todani at this time, as you should well know. Why do you attack me in the middle of the night when you could have sent a courier in the daytime?" Hamrick rubbed his shoulder and accepted a small scroll from a jet-black hand.

"Read it and ask questions if necessary," the voice demanded.

Hamrick nodded nervously and cracked the seal on the scroll. Oddly, it was a regal seal on the missive that he did not recognize. Reading it, his eyes widened, and he began to shake his head.

"So, the Todani are moving to attack Orus and his ragged band. The Todani will breach our borders and raze the fortress and township of Redemption. The humans, Elves, and Galdrissen problem will be solved. What is the problem? Why all of the secrecy?" Hamrick sighed in relief. "You Todani have a flair for the dramatic, don't you think?"

"That is all you gleaned from that warning, good King?" The eyes chuckled softly in the darkness, responding, "Lyax will move against Orus and his allies—your true allies—you fool. My Mistress thinks that if you are capable of betraying those allies, who she thinks trustworthy, why not suggest that you go even further and betray King Lyax? It is definitely in Dornat Al Fer's interests to stifle the plans of Lyax. His endgame is to ultimately isolate the Dwarfish Kingdom, ostracized by the Rynn for its betrayal of its friends, and then to use the ensuing mayhem that is sure to come to his advantage. He fully expects the remnants of Orus's forces and alliance to attack the Dwarves in retaliation. When your forces move from our borders to quell the coming insurrection, Lyax will see his opportunity and strike. He will take his jewel right from under your nose. Do you fear the rule of Orus? You should fear your rival Lyax."

Hamrick heard these words and was concerned. The messenger's assessment made too much sense. He knew that the Todani were not to be trusted, but out of jealousy and personal pride, he made a deal with the Underlord to quell the rivalry with the humans. Hamrick paced nervously, knowing he had made a grave error, and knowing that it would be impossible to stop the wheels from turning in time.

"Can you get me intelligence?" the King asked the invader.

"To what end?" the eyes responded.

"I intend to preemptively strike the Todani before Lyax can recover from his troop movement," Hamrick responded thoughtfully.

"I can collect the information you seek, but I have one demand from my Mistress."

"What is that demand, messenger?" Hamrick asked.

"King Lyax must die, and Princess Vyqua will assume the throne in his stead."

Hamrick nodded, but wondered what internal strife was eroding the ruling family in Haeldrun Ir.

"I will need information about troops—locations, fortification, logistics—the usual, battle planning reconnaissance. I will need it within a day or so. Can you deliver that quickly?" The King waited for the answer as the intruder thought.

"It will take me at least a week to accomplish what you require. That includes travel to and from our nations. I will be forced to meet you this way again." The eyes smiled, revealing pearly-white pointed teeth in the inadequate lighting. "I will not use a knife to get your attention the next time, friend."

"I should hope not. I will keep our conversation quiet. Tell your Mistress that I thank her for your visit." Hamrick stood up straight in his bath towel.

The scene was ridiculous in the eyes of the invader, who just nodded and snorted, disappearing into the darkness. The King went over to his steward and rolled him over. Within minutes the young lad woke, feeling a bit nauseated and confused, but otherwise all right. The King sat him up and gave him a bit of water to drink, then dismissed him and went to his wardrobe to find fitting nightclothes. He looked around in the shadows apprehensively. He was unsure whether he would ever get to sleep.

* * *

Orus and the eight legions he now mustered prepared to march toward their primary objective of Whaleford. Vynwratha formed several thousand of its Rangers and moved northeast into the forest. They would meet up with the Hodan as they converged on Whaleford. Thankfully, there was no perimeter wall to speak of, save a post fence here and there. The city was surrounded by small villages and hamlets whose most prominent function was farming. The Dwarves held their ground at Redemption and watched as the allies left in different directions.

Days earlier, Kepir sent word by messenger to Ynus-Grag to warn the Orcs of the massive troop movements. Hodan did not want to meet the Orcs on the road to the Todessen over a misunderstanding. Two days prior to the departure of the Hodan army from Redemption, the Hodan navy began its harassment of the Todani on the shoreline and in the ports of Whaleford. The resulting wave of refugees began to flow toward the Dwarfish borders. It was a massive migration of Humans and Galdrissen. Whaleford was in disarray, just as Kepir had predicted it would be.

The Todessen occupiers formed defensive positions in depth completely surrounding the ruined Temple of Haya. The unit Commanders realized that they were losing ground to a new threat of the human underground resistance. The humans attacked haphazardly in pinch points formed by roadway intersections near buildings and bridges, or in blind spots where advancing troops could not see. The Todani Commander pulled his remaining forces back and held the Temple while he waited for his brothers and sisters to arrive from the northwest. The leader knew they were at least a week away. It was looking hopeless, but he knew they still had options if he could only hold the Temple.

"Kepir, are all of the human refugees out of their forest fortresses and in the main city walls at Redemption?" the Hodan King asked, looking over a field map once more time while on horseback.

"Sire, they are in the fortress, but many still flee to the gates from the mountains." Kepir sat ready for his orders.

"That will be the responsibility of the Dwarves," Orus scowled. "They had better hold up their end of the bargain."

"Agreed, My King," Kepir said. "I will take my leave and tend to my forces. Are you sure that you will not reconsider my request to join my men in the field?"

"No, Kepir, I do not trust those damned Dwarves." Orus looked at his friend with sincerity. "You, I trust. Protect Jaruz, Dryna, and the rest of them. Uilam will stand with you. You are all that they have if we fail."

Orus nodded and then turned, barking out orders to his legion Commanders. There was an echo of affirmation and then the clatter of thousands readying for the long march eastward. Many traveled light, in leather armor and camouflage suits, carrying swords, daggers, and bows.

Kepir smirked at his King's words. "Failure is not an option to a Hodan. We will succeed or meet in Aeternum, my brother."

* * *

The battle raged, door to door, through each hamlet and village. The countryside was on fire as the masses of noncombatant civilians fled west, running as expected, into the mountains and forests. The Hodan legions fought house to house in the near-abandoned city and surrounding settlements, routing out any Todani resistance they encountered. They found little, but the little they found was fierce. What Orus did not expect was a citizen militia underground, which was surprisingly proficient in wreaking havoc on the occupying forces of the Underlord. Kren, contacting one of the Whaleford scouts through one of his own, arranged a short meeting with the loose leadership of the underground, asking them to continue to harass the enemy at will, and that they did to surprising effect.

Hours passed, and the sun moved up high into the sky. By the early afternoon, Hodan was tired and bloodied, but far from finished with their mission. The legions met the Elfish Rangers at the temple in the center of the city by mid-afternoon. As he rode to an elevated position, the Hodan King surveyed the locale.

"Kren, what are we dealing with?" Orus asked in a professional, disconnected manner.

Kren answered similarly. The humor and banter were absent from his person. He was different. This was not lost on Orus, who looked at the camouflaged face of the bush that spoke.

"Your Majesty, around four-thousand Todessen are dug in around that place. They have siege weapons, and their cavalry is equipped with warhorses and mass weapons. The scouts are within striking range and undetected, as are several thousand Elfish Rangers to the north of the Temple. We have the numbers, but we have no idea what is below ground. They may have specialists and mages there also. Is it true what I have been told? Master Kepir said he met a mother Dragon down there? Under that?"

Orus sighed, then spoke. "Yes, Kepir met a Dragon, and she is the mother of others who are imprisoned in that Temple. I would wager that they need to hold that position, because it is the location of their secret weapon. I will venture a guess that the Dragons are what they seek to use against us. It may be too late for the souls beneath this den. If they are like the black Dragon who attacked Kairoth in Sudenyag ... If we can turn them to our side, though ..." The King trailed off in memory. "Let me just warn you, son, if it is the same, there is nothing we can do to stop them except kill each one with everything we have at our disposal. The battle between the Golden Queen and that demonic aberration in Sudenyag is something I will never forget."

Kren nodded silently, noting the look of concern on his King's face. "We must be victorious, My King. There is no other option."

Orus smiled at the statement. "Then, son, let us kill what we can see and deal with the unknowns when we get there. Unleash the Underworld on these spawns of Haeldrun. Make them wish that they had never seen the sun. See if you can get a team in there to see what we are moving in on. Also, see if the Dragons are not turned to the darkness. If they are not, we must figure out how to get them out of that place. By Kepir's own account, the doors do not seem large enough."

"Yes, Sire," the shrub responded, and quickly it melted away into the distance.

"Commanders, sound the horns. Let the field know that it is time for these Toads to be sent to the Underworld. No quarter!" Orus ordered.

The horns were sounded, and the roar of armies filled the air. Orus watched with concern as the grasses of the fields rose in front of the lines of the enemy, using fire and explosives against their foes. Many Todessen shrieked in fear of Kepir's men, running toward the Temple, but as they ran from their positions, away from the unseen, the swarm of quite visible regular coalition closed on them. The entrenched Todani forces fought valiantly and with deadly capability. Orus watched on solemnly as he witnessed great swaths of human and Elfish warriors swept under the Underlord's boots. The Hodan King's upper lip twitched angrily. Time to grind them to dust.

"Use everything we have to destroy this emplacement, Kren. Breach their lines. Kill them all. For glory and honor," Orus stated with a stone face, galloping to the front lines.

For several hours, the battle raged with neither side gaining an advantage, but sheer numbers of Hodan and Elf eventually overwhelmed the spirited defense of the Todani. Many scrambled into the Temple and were pursued, not only by the Dole'kyn, but also by the Vyn. By nightfall, the battle was won. The carnage was everywhere. The Hodan and Elves chanted slogans and war cries back and forth, exhorting each other for their roles in the victory, each time the cheers were louder. Humans lined the streets of Whaleford to behold their deliverers. None stood out plainer than a man on a white horse, in black armor with a white lion on his breastplate.

As Orus nodded at the victory of his legions, he sat upon his warhorse, looking at the nonstop stream of refugees making their way west under cover of the coalition troops. Little did the King or his coalition know, but many of the refugees were wolves in sheepskins. The Todani specialists mixed in with the humans and Galdrissen running from battle. When the Todani were safely out of view of their enemies, evading even the Elfish and Hodan Elites who patrolled loosely in the northern forests, the retreating forces rallied as planned in the woods, east of Redemption, and within striking distance of the human mountain settlements. There, Haeldrun's devoted set large signal fires. Looking to the north, more Todani Raiders waited. The invaders gathered, asking the Underlord for his assistance.

* * *

Redemption was quiet. The villages and fields that dotted the landscape outside the city walls were now deserted and dark. No fires lit the horizon; Even the moon hid behind the clouds, and a light rain had begun to fall. The Galdrissen huddled en masse in the large longhouses that were built for just such a situation. The people of Redemption and those of the human settlements sat with heavy hearts. Each grimly contemplated the fates of the brave warriors, fighting to save souls just like them in killing fields just over mountains to the east. With every passing hour, more refugees arrived from the north, south, and east. The fortress was bursting with humans and Galdrissen. The cries of refugees of every race were heard in every corner.

Kepir reported to Redemption several times since the alliance began its invasion of Degran-Eras. It had been several days, almost approaching a week since he had returned. The Hodan leader had briefed Jaruz on the defensive situation of the fortress and surrounding hamlets. The scout's demeanor was hurried and abrupt, but he always made a point to meet with the Dwarfish leader and Dryna in the baronial chambers. Uilam, while eavesdropping, could hear the concern in Kepir's reports as he told the pair of his suspicion of Dwarfish betrayal and the new crisis—the inability of the fortress to house the people who continued to arrive from the east. Later in the day, the Hodan leader witnessed the validation of his suspicions, as he watched as the Dwarfish forces picked up their camp and moved westward at least a mile or more. It was just as Kepir had feared and Orus had guessed. The Dwarves had no intention of intervening. They would not be in range to offer an adequate defense in the case of attack from the east. Uilam repeated the report to his men. The official Dwarfish story was the past few rainy days had made the camp untenable due to mud, but Uilam smelled a rat.

Kepir's men verified the field was indeed a bit muddy, but no muddier than in any other campaign or peacekeeping mission. Their leader was not convinced of the innocence of the troop movement. He put the specialists and Uilam's unit of one-hundred humans and Galdrissen on alert.

Uilam walked the walls, checking on each emplacement. The defense was well-manned and supplied, but he was not confident of their position or ability to repel a large force. He had been here before. Now there were one-hundred times the charges for him to worry about. The young warrior shook his head and uttered a quick prayer.

"Commander," Uilam said officially.

"What is it, Uilam?" Kepir asked, responding as if he already knew what the young man was about to say.

"Those self-serving little bastards sold us out, did they not," the young warrior stated, more as a matter of fact than a question.

"Aye, I believe that you are correct, Lieutenant," Kepir responded calmly. "It has now fallen to us to raise the fury of Hodan upon all who would harm our lands and our people."

CHAPTER 13

Uilam looked at the longhouses. "Understood, Sir. We will not run."

Kepir smiled. "I know that you will not. You and those you led did not flee the last time. I have no cause to question you or your people, son." Kepir nodded, and Uilam left to take a position above the defenses.

* * *

Darkness crept over the land as the sun dipped below the eastern mountain range. The temperature also dropped into the high forties, and Uilam could see his breath escaping the woolen scarf that was wrapped around his cheeks. All positions were ready, but for what kind of threat was the young Lieutenant's question. All was quiet. He scanned the horizon expectantly with a spyglass trained chiefly on the eastern forests. There was movement off to the southeast, but the young warrior could not make out what it was. It could have been deer or a hunting pack of wolves, for all he knew. Still, he observed.

"Anything to report, son?" Kepir whispered, entering the small balcony where Uilam stood vigil.

"Random movement on the tree line, Sir, but nothing definitive," Uilam responded, still looking with his glass.

"I will send a scout team to investiga ..."

Kepir's statement was cut short by a burning arrow that streaked across the sky.

"Incoming, Sir. We need to sound the horns now!" Uilam shouted, blowing his own.

Kepir's eyes opened widely as the woods emptied into his killing fields. He had prepared, but there were too many.

"To arms! To arms! The enemy approaches!" the Commander shouted, sliding down the ladder and sprinting to the courtyard. He was met by a platoon of his own Elites. "Take positions and kill until you can continue no more. Pass the word to the rest of the legion! For Hodan!"

The small group bowed and stated angrily in unison, "For Hodan!"

Kepir watched as death melted into the darkness from where he sat. Smiling with a twinge of excitement, the Hodan Elite readied his blades and checked his bowstring.

Outside the fortress walls, the fields around Redemption were set ablaze by Kepir's men. Uilam smiled as he watched flora and fauna seemingly spring up everywhere, decimating the incoming Todani, but soon his smiles turned to concern, as he realized that the specialists were overwhelmed and that the first of the Todani Raiders were making it to his walls.

"Kill them as they climb, gents!" Uilam said, joining them in the courtyard. "Archers! Kill them at will!"

* * *

Edmund had seen enough. Hopping down from his perch, he ran to the nearest engineer. "Where are the mallets? Where are the axes, Dwarf?" the young warrior demanded.

"Here, My Lord!" the old Dwarf in the funny hat said in fear, looking upward.

"Look at me, Dwarf," Edmund said in a stern voice. "Hand them out to whoever comes here. Do it!"

The older Dwarf calmed and looked at the young man, nodding in affirmation.

Edmund ran to a huddled mass of humans. They were screaming and crying out for deliverance. The warrior was not pleased. He stood on a cut stump and shouted to the crowd of humans in front of him. "Be quiet, you sheep!"

There, a huddled, cowering crowd whimpered as the young warrior, clad in chainmail, addressed them angrily. "Every man, stand up and follow me over to that wall!" The warrior pointed to where the Dwarf stood near a pile of building implements. "The Todani are here for your wives and children! Will you cower in your own piss or kill them with us?!"

"We can't fight them," a random male voice responded.

"Why? Because they are demons?" Edmund responded, as an arrow impacted his shoulder. He fell to one knee, then stood as if nothing had occurred. Breaking off the head of the arrow, he pulled out the shaft. It was a superficial wound, but the people were in awe of the young man's restraint and lack of fear. His eyes glowed a bluish hue. It was visible in the darkness. The people watched in awe.

"They tried to kill me once, and they failed. My brothers died here to save the Galdrissen. Now, the Galdrissen allow you to hide behind their walls! They feed you out of their stores! They clothe you with their blankets! Yet, you will not even stand with Hodan against those who would snuff the lives of your families for a laugh? You are NOT men. You are not even sheep. You are lower than the dust upon my boots," Edmund spat.

"Who are you to demand we do anything? You are no one, boy!" a voice shouted.

"I am a man, you cowardly fool. I am a Sergeant under Master Kepir, of Hodan. We serve the King, Orus, of Hodan. We are heroes. Join us; fight for your lives. Fight for the lives of those you love, or when our righteous blood is finally spent, while you watch us die in vain, know that you put your own heads upon the blocks of your oppressors' executioners, for there will be no quarter given this day. Of that, you can be sure."

Random voices shouted desperately for reinforcements and arrows. Edmund scoffed and turned away from the crowd in disgust.

"Wait," several voices cried out. "We will go."

Within minutes, the men kissed their wives and children goodbye, prayed quickly, and one by one joined Edmund by the Dwarf handing out axes. Nodding, Edmund welcomed each man to Hodan personally. Looking off at the crowd, the Galdrissen were herding the women into the caves, longhouses, and towers. It was standing room only.

"Someone, get these arrows to those archers," Edmund demanded loudly, and his shout was answered by five young boys around the ages of ten to twelve years. They grabbed bundles of arrows and ran off toward the calls

231

for ammunition. "Keep your heads down!"

* * *

The Todani came with a fury, unseen by the human defenders in a hundred years. The fortress walls held steady for most of the fighting, as the supply lines kept the archers firing, while the oil pots kept the fires burning. It seemed that the first wave was repelled, but the defensive victory was not without a cost.

After the first wave failed to breach or scale the walls of the palisade, due to Hodan archers, the Todani arrived with archers of their own. The Todani bows were much like the Elfish bows of the Vyn, and their range was considerably better than the human variety. Soon, the Hodan archers were pinned down, fighting fires from flaming arrows, or shot dead in their positions.

Uilam had seen this before. He grabbed his Sergeants and shouted, "Get the civilians to the cave now! Cram them all in there if possible! If not, arm the boys and men! Then fill that passageway with the warriors of Degran-Eras!" Uilam stood tall. "We were adopted by Hodan! It is time to earn that title, gentlemen!"

Edmund motioned to a five-hundred-man platoon of human men near the main fortress gate. They had shored it up with logs as makeshift battering rams began pounding the main entrance. The human platoon sat silently in the darkness. Uilam smiled, noticing that they all had large hammers or axes. The Lieutenant nodded as he saw that most of the refugee women and children were already tucked away, as safely as could be.

"Your doing, Sergeant?" Uilam asked Edmund.

"Yes, Sir. I saw a need and filled it as trained," Edmund responded saluting.

"Move those axemen to the mouth of the cave and have the specialists reinforce the longhouses and tower. The archers are doing the best that they can at the walls. The gate will not hold for long, and the walls are showing signs of failing. I have no idea where Master Kepir is." Uilam frowned and swallowed hard. "I only hope if he went to Aeternum this evening that he sent twenty of them to the Underlord."

"As you order, Sir. Luck in battle, Uilam. I love you, brother. I stand here today, because of you."

"I think you have that backward, Edmund. It is I who owes you," Uilam responded, running to the tower to inform Jaruz of the situation.

* * *

The space within the cave was a standing room only affair, and the entrance was filled with rank after rank of armed human and Galdrissen warriors. The remaining specialists and warriors formed a mass unit outside the door and awaited the onslaught to come to them. They could hear the enemy war cries from within the now burning and crumbling walls of Redemption.

"We shall ne'er forget the treachery of the Dwarves!" Kepir growled. "Its stench will remain as long as a Dwarf draws breath upon the Rynn."

"I am sorry, Kepir," Jaruz said, tearing up. "I never imagined that Hamrick was such a wretch. I am ashamed of my heritage."

"Be not troubled, Jaruz, for you are a friend. I consider you of Hodan, not of Dornat Al Fer. Your honor is intact, and you do not share the stain of those people," Kepir said, extending his hand. Many Hodan in the tower war room around the two nodded.

"Then I accept and hope that the Gods deliver Hamrick's head on a pike to Orus when this is all resolved!" Jaruz shouted.

The troops shouted as they saw the first Todani Raiders breach and scale over the walls. "Huzzah! Huzzah! Huzzah! Long live King Orus, of Hodan! Death to all who oppose him!"

The warriors in the war room quickly exited into the courtyard to join the fray.

"Stand READY!!!" Kepir shouted as more and more of the enemy gathered near the portcullis.

Then the Todani opened the gates.

* * *

Against Kren's wishes, Orus and a contingent of his men made their way into the Temple passageway with the specialist's unit. The King had in tow Ega, the mage. After much arguing and debate, the High Priestess knew she had no other option. Orus, in turn, promised Ma 'Dryna to protect the girl from harm. The Champion remembered that the High Priestess's eyes glowed amber as she promised him a painful death if anything should befall the mage. Orus looked at the trees and animals with suspicion, but there was no sign of that sort of power here. Dryna was changing, but Orus had no idea what Likedelir had in store for her.

"Stay close to me, young lady!" Orus chided the mage.

She smiled, then nervously joked, "Yes, father!"

Orus was caught off-guard by her remark. He held her face in his hands for a moment, looking intently into her eyes. "Make no mistake, young one, I will protect as if you were Faylea herself, but this scum would sacrifice you like an animal to the Underlord."

Orus released her. He was genuinely concerned that something would happen to her. His worry brought a smile to her face.

"It is good to know that a King cares so much for the likes of me," Ega remarked.

"Just stay close to me," Orus demanded as a skirmish erupted around a ninety-degree corner.

A random human voice declared, "CLEAR!" The column continued down the long switchback passageway, eventually reaching the sanctuary that Kepir had described.

"We are here, girl," Orus lectured. "Stay close."

"Yes, Da!" she responded, smiling and touching his side.

Orus frowned at the idea of putting her in harm's way, but she was the only one who could do what needed to be done. A voice called out with a large growl simultaneously filling the chamber. Several specialists faded into the darkness.

The voice continued. "You are Kepir's friends, are you not? See how you hide from even my eyes! Beware the shadows, humans!"

Orus spoke. "Are you the Dragon who speaks, or a Toad who needs to have her tongue removed?"

"You must be Orus. I know of you and of your part in the Arondayre! I am the Dragon, King. There are hidden foes here. Beware."

"Stay out of the shadows men, I have seen this in Sudenyag. The Denir may be present."

Ega lost all joviality and looked at Orus with fear. "The Denir, My King?"

"Yes, I do not jest," Orus said seriously, as mayhem began to erupt in the chamber before him.

Several specialists screamed in abject terror, bolting from their corners and attacking anyone or anything within their sight. Their eyes were wide and white. They screamed out nonsense to everyone who was unaffected, but to them, the terror they experienced was very real.

"Set everything that can burn on fire now!" Orus demanded as he grabbed a torch from a nearby sconce. "They hate fire and real light. Magical light does no good!"

The number of affected began to grow, and the violence began to increase. Ega, from her vantage point, noticed a figure beside the altar, between two statutes. She looked over at the dark area behind the sanctuary to where she guessed the Dragon to be. She could not see past the fires.

A voice entered her mind. "Hello, mage."

"Are you a Denir?" Ega responded, but without fear.

"Hardly, child, I am a Dragon."

"Can you kill that Todani near the altar? I believe he causes the Denir to exist on our plane." Ega's eyes were glowing amber.

Orus looked at her with concern. "Are you all right, child?"

Ega smiled. "I am fine, My King." Then the girl turned to the Dragon. "Well? Can you kill him or not?"

"The rod he holds in his left hand will not allow me to attack him or anyone he deems friendly. If you could get it for me, I would be eternally grateful, young one." The Dragon chuckled.

"I will see what I can do," Ega replied, raising her hands.

Orus recognized the hand gesture as preparation for magic and shouted to his men. "MOVE!"

Above the Priest by the altar, a small dark cloud appeared. Ega's runes glowed white, lighting the area immediately around her person. She uttered something in the Todani tongue. Three bolts of lightning struck the distracted Priest, knocking him off his feet and to the floor.

The Priest shrieked in Todani. "No! You fool! What have you done? My master will devour you all!"

Ega replied, her hair floating gently and eyes still glowing. "Give me the rod, pig!"

The Denir swarmed the Galdrissen girl, but Ega stood unharmed. She looked through them at the Priest who scrambled to heal himself.

"The rod, or I will make your death one of epic despair and agony," Ega said, as her runes began to glow a brighter white. Her eyes blazed like molten gold in a crucible.

Orus motioned for his men to stand back.

"You think that you are the only one with power, my dear," the Priest smugly replied. He chanted, and the rod glowed blue.

A voice in Ega's head shouted. "Run away!"

But it was too late. The Dragon turned and rained fire down upon the mage. She instinctively flung up a shield, but the power of the Dragon breath was too much for her, and she took the brunt of the attack. Reaching into her satchel, she retrieved a small, green vial and drank its contents immediately. Exhausted, the young Galdrissen woman sat, her clothing smoking, her hair singed, and one side of her body severely burned. Orus was livid.

"You bastard son of a whore," Orus muttered.

The Hodan troops backed away from their King in both fear and awe as he too began to glow faintly. Runes appeared on his face and hands. The King's eyes were bright as the light of the sun. They were, in fact, so bright that the Denir shied away from his gaze. The Priest cowered in fear, wondering what this might mean.

"Give them the rod, Priest," an ethereal growl barked.

The Priest convulsed violently, then stopped moving, answering, "You have no power here, son."

"Oh, but do I not, father?" Orus replied to the weakened Priest, springing forward and pummeling the robed figure.

The Hodan stood in awe of their King, who was shrouded in white light, while locked in battle with an enemy Priest, who was now so blackened that it appeared he consumed the light around him. They tried to rush the room, but as they attempted to push in, the Hodan were attacked by the shadows, and the Denir created mayhem in the ranks. There was nothing they could do. Dejected, the legionnaires stood helpless at the entrance to the sanctuary.

"Why do you resist me, Orus?" the priest hissed. "You have no reason to care for these vermin."

"I have every reason to wish your minions the death they deserve, Denir," Orus retorted.

"Denir?" the voice chuckled.

"Kill the Priest, Champion, and my father will be sent back to the Underworld," an image of Likedelir said, appearing beside Orus.

"Your father?" Orus's snarled as his eyes widened in realization. A toothy grin followed as he leered at the robed figure. With glee, the Champion declared, "My Lord gives me my wildest dream, or as close to it as I will ever be! Die, Haeldrun, and go back to your fetid, dung-filled hole within the ground!" Orus then drove his sword into the heart of the Priest, who was still clutching the rod.

Likedelir vanished, as did the presence within the Priest. The room's darkness dissipated like a fog and the Denir shrieked, fading in the light of random fires. Orus stood alone, holding a sword in one hand and the dismembered arm of a Todani Priest in the other. The hand of the arm still clutched the rod and would not release it. A bloody pile of rags contained what remained of his adversary.

Orus fell to one knee to catch his breath. The King stumbled over to where Ega lay. He called for his field physicians and water. The girl was conscious and sipped a bit from the skin. She was alive, but in extreme pain. The potion she had drunk earlier had done its job, saving her life, but Ega was still far from all right. She motioned for Orus to come closer.

"Father, bring the swine's arm. I must take possession of the rod." Ega smiled. "You did it, My King."

"We did it, young lady. Now, do what you came here to do and let us get you home," the King replied softly, handing the Priest's arm to the Galdrissen mage.

Ega uttered a few quiet words, grasping the rod, and the hand that held it released its grip, as if it handed it over to the girl.

"Release me, girl," a voice said within Ega's head.

"I release you, Dragon," Ega said plainly. The Dragon roared in jubilance at being free. Ega sighed and fell asleep in Orus's embrace.

"Healer!" the King bellowed.

A healer ran to the King, checking the mage's condition. She determined that the mage was simply exhausted from combat and her injuries. Her actions had taken a toll.

"Sire, she needs a better healer than I. I am but a field medic. I suggest that we make a litter and get her out of here as soon as possible."

"Make it happen immediately, gentlemen!" Orus ordered, looking at the face of the sleeping girl in his arms.

The Hodan made a litter from available materials, placing Ega upon it.

As this was happening, everyone in the chamber became acutely aware of an immense stirring in the darkness before them.

THUMP! THUMP! THUMP! ROAR!

Orus ordered that Ega be laid down gently. His remaining men formed behind him. He took position right in the path of a white-scaled version of what he had seen on the Arondayre all those days before.

238

"Are you my Dragons now?" Orus asked, wrinkling his forehead in puzzled expression. "Is that how it works when you are a Champion of a god?"

The Dragon laughed loudly. "I am no one's Dragon, nor are my children anyone's property!"

"No disrespect intended, great Dragon, but my God is very stingy with information!" the King shouted sarcastically at the ceiling.

"I will aid you, human. You have saved my children and me from the Underlord," Henargya replied, bowing her scaly head slightly.

From behind her, several juvenile Dragons could be heard calling for blood. Orus looked over the Dragon and into the darkness with concern.

"They will be no problem, human. They are young and stupid. They have also had a rough go of things these past two decades or so. They are angry and want blood. Understandably so … I will ensure that their ire is pointed in the right direction."

"How will you escape from this place, Henargya? The doors are too small and the passages only eight feet," Orus stated.

"The walls behind us are only a few measures thick. The stone cannot hold us now that we are loosed. My children and I will be free in no time. The wall will open over the eastern side of the cliffside if I am not mistaken. We shall emerge over the beaches and the seas." The elder Dragon smiled and growled out something to her agitated children. Each growled back in protest. She rolled her eyes impatiently. "Children can be so obstinate! We will meet you over the mountains at the fortress Kepir informed me of."

"Oh, one thing, Dragon, if I might," Orus added. "The black ships on the seas that sound like they harness the thunder, they are my men. You will know them by the standard on their sails. A lion. They are not Toads. Please, do not destroy them!"

Henargya smiled and laughed. "We will keep that in mind, my deliverer. Now, leave this place, and we will burn it all to ash after we make our exit out of this dungeon! When we have a proper door to this prison, I think the space will make a perfect new home."

The younger Dragons roared in the distance, again in protest. Henargya closed her eyes and shook her enormous head in frustration.

Orus bowed, as did the Dragon.

"Let us go, Hodan! Out! They are going to burn this stinking chamber pot to a crisp. No one wants to be anywhere near Dragon fire!" Orus, remembering, looked at Ega and frowned.

The men quickly left the sanctuary and made their way to the surface. Once there, it was evident that victory had been claimed by Hodan and the Elves. The camps were set, and the survivors were eating rations. As Orus and his remaining men carried Ega out of the mouth of the Temple, the cheering of the Hodan and remaining civilians filled the air. It was soon interrupted by a ground-shaking explosion east of their location. People ran in all directions seeking cover, not knowing what could have dealt such a blow as to open a cliff side, facing the sea. Out of the dust and debris, a roaring presence could be heard. Into the sky above flew a giant ancient white Dragon and several adult Dragons of varying shades, followed by many young. The survivors of Degran-Eras shrieked in fear.

Orus held up his hands. "Fear not, my people, they are our friends! For the love of the Gods, DO NOT attack them!"

Kren had the signalmen blow the horns, calling for a stand down. The military was distressed by the sight of Dragons but relaxed their posture as ordered. A short time later, Orus gathered his leaders and told them the tale of the Temple. Most were comforted by the news, but everyone was concerned as they watched as the thunder-lizards circled northwest toward the forests. Randomly, here and there, the large one would stop and belch flames down on what Kren reasoned must be some unsuspecting Todessen patrol.

Occupation forces were set. Security was established, and word of the human victory spread northward like wildfire. Orus looked at the young unconscious Galdrissen girl in his charge.

"Kren, we leave for Redemption at first light," Orus ordered.

"Understood, Your Majesty. I will bring a platoon as security," Kren replied, nodding.

"The Dragons are following something west. I am not sure what they see, but they are burning the forest. We need to get home soon. Bring a legion instead of a platoon. We may need it." Orus saluted.

"Understood, Your Majesty. I will include a hundred of my own men if that pleases you," Kren replied, returning the salute.

Orus nodded, looking at the burning forest. He was worried.

* * *

Kepir was battered and bloodied. The civilian warriors, when pressed, fought passably, and with the support of highly trained specialists, the Todani invaders died in droves, as they spilled into the open fortress gates. Still, the alliance dead numbered in the hundreds. For the moment, things seemed oddly quiet. It was almost dawn, and Kepir could see Uilam helping an obstinate Edmund to the medical tent. The Sergeant was covered in blood, his and his enemy's, and the boy could barely stand. What impressed the master the most was that Edmund still gripped his sword while two arrows protruded prominently from his left shoulder. The master chuckled as Uilam began shouting at Edmund to sit down.

"Sit down! Shut your hole! Let the doctor fix you! You insufferable horse's ass!" Uilam was livid.

"Ah, you shut it, Sir! There are more out there! I will not sit by and knit with the women while those scum still breathe." Edmund made a profane gesture at his friend.

"Ass!" Uilam said, laughing. "Just heal up and get a potion in you or something. I don't think we're done yet."

"I'll just sit here on my lazy ass and watch you fight, Sir! Yes, Sir!"

"SHUT up!" Uilam said, storming off toward Kepir.

"What an insubordinate little bastard," Kepir chuckled loudly.

"That he is, master, but he's the best man I've got," Uilam said with pride.

"It is good to have brothers to stand with you, son." Kepir smiled. "Now, get up on that platform and see where our friends have run off to, would

241

you?"

"At once, Sir," the specialist replied, bowing and lighting off to a nearby ladder.

Once up on the wall, the young man pulled a spyglass from a case hanging around his neck. Raising the glass to his eyes, he gasped at what he thought he saw. He dropped the glass, blinked hard, and then looked with his naked eyes. He could see something, but it did not make sense. Again, he lifted the glass and gasped at his discovery. Something big was airborne to the northeast. The Todani forces seemed to be massing to the north of them on both sides of the mountain barrier. There were thousands from what he could see from a distance. They had stopped their advance, and there was some indication that they were now in a defensive position. Some signs pointed toward the possibility that they were trying to tactically withdraw, but the mirage the boy kept seeing could not be true, could it? Uilam shook his head in disbelief. This had to be a Todani trick to make him drop his guard.

Kepir called up. "What do you see, warrior?"

"You won't believe me, Sir. I don't believe me," Uilam responded in shock.

"Well, try me, son," Kepir responded impatiently.

"There are thousands of Todani regulars northeast of us moving in from the eastern and western side of the mountains." Uilam paused. "That much I can confirm, but the rest may be a result of me finally losing my mind."

Kepir made his way below, to his man. "What do you see? Just tell me now," the Commander demanded.

"Well, Sir, the forest is burning, as are many Todani. The fire appears to be coming from an unknown number of Dragons flying over them. I think they are Dragons. I have never seen one in real life." Uilam looked at his Commander in awe.

"That makes sense," Kepir said expertly, climbing the wall without a ladder. "Let me see."

Uilam handed his Commander his spyglass.

"Haha!" Kepir exclaimed. "They did it!"

"King Orus and the alliance won?" Uilam asked, smiling.

"That is the Dragon I saw in the Temple ... long story ... His Majesty freed her and the children. The Todani sought to use them against us." Kepir laughed loudly. "The joke is on those fools! They are reaping the wages of their atrocities. Dragons do not forget, and they live an awfully long time!"

Kepir slid down a pole to the ground. Looking up a Uilam, he ordered, "Have a team secure the interior perimeter; secure the gate as best as can be. Shore up the walls. Have a party collect the dead, say the prayers, and burn them before the night ... Outside the fortress. You hear me? Outside."

"Yes, Sir." Uilam responded. "I will also have the men search for survivors and injured, in and around the fortress."

"Good idea, son. I must tell Jaruz and Dryna the good news." Kepir smiled up at the specialist and ran to the tower.

* * *

"Dryna, I have news! Where is Jaruz?" Kepir asked the Priestess, who looked up at him with reddened eyes.

"He is here, Kepir," she responded, gesturing to the gurney that she sat beside. The Dwarf on the litter was severely injured. His bandages were soaked in blood, and he was barely conscious.

"What happened, Jaruz?" Kepir stared down in horror, clutching the Dwarf's free hand.

Dryna spoke. "There were two Todani in the medical facility here at the tower. They struck after everyone left to meet the enemy within the fortress. They were much like your specialists, Kepir." Dryna sobbed, continuing. "They came for me, but Jaruz killed them both, but not without a brutal battle. His bravery was unmatched. My love was already in here for other injuries. He was no match for two raiders while hobbled."

Jaruz stared up at his love, pulling her toward him. He kissed her gently. "I love you, Dryna. I told you that I would defend you to my death. I meant it."

Dryna's tears fell on her man's face. "You fool, you cannot die. I am not finished with you yet."

"I only fear that I cannot protect you now. Kepir, please," Jaruz coughed, wincing in pain.

"Of course, brother. I will take your post if the gods will it. But you are not gone yet." Kepir smiled, but he knew it was only a matter of time. "Brother, your valor has preserved the people. You and all the others who were injured or fell in battle protected the innocents long enough for the Dragons to arrive."

"Orus did it!" Jaruz coughed, but he was smiling.

"We did it, my brother. Orus, you, I, and all the others. The Todani army came in force. The Dragons are turning them away from us. If they do not scurry back to their holes in Haeldrun Ir, they will be consumed in Dragon fire. We are saved." Kepir noticed the grip on his hand began to loosen.

"No! No! Nooooo! You cannot leave me, my love. What am I supposed to do without you!?" Dryna cried out in horror.

Jaruz's eyes stared blankly ahead. His chest stopped rising and falling. His face still smiled. Dryna buried her face in his beard, wailing at the top of her lungs. Kepir reached out to put his hand on her shoulder, but she would not be comforted. Kepir swallowed hard as a tear rolled beneath each eye. He lowered his head and prayed for the first time in many years.

Chapter 14

Kren gave the orders. His men set up hasty defenses dispersed throughout the baronial lands of Whaleford. The fortifications were meager, but specialists and the Vyn augmented the positions as best as could be expected. All was quiet, and with the quiet came the survivors of the region. From every nook and cranny, every hole in the earth, every hidden root cellar and cave, men and women poured into the streets, their children in tow. They were filthy, hungry, and exhausted. Every man had a dagger, ax, or club at the ready as they moved forward to meet their saviors.

Orus sat on horseback; he was concerned with Ega. Nothing else had his attention at the moment.

"Sire, there is something you should see," Kren said seriously.

"Not now, Kren," Orus replied quietly. "I have more important things to tend to."

"But Sire, this is very important. You must see."

"All right, Kren, if you insist, but it better ... be ... important," the King stammered, looking at the city proper from his hillside vantage. "Oh my Gods. Where did they come from, son?"

"It seems we have inherited our own Sudenyag, Sire." Kren chuckled loudly, then cleared his throat.

Orus rubbed his face and took a deep breath. "You may be right, Kren, you might be right. Harun would laugh so ... would Famlin ... I would never hear the end of this."

"Will you meet them before you go?" Kren asked.

"I will. Let us go." Orus mounted his horse, leaving Ega in a covered wagon, in the care of his best physicians. "Come to me if her condition changes, Priest."

The chief healer nodded, bowing.

Orus rode toward the crowd with a contingent of fifty specialists flanking him on his left and right.

* * *

Uilam and Edmund stood side by side. The healers had bound the younger's shoulder after removing the arrows. After a couple of healing concoctions were administered, Edmund declared himself fit for duty, much to Uilam's chagrin. The Sergeant would not be denied, even with the threat of court martial. Kepir snickered at Uilam's dilemma, but the situation at the fortress did not afford the Commander time for derision. Somberly, he looked about at the display of butchery and havoc left in the wake of the Todani charge.

There were two large, shallow pits dug several hundred measures from the fortress walls. Each had a substantial heap of corpses piled within it. One pile was for alliance fallen, the other Todani. Kepir understood the petty hatreds of men, he had felt them many times in the past, but as he looked upon the carnage before him, he understood one thing—the dead were dead, no matter who they were.

New Priests of Likedelir and old ones for Haya made prayers for the dead of both sides. Kepir nodded, then lamented his losses. One body was set aside on an altar that was prominently displayed in front of the tower entrance. It was covered in gauzy gold cloth. He had been washed, then dressed in his finest clothing and armor. The Dwarf was covered by his shield, and his sword was placed in his right hand. Jaruz would be sent off as a Hodan Elite. Many who passed by paid their respects, donating small offerings for his pyre. Kepir hoped his King would return soon, or the specialist would have to do the honors without him.

"Edmund, would you set those swine on fire for me?" Uilam asked sarcastically, looking at the pile of Todani, which was taller than he. Wood, oil, thatch, and kindling were intermingled with the twisted faces of death. Immediately after saying the words, he regretted them. They did not look so evil while dead. They just looked to him like dead people. The Lieutenant was saddened.

Edmund grunted affirmatively. Strangely, the boy bowed slightly, oddly saluting the enemy fallen. He dropped a lit torch into the pit, and immediately the pitch ignited, spreading fire to all points around the pyre. Kepir wondered about the boy as he watched. Uilam witnessed solemnly, bowing his head and asking Likedelir for forgiveness.

In the alliance pit before the Lieutenant, were hundreds of his own countrymen. The Priests had long ago said their prayers, and the people donated a collected tribute of food, drink, clothing, armor, weapons, and coin. The small symbolic cache was placed at the edge of the massive pyre for the souls in their new life in Aeternum. Uilam bowed, then stood tall, saluting his fallen comrades, while muttering a prayer and throwing the burning torch he held into the center of the pit. A similar scene as the first developed, as the hole was engulfed in flame.

* * *

The smell of burning flesh was overwhelming as smoke filled the air, but mercifully, the winds carried the smoke inland and away from the fortress walls. The Dwarfish leadership sat in their camp, a mile or two away, watching the fortress with interest through their spyglasses. The aroma of death surrounded them. Many warriors in the company of Dornat Al Fer felt an unbearable shame as they watched the scene.

"Rider," the Dwarfish Commander called out.

"Here, Sir," an older Dwarf responded.

"Take this message to His Majesty. Do it quickly. He will be very concerned about these developments."

"As you command, Sir," the Dwarf responded, taking the satchel and riding northwest.

"Gentlemen, this is going to get worse before it gets better—if it gets better at all," the Commander said to his Lieutenants.

* * *

Kepir snapped out of his melancholy daze and marched to where his two senior leaders watched the bodies burn. "You two there!" the Commander barked. "I need you."

The two snapped to attention and then ran to their leader. Uilam responded, "What is your need, Sir?"

"Organize the remaining warriors, specialists, and civilian warriors. I intend to march to the Dwarves and confront their treachery." Kepir's eyes were steeled. His words were stoic, and one could almost feel a chill in the air as he said them.

"At once, Sir," Uilam responded, nodding at Edmund, who nodded once. They both ran, calling out to the masses.

"Jaruz, your death is one thing with which I cannot abide. If His Majesty is wroth with my decision, I will spare him the trouble and take my own life. These haughty turncoats will not sit there in their camp eating venison from our stores while they mock us. I will have their heads."

* * *

Orus and his men stood before a large, unruly mob. They had all the makings of an insurrection, and that was all right by him, just as long as they joined his coalition. Angry voices spoke up, as many in the rabble tried to silence them in fear of the new invading force. The people were tired of oppression. They were at their wit's end. To Orus, it seemed that they were prepared to die, rather than be slaves to a new master. The Hodan King smiled at this turn of events.

"Who are you? What does YOUR army desire of our lands?" a random voice catcalled.

"You think it is your turn to put your boot on my neck? I would rather kill you or die trying, invaders!" another angry voice declared.

Orus was intrigued. They were ready. They only lacked a plan and leadership to unite them. He hoped to fill the void. The King raised his hands, asking for the crowd to allow him to speak. The Hodan specialists were slowly surrounding the thousands of souls who packed the main city square and surrounding roadways.

"Kren, where are they coming from? I had no idea how many hid. Where were they hiding?" Orus was amazed.

"I am not sure, Sire, but you had better win them over soon, before we end up fighting the people we came to liberate." Kren was signaling toward the horizon. Orus knew there were specialists out there somewhere.

"Good people! Pray attend!" Orus bellowed.

The din slowly settled to a murmur. Rows of desperate faces now looked at the unknown warrior in wonder and fear. Orus thought of when Puryn and Adasser stood on the platform in Empyr. He had wondered what it felt like when Queen Falda laid that crown upon his head and left him to rebuild all that was before the Scourge had taken it. He knew now. Orus was never truly afraid in his adult life; he had accepted his death years ago, when he took on the mantle of a Hodan Elite, but now, he held the lives and welfare of so many downtrodden in his hands. Hodan's rebuild was comparatively easy. A nation of warriors could do anything, but these were street urchins, women, and old men for as far as his eye could see.

"Well, get on with it!" an old voice cackled from the back of the crowd. The comment elicited a chuckle from the people in attendance.

Orus smiled, stifling a laugh. "I am Orus, King of Hodan. I come from

249

across the sea. I left my home to defeat the Todani, here and anywhere else that I find them."

There was a murmur of subtle approval among the masses. Many heads were nodding, but many still held their tongues, unimpressed.

Orus continued. "We have defeated the Todani here! I have made an alliance with Elf and Dwarf, as well as a truce with the Orcs to our east. The large green ones wish to trade, not fight. They desire fish and stone. With this alliance and newly formed trade routes, I dream of a day when Whaleford is a strong capitol for a free human kingdom!"

"Ah, what you are going on about, fool?" a voice derided loudly from the pack. "You kill a few Todani scum in a village and call yourself a conqueror!? What will you do when they come back with reinforcements? You have killed us all! They will not take this rebellion lightly. The Todani will come and crush everyone, King of wherever!"

Kren was visibly irritated and scanning the crowd. Orus saw it plainly and looked at his man, raising his hand for him to cease.

"All the Rynn has joined me in alliance to defeat the evil to the north. We together hold the keys to your freedom and salvation. You must join our cause for us to have a chance at redemption. Humanity cannot be the fodder for evil, unless it chooses to allow evil to run unchecked." Orus paused.

The crowd seemed to be warming to Orus, but an undercurrent of suspicion and doubt held fast in their hearts. They had not stood openly and proudly against oppression in generations. This stranger promised the world, but only had a handful of warriors with him. Where were his vast armies?

"If you command so many, great King," another voice said sarcastically, "and you have the Dwarves in your alliance, where are your vast numbers and where, pray tell, are the Dwarfish legions?"

Orus nodded. "The Dwarves protect our rear guard inside of the Kingdom of Dornat Al Fer. The Elves are here, and my numbers are under your noses! Gentlemen, ladies, reveal yourselves to our new friends."

Kren signaled, and from thin air, a thousand specialists swarmed the crowd, surrounding them. The effect was one of alarm and terror.

Orus raised his hands and bellowed. "Stand down, warriors! Good people, be not afraid! These are your warriors and protectors. They are not your oppressors. We seek to let you live in the sunshine and fresh air. I seek to restore your farms and workshops! I seek to make this a nation once more."

The people formed a large circle with their children running to the center instinctively. Orus watched as thousands of knives presented themselves to the specialists who stepped beyond the reach of the spooked civilians. Soon, calm returned, as the people realized this was not an attack, but instead a demonstration of power.

The critic shouted again. "Well, you have some might, but how will you stop a thousand legions of Todani, er minus the one or two that you dispatched today? We, even with the Elves, cannot face them—especially if those cowardly Dwarves only help from within their borders."

Orus knew the voice had a point. "Well, we are forming our own forces. With many of ..."

As Orus continued, his voice was drowned out by a collective scream of horror. People, as well as Hodan specialists, ran in every direction seeking cover. Soon, the exits of the large square were fouled with people trying to squeeze out through side roads and doorways. People cowered in place, in fear. A large shadow blotted out the sun over the King. And then another.

Closing his eyes, he muttered a prayer. "I hope you are paying attention, My God."

As Orus prayed, an unceremonious crash occurred directly in front of him. Kren and his men surrounded the King instinctively, and the crowd screamed again, but there was no place left to hide. There, in the courtyard, was a copper Dragon with green stripes and a white Dragon with black spots. Both appeared to be young, and Orus was privy to their thoughts. They were arguing.

The copper shouted. "Friends!"

The white hissed. "Not friends. Kill!"

The copper growled and threatened the other. "Nooo! Friends! No Eat!"

"Not friends, EAT!" The white roared at the crowd.

The copper one, being larger, raised up on its hind legs and lit its sibling on fire, albeit temporarily. It screeched in pain and cowered to the copper.

"Fine! Not Eat! Friends!" The white one sat like a tamed wolf biding its time in irritation, disappointed.

Orus looked at them both. *Friends?* the King thought.

"YES!" the white grudgingly agreed.

The copper nodded. "Speak to them."

The crowd was amazed as Orus dismounted, walked over to the cowering white Dragon, and stroked its scales gently.

There was a collective murmur. "What manner of man tames Dragons?"

"I am your friend, white. When you are ready, I will know your name, and we will be true friends," Orus said genuinely. The white cocked its head, listening intently.

The white lizard lowered its head and looked eye to eye with Orus, almost purring as the King stroked its scales. Its eyes darted upward looking at the menacing gaze of his sister, the copper, and then he quietly laid down, much as a dog would do at its master's feet.

"Good people, these are my friends. I do not own them, nor do I command them without their consent. They despise the Todani with decades of pain to remember them by. They are also our allies. What do you think now? Will you join me? With a union of the people, a vast army of trained warriors, the advanced naval weapons of the Vyn, Dwarf, and Hodan, who can oppose us? Especially when being backed by creatures and fierce as these. The days of Todani rule are numbered. What say you, Degran-Eras? Will you join me and reestablish your kingdom to its rightful place of honor?" Orus waited.

As it was with every rowdy crowd, one voice cried out and started the call. Other less brave souls, seeing the jubilance and hope displayed around them, slowly joined in the celebration. Before long, the square was full of cheering souls, raising their fists into the air.

The white Dragon sat up slowly, watching the people cheer him. He was not accustomed to praise of any kind, only abuse. Smiling, the white looked to his sister, the copper. She smiled back, nodding.

"NOT Eat! Friends!" the white said.

Orus chuckled.

* * *

The Todani march toward Whaleford and Redemption had been halted by a brood of Dragons with a vendetta. They flew in, taking turns burning lines of Todani warriors as they hunkered down within the trees for cover. The forests blazed brightly. Their fires could be seen for miles within Degran-Eras and the Kingdom of Dornat Al Fer. Dwarfish hamlets began taking their livestock into their barns and securing all the provisions that they could gather, as unconfirmed reports of the return of marauding Dragons were retold in every tavern in the eastern provinces. The Dwarves were afraid.

The Dwarfish defense forces, slightly a mile from fortress of Redemption, also heard these tales, as fleeing villagers begged them to save their towns. So far, the Dragons were preoccupied with something in the mountains—and no one dared to venture close enough to determine what that would be. The worry was that they would tire of that sport and look for something new to entertain them.

To make matters worse, the Dwarfish troops camped near the human fortress were experiencing a significant morale drain after many realized the gravity of the betrayal the leadership in Dornat Al Fer was involved in. Many of the officers and foot soldiers were a nudge from open rebellion, and the Commanders knew it. Now, reports of an advancing alliance militia from Redemption met the Dwarfish leader's ears.

The Dwarf was concerned until he saw them. Most were farmers with field implements led by a small contingent of Hodan Elites. The legion Commander knew he had the numbers to crush this rabble, but then he reconsidered, wondering where the Hodan scouts might be. They were never in direct sight, but an ever-present threat, just the same.

"Send a rider to intercept and ascertain their intentions, Lieutenant," the Commander stoically ordered.

"I know what their intentions are—and I can't say that I blame them," the Lieutenant murmured a bit too loud.

"Do you have something to say, Sir?" the Commander challenged.

"No, Sir! As you command," the Lieutenant declared, barely holding back his disgust. The tone was not lost on the Dwarfish leader.

A rider was dispatched under a white flag. He rode with purpose toward Kepir.

* * *

Kepir saw a Dwarfish rider coming. He sent his own to intercept. He was in no mood to talk. He carried the favor of the King of Dornat Al Fer. It had been given to Jaruz as a token when they defrocked him and took his command from him. When he was sent to the eastern frontier, the Dwarf put it in his footlocker and forgot about it. He turned his back on his own people to join Orus, and the specialist considered the Dwarf as much a Hodan as those he had sailed here from the Ert with. Kepir did not take that lightly. He would return this favor to the Dwarves and challenge the Dwarfish Commander to a duel for the honor of his kingdom. If he disagreed, Kepir would kill as many Dwarves as was possible before his unit was destroyed.

Uilam and Edmund flanked the Commander, who calmly ordered, "Do we understand our orders, gentlemen?"

Both young men responded affirmatively. Uilam smirked while looking at Edmund. The younger was wearing a new Lieutenant braid proudly.

"What are you looking at, Uilam?" Edmund scowled knowingly, then the boy laughed.

"Enough foolishness, men," Kepir scolded. "The time is at hand for retribution. Hodan will be avenged by my hand, or I will take it out of all of their hides with my men."

After a moment or two and an exchange between the delegates, the riders returned to their respective camps. The Dwarf notified his Commander with Kepir's challenge and the Hodan messenger held out a scroll to his leader.

Kepir broke the seal. "It seems that the Dwarf is not happy with our 'aggressive' posture. He wishes us to cease our approach and return to our fortress immediately. Obviously, this fool thinks us to be under his command. I will show him otherwise."

"Your orders, Sir?" Uilam asked.

"Continue forward and alert our prepositioned scouts to stand by to engage on my command." Kepir looked at both young men with all seriousness, stating, "This is a Hodan custom. It is not your fight. If you wish to return your people to the fortress, do it now. I will sever our ties to the Dwarves with this action—if in fact, there ever was an alliance, aside from some flowery words a herald scratched on paper."

Edmund wore a hurt expression. "I will not turn."

Uilam responded. "Who are we, if not Hodan, Sir? We were not a people until we became a part of yours. Now, we are bound by blood, Sir."

Kepir smiled. "As you wish, young ones, as you wish!"

* * *

The Dwarfish Commander cursed as he read Kepir's missive. "The nerve of that human dung! Who does that nobody believe himself to be?"

A Lieutenant rolled his eyes. "Apparently, Sir, he is the right-hand man to Orus himself. He is also a skilled Hodan specialist. I would imagine him to be very skilled in the combat arts. Perhaps, we should have aided them in their fight. Vice sat on our hands as you commanded."

"You will hold your tongue, or I will have it on a plate, soldier. You forget your place!" the Commander blustered.

"Will you face him and spare your men, or will you risk our lives to hide your shame?" the Lieutenant continued spitefully. "If I survive this encounter, I will petition the King for my release. I will tender my resignation. I have lost faith in what I do. Once, we were the protectors of those who were weak, and in need of a shield. Now, we coddle a vain King's folly." The Lieutenant turned to go.

Swiftly and with precision, the Commander drew his blade and deftly drove it into the back of the departing officer. There was the sound of a blade penetrating flesh, a shout of pain, and a short gurgle, and then the dissenter slumped over dead on the floor. When the Commander turned him over, the look on his face was one of expectation, vice surprise. That is what bothered the Dwarf the most about the incident. That soldier despised him so much for the betrayal of the allies that when his Commander, in turn, betrayed him, it was almost as if the victim expected it and was not surprised in the least by the treachery. The fallen's face spoke loudly in death of what countless others thought of their leadership.

"If Hodan wants to fight, we have the men and the resources to send them all to the Underworld. We will fight them. Prepare the legion for battle. Rally the men," the Commander ordered.

The watch rang bells and sounded horns to muster their forces. Hodan was scarcely a quarter hour away.

* * *

Ma 'Dryna was distraught and angry. She wanted the Dwarves to pay for the death of her beloved. Now, less than one day after all the death and mayhem had subsided, Kepir marched off to certain death against a superior Dwarven army. She prayed earnestly to her god. As she did, voices filled her head. A cacophony of angry shrieks and sentiments, visions of fire, and of eating charred Todani. Abruptly, the High Priestess shook from this nightmare, drenched in sweat and shaking.

"What was that evil?" she muttered alone.

"We are not evil, Priestess," a reptilian voice answered. The Priestess felt a cold-blooded wave of scales in place of her skin momentarily and stood abruptly.

"Who said that!?" Dryna shrieked, rubbing her arms.

"I am Henargya, a friend to Orus and Kepir. Who might you be, Priestess?" the voice demanded.

Dryna was standing, hugging herself and speaking out loud. She was having a one-sided conversation in the medical facilities, while several acolytes watched with interest. Those watching guessed that their Mistress must be having a vision.

"I am Dryna, High Priestess of Likedelir—a Galdrissen. I am also the friend of Orus and Kepir."

"Excellent! Then we will not have to kill you," the voice responded happily.

"Kepir is in danger. Are you nearby? The Dwarves will kill him. He has no chance with the army he possesses, but these Hodan are too proud for their own good." Dryna waited for a response.

"Kepir is in need? I will send a couple from Whaleford. They will come within the hour. Be ready."

"From Whaleford? That is several days' ride? Be ready for what?" Dryna pleaded, but the voice was gone.

* * *

The crowd had dispersed, and Orus and Kren were eating some rations while looking over a map of Whaleford. After determining that the last of the Todani occupiers had fled to the north, been killed by patrols, or eaten by Dragons, the two men came up with a plan to set the defenses and begin to rebuild. Dragons of various ages and sizes flew overhead and perched on cliffsides in plain sight. It was as if they wanted to be seen. They were the deterrent that Orus had prayed for. He thanked his God and put his plan in motion.

"Kren, let us get a move on. Give the orders, and let us depart immediately for Redemption." Orus looked at his surroundings.

The King watched the two Dragons near him. They had not left his side since they had arrived so suddenly, but as if lightning struck it, the white one jerked up straight and grinned maliciously, looking at the copper.

"NOT friends! Kill!" The white licked its maw and laughed.

Orus swallowed hard, reaching for his sword.

The copper saw this and spoke. "We leave for fortress. Mother sends. Not friends there. Must go. Will return."

Orus asked, "The fortress is not safe?"

The white simply responded, "NOT friends. EAT!"

The copper shook her head. "Enemies without. Fortress stands. Mother sends us."

And with that, both thundered up into the sky and were over the mountains within a half hour. Orus sat dumbfounded. He looked at Kren, who shrugged.

"They are fast. Good," Orus stated. "Let us go to Redemption, now!"

The orders were sent out to reaffirm the King's plan, and then the King and his men moved out for home.

* * *

Kepir's men stared at an entire legion of the famed Dwarfish army. They were not carrying wooden weapons now. They were in full plate mail, carrying shields and swords. Each side was flanked by one-hundred crossbows. There were at least one-hundred cavalrymen. The Hodan specialist showed no sign of backing down. He was resigned to die for the honor of Hodan, and he would take as many of them with him as he could—unless their cowardly leader would accept his duel. Kepir thought the traitor would not.

"You are out-matched, Hodan. Retire to your fortress, and I will let you live for another day. If you choose to engage this army, I will destroy you. Every living soul. No quarter!" the Dwarfish Commander declared proudly amid his thousand or so shieldmen.

"Know, worthy opponents, that I, Kepir, of Hodan, challenged your Commander to single combat—to the death, rather than risk the lives of men who had no part in the decisions that led to the betrayal of my people and our alliance." Kepir paused for effect. The field was silent. "He refused, as most cowards do. He would rather you would fight and die for him as if he were a damsel in distress, the horse's ass."

The Dwarfish ranks murmured as many chuckled out loud in disgust. Kepir knew that they did not want this fight, but he also knew that they would engage if told to do so, just as he would if placed in the same predicament.

The Dwarf Commander raised his hand confidently. "Enough! Leave this field, or prepare to die!"

"Hodan! Shield wall up!" Kepir responded. About fifty men and boys cobbled together a shield wall flanked by thirty or so archers. It was certain death. The large bonfires lit the field a bit, but the Dwarves had the advantage, fighting in the descending darkness. They could see in the black of night.

As the charge began, Hodan was encircled. Kepir nodded to his men as if accepting death as a certainty. Swords raised, they prepared for Aeternum.

A loud screeching voice declared from above, "NOT FRIENDS!" No one who heard the growl understood those words but Kepir.

Recognizing the angry growling of his new scaly friends, the Commander shouted, "Get down, men!" as a line of fire erupted from the sky onto the Dwarves.

The Hodan instinctively huddled together with the civilians who dared to follow them into battle in the center of the group, looking fearfully to the pitch-black skies. In the darkness, the sound of leathery flapping wings, screeching, and growling made even the bravest man close his eyes and pray.

The Dwarves ran, shrieking in all directions. Breaking ranks, they became separated. Shrill screams filled the darkness as some were snatched up off the ground. Kepir and his men heard the din, watching expectantly, as limbs fell to the ground from the night above. Unable to see past the firelight, they were forced to sit, watch, and pray that they were not next.

An hour passed as many Dwarves died or ran for their lives. The Dwarfish encampment was now in flames, lighting up the countryside. Kepir sat with his survivors, watching the show. Nine out of ten Hodan challengers survived the Dwarfish charge and the mayhem that had ensued thereafter. It was quiet for the moment, but Redemption's warriors decided to huddle in place until light so they could effectively see what they were dealing with. None of them believed they would actually be able to deal with the unseen threat, but seeing the enemy allowed them to at least try to defend themselves the best that they were able.

A few hours later, while Hodan tried to rest, the legion shieldmen were forced to form square, hearing the return of flapping wings. Two loud crashes in the darkness and just out of sight caused a momentary murmur among the Hodan. Then there was a thunderous thudding of heavy steps as two Dragons made their way toward Hodan's position. Kepir stood and looked.

"Get down, Sir!" Edmund pleaded.

"What difference will it make, son?" the leader replied.

"Kepir FRIEND! Not Eat!" A large white reptilian head moved out of the darkness and down to eye level with the Hodan leader.

"I am Kepir," the specialist said, swallowing hard.

Then another voice responded. "Apologies, Master Kepir. He is still a young one. Mother sent us to help. Dryna also."

"Dryna?" Kepir asked incredulously.

The white juvenile responded with apparent disappointment. "Dryna FRIEND ... NOT Eat."

"Eat the Dwarves!" the copper responded in an exasperated tone.

"Eat DWARVES!" the white said gleefully, running off into the darkness.

"You are the Dragons from the Temple? Henargya is your mother?" Kepir asked.

The copper responded. "Yes, warrior. Our Mother. Dryna is a friend, too. Must go back. Orus comes."

"Orus comes!?" Kepir exclaimed.

Edmund and Uilam asked simultaneously, "Are you talking to those creatures, Sir?"

"A long story, my friends. The two who saved our skins are here apparently at the request of the High Priestess. Perhaps, her God favors us after all. The King returns to the fortress. We must depart for Redemption immediately."

Groaning, the exhausted militia picked up their weapons. They stole a few horses that were not eaten and a few carts that were still functional and collected the Hodan dead and any salvageable weaponry they could find. Another day for pyres tomorrow.

The Hodan trudged back to their beaten fortress.

In the distance, Kepir could hear a roar and crunching. In his mind, he could hear, "Dwarves, tasty!"

The specialist swallowed hard and shuddered at the thought. The carnage of the two Dragons was inescapable and surrounded Hodan as they marched away. In awe, the legionnaires pondered the scene. The fact that this destruction required only the efforts of two Dragon whelps was not lost on the humans as they wondered about adults they had not encountered yet. These were the children. These Dwarves were not farmers. Even though they had been caught off guard, they were still a formidable force to be reckoned with—a feared band of professional warriors.

The men were secretly worried about the prowess of adult Dragons and what would happen to their own person if they were accidentally angered.

Chapter 15

Whaleford was secured. The last of the Todessen forces were routed by the Vynwrathian Rangers as the Scourge fled north. The Dragons had stopped the southward march of the northern enemy at the nearby mountains northwest of the famed Degran Jackrabbit Canyon. There, Hodan scouts reported that thousands of the enemy camped, licking their wounds and trying to regroup. It would be some time before the aggressors were capable of mounting another push toward Whaleford, which was now several days march south of their position. The enemy apprehensively held their ground, their leaders fearing that an attempt at advancing on their goal would inevitably be met with new attacks by the Dragons from the sky and Dole'kyn or Vyn attacks on the ground. The Scourge still outnumbered the human insurgency by a factor of two to one, but they were down to half of their army in a few short days. They were now scattered and poorly supplied, having lost their only southern logistics depot at Whaleford, and they knew they were too far from home to hope for help from Haeldrun Ir.

* * *

It seemed to Hodan that the Todani were in no hurry to test the field, and their hesitation gave Orus and Vynwratha the chance they needed to consolidate their forces. The two kingdoms deployed them strategically, forming a hasty, but solid defense north of their new port city. Orus's navy owned the seas to the east and south of Whaleford. The Orcs witnessed the prowess of their new neighbors to the east and immediately signed a binding truce with the Commanders of the human legions. Overnight, Ynus-Grag began permitting Hodan ships to dock at their crude Orcish harbors in the southern kingdom.

The Orcish Chieftains were encouraged by the human and Elf victories on land, but the lasting impression of Hodan strength was steeled when they witnessed four Hodan ships engage the feared Todessen navy, south of their own shores. On three separate occasions, the Todani pushed their advantage, but each time, the encounters resulted in the humans chasing off the aggressors from Haeldrun Ir. Only once did a Todani vessel dare to challenge the Hodan at sea. After a short, but loud engagement, the enemy ship listed to one side, burning and sinking far off the southern shores of Ynus-Grag. The Orcs celebrated their newfound security with a feast. Not long after, the Orcs decided to strengthen their bond with Orus, and a delegation was sent to Whaleford, pushing for a tentative alliance with the human kingdom.

With this unexpected addition to Orus's coalition, Whaleford was secure on every side, but the north.

* * *

Orus was wroth. His anger was felt by anyone in his immediate vicinity. Angrily, he sat at a table in his small command tent, sipping mead. The smoke of the endless pyres polluted the morning air. One pyre, in particular, fouled the morning more than others, in the King's opinion.

The Dwarf was laid atop an altar built for a King. His armor was spotless, shining gold. The warrior held his sword in his hand as if readied for battle. Orus had paid his respects, consoled the devastated Dryna, and dropped a small bag of coin at the site. Words were said about the deceased, many songs were played, and the people cried for their deliverer. The scene stoked the anger of Orus.

The command tent's flap was open and flapped gently as a slight breeze kicked up. The Hodan King looked toward the destroyed fortress. He saw refugees crammed in every nook and cranny. He sighed, drinking more.

"They come from the north, My King," Kepir said as a matter of fact. He was speaking of a new development—Dwarves.

"You say that Hamrick left us all to die here?" Orus replied calmly, watching the short-statured refugees begging for mercy from the Degran guards.

"Yes, Sire. That swine pulled back his troops as we had feared that he might. We were able to capture one of the Dwarfish General's scribes who wasn't eaten by that white Dragon," Kepir spat out of the tent door in disgust.

"Ah, so, how did that go, brother?" The King's face sneered, knowingly.

"After an hour of *interrogation*, my men were able to extract knowledge that my King should know."

Kepir was deadly serious. Orus only saw that face on his friend when the subject he was about to talk about involved necessary evil. Looking at his own left upper arm, Orus could still see the tattoo of another life—a wolf, howling at the moon. Long ago, Orus had burned the moon from his arm with a brand, in penance for the things that Kepir was about to suggest. Kepir had the same tattoo. In days gone by, Orus's King had listened to similar reports from Orus himself.

"Brother," Kepir said uncharacteristically to his King, "we have been through much together. Much of it, we shall never speak of again. War is an abomination, and killing is killing, but we know more than most of how brutal battle can be."

Orus frowned, staring at the moon above Kepir's tattoo. "What do you have for me, my friend?" the King somberly replied.

"The scribe squealed to save his own life, as we knew that he would. His report was that Hamrick is in league with the Todessen in Haeldrun Ir. He said the Dwarf signed a peace treaty with the Scourge to secure his hold on the lands. The agreement was that Dornat Al Fer's legions would pull back and allow the invasion of the Toads to occur unimpeded." Kepir stood, pouring himself a mead, and threw it back in a gulp.

"Hamrick did this? Are you sure?" Orus responded, knowing the report was accurate.

Reaching into his pouch, Kepir retrieved a vellum and handed it to his King.

Reading it, Orus scowled, sighing forcefully. He looked at his friend with reddened eyes, gritting his teeth.

"We should be smart, My King," Kepir said, returning to a professional soldier once again.

"They must pay, and dearly, Kepir."

"Agreed, but to what extent, Your Majesty?" the scout responded.

"In elder days, I would have mustered my legions and marched into Dornat Al Fer, burning it to the ground, but alas, we barely hold Whaleford, and we have Orcs holding our western flank—who would have guessed that five years ago?" Orus stood. He began to pace angrily.

"True, My King. Hodan cannot march into Dornat Al Fer and win in a face-to-face match-up, but we have the means to make them pay."

Kepir's lip curled back, reminding Orus of a snarling wolf. The image it conjured stirred memories that made Orus smile momentarily.

"He needs to die for Jaruz, Kepir. Perhaps his whole family should perish in retribution?"

To Kepir, Orus's face looked darker than it had in ages.

"My King, our vow. Remember the words we promised after Jabir!" Kepir closed his eyes to collect himself.

"Yes, yes!" Orus bellowed angrily. "I know what I said. I know what I meant. I know what we need to atone for. Do not lecture me!"

"My apologies, Sire," Kepir said, looking downward in shame.

"No apologies, brother. You have said nothing wrong." Orus scratched his beard, collecting himself. He drank another mead. He had consumed quite a few by this time.

"What would you command, Sire?" Kepir asked, standing tall.

"Kill him. Kill Hamrick," Orus said curtly.

"It shall be done, Sire," Kepir said, preparing to go.

"Wait." Orus ordered. "Kill him, but make it look like his allies to the north did it. Do it silently. Do it personally, brother. I trust only you to get in and get out without being found. Make it look as if the Dwarf was killed by the hand he took as a partner over his trusted alliance."

"Yes, Sire. It shall be done. I will depart at sundown. It will look as if a Todani assassin infiltrated their palace and killed him with poison and Todani blades." Kepir looked at the decimated fort before him. "Gods know that the dung from the north left me plenty of their blades and tools of the trade."

"Good," Orus said with a twinge of guilt in his voice. "This is just retribution. If we are lucky and they are caught in this ruse, the remaining royalty may seek revenge and attack the Toad Kingdom directly. That would get the Todani attention, and quickly."

"Perhaps." Kepir said, nodding and finishing off another mug the King had handed him. "And if we are even luckier, the Toads might just pull back a good portion of the forces to our north to reinforce their own kingdom's borders."

"We shall begin conscripting regulars in the morning." Orus said plainly. "Tell your Commanders that any able-bodied man or woman between fifteen and fifty will be required to train with the Hodan military. Everyone must be able to put up a fight if we are to secure a homeland. This is not optional."

"As you command, Sire." Kepir said, bowing. "I will pass the word, gather my things, and attend to my mission. If I am captured, it has been an honor serving with you, Sire, and a privilege to serve the Champion of a God."

"Do not die, brother!" Orus said with a hint of sadness. "I would miss your company."

Kepir nodded with a brief smile, leaving the tent to attend to his mission.

* * *

It was night. The specialist crouched silently behind a large pile of rock that was stacked off of the side of a large road. It was a brisk evening, and the sky was overcast. There was no moonlight, but Kepir remained hidden, as he looked out over the well-lit route. The paved road was impressive, and it stretched off toward the woods to the west. There, it met a big intersection that sent similar thoroughfares north, south, and east, while the original route continued off into the tree line and out of sight toward the western horizon. This was the main entryway into Dornat Al Fer. Guardhouses and sentry posts were located all along the route to the main gate to the mountain kingdom.

It was dark, but the assassin knew that his short foes were very capable and could see as well in the darkness as in the light. Using caution, he kept cover as well as he could manage, creeping closer to his objective—the main entrance. He moved toward a commotion. There, he found a small guard hut with several guards bantering, drinking wine, and throwing dice at a table. These, the specialist surmised, were the higher-ranking guardsmen. The peons would be walking the wall or covering a guard position. Kepir thanked the Gods as the game had taken on a bit of a party atmosphere. The Dwarves were into their bottles and laughing loudly as they told stories of glory days. The noise and inattention made his movements that much easier.

Kepir used the racket as cover, making it to the gate without incident, but just before he was able to enter, he came upon a young Dwarfish sentry at his post who stood in his path.

"It is your lucky day, son," Kepir whispered under his breath, reaching for a needle and a bottle containing an agent created to temporarily incapacitate its victim. Hiding in plain sight, he snuck up behind the young sentry, drugging him.

"Thyriz! Where are you, boy?" An older Dwarf cried out in irritation from a location not far from the unconscious sentry. "If you're sleeping, I'll kick you in your arse, boy!"

The Dwarf made his way with irritation, directly to the position occupied by Kepir's victim. Expertly, the Hodan hid in shadows and found concealment behind a stack of crates nearby. The specialist witnessed the anger of the Dwarfish Sergeant, who was not amused with his *sleeping* sentry.

"You lazy son of a whore!" the Sergeant bellowed, kicking the young man in his backside, "Get up!"

Thyriz, the sentry, did not move. This concerned his Sergeant, who softened his approach.

"Hey, boy! Are you all right?" the Sergeant questioned with concern, rolling the younger Dwarf over and onto his back.

The Dwarf squad leader could see the boy was unconscious and unresponsive, although there was no obvious sign of attack. He was breathing, albeit when the Sergeant checked, his eyes showed white, as if they were rolled back in his head.

"Help! I need a healer over here and now! Hurry up!" the elder Dwarf shouted.

The Sergeant was now fully occupied with the urgent matter of his sentry's health. Kepir took this new disturbance as his cue to depart the area, sliding quietly within the available shadows into Dornat Al Fer. Moving carefully toward the main gathering places of the large city under the mountain, he stopped to listen to conversations on the street. Taking the information that he had gathered and comparing it to what he heard from the locals, the assassin tried to ascertain if the intelligence obtained from the Dwarf captive at Redemption was genuine or a just lie to save his skin. Kepir looked at his hand-drawn maps and oriented them appropriately. To his surprise and disgust, he realized that the Dwarfish captive had spoken true, spilling all the information necessary for the Hodan specialist to carry out his covert plans. Shrugging, he rolled up the skins and quietly stuffed them into his satchel.

* * *

It had taken several more hours to navigate the vast halls of Dornat Al Fer without detection. A few close calls with the locals now had the specialist moving with extra care. The eyesight of Dwarves in the dark was a primary concern, but the Elves of the Ert had shown the humans ways around it. Using elemental Elfish magic and meticulous camouflage techniques, the professional scout managed to avoid contact with Dwarfish residents, civilian or military.

The door before him was enormous, even by human standards. Kepir guessed a full-grown hill giant could walk into the Dwarfish royal chambers without even stooping to avoid the top of the door. Periodically, a guard or a servant would open the large entryway. Kepir could see that the doors were at least four inches thick. They appeared to be jewel-encrusted, he guessed steel-reinforced, and for good measure completely encased in solid gold. When the activity at the entrance began to wane, the Hodan warrior made his way as close to the entryway as possible, while avoiding detection.

Kepir searched the area for an alternative way in, spying a window that was propped open above the large golden doors. It was at least twenty feet up a sheer wall. The scout figured it was open for air circulation. Its size and shape would be exactly what was needed, if he could not directly walk in the entrance when the doors were opened by those who were coming and going. His only concern was that he could not see, from his vantage, whether the opening was barred or not.

While looking for a way to climb up a sheer wall in front of a well-lit and guarded position, Kepir hid. He knew there was no way he was going to get into that window without the guard finding him. As he thought of the other alternatives, the scout ducked farther into the shadows, hearing a voice approaching from within the royal chambers. It was muffled by the stone and metal, but he could still make out what was said in the Dwarfish tongue.

"Good evening, good lady. I will return in the morning!" a young female voice said enthusiastically.

"Be well, girl. I will tend to his whims while you are gone!" the older voice replied, chuckling. "Bring me a scone or two tomorrow morning, will you?"

The door cracked open almost silently. "Of course, Beletha! I will bring the blueberry ones you love so much!"

A guard acknowledged the lady-in-waiting, and she curtsied properly to the man-at-arms. "Good evening, My Lady." His eyes were on the lass before him. As he smiled at the pretty girl's face, his admiration was interrupted by a random movement that caught his eye. He snapped his head smartly toward the shadows, looking intently for anything out of the ordinary. When he found nothing, the guard rushed to the closing door with his sword drawn on a hunch. Searching intently, the sentry found nothing to speak of, except the familiar face of the older lady who relieved his love interest of her duties every night. Still feeling that something was amiss, but finding nothing out of the ordinary, the sentry shook his head, reasoning that he was just tired or seeing the brazier fires reflect off of the gilded doors to the chamber. He returned to his post outside, closing the hatch securely behind him. He looked up expectantly, but the girl was gone. Sighing, the Dwarf guard resumed his position, sheathing his sword.

Kepir let out a relieved sigh, lowered himself to the floor silently. He held a poisoned Todani dagger in his hand. The guard did not know how fortunate he was that he had left when he did. Kepir had fully resolved to kill the Dwarf, but relented as the sentry decided to walk out of the door.

"No need to make a mess when no mess is needed," the voice of his mentor and trainer echoed in his mind.

Before moving gracefully through the darkened antechamber, the Hodan swiftly bound the handles of the doors together. Then he pulled out a set of tools and expertly worked the large lock, securing the golden doors so as to at least delay further interference with his objectives. Down the hall, he could hear contented humming and even a bit of singing. He slid silently by an open kitchen where an older Dwarfish lady was making a meal for herself. Looking around intently, the assassin gathered that there was only a skeleton crew working during the evenings. Nodding in approval, the specialist continued down the darkened, ornate passageway unhindered.

Minutes later, judgment had found its way to the King's door. Kepir heard the familiar voice of a nobleman lecturing a young lad on the virtues of his servitude. The conversation sickened the assassin, reinforcing his resolve, as he was forced to listen to a lecture about how *fortunate* the lad was to polish the King's shoes and wash his dirty underclothing. Kepir's anger began to burn brighter.

"Boy, your family is well-off, because of our benevolence. Never forget that. Never betray he who feeds you."

Kepir beheld the inner chamber through a small window in the door designed for a sentry to check someone desiring entrance to the royal sleeping chamber. The Hodan warrior saw no such sentry. He only saw the boy picking up shards of gilded Dwarfish pottery. Apparently, the boy had dropped a washbasin or vase. The King was lecturing him.

"I apologize, Your Majesty," the boy replied with penance. "I will do better, Sire."

The boy bowed, opening the door, leaving it absent-mindedly ajar in his hurry to escape, and Kepir slid into the corner of the royal sleeping chambers, as if a venomous shadow. There, the assassin stayed, looking about the spacious sleeping quarters in disbelief. This King's bed chambers dwarfed Orus's entire palace at Warrior's Crossing in Hodan.

Why would this dung betray those who have nothing, when he and those he loves have everything? Kepir pondered silently, never taking his eyes off of his prey.

The specialist reasoned. "Pride was an answer. Envy another."

Sliding out a blackened blade, the Shadow of Death coated it with the vilest of Todani poison. Kepir's merciless eyes waited for his chance.

* * *

Orus looked out over the field before him. All around Redemption, the call had gone out for those between the ages of fifteen and fifty to report for training as foot soldiers for the glorious legions of Hodan. Orus knew that very few of these refugees would actually make the grade and join the ranks of an actual legion, but he needed warriors, and badly, at this point.

The King of Hodan reckoned that he had gained just shy of ten more legions of warriors from the rabble that migrated to his broken fortress. To the old warrior's surprise, almost five-hundred Dwarves actually showed their faces. They huddled together on the right flank of the gaggle of the Rynn's downtrodden. As the King watched, he detected the fear and desperation on the faces of these shorter, but better-fed additions to his military forces.

"Lieutenant," Orus said to Uilam, who was standing nearby, "go over to that group and ask them of their intentions?" The King gestured toward the Dwarves.

"At once, Sire." Uilam saluted, grabbing a squad of his own men. They made their way to the Dwarfish group.

The Dwarves stood closer together as they saw the riders approaching. Some held hands. Older Dwarves leaned on each other with tears in their eyes. There were young, old, men, and women. A few of the rabble had armed themselves with farm implements. Uilam knew them well. They were peasants from the northern and western villages destroyed by Dragon attacks. They, too, had no place to call home, and it looked as if their King had abandoned their families to die from fire or starvation. They had turned a blind eye to Redemption and watched it burn on two occasions. The young Lieutenant was torn between pity and disgust as he dismounted his steed.

"Who is in charge here?" Uilam demanded.

The crowd murmured. They looked around bewildered. There was a buzz of confusion.

"Silence!" a Sergeant growled, producing a flail, which resulted in the Dwarfish ranks tightening their group and staring at the humans with fear.

Uilam nodded at his man in approval. "All right then, if you have no leader, I will appoint one for the time being."

Uilam looked around intently, finding one Dwarf who seemed unfazed by the situation he was in. Nodding quietly, Uilam pointed at the Dwarfish middle-aged man. "You there!"

People looked around in confusion and then behind them.

"Move!" Uilam demanded harshly, pushing into the crowd with his men around him. The people parted widely, but one Dwarf stood silently, closing his eyes expectantly. Uilam smiled at the demeanor of the Dwarf.

"My Lord, what can I do for you?" the Dwarf replied sarcastically. He was not impressed, nor intimidated by the lad in armor.

"Who are you, Dwarf?" Uilam interrogated. "Why do you not wet yourself like these other goat-herders?"

"I have seen my share of warriors and battles, son," the Dwarf said with a bit of condescension. "Your little display does not intimidate me. I have seen the Hodan fight before."

Uilam was intrigued. With a furrowed brow, the legionnaire questioned the Dwarf further. "If you had, then you would know not to trifle with King Orus, of Hodan."

The Dwarf frowned, looking back at the pyres. "I knew Jaruz, boy. I knew him before you were born. We fought side by side. I know Orus as well."

Uilam perked up at the statement. "You knew Lord Jaruz ... Orus? How? When? A likely story. You would say anything to save your sorry Dwarfish hide."

"Stand down, lad," a deep, familiar voice said calmly as he trotted up on a large white warhorse. "He did know Jaruz, and I know him."

Uilam turned to see Orus had come to find out what the delay was. Uilam bowed with respect, sheathing his sword and stepping out of the way.

"Orus, how have you been, old friend?" the Dwarf asked.

"I have been well, Tavro." The King looked around. "That is, until this recent Dwarfish treachery. That is why I sent my zealous man to question the intentions of this group."

Tavro snorted. "He is a bit full of himself, old man," the Dwarf quipped.

Tavro smiled wider as he saw Uilam begin to protest, but immediately cease his complaints when Orus raised his hand preemptively.

"It's been over five years. Where have you hidden yourself?" Orus asked.

"Almost eight! I was reassigned after they defrocked my mentor and sent him here," the Dwarf said plainly. "I did my time, resigned my commission, and had a farmstead a day north of here. I always told myself that I would ride here and see him again for old time's sake, but alas, the farm never gave me a chance. We were poor, but happy there. It seems the gods have treated you well, good King."

Orus saw Tavro wipe a tear from his eye and listened intently.

"I had a wife and a son," Tavro said, frowning.

Orus keyed in on the word *had*, nodding silently.

"Dragons came and then the Todani who ran through us, doing what Todani do. When I heard about what happened here, I knew it was Hamrick, that bastard." Tavro's fists clenched, and his face twisted. "That dishonorable ass has tainted all of our people with his treachery! He should be sent to the catacombs where he belongs."

"So, what of your intention, Sir?" Orus responded seriously.

"Well, I have nothing to lose, Hodan." Tavro's face was blank. Sadness hid behind his eyes, and he had begun to wring his hands as his lip began to quiver, ever-so-slightly.

Uilam interjected. "That is King Orus, to you, fool!"

Orus raised his hand again, quieting his man. "Be that as it may, what is your intention?"

"I would raise an army of my people to fight alongside Hodan to redeem our honor and earn a place to live in peace, outside of the taint of this kingdom," Tavro spat in disgust.

Orus raised his eyebrows, looking at Uilam. Uilam shrugged, nodding in response.

"Get with my Lieutenant, Uilam," Orus pointed at the man to his left. "He will get you equipped and assign you to the proper trainers."

Tavro bowed. "Thank you, King Orus. I will not disappoint you."

"I remember who you are, Dwarf. Jaruz always spoke highly of you. He thought of you as the son he never had. Now, we avenge him, your disgraced people, and the betrayed of Degran-Eras. No longer will this rabble be of many places. We are all Hodan now. Time for you all to learn what that really means."

"Gentlemen, ladies," Uilam said with newfound respect, "let us make our ways to the fortress and see what we have available in the way of armor and weapons. We have a fine selection of Todani wares."

Uilam's men chuckled, as did Tavro. The rest of the Dwarves did not see the humor in the statement.

* * *

Kepir found himself in the bathhouse portion of the King's night chamber. A Dwarfish young woman was washing the King's back. The assassin waited patiently as she not only cleaned her King, but also massaged his incredible vanity. Listening to the Dwarf prattle on about his exploits on the battlefield and with the ladies made the assassin nauseous. The lady smiled politely and nodded periodically, pretending to hear everything the old King said, but Kepir knew that this one had learned the art of selective listening long ago.

"Thank you, my dear," the King said in approval as the young woman helped him into a night robe.

"Yes, Sire. It is my pleasure," the young lady stated respectfully with a smile that appeared genuine, but Kepir knew she had also learned that skill a long time ago.

"You are dismissed for the evening. Please tell the lady on duty when you leave the residence. She is all that is left for tonight, except for that damned, clumsy little boy." The King smiled, thinking of the lad. He really was fond of him.

"Of course, Your Majesty. Be well, and goodnight," the young woman said, bowing and leaving the bathroom.

She closed the door securely, leaving the King to his own mutterings as he looked at his face in a polished golden mirror. He could see the lines of age creeping up at the edges of his mouth and eyes. Lamenting his present reflection, he was startled by when a dark figure appeared, as if from thin air, behind him.

"Oh, my Gods, you startled me, you fool!" Hamrick whispered, as if he knew that Kepir was coming.

Confused, the assassin remained in the shadows and kept his blacked face below his hood. He said nothing.

"You brought me the information I require to carry out our plans, did you not? Well?" The King looked with anticipation at the black shadow.

Kepir nodded once and motioned for the King to come over to where he crouched. The assassin reached into his satchel as if he was retrieving papers, but feeling around in the bag, he knew that there were only vials filled with various ways to die. He pulled out his small roll of maps, showing them to the King.

Smiling, Hamrick sauntered over confidently to the dark figure. Kepir stood ready, dagger palmed, his eyes darting around the room in search of anything that would interfere with his plan. There was not a soul present, but the King and him.

"Why so secretive, friend?" Hamrick asked, holding out his hand expectantly.

Without warning, Kepir struck with vicious precision. Hamrick had a look of confusion on his face as the dagger severed the Dwarf's vocal cords without puncturing a major artery.

The cat wanted to play a bit longer with his mouse. Kepir eased the monarch to the floor as he gurgled in protest, clutching his throat. The Dwarf's face twisted in horror as he realized he had been betrayed. The taste of his blood was rancid, and he felt his jaw locking closed as his body tensed up involuntarily. Muscle control was rapidly failing, and the pain of full-body cramping began to take over. Hamrick now writhed in pain, but his movements were involuntary. The shadowed attacker now stooped with malice over the paralyzed body of the King of the Dwarves.

Whispering in his victim's ear, Kepir hissed, "King Orus knows of your treachery, you vile worm. My liege sends his regards. This poison is a gift of the Toads defeated at Redemption. They used it on many innocents while you fattened yourself, here in your chambers." Kepir smiled revealing white, but entirely human teeth.

Hamrick struggled, but could not move. He was losing his vision. In the blurry, dim light, the dying King took short, sharp breaths as the Dwarf felt that his killer's face resembled that of a Denir, come to snatch his soul to the Underworld. Struggling to live, he knew it was no use. Still, he struggled, knowing the end was near.

Kepir watched over his victim, pretending to enjoy the moment. The smell of fecal matter and urine now filled the immediate area. It would not be long now. He must see the end, to be sure. The assassin decided to rub salt in the wounds of his helpless mark.

"Know this ... as the Denir claim your wretched soul ... when you are forced to roam the catacombs for eternity ..." Kepir lowered his face nose to nose with the victim. Death was imminent as the stench wafted from Hamrick's lips. "... Your wife and children will join you shortly. This is all of your doing."

At this point, Hamrick was without the use of any bodily function, but his eyes, and tears fell freely from both of them. Kepir could see his pleading as the Dwarf faded, facing eternity, and the sentence he had left for his loved ones.

The assassin scanned around his position. It was still quiet, save for the sound of brazier fires and a bit of industry from somewhere outside of the sleeping chambers. He looked at the King again. He was dead. His face was an expression of death and pain. The body was twisted unnaturally and covered in feces and urine. Kepir decided to leave his victim's eyes open in that look of pleading terror. The Hodan warrior knew everything he told the Dwarf was a bluff. He would not dispatch the entire royal family, but he wanted to make the traitor suffer as much as possible before he went to the other side. Fear was a powerful tool, and Kepir used it well.

Gathering his things, the specialist changed clothing, burning his old tunic and pants in a nearby furnace. He cleaned the area, covering his tracks as only a Hodan scout or Todani assassin could do. Looking back over at his handiwork, he felt a pang of guilt. It had been over ten years since his last assassination. He had killed many on the battlefield, but he had really come to hate this kind of work.

His regrets would not fade quickly as he looked at the twisted corpse before him. He knew that somewhere there would be wailing and despair, for even a wretch like this had those who cared for him. There were at least a few close friends and family who knew him and loved him.

Kepir slithered quietly and invisibly out of the chambers. He had traveled half a day's ride from the gates of Dornat Al Fer when the first servant found their King in his bathrobe on the floor.

Chapter 16

"Who did this?" the Todani roared.

"We have no idea, Sire," a scribe replied with a bit of fear.

The Todani King threw his goblet across the obsidian-walled room. It clattered across the shiny, black, floor and its gold glimmered in the brazier light of the large throne room. Many attendants scurried here and there, feigning industry, while trying to avoid the gaze of their furious leader. All present knew that Lyax was known to be an unbalanced King. No soul knew if they would be the recipient of his ire, even if they had no hand in what had caused the King's misfortune. Innocents were often killed to defuse the tyrant's mood. No one wished to be the sacrifice of the day.

"Sulfga!" the King bellowed, "get your ass over here, now!"

"Yes, Sire," a more prominent, armored warrior replied loudly, jogging before the throne. He bowed.

"What in the Underworld is happening? What assassin killed our fool in Dornat Al Fer? This has all of the makings of a stupid move that you would make. Did you order this?" Lyax stood drawing a sword from a scabbard hanging from the arm of the throne. Two guards with long, boar spears stepped forward to aid their King if needed.

"It was not I, Your Majesty. I swear," Sulfga responded without batting an eye. He stood stoically.

Lyax sighed, sitting and sheathing the sword. "Sulfga, why? We had everything going to plan. Who would do such a thing?"

"The Elves perhaps, My Liege? They are quite stealthy and ruthless!"

Sulfga offered.

"Hmm," Lyax nodded, "astute observation for an oaf."

Sulfga nodded and stood taller after the guarded compliment.

"But it makes no sense, General," Lyax said, rubbing the back of his bald head. Two Todani girls moved up to their King from his flanks and massaged his shoulders with care. The King nodded in appreciation.

Sulfga furrowed his brow. "They hate the Dwarves for Edhelseere. They fought them for almost a century over that slight."

Lyax calmed, trying to collect his thoughts. He replied, "True, but Lourama allied with the Dwarves after the return of their lands. We have recently seen them fight together on the field of battle. The Vyn have even made peace with Orcs!"

"Not so, Your Majesty. If you would entertain my reasoning," Sulfga stated respectfully.

"Go on, man. What do you have to say," the King skeptically said, rolling his eyes.

"When have we seen the Dwarves come to anyone's aid, except to provide flank security for the humans?" Sulfga stopped, awaiting permission to continue.

Lyax rubbed his thin chin hair. "Go on."

The two girls stopped their ministrations and stepped aside, bowing to their King.

"I have never witnessed the Dwarves march to battle in aid of the Vyn. To be truthful, Your Majesty, they never marched to defend their human allies either. If anything, they were the Hodan's rivals in most instances. Hamrick resents Orus—er, he did resent. He hampered that human's gains with every step the Degran earned." Sulfga stood silently, awaiting his King to process his proposal.

"You know, Sulfga, you amaze at times." Lyax smiled, accepting a new goblet of wine as he continued. "You are correct, General. I have not actually witnessed those little motherless whores to the south do anything, but try to maintain their grip on power. Everything was done to maintain the status quo. The only time they were actually deployed to aid the humans," Lyax stopped mid-thought, laughing loudly, "they pulled back, didn't they—left the fort to our raiders!"

Sulfga nodded and bowed in recognition of his King's words, adding nothing.

"Give this man a drink, porter," the King ordered. "A toast, Sulfga! To Vyn atrocities! May they turn the Dwarfish focus southward."

The General raised his glass, quickly swallowing the vintage.

"But Sire, no one knows of our agreement with Hamrick—and our Dwarfish spies tell us that it appears that a Todani assassin performed this kill. I have to say, if the reports are accurate, it does appear that one of ours did this—or one who knows our ways too well."

Lyax grimaced at the words of his General, but he knew that he was right.

"Your Majesty, may I suggest that we pull our armies back to Haeldrun Ir. The Dwarves will surely march on our port city in retaliation. This battle has been coming for over a century, Sire." Sulfga frowned and handed his empty goblet to the nearest porter.

Lyax nodded somberly. "Pull our armies home before those damned humans, or their Dragons, kill them all and leave us defenseless. What of the Dwarfish legions? Do they move northward yet?"

"Scouts say they are gathering at the Dwarfish capital, Sire. It will be soon."

"Set the defenses. Call our navy back to defend our shores. Bring back the deployed forces in Degran-Eras, but leave a deterrent force to stymie any human aspirations. That fool, Orus, only has six or seven legions of trained men. Leave enough to make it very costly to attack our territories. I am almost certain he will see an opportunity to push his borders. Do your best to make it a costly expedition, Sulfga."

Lyax sat back wearily on his throne with a thump. He pressed his fingers into his forehead, as if he felt a headache coming. The two girls appeared again to the appreciation of their King.

In the shadows, just out of view, Vyqua listened intently to the report of the General. She hid her smile behind a veil. She wondered if her assassin-suitor had killed the King for some reason, while attempting to deliver the information the Dwarf had requested. She had not seen her admirer in some time. The Princess had no answers, but things were now in motion. Quietly, she exited the throne room and made her way to her private quarters.

* * *

The family of the fallen King was not seen publicly for several days, as the people of Dornat Al Fer all publicly mourned the passing of their monarch. The absence was not out of the ordinary, and many saw it as business as usual. Still, all the people of the kingdom wore traditional black clothing, and all revels were postponed for later dates. All knew that the Queen Mother had assumed the crown, and with that, nothing would seemingly change for the foreseeable future. Many held the royal family in respect, but the lack of interaction with the commoners of the realm was noted by the average soul on the street. The average Dwarf felt no real animosity toward their royal family, but they did not know their rulers very well either. One crowned head worked as well as another in the reckoning of many. Most simply saw them as a figurehead that sat in power over everything, but the average Dwarf had had no emotional investment in whoever was seated upon the throne. Real-life struggles and everyday industry were more of a concern. Providing for their families was their priority. It was not as rosy in the hamlets and villages as people in the capital believed. Many poor struggled, and the death of one wealthy, pampered monarch was of little consequence to the farmer in the hills.

The lack of any interactive leadership left most folk more apt to identify with their local lord than the King. The death of Hamrick, the senior, was shocking, but did not stir the public emotion that the Queen imagined it would. In her grief, she was disillusioned with the crown, quickly deciding to hand rule over to her son, who was barely of age to be considered an adult.

"They dress the part, don't they, my boy," the Queen said with disdain, looking at the military uniform her son wore. He was adorned as a hero, but had never held his sword in opposition to anything other than a practice partner.

"Surely they do, Mother," the young Dwarf replied smugly, looking at the cords and ribbons that adorned his attire. Each meant something, but the boy did not know what any of it represented. He had never been interested in the military until the death of his father.

The Queen Mother preened her son's uniform. She checked every seam and hounded her ladies-in-waiting to make sure that all was perfect. Squires polished the royal sword and shield. Hamrick II did little to nothing, other than stand around with entitlement, receiving the labors of those who served him. The servants sighed, seeing that nothing would seemingly change with the new King's disposition. All went about their usual business, pretending to be grateful, smiling to the faces of those they served.

"Now, my son," the Queen said lovingly, "show these ingrates who you are. If they will not mourn your father, make them love you."

The Queen stood proudly, looking at her son in full dress uniform. He looked very much like her husband had when the two met all those years ago.

"Once I am King, I will avenge the death of Father with a river of Todani blood," the Dwarfish Prince replied with angry confidence. "Rest assured, Mother, I will send our forces to burn and pillage the lands of those wretched savages to the north. They will not escape punishment for their treachery."

The Queen clapped at her son's speech. She kissed his cheek, eliciting a smile from the young Dwarf who hugged his mother tenderly.

"Do not fear, Mother. I will carry on. The Dwarves will remain when all else is pulled asunder. Haya blesses our virtuous nation for all of the years we have protected the light."

"The Generals have assured me, son, that the armies are almost readied for the invasion of the wretched northland."

"Excellent news, Mother," the Prince said, taking his mother's arm as her escort. "We will make them pay, as Father did all of those years ago."

"Let us go, son," the Queen said beaming at her only son. "Your crown awaits."

The two left the chambers, where barely two weeks prior, the King was found dead on the floor. The Queen's eyes strayed to the very spot where her Hamrick was found. Frowning, she dabbed her eyes with a handkerchief, swallowing hard, and then turned back to her son's serious face. He was doing his best to maintain an air of strong, balanced leadership, and this made her smile.

A carriage waited outside of the royal chambers. It took the remaining royal family down long gilded streets. The city view rose out of sight, stretching upward into the darkness of the cavern ceiling hundreds of feet above. Smaller, dimmer lights lit the higher city elevations. As the carriage processed with guards in tow, peasants, commoners, and merchants lined the streets with flowers, cheering for their leadership as the royals made their way to the coronation ceremony of the new King.

Rumors of renewed war with Haeldrun Ir circulated, and the public mood was tense. Many mothers and fathers worried for their sons and daughters, serving in the new boy King's crusade for vengeance. Many lamented that many more, who had lacked much, would die to avenge the death of one who none of the commoners truly knew in the first place.

The armies were almost set. Dwarfish spies, sent by the Hodan to ascertain the situation, could see that the massive open fields before the gates of Dornat Al Fer were covered with countless squares of white tents, horses, and siege weapons.

It appeared to those looking on that Hamrick II was intent on sending his entire kingdom after Lyax and the Todani. The mood was one of apprehension and second-guessing, not inspiration. Peace had been the norm for so long. The Dwarves had forgotten what the reality of war was. The public did not like the view from where they sat.

* * *

Kepir had returned to the command tent during the evening, nine days prior. His confidential report was for the ears of King Orus only. The two men exchanged greetings and news, then told stories at the table while drinking much mead. From time to time, they shed a tear or two over the past while sipping from their tankards. Puzzled, the porters listened to the Hodan men talk. All folks who were present were confused by their speech, because neither man was speaking a tongue that anyone other than the King and his man seemed to understand.

"He suffered, Sire. I saw to it," Kepir slurred.

Orus pursed his lips, nodding. "I reckon that he earned his exit from this world."

"That he did, Sire!" Kepir replied, forcing a smile.

"To Hodan and all of her allies! May all who deal treacherously with her be ground to fine dust," Orus declared, raising his glass.

"Here! Here! Sire!" Kepir howled.

Uilam could hear the revel from where he stood outside of the tent. He knew something was bothering Master Kepir when he returned from his scouting mission, but he knew not what it was. He suspected, but he kept his suspicions to himself.

"Edmund," Uilam called quietly.

"Yes, Captain," Edmund replied with snark.

Uilam smiled at Edmund's attempt at a curtsey in armor. The Lieutenant almost fell over in the attempted sarcasm.

"Ass," Uilam chuckled. "Seriously, Ed. What is the status from the front?"

"Not sure, Sir," Edmund answered with concern.

"Well, give me your assessment, man," Uilam poked.

"My scouts tell me that the Todani numbers are dwindling, Sir. They still occupy well-protected positions, though, and their embattlements are formidable." Edmund looked around to see who was listening. "They do seem to be moving north. I figure that they move away from us and most likely back toward their new front with the Dwarves? Rumor has it, Hamrick was murdered by a Toad assassin. Hamrick's whelp is now King and wants Lyax's hide for it."

Uilam shook his head gently at the exuberance of his friend's report. "This means that we will be moving north soon. I wonder how much territory His Majesty will push to claim?"

"Well, with the progress of the new recruits, we will have our hands full. They are not the champions of old by any stretch of the imagination, Uilam."

"I'm sure the leaders of the champions of old may have said the same thing about their recruits!" Uilam smiled.

Edmund thought for a moment and then nodded reluctantly. "Probably so. Look at us, brother!"

"Agreed," Uilam responded humbly. "Inform the Degran Commanders that a tactical planning meeting will occur tonight in the tower. All are required to attend. We need to assess our capabilities and prepare for an invasion of the north."

"Always thinking ahead, eh?" Edmund said, pretending to be put off. Then the younger man winked. "That's why you're the Captain now, and I'm just a lowly Lieutenant!"

"Off with you, you damned fool!" Uilam said, laughing. "We need to be ready when the King tells us to move out. That is the Hodan way."

"As you command, Sir," Edmund responded earnestly, saluting and going to pass the word to the Commanders of the Degran reserves.

* * *

The Elves sent reinforcements to aid in the Degran push northward. The combined forces of the Vyn and Hodan crushed most of the half-manned Todani defenses. The Hodan losses were moderate, but still proving to be costly. Orus, upon seeing that his Elites were starting to be spread thin, called a halt to the push northward, just above the former barony near the Jackrabbit Pass. There, the Hodan and Vyn liberated thousands of humans and Galdrissen from the grip of Todani servitude. The results were immediate. Orus gained another ten to fifteen untrained legions of militia. Most were of questionable fighting fitness, but each was accepted and sworn into the reserves of Degran-Eras. Soon, Kepir and his trainers were overwhelmed with green recruits needing to be whipped into shape.

Within another six months, twenty thousand ragtag militia became passable Degran legionnaires. Most were relegated to posts within the walls of hasty border defenses and told to hold at all costs. The Hodan trained Degran and the Elites pushed the advantage on the open battlefield. This was not put upon the new armies, for Orus did not feel that they were ready. Many Degran felt the familiar sting of shame, as foreigners fought on the field while they were ordered to stand guard duty.

Little did the discontented know, but their time would soon come. Orus and Kepir knew that very few actual native Hodan were left in the legions now. Of the original five legions that sailed from the Ert, thousands had been lost over almost a decade of war. Orus and Kepir estimated that one pure Hodan legion remained and three of the original warships they had sailed over on. The rest of the army was constructed by the best of the Degran volunteers. The local forces were living up to their new title of Hodan Elites, but they were very green. Orus looked out over the fields of golden armored warriors and smiled. The humans had once again risen to take their place under the sun again.

"Kepir!" Orus said optimistically.

"Yes, Sire?"

"How many more legions do you think you can construct from this new gaggle?" Orus asked, pointing out over a field of tents below his position.

Kepir's eyes opened wide with frustration at the question. He sighed mournfully. "Sire, four maybe?"

"Fifty-thousand souls down there, and you tell me only four-thousand are capable?" Orus was miffed.

"Fine, Sire, maybe six, seven at the most," Kepir relented.

"Better. Make it ten, and we have a deal," Orus chided.

"But Sire! TEN?" Kepir protested.

Orus smiled and crossed his arms, raising his eyebrows.

"Yes, Sire ... ten," Kepir said, muttering curse words under his breath in a foreign language. He rolled his eyes, shaking his head as he left to conjure up warriors from the rabble he saw living within the tents below.

"I heard you!" Orus laughed, making a profane gesture at his best friend.

"I know!" Kepir said, walking away and returning with a mock salute.

The specialist called to his leaders. The team gathered, leaving to inspect the existing units and to glean those who would make up the next ten Hodan legions. Kepir knew the King planned to push again soon. The Hodan had already claimed half of the destitute human territories.

Hodan's alliances held firm with the kingdoms of Vynwratha and Ynus-Grag. Orcs began voluntarily patrolling the Dwarfish borders as Dwarfish refugees began to stream to the edge of Whaleford territory.

After several reports of engagements with the refugees, Orus sent an emissary to the Orcs, asking that the Dwarves be allowed safe passage to the lands of the humans. The Hodan King reasoned that the Dwarves were educated, skilled workers, and inventors. The people of Dornat Al Fer were industrious folk. They were not at fault for the folly of their King. Orus would grant them asylum and use their skills and talents to strengthen his new kingdom.

If spies or saboteurs were found to be hiding among the displaced, Orus knew they would not live to see their next day. This the Orcs gladly promised.

* * *

Several intense, bloody battles between two of the greatest armies the Rynn had seen in a century had taken their toll on both sides. The Todani pulled back to their hardened defensive positions, giving up a few miles of territory to the overwhelming flow of Dwarves into their lands. At the newly fortified positions, the resistance of the Todessen stiffened significantly, massacring the overconfident Dwarfish units that had overextended themselves. The Dwarfish Commanders foolishly believed that the Todani were on the run, when all that had happened was a tactical withdrawal and reinforcement. The Commanders of the Dwarfish military, seeing the error of their ways, decided to dig in where they found the advantage, and sent couriers to Dornat Al Fer to inform their King of their situation.

Newly crowned King Hamrick II was angered by the inability of his military to push through to Haeldrun Ir. He had used entire might of the Dwarfish nation, but still, they could not defeat the Todani single-handedly. The young Dwarf leader was miffed that all had not happened as he had envisioned it. Hamrick II's frontline Generals sat apprehensively waiting for the next ill-conceived set of battle plans to arrive at their location.

Hamrick, the junior, and his military advisors sat around a large war table discussing options. The Generals looked silently back and forth between each other. They said nothing, but their worry was apparent. They did not think their King was up to the task, but the young man insisted on making tactical decisions, even when they flew in the face of advice or reason.

"What do we need to do, General?" the King asked in dismay.

"Hold our position and hope that Hodan stirs enough mischief on the eastern borders, My King. That Orus is making a big dent in the holdings of the Todani. They will not be able to ignore them much longer."

The young King was flanked by his advisors. He looked at his High Priest of Haya. The haughty, robed figure wore bright white robes and a mithril coronet on his head. The King had never liked this Priest. He always felt like the man thought himself superior, even to the crown.

Hamrick said plainly, "What say you, Your Holiness? Does the Goddess withhold her blessing, because we do not do her will? Or does she hold back her blessing, because we lack the faith to trust in her and charge headlong into battle?" The King stood expectantly with his hands on his hips.

"It is hard to say, My King," the Priest politicked. "Perhaps the Goddess is weary of war and death? Perhaps she waits for us to truly rely on her benevolence and not our pride and strength?"

The King was not convinced. "Do you speak for Haya or yourself, old man? Does she even visit you anymore? She has been silent for many of these past few years."

"My King, the Goddess does as she pleases. I am not able to tell her what to do," the Priest offered.

"You are correct, Priest," the King said with little interest. "You cannot tell me what she wants, and you cannot dictate what she would have us do. I wonder of your significance these days."

"I will take my leave then, Sire. I can see that you are vexed and tired. Just remember that the Goddess says, 'All retribution is dealt with a two-edged blade. Each hand which grips it will bleed its fair share.'"

The young King bowed out of tradition to the Priest. He had a scowl on his face at the holy man's rebuke.

"To the Underworld with Prophets, Priests, and so-called allies. We need none of them. Hold your ground. Watch for the Todani to ease up on their defenses, if they do indeed divert forces to the damned human invasion to the east. Call up conscripts, train them, and send them to reinforce our forces."

"Yes, Sire," the General replied.

* * *

Ma 'Dryna fussed over a bandaged patient. The old Dwarf kept trying to sit up and leave the infirmary. His wounds were not closed, but he continued to insist that he must return to the lines to redeem the honor of his people. Dryna rolled her eyes at the word honor. She was sick of it being bandied about like a word with no meaning. It was not a slogan, but a way of life. It was one word that her love had given his life for. It had been almost a year since the death of Jaruz, and the High Priestess of Likedelir remembered his last moments as if they had just occurred.

"Dryna, why do you hold on so?" the old Dwarf in bandages asked her with a calm voice, sitting back against the wall of the clinic.

"Hold on? Well, because your foolishness is going to get you killed, old man!" Dryna said as a matter of fact.

"All Dwarves die, but not many can say they earned the gold in the bags on their pyres," the old man sneered back.

"Silence, you old fool," Dryna said, frowning. She swallowed hard, remembering a pyre that burned not so long ago.

"Jaruz earned his," the soldier replied, as if he'd been there with him in the battle.

"Were you there when they cut him down!?" the Priestess shrieked angrily. "Do not lecture me about honor!"

"In fact, I was there when they came," the old man said calmly.

Dryna stared hollowly at the Dwarf before her. She was crying.

"I saw many die and enter the gates of Aeternum that day, and so many other days, too."

"You are full of stories, aren't you, *hero*," Dryna mocked, pulling out a blanket and loosely draping it over her talkative patient.

"I have seen the Todani atrocities here and in other lands. I have seen the atrocities of Dwarf, human, Elf, and Orc. All are without virtue. All have need of redeemers to wash away their stain." The old Dwarf lounged casually.

"Certainly, there are those who redeem the lot of us all, but why do the gods take them from our presence? Why not let them lead us in their virtue?" Dryna's tears had dried, and she sat back in her chair.

The old Dwarf said plainly, "My Priestess, he watches and waits for you. He will not be going anywhere! You, I wager, have more to do here, so do it! Remember him, but do not allow it to become a convenient escape from the trials that await you." He coughed. "May I have a drink of water, Priestess?"

Dryna turned for the pitcher. "Certainly."

As she turned back after filling a wooden cup, the bed was empty except for her satchel, which sat on the covers where her patient had laid. Tentatively, she opened the leather case and removed the leather-bound, jewel-covered book, opening to a place marked by a ragged raven's feather.

The passage read, "Today an old acquaintance visited the High Priestess and told her to get on with it."

Dryna slammed the book shut and shouted, "That son of a ..."

Her statement was interrupted by a distinct chuckle within her head. Dryna rolled her eyes and shook her head.

"What is wrong with you, My God?" she asked the thin air to many who looked at her with concern.

Dryna smiled, eagerly picking up her book and leaving the medical tent in search of dinner. She was sure that there was more to read in her tome, but she was unsure if she really wanted to hear it. It had been a while since her god had contacted her, but she was encouraged that he had finally listened to her prayers.

* * *

The new Degran armies began training, and with that, Master Kepir and Commander Kren found many souls who would fit in nicely with the Hodan Elites. The young—and not so young—filled the ranks of four more Hodan Elite legions. Orus now had at his disposal his original five Elite units and almost thirty legions of regulars and reserves. Estimates of the entire war machine were in the area of fifty-thousand souls—foot soldiers, archers, cavalry, mages, healers, naval forces, and logisticians. The King of Hodan called a meeting of his Commanders to plan for the new northern push to liberate more of Degran.

Orus felt the Degran were ready. Eight months without any actual conflict was enough time. It was late summer, and he knew that the weather was likely to take a turn for the worse within six to eight weeks. The time was now to push forward, while the Todani were busy with the Dwarves and their static war front.

"Sire," Kepir reported, "the Todani have a new problem far north of us—to the borders of northeastern forests."

"What good fortune has Likedelir given us today, my friend?" Orus asked, looking to the north.

"The Dragons, Sire," the specialist replied. "They're back and giving the Scourge a serious thrashing near the dense forest edge."

"Why there?" Orus asked with interest. "What interests our scaly allies so?"

"Unknown at this time, My King." Kepir said with thought. "But whatever it is, it has the Todani cut off from reinforcements. If we push now, we can take the rest of the lands before the winter."

"Good news!" Orus exclaimed loudly with a chuckle. "But, brother, can we hold it?"

"With the Dragons, Sire, we can hold this continent," Kepir reasoned, then added, "but to be true, I do not trust them."

"Why so?" Orus asked with concern.

"Sire, they are ancients. Even their adolescents are as old as our elders. They are not in this fight to secure our new homeland." Kepir sighed.

"Aye, brother," Orus said, scratching his beard. "What is in it for them? Revenge ... but then what? Henargya knows what she wants, that is to be sure. She is older than everyone in the five legions combined, I would wager."

"I suggest that we do not anger our tentative allies. We should appease them as much as possible—as long as they are working toward the same goals as we are." Kepir was thinking like the calculating tactician that he always was. He had a knack for seeing the long game. It was one of his unique talents.

"Agreed. No need to stir that bee's nest when it is not necessary. If the Dragons are killing Todessen or Dwarves, it is of no concern of ours—except that it leaves less of those bastards for our folks to personally deal with!"

"I will keep a scout north at all times and rotate them weekly to get updated information on the northeast mountains, Sire."

"A wise idea, as usual, my friend. Let the Commanders of the legions, Elites, and regulars know that they must prepare to move north. We leave in three days."

Kepir bowed and left the command tent to gather the leadership in preparation for the last push northward.

Chapter 17

Hamrick II could hear the sound of sabatons slapping against the stone floor and the huffing of the approaching messenger. The courier was in a hurry and had something of great importance that he thought the King should know. Annoyed, the petulant, younger monarch sat up in expectation of bad news.

"Your Majesty," the courier wheezed, catching his breath, "I have news from the front, Sire!"

The King paused, allowing his man to catch his breath. It looked as if the man had run all of the ways from the front to tell him his tale. The soldier was bent over unceremoniously, drawing breath with labor.

"You there," the King ordered, "bring the man some water, immediately." The King waved his hand.

The order was complied with to the appreciation of the armored Dwarf who gulped down the water. Hamrick, the junior, was disgusted by the way the commoner allowed the water to run through his beard and down onto the floor. Servants had begun to dry the mess before the King felt the need to say anything.

"What news have you, courier?" the King demanded.

"The humans have driven the Todani from their lands. They have complete control of Degran-Eras—that is, except for the territories known as the port city of Haeldrun Ir."

The King was intrigued. The Todani were running for the first time in over a century. The humans were proving to be a worthy adversary after all. The monarch paced, hands clasped behind his back in thought. Then he spoke. "So, the Todani are defeated? They retreat to their city with their tails between their legs?"

"Yes, Sire. They are looking much worse for wear since engaging the humans and Elves in the forests."

"Fools. To fight Elves in the forest is to invite defeat. And that Orus is not to be taken lightly either!" The King snickered. "Fools. The lot of them. How are their defenses fairing after being soundly drummed out of Degran?"

"My King, it appears as if they are in disarray. I was told to give you this scroll and to emphasize that our Commanders at the front believe that this may be the time to strike. The Degran have given us the opening that we have been waiting for—a crack in the Todani defenses to exploit."

The King nodded, reading the scroll that the messenger had handed him moments earlier. It said much the same thing as what the man had relayed.

"My good man," the King said, scrawling down his response on a parchment handed to him by a scribe. "Tell the generals, no quarter."

"Yes, Sire!" the man barked, placing the missive in his satchel, and then turned, running off.

* * *

Princess Vyqua sat in her bed chambers in silence, pretending to pray. She was far from pious. For many years, the young Todani woman had plotted to kill her father and take his place as ruler of the Kingdom of Haeldrun Ir. She set in motion treachery after treachery in attempts to destabilize his rule and strengthen her position as rightful Queen. Unfortunately, to this point, all of her machinations had come to naught, but new developments on the war front had buoyed her waning hopes of ever seeing any of her aspirations come to fruition.

The humans had routed her father's men at the forest. Most Todani disliked the region, because the forests were always a place of death for a Todani. Rumors of monsters and Elves permeated the bedtime stories Todani mothers told their children to get them to behave. The story was always similar—Vyn Raiders would arrive in the night, killing Haeldrun's children. The mad Elves would always capture a few young Todani whelps to roast upon a spit during their victory revels. Then the Elfish fiends would eat the children.

Now the boogeymen of the Todani seemed to be more alive than ever before, with the Hodan, Degran, and Vynwrathian armies defeating the armies of Haeldrun Ir in the forests named by the ancient Degran as Drakyn Ignyris. Rumors of Dragons, friends, and foes were whispered in every corner of the kingdom. The people were on edge. The scary firelight stories were becoming a reality before their eyes. The elders grumbled over incompetence, while the younger feared the coming Scourge.

* * *

The Todani pulled back and regrouped by the trees. Half of their army had fled westward, presumably to rejoin their kin within their home kingdom. The hard military push of the Hodan had forced the Todani to withdraw deep into the northern territories.

"Commander, the humans come. I see them. You are ordering us to enter the wood?" The Todani Lieutenant looked at his leader with dismay.

"Yes, we must use the woods to augment our dwindling numbers. The humans will not be able to freely maneuver in tight quarters as much as they can out on an open field! Give the order!"

"But Sir! Where are the Vyn? Where did they go? Do you not think that they might meet us in the damnable forests? That's where they prefer to fight! If we enter there, we may cut our own throats." The Lieutenant was looking at the Commander with a face that almost pleaded with him.

"Die here or die there. What difference does it make, son!?" the Commander asked smiling. "We have no choice. Sound the horns."

"Yes, Sir!" the younger Todani said, blowing into a horn and sounding the retreat.

The Hodan and Degran armies followed closely behind.

* * *

"They flee to the trees, Sire!" Uilam bellowed as he rode forward, exhorting his men from horseback.

"That they do, son," the King said as he watched thousands of Todani melt into the woods.

The Hodan warrior hoped the Vyn were in position, but his allies did not have the necessary time to set up a proper ambush, so Orus was skeptical that it would go as well as Lourama had predicted. Battle was always adlib, and this was about as random a battle as the King had encountered in some time. The Todani were losing at every turn, but in their retreat, the viciousness of their tactics was taking its toll. The forest could be an advantage, or it would aid the Todani in holding out longer—perhaps long enough for reinforcements. Orus could not allow that. His army was inexperienced, worn out, and without proper support. Many had not eaten in days.

"Kepir, take your men to the other side of the forest and set up an ambush there. Tell Edmund to drive the Todani out the other side of this forest and toward your waiting specialists. We cannot assume that the Vyn are ready to do their worst, but if they are, you drive them through a Vyn gauntlet and into your trap. They should be ready to die or surrender by then. If not, we fight it out after we thin that herd of evil down to a manageable size."

"I will pass the word, Sire. Luck in battle!" Kepir said, goading his horse to a gallop.

"Luck in battle, brother!" Orus said, waving at his friend.

298

* * *

The Dwarfish armies left their embattlements on the field and marched northward, as Lyax had feared they would. Soon, peaceful Todani farming collectives, villages, and townships south of the port city of Haeldrun Ir were razed. The King of the Todani could see the smoke rising on his southern flank. His armies were sorely outmatched. The Todani were stretched too thin when the war began. Now the Dwarfish legions, reinforced with militia consisting of barely trained teenage boys, pushed northward with ease.

"Sulfga!" Lyax raged. "Why are the Dwarves advancing so easily? What can be done to stop their advance? They pillage at will. How has it come to this?"

"Sire, we will reinforce with those who made it back from the eastern border. We will make it so bloody at the city walls that the short invaders will be forced to return to their holes in the ground."

"Make it so, Sulfga, for time appears to grow short! There is now some unrest in our own streets! Soon, we may need to put down a nascent rebellion of our own populace! We must get control of this situation, and soon, if we are to survive."

"At once, Sire!" the General acknowledged and left the room.

From the shadows, one man watched the King with interest. Smiling, the assassin slid like a specter out of the room to seek out his only interest in this world, Princess Vyqua.

* * *

In the Temples to Haeldrun, the common Todani sat, dejected and hopeless. Two great nations pushed from the east and the south. They watched as the Dwarves marched over their fields, burning the late summer crops.

The enemy did not stop there. They burned the silos, which were close to full of grain, killed the livestock, and then turned to the residents of the regions they sought to conquer.

Dwarf legionnaires captured entire families of Todani. They would often beat the men to death on site, corralling the women and children into their homes or public buildings. There, the Dwarves would pray to their Goddess and set the buildings on fire, residents within. The screams and pleading of the Todani met deaf Dwarven ears, for the hate of a century had sealed the hearts of the warriors of Dornat Al Fer.

Haeldrun was stirred from whatever evil he was presently engaged in by incessant prayers and the random, but frequent pleading screams of his devoted followers. Soon, the Underlord looked up from the catacombs to see what had disturbed his children so. There, he saw the children of the light and their brutal display of piety.

Chuckling, the Underlord shook his head. "Children of the light." He laughed outright. "How dare you, Dwarves! How dare you condemn my children when they are ironically the innocents in this affair."

Haeldrun looked over at several Denir, who were wandering about the catacombs, looking for lost souls to torment. He thought long and hard about his response, and then he had it.

"If *She* can use a Dragon to squash my invading armies on the Ert, I will return the favor. I will use one of her tricks upon the Rynn."

The God was angry. He would make the Dwarves pay. Haeldrun called out into the darkness. Patiently, the God waited for his answer. A loud growl—one that was so low it was more of a feeling than a sound—filled the catacombs. Haeldrun nodded.

"Scoria, my pet," the Underlord purred, "it is time, my love. Go forth and save my children from these Dwarves. Then incinerate those annoying humans, once and for all."

Two big, white eyes snapped open. Two sets of eyelids blinked as jet-black irises adjusted to the darkness. The Dragon laughed, shaking the tunnels around him, then disappeared into thin air.

CHAPTER 17

＊

Orus was entering the forest. He could see that the Vyn had not been ready as he had feared. Still, the Elves and his Degran legions were doing their worst, and it had the desired effect, driving the Todani miles into the dense forest and toward the open foothills on the other side of the trees. As badly as the Scourge were taking casualties, they seemed as if they were inflicting their own at a rate of two to one.

"Uilam, get control of the lines. Tell your leaders to advance with purpose and cohesively!" Orus was concerned with the loss of his numbers so close to the border with the Todani. He continued. "Use caution and push them out of the forest. Kepir and his specialists are waiting for them there."

Uilam raised the Degran standard and blew a horn, calling out to reform on his position. Within five minutes, the unit formed and marched cohesively toward the enemy lines that were rapidly pulling back toward the foothills to the delight of Orus.

As things appeared to be going as planned, the Hodan King smiled smugly from his saddle. Moments later, his smile would turn to a look of horror. Somewhere off in the distance, echoing off of the hills from every direction, a sound that Orus had hoped he'd never hear again filled the air. Everyone—friend, and foe—froze where they were and stared at the skies to the west.

The angry, booming roar of a thunder lizard filled the air. This was unlike any Dragon he had heard since Hodan had arrived on the Rynn. The sound dwarfed that of the Dragon Mother Henargya's roar when she freed herself and her children from their prisons at Whaleford.

Horses panicked at the sound. They bolted in all directions. Hodan, Degran, and Todani cavalry ran in all directions; some were thrown from their mounts. Entire units began to run eastward in panic and away from whatever had made that sound. Orus moved quickly with the mass exodus from the trees. He squinted, looking as the opposing armies seemingly forgot they were engaged in a battle. Comically, the foes ran as one, as far from the roar as possible.

"Now what?" Orus lamented, finding Uilam in the fray.

"What in the Underworld was that, Sire!?" the boy asked, flushed.

"That, my boy, is a very large lizard. One that I hope is on our side, but from the direction that sound is coming, I seriously doubt that it comes to aid us. We must regroup and prepare for the worst, for it comes, and soon!" Orus goaded his horse and called his Captain. "Let's go!"

* * *

"Sir, we have the Todani on the run! None of the Scourge from the last village escaped to warn the enemy."

"Good work, Sergeant," the Commander said formally. "Prepare to continue northward to the city, proper."

"Yes, Sir!"

The Dwarfish Commander could see the gates of the former Degran port. It had been under Todani control for over one-hundred years. Today, the Commander reckoned, it would change hands once again, but this time to the Dwarves. The Dwarf sat in his gilded armor, the favor of the King on his belt. The cloth was stained with black blood. Arrogantly, he looked over the lands, figuring that the King would grant him the choicest piece of land once the pesky Todessen infestation was taken care of. As he readied to drink from his canteen, his assumed good fortune changed drastically.

A booming voice filled everything at once, it seemed. It said plainly, "Foolish Dwarves! Do not think that you will wipe my children from this place so easily? Little hypocrites who claim the light! You are as ruthless as any of my own creations! Haya will not be pleased by your barbarity! Wail, but know that my dearest will not save you, for the gravity of your sins!"

The ground shook again as the voice continued in its rebuke. "Scoria, my child, purge the lands of the hypocrites! Cleanse them with your fire!"

With that statement, the ground shook violently, and then, as if it was an

302

illusion, a large reptilian head, neck, wings, and body began to emerge from the very soil itself. When the creature was entirely in view, it stood taller than any of the castle towers. The immense lizard was obsidian in color with white eyes. Their large black pupils shrunk as they received their first light on the Rynn. The Dragon stretched its gigantic wings outward, letting out an earsplitting roar and then a blast of fire that set a Dwarfish legion's front rank instantly ablaze.

Mayhem then proceeded to occur. Horses ran in all directions, as did Dwarves, Todani, and livestock. The disarray on the field had stopped the advance of the Dwarves cold. Commanders who had control of their wits were frantically blowing horns, calling for their lines to reform, but to no avail. That is when the Dragon lit off into the air and began killing Dwarves at will.

The Todani cheered their god from their embattlements, witnessing the enormous black Dragon swoop down upon the invading Dwarfish armies with ease. The Dwarves were running southward for their lives.

"Rider!" a Dwarfish Commander screamed in terror at a young Dwarfish squire beside him. "Ride to Dornat Al Fer and warn the King! All is lost here! All is lost! Ride for your life!"

* * *

Kepir and his men had heard it, too. It was a sound that the specialist had thought to never hear again. It sounded to the Captain as if Maradwynne had once again joined the fight against the darkness, but the assassin knew that the Golden Queen would only come for Puryn of Yslandeth. She had never shown herself again after the Temple at Sudenyag. The specialist now wondered if there was another Golden Queen to worry about. What if she was not taking sides this time, or worse yet, was in opposition to his allies. The men frantically gestured to their Commander in confusion, using hand signals.

As the Hodan remained hidden and observed the forest, they saw a strange sight. Todani, human, and Elf were running out of the woods at breakneck speed. They were not in any sort of order or in any coherent unit or grouping. All were running for their lives, and in that terror, they had forgotten the battle at hand.

Kepir sent out hand signals. "Remain hidden. Observe. Stand by." His men responded with affirmation and did not move.

Eventually, the gaggle of mixed armies realized the folly of their escape plan. Each warrior gravitated to allies forming small groups and then rallying on opposite sides of the field. The Todani were vastly outnumbered by the Vyn and Degran at this point. Kepir had not even factored in his own unit when calculating strength, and he estimated that it was at least two or better to one in favor of the Degran armies. The specialist could see with his spyglass that Orus had found a few of his leaders and begun the process of organizing the gaggle that was once his proud and disciplined force.

Dragons from unknown places tended to be disruptive, and the Degran armies did not seem to be immune, despite their training.

For some time, both armies stared across the field, one at the other. Neither made a sound, listening for more from the east. The sound of loud screeching and roaring was heard off in the distance. Neither side knew who was on the receiving end of whatever was making all the racket, but each hoped it wasn't their side.

It was eerily quiet for a battlefield. After an hour, the relative peace was broken by an unceremonious crash nearby Kepir's location. From high above, something significant, scaly, and copper-colored landed and looked directly at the specialist while sniffing furiously.

"I see you, Master Kepir," the lizard said within the specialist's mind, squinting as if she really did not.

"Ah, thank the gods it is you, Henargya!" Kepir said, revealing himself.

"Why do the armies gather here? Why do humans, Elves, and Todani seem to gather at our doorstep?" Henargya asked with a bit of irritation.

"Oh, great Dragon, please hold a moment." Kepir raised his hands, asking for a chance to explain.

"Explain," Henargya said angrily.

She was very defensive, and Kepir did not understand why.

"We are trying to push these Toads out of our nation, Great One," Kepir stated calmly. "Your children aided us greatly in the past. We have almost freed our lands from the grasp of the Underlord. We were fighting in the trees when …" Kepir pointed to the east as a series of loud, angry howls met his ears.

"What have these imps done?" Henargya moaned.

"What is it, Dragon Mother?" Kepir asked with concern.

"It is an evil I have never felt before, Master Kepir." Henargya paused and quickly changed the subject. "Tell Orus, the Dragons claim the mountains to the east. They will be ours. There will be no negotiation about it."

"I am sure that he will not object, my friend!" Kepir said, trying to lighten the mood. "Why do I sense such worry in your tone, Great Protector of the Dragons?"

"The one who beckons from the east is straight out of the bowels of the catacombs, I fear," the Dragon said with great certainty and sorrow. "The Dwarves must have caught *His* attention with their attacks on the people of Haeldrun Ir. Gods will only stay silent for so long, I fear. Now the Underlord has responded—and with fire."

"Is there anything that Hodan can do to help?" Kepir asked with honest intent.

"Know this, friend," Henargya replied as if whispering a secret, "these vile rodents pilfered my eggs and those of others that laid dormant in dens for thousands of years throughout the lands of the Rynn. They put them in their evil Temples and sought to turn us to the darkness, so I thought, but it appears that I was mistaken."

"But we saw it with our own eyes," Kepir said, confused.

"It appears that they didn't seek to turn us after all, my rescuer. They were diverting the energy of my unborn kindred to create that monstrosity. The evil I feel, over there, near Haeldrun's children, is most definitely a Dragon, but one born of evil itself."

305

"How do we defeat such a foe?" Kepir asked in horror.

"You do not," Henargya said plainly. "My children and I will do what we can, but you could help us in another fashion if you wish."

"What is your need? My brother, Orus, would never turn his back on such an ally as you." Kepir smiled, but his fear was evident to the Dragon, who knowingly nodded.

"We will engage the evil when it eventually arrives. We need your people to travel to the mouth of a large cave and to defend it against anyone who would enter there to do us harm, for we have put all of the eggs we have collected—mine or others—in that cavern. They will hatch and continue our kind. Our numbers are perilously low at the moment—scarcely forty of adult age remain from thousands at our peak!" Henargya lamented.

"I will tell Orus. We will defend your children. Do not worry. But how will we know where the cave is when we arrive?" Kepir questioned.

"A young fool of a Dragon, white with black and copper spots, will greet your people when you near the mountain. He remembers what you and King Orus did for him. He will not forget. That one is wily, but not without his merits."

"Ah, that one!" Kepir said nervously, remembering the younger Dragon's temperament. "The one who looks as if his colors are blurred or smudged? For ease of remembrance, I will refer to him as Smudge, if that does not offend you, Mother?"

The Dragon thought for a moment and shrugged. "I will ask him." She paused for a moment and then responded to the specialist. "That will do, human. He does not object."

"I will ride to King Orus. Be assured that our armies will depart soon. I do not think that the Todani will advance from their hasty defenses while they see you here, so we should be able to move freely."

Kepir made hand signals, and the bushes of the field rose and ran toward friendly lines. Kepir bowed and did the same.

"Oh, how I love the magic of Elves. I did not see them at all. Sneaky humans!" Henargya watched as the specialists retreated.

The Dragon Mother growled at the Todani, who responded by turtling up below their large shields and presenting sharp points in all directions. The Dragon chuckled and flew high to see what she could see, concerning her adversary to the west. She knew that losing was not an option, or her line would be lost forever.

* * *

Smudge met the Degran on the road two hours later as they traveled to where Henargya had asked. His unceremonious crash landing and screeching terrified several of the reserve units. Kepir restored order, calming the skittish warriors, and then the Dragon led the Hodan, Degran, and Vyn to the mouth of a large cave. There, Orus and his Commanders gave the army the order to rest. Many laid where they stood and gladly slept for the first time in two or three days.

One unfortunate platoon of Degran was not so lucky. They had drawn the watch. It was Uilam's band who drew the shortest straw.

Wearily, Edmund saluted his Captain. "Glad to be of service, brother!"

Uilam sighed with exhaustion. "Set the pickets, Ed. We have Toads in the area."

The Lieutenant replied professionally, "Right away, Sir. Be safe."

* * *

The destruction of the immediate threat at the city walls did not quell the unrest within Haeldrun Ir. The commoners were up in arms over their treatment. Families who had lost loved ones protested openly in the street. Lyax was under immense pressure from all sides. The war was taking its toll, but for the moment, that seemed to be under control, due to the favor of the Underlord. Still, the losses of homes, family members, livestock, and food stores had taken their toll on public sentiment. The people were angry. Lyax hadn't taken these things from them, but old reports began to circulate of the assassination of the King of the Dwarves, pointing blame straight back at their monarch. Everyone knew that this sole action had brought about all of the ills which had recently befallen the Todani nation.

Princess Vyqua was elated by this recent turn of events. To feign interest in the war effort, the Princess had begun a daily public spectacle, where she would personally sacrifice a calf or goat to the Underlord at the main city temple. She would make a great public show of it and then send the burnt offerings to the Underlord with the pretense of gaining his favor. The number of worshippers increased daily with the level of the people's suffering. Every day, the average Todani saw their Princess praying for them and for their kingdom, while the King hid in the throne room directing the destruction of his people. Now, the prayers of the Princess, said as an advocate of the commoner, were answered by Scoria, the Dragon. Many attributed this excellent fortune directly to Vyqua's persistence in petitioning Haeldrun's mercy.

"Princess," the shadow hissed, "his reign is weaker than ever before. I have spread the tales of Hamrick's death in every dark corner. I have fanned the flames and goaded the mobs. What is your command?"

"Hold your hand a bit longer, my devoted," Vyqua cooed to her admirer. "Soon enough, we will rule and return our people to their rightful glory."

The Princess looked at the covered face of her devoted, imagining what sort of man this Todani was. He was not too large and not too small. A wiry, agile kind of warrior, well-suited for his chosen profession, but the future Queen could never see his face. She imagined it to be the face of death, or perhaps a Denir incarnate, but he served her purposes and had never failed her.

"As you wish, Your Highness," the eyes below the hood responded. "I live to serve you."

The Princess smiled at her admirer, who stared a moment longer than was perhaps appropriate. Vyqua knew that this man was fanatical in his devotion. Soon, she would use that adoration to focus his deadly skills in repayment to her father for the deaths of so many she had loved as a child.

The streets in the commons were burning within the city of Haeldrun Ir. The enemy was now within the walls, as well as without. The humans were not the only threat to Lyax, and Vyqua relished every moment of discord, envisioning it as a step closer to the end of her father and his rule.

* * *

The ebony Dragon flew effortlessly above the retreating Dwarves. He had eaten his fill and decided that there was no rush in dealing with the southern Scourge. Scoria laughed as he envisioned them scurrying back under their mountain like the rodents they were, relying on the fortress doors to seal out any threat. The Dragon smiled, revealing rows of jagged teeth as long as swords. He felt his fire would be enough to eventually buckle the doors of any fortress. These infidels would not escape the wrath of his Lord, Haeldrun. He would ensure that they all suffered.

Sniffing the wind to the east, the Dragon smiled.

"More vermin! Humans, Elves, and my Lord's chosen!" Scoria turned toward the east with interest.

The Dwarves continued scrambling southward as rapidly as possible. Occasionally, a brave band of fools would launch a volley of arrows at the thunder lizard. Every projectile bounced harmlessly off of Scoria's scales. While the thunder lizard contemplated his next move, he absent-mindedly burped a burst of flame at the annoying archers, incinerating the lot within a minute or two.

"I must investigate." The black Dragon started flapping his wings and moving at incredible speed eastward.

Chapter 18

The riots could be heard off in the distance. Vyqua heard random chants demanding her ascension to the throne. It was somewhere between pride, flattery, and terror that she realized that she was out of time. Her father would hear those cries also. In the past, others in line for the throne were summarily executed or died unexpectantly for much less. Vyqua would not wait for the assassin's needle or a poisoned glass of wine.

She lit the signal to summon her devoted. It was small and hung from a black metal chain. The stained-glass candle holder illuminated as the candle burned. The shadows of her quarters were tinted crimson by the light shining through the blood-red glass of the lantern. It would not be long now.

* * *

Sulfga was not an intellectual by any means. His education was a result of a series of bad decisions that had landed him in a Todani prison. There, the young street thug honed his only proficiency-killing. The prison guards would often choose two of the largest or smallest of the prison block, dragging them out of their cells and into the fighting pits where bets were wagered on not who would win, but instead on who would survive. The rules were simple in the pits—kill your opponent. If you survived the ordeal, you were rewarded with a bonus meal and another day to live.

Sulfga was chosen from the rabble by the King to be a gladiator of sorts. The giant, muscular, Todani warrior would spar, killing anyone who dared to stand against him in the arena, much to the King's delight. Soon, Lyax had promoted the young Sulfga to one of his personal guards. When war came, Sulfga further proved himself on the battlefield and gradually made his way up the ranks. When the Vyn finally attacked the harbor, close to ten years earlier, Sulfga had positioned himself politically to assume command after the untimely death of the former Commander.

The General knew the Princess was behind the unrest. If not all of it, a good portion of the rioting was orchestrated by the malcontent little girl. Sulfga reasoned that if this rebellion grew to be unmanageable and Lyax was deposed by force, Vyqua would seek the General's head to display it on a pike. He would be made an example of what happened to those who endorsed her father. He was not about to allow that to happen.

Lyax stood milling about nervously. He no longer disparaged his General, instead leaning on him for support. The King trusted few, but he trusted Sulfga to a fault. The circle around the King was shrinking by the day. Sulfga had never been proven anything, but trustworthy.

"Sulfga, we must put down these insurgencies!" the King bellowed in frustration. "Bring me that damned girl. I know this is of her doing! It has all the markings of what one of my spawns would do!"

"At once, Your Majesty," the General declared, bowing and exiting the room with several guards in tow.

The King looked at one of his servant girls, smiling deviously. "Perhaps I will just have to make more heirs to replace these treacherous whelps my last whore produced."

The young woman bowed timidly while smiling politely. She was afraid.

* * *

311

"They come," she said, looking into the darkness. "We knew that they would. Father is a lecherous bastard, but he is no fool." Vyqua sat upright in her chair, trying to calm her nerves. "Meet me in the throne room. Father will undoubtedly run on with a long, rambling speech about family loyalty and such—the lout knows not what those things mean!"

"What then, My Queen?" the voice hissed gently.

"Kill him. Send him to the Underlord!" Vyqua heard the door handle rattle. "Go! Now! They are here!"

The shadows shifted momentarily, and she knew that he was gone.

"Princess Vyqua," Sulfga bloviated, "His Majesty requests your presence!"

Two guards roughly grabbed the Princess. A foot soldier tied her hands tightly behind her with leather cording. Forcefully, the Todani guards pushed the young Princess down the hall to meet her doom.

Vyqua protested her treatment, even mustering tears when pleading for her life. In reality, she was barely holding back her excitement. Her plan was finally on track, and she could see the light at the end of the tunnel.

* * *

The throne room doors were thrown open, and Vyqua was dragged into the room with much protesting. She averted her eyes from her father, who was engaged in acts with her servant girl that should have been relegated to the royal sleeping chambers. The Princess was not surprised. Her father was a pig, and she expected nothing less.

"AH! My dear daughter," the King sneered, "come closer. We are all but finished here—for now."

The King looked menacingly at the barely adult servant girl he toyed with. The young woman scrambled to gather her clothing and backed away half-nude, bowing in embarrassment and shame. Her expression was not lost on the Princess, who looked at her father with angry disgust.

"Truly, father," Vyqua spat like venom, "she has not even reached my age.

It does not bother you that you violate young ladies, young enough to be your own daughter? Lecherous tyrant!"

"Silence, you impetuous little imp," Lyax responded, tying his robe around his waist.

The riots were louder now. Vyqua's name was now more prevalently heard above the din.

"Sulfga, will you let this pathetic lump direct you to cut your own throat? You hear the calls from the streets for his demise. Free me. Join me. The reign of Lyax, the insufferable, is over!" Vyqua smiled with malice.

Sulfga said nothing and looked at his King, who nodded. The Todani warrior swung and made contact. The Princess could feel the gauntlet impact her cheek, and immediately, the taste of iron was in her mouth and her vision blurred.

She slurred, "So be it."

* * *

High above the argument, a dark, menacing cloud hid in shadows. The specter floated effortlessly above the scene below. From his vantage, he spied two door guards, General Sulfga, a few servants, his target, and his beloved. Assessing the tactical situation, the assassin moved away from the main event, using needles to poison the door guards. Like a spider, he crept upon them. They did not see it coming. Within a minute, both lay dead, still foaming at the mouth, as the assassin effortlessly disappeared once again.

A ghost, the specialist glided silently. He dodged two servant girls, only to be detected by the third, who was crying silently while carrying her clothing in a ball in front of her naked body. She stopped, startled at the eyes that stared at her as she sought to depart the room in shame. Smiling, she bowed to the specter and then ran from the room. Stepping over the two deceased door guards, she realized that death had come for Lyax, at

313

last.

The assassin watched from behind the thrones now. He was only five feet from the General and seven to eight feet from his Princess. When the General struck his love, he had seen enough.

There was a blur of movement. Lyax saw it coming, but could not move out of the way. The assassin moved like a shadow, as fluid as smoke. Death made a straight line for the King's position. The target's eyes widened in realization and fear.

"Sulfga!" the King bellowed, as the assassin buried his poisoned dagger in the neck of the surprised King.

The General knocked the Princess to the floor with another blow, dazing her momentarily. He drew his sword, advancing on the smiling assassin who had turned to meet him. The Todani rolled left and then pulled his short sword, but Sulfga was not a novice or a fool when it came to war. The assassin knew that many of the tricks of his trade would not work against a ready, seasoned warrior. He was forced to stand and fight, or run and leave his beloved to deal with this man.

Lunging, the assassin slashed at the General's leg, hoping to hobble him and reduce his mobility. It did not go as planned. Sulfga parried with ease and delivered a vicious knee to the side of his opponent, knocking the specter sideways and onto the floor. Rolling over and flipping to his feet, the disoriented specialist shook his head and attempted to come up with a plan.

Sulfga struck again, this time faking a slash and changing his blow mid-strike. Instead of the blade, the General struck the hooded figure with the pommel of his sword hilt. The blow sent the assassin reeling, blood running freely from an open gash on top of the man's head. Sulfga, seeing his opponent staggered, pushed his advantage, again hitting the dazed, lighter, Todani man across the face, this time with a vambrace.

The assassin knew that he was in trouble. Unable to see clearly, and unable to gather his balance, he stabbed wildly until his blade struck true. Sulfga grunted, receiving a sword blade through his left side, but the General was not deterred. Remembering the many battles he had won within the arena, the older warrior grabbed the hilt of the assassin's sword, pulling forward until he was close enough to drive his own blade into his enemy's chest.

Vyqua closed her eyes. Strangely, she felt sorry for her devoted. She would miss the presence of someone in her life who only wished for her and not what he could gain from her. Guilt flooded her heart as she thought of how he died in vain. She had never loved him. She had never even seen his face.

Getting to her feet, Princess Vyqua walked over to where the deceased King had kept his sword hung from his throne. She managed to pull six inches of the blade out of the scabbard and to use it to saw through the leather thong that bound her hands. Rubbing her numb wrists and hands, she walked over to where the three were lying.

Sulfga was on his side, silent, the King lay face down in his own vomit, a dagger in his throat, and the third, mysterious figure who was clad in black cloth, was lying on his back, with a long sword in his chest. Kneeling beside the still body, the Princess satisfied her curiosity.

Removing the head covering was a bit of a task. It was a hood over a gauze-wrapped head. The body was covered in a suit made of silk and linen. It was black, dark gray, and had flecks and spots within its pattern. When the Todani woman had finally unwrapped her prize, she was shocked at what she found. He was nothing as she had imagined him to be. Here was no leper. His face was not a twisted, burned, freakish display as she had envisioned.

His cold blue eyes stared back at hers as they had many times before. His skin was pale in death, but still bronzed and youthful. His long, silky hair fell gently from the headdress he wore. There was a small scar on his right cheek, but otherwise, he was perfect in her eyes. He had chosen her, but she knew, from looking at his face, that he could have had the hand of many a maiden in the kingdom. Still, he loved her to his death. One thing stood out above all other features. The runes on his skin were gold and silver.

Tears fell freely from the eyes of the Princess. She gently hugged her champion and then set him down on his back. All of the fiery malice that she had stored up in her heart cooled to dying embers within minutes of her tears. She surveyed the damage she had created and no longer wanted the throne. In fact, all that she now wished for was to be far, far away from this palace and the crown.

"I am sorry, my devoted," the Princess sobbed, kissing her savior's forehead and closing his eyes. "I have failed you, and I do not even know your name." Frowning with grief, she begged for forgiveness, although she knew that her god cared not for such things. Her fingers traced the golden runes on his cheeks, while she sat in wonder of the Galdrissen who had died trying to free her.

"Why is there so much suffering?" Vyqua asked, standing. She walked over to Sulfga, and much to her surprise, he was not dead. She contemplated cutting his throat for killing her devoted, but decided that Sulfga was only doing what he was supposed to. He was not at fault for the sins of her father. She resolved to allow him to live, calling out for help. The Princess awaited the roving guard to arrive.

The King was dead, but Sulfga lived on. The assassin had apparently not poisoned the sword he was using before the battle. Sulfga guessed the Galdrissen reasoned, poisons were good for some tasks, but against an honorable foe, they were taboo. The Todani laughed at the reasoning of the followers of the light, but he was not complaining. After the Princess had called for help, the guard brought the healers to the throne room. They mended Sulfga's wounds.

Sulfga would not make the same mistake as his enemy had. There would be no pardoning of the Princess for her treachery. Her gesture of mercy went without reciprocation.

* * *

Sulfga sat on the throne, the crown upon his head. He smiled smugly as he remembered the look of shock on Vyqua's face when he called the guard to arrest her for treason. The foolish girl spared his life when she should have finished the job that her lover could not complete. The warrior pushed his advantage in her moment of weakness. It was how he did business.

The riots were eventually crushed by the new King's men. Thousands were arrested and condemned to die in the vast dungeons below the palace, and Vyqua was among those imprisoned. Sulfga wanted to watch her beg for her life. If he could manage to break her spirit, he reasoned that she would perhaps be tamed and become a handsome mate. She was a gorgeous woman, but a bit much to handle. Despite the consequences of resisting the new King, the Princess made it clear that she was not interested in his proposition.

Vyqua had been in prison for many weeks. She had prayed to her God for deliverance, but as usual, Haeldrun was off doing whatever it was that gods do when they are busy. The overcrowded mass cells teemed with Todani prisoners. Sometimes, out of necessity, they milled about. On the most miserable of days, when the cells were so full of condemned souls, there was not even room to sit or lay down. Sanitation was non-existent. Many died every day of malnutrition and disease. The deaths of so many made the crowds question everything that they had accepted to this point. Gradually, there came a change of heart in many of the survivors.

Vyqua walked the cage like so many others. No one knew she was the Princess. They simply saw her as another educated Todani who had said the wrong thing and enraged the new tyrant who sat on the throne. She suffered with all the rest, but to those who were observant, there was something in her demeanor that seemed different. She did not lie down to die as so many others chose to do. She helped where she could, going hungry, giving up her gruel or molded bread to help some random starving child or old person. Many Todani took notice of her actions, and even the thieves' guild watched silently, making sure that Vyqua was untouchable in the cell. Anyone who sought to harm this Todani woman would face the wrath of the many she helped throughout her weeks in that abyss.

A hungry old man in rags coughed in the corner of the cell. "My lady," he begged, "a scrap of bread for an old beggar?"

Vyqua sighed sadly, looking at the pathetic lump of a man before her. Her stomach rumbled. She had only one small loaf of moldy bread in her hand. She thought about it and then tore off a piece, handing it to the wretched old man.

Sitting up with new life, the old man snatched it out of her hand greedily, but then repented. "I'm sorry, Princess. My manners are a bit rusty in here."

Vyqua sat wearily beside the twisted frame of a man. "As are mine. You know who I am?"

"It is plain to see, My Queen," the old man said, bowing his head and tearing off a small piece of bread with his ragged teeth. "You rise above and keep faith when *He* has abandoned the downtrodden—once again!"

"I have long lost faith that the Underlord will do anything that is not in his own interest." She looked around to see if anyone was listening. "There has to be something better than all of this, My Lord," Vyqua said wearily, tearing up.

"Oh, but there is, My Queen." The old man smiled, his grin toothless, save for two or three dispersed here and there. To Vyqua, his mouth resembled a crooked jack-o-lantern, and this made the Princess snicker.

"What is there for us? We are forsaken, old man." The princess moaned quietly in defeat. "Here," she motioned, covering the old man with a ragged blanket.

"You are too kind, My Lady," he responded. "Your heart is not the same as it once was, now, is it?"

"What do you know about it, old man?" she snapped self-consciously. "I have too much to atone for. No other would claim me, but the Underlord!"

"We all bear the marks of our sin, my dear, do we not?" the old man mumbled as he slipped off to sleep.

Vyqua leaned up against the rocky wall nearby. She looked at the old man fondly. Something about him reminded her of what she had always wished her father would be.

"I am of no good use, Sir. My only virtue is my vice," Vyqua spoke quietly, closing her eyes as tears trickled down from their corners.

The old man was awake, staring at her while she slept. Likedelir smiled gently, saying, "It is never too late, my dear." Muttering, the god rolled over and closed his eyes.

* * *

The guard blew their horns within the dungeon chambers. Most times, it was done more to wake the prisoners from the mercy that sleep brought, rather than to notify them of anything important. This horn, however, was vital, as it sounded that it was feeding time. From outside the bars, the guards heaved stale loaves of bread, questionable pieces of meat, and mostly swill, unfit for a swine, into the crowd. The Todani swarmed like rabid animals. Vyqua was annoyed by the scene, but walked the edge of the fray. She worked her way carefully into the maelstrom finding a stray loaf and some wilted cabbage. As she turned to go, she saw a young girl.

The Todani lass was of primary school age and looked as if she had not eaten in days. There was no parent in the immediate area, so Vyqua figured this girl was apparently on her own, and doing her best to find something to eat. She had found a wedge of hard, moldy cheese, and a small stale loaf of bread, not unlike what Vyqua had. The girl was on the floor of a filthy cage, clutching the rancid food with all of her petite frame's might. Two men were beating her, trying to coerce her into relinquishing her find. She screamed in pain, but was not giving in to their demands. Vyqua's eye twitched as she growled angrily.

Hands on her hips, the Princess howled at the two men badgering and beating the young one, "Get off of her, you two oafs!"

One of the two stopped kicking the child and turned to the Princess, slapping her hard across the face. "You shut it, or you're next, love."

Seeing that she was getting nowhere with the attackers and that the young one was now battered and crying, the Todani Princess stepped in angrily. "You swine! No, swine are more honorable than you are!! You are the ass of a swine!!! No, even lower! You are what comes from the ass of a swine!!!!"

The one who had slapped her turned again to deal another blow. "I told you to shut your mouth, woman!"

"I do not care for your attitude, My Lord!" the Princess said, kicking the man in his groin as hard as she could muster.

The filthy mongrel fell to the ground, clutching his testicles and moaning. He laid on the ground, writhing in pain.

Turning to the other, she could see that he was even more substantial in stature. This Todani man had taken to beating the young one with a belt. Without thinking, Vyqua slid in between the attacker and the child, shielding the young one from her abuser. The leather strap cracked across the back of the Princess, and she let out a sharp yelp from the pain.

"You will not beat this child any longer. What is wrong with all of you!? You fight each other as if we are enemies! Do you all not see that we are the only thing each other has now! Will you give them the satisfaction of killing one another over a spoiled piece of cheese and moldy bread?"

As she finished her statement, the man stopped swinging. The crowd was silently looking at her. Vyqua stood, turning to those who listened, asking, "What are we doing here? Why do we settle for this torment while we still walk upon the green? Do we not live? Do we not have dreams? Do you not love some and hate others?" Vyqua looked at the man with the belt. He had dropped it and cowered in shame from her words.

Vyqua stood, brushing the refuse from the tattered rags that wrapped the child's body. She helped her to stand. The young one immediately hugged the Princess around her waist, sobbing.

"Todani are not savages. We are a proud people." Vyqua brushed the young one's filthy hair. "No child should suffer this fate while praying to ANY God who is thought to be worthy of the worship of his people!"

The crowd began to murmur of heresy, unsure of the statement. A random voice cried out, "Hush! Let her speak!"

Vyqua struggled for the words she felt in her heart. She looked down at the little girl's face below her. She now knew why the men had beaten her so. Smiling widely, the Princess saw the golden runes upon the young girl's face. She was a Galdrissen. The Princess thought of her deliverer, who died in the royal chambers. She knew that he had found his way past the catacombs—at least Vyqua hoped. The girl looking up at her, beckoned for the Princess to stoop so she could whisper in her ear. The Princess complied.

"He will have you, My Lady," she whispered. "If you call out, he will come to you."

Looking up to the crowd, the Princess smiled. She let go of past hatred, anger, and strife. "What good is a God whose only mission is to kill all that lives? He created us to kill!? I, for one, reject this folly! I wish to live in peace! To love and raise my own family! To prosper with, and not off of my neighbor!"

Vyqua finished speaking. She staggered, regaining her balance, and immediately felt overwhelming nausea. The crowd around her was still silent. Falling to her knees, she called out to the sky for help.

"Help me, my God, for I no longer wish to live in this darkness!" the Princess shouted loudly with her eyes closed.

"He comes, My Lady," the small girl said with a tooth missing in her smile.

Vyqua felt her skin burning. She cried out in pain, but it was over within a moment. The smell of burnt hair and ozone permeated the air around her person as she slowly opened her eyes. The world seemed different now. Things looked different. No longer did her surroundings have darkness or a shade around it. The Princess saw light in every corner of the gloom. Returning to the moment at hand, Vyqua again looked at the young one, astonished at the newfound peace that she felt in her heart.

"Look at your runes, My Lady! They are wonderful!" the girl exclaimed.

Vyqua looked. Her runes were the brightest gold. They were almost luminous. "What has happened to me, child?" she asked.

"He has claimed you, because you called. My God has come to many in this hole. He has even changed your black eyes to ice blue, though you cannot see them yet!" the girl beamed at her protector.

A random Galdrissen woman handed the Princess a shard of a looking glass. Vyqua saw her light skin, illuminated with golden runes that seemed as if an artist had painted them onto her skin. She looked at her face. Her jet-black hair fell, matted over her dirty face. Two eyes, much like those of her devoted, stared back from her reflection.

As Vyqua stood, she heard the cries of others who called out to the new god. Many others cried out throughout the day. Before the evening, three in four within the dungeon had become part of the Redeemed.

When news of the conversions reached Sulfga, he shrugged, deeming himself too busy to deal with traitors at the moment. The war continued to go badly. He feared that another uprising of the commoners was only being averted by his declaration of brutal martial law. His royal coffers were emptying rapidly from the expenses of suppressing rebellion and defending the city walls. The new King knew that he would have to negotiate peace soon. If he could not find a way to bring about a cessation of hostilities, his nation would be physically and financially ruined. A few more Galdrissen in the world was not the concern of King Sulfga, the venerable. Saving his own hide was.

Chapter 19

It was getting dark, and Orus was concerned. Nothing was happening in his immediate vicinity, but something immense cried out from the west earlier, and then had gone silent after that. The Hodan worried about a surprise attack by a Dragon, especially as nightfall approached. The Todani forces had retreated into the edge of the forest and held their position. They had not fled to the surprise of the Hodan King. Silently, Orus wondered if the Todani were regrouping and awaiting reinforcements. He did not know how close to the truth that the assumption was.

Kepir scouted the enemy camp. They were well-organized and equipped for battle. The Todani unit, now that it had collected itself, catching its breath, regrouped as a formidable, but outnumbered crew. The Hodan spy skulked in the darkened corners of the wood, listening for any discussion of their plans, but the camp was oddly silent, as if they were waiting upon something ominous. After a short while, the specialist could see that the entire group was praying and meditating. Nothing good came from the Todani beseeching aid from their god, the Underlord. Kepir left the area and returned to his own lines to pass the word to Orus.

* * *

Dryna was in the cave, as far back as her healers could be. She could see the thousands of humans, Elves, Dwarves, and Galdrissen standing shoulder to shoulder in the large entrance. She was impressed by the scene, but worried for Orus. He had pushed so hard to finish. He had come so far, and now, the Dragon threatened all the Degran nation had gained. She closed her eyes and whispered a prayer to Likedelir for deliverance, and then turned to her nearest girl.

"How are they doing, lass?" the Holy Mother asked.

"They are comfortable, My Lady, but many will not see the 'morn." The girl's shoulders dropped with the statement, and she frowned.

"War is for fools, child. The sooner we figure that out, the better!" Dryna patted her on the shoulder and went about changing the dressings of those she thought could be saved.

* * *

The sky was overcast, and the moon was a hazy sliver in the black sky. It looked as if rain would fall at any moment, but not a drop had fallen yet. The Todani slept in shifts around small fires. Others stood watch, ready to sound the alarm if the Hodan left the cave they hid in, far across the large open field between the two armies. The uneasy sleep was the first that they had experienced in days, but it would not last. It was not the Hodan who disturbed those who rested, but something even more terrifying.

* * *

Scoria hovered over the field, flapping his large leathery wings. From his vantage point, he could spy the Underlord's children huddled against a backdrop of the forest. Across the field, inside of a cavernous opening in the side of the mountain, the Dragon could plainly see firelight dancing. The humans and Elves would be there in force. The black Dragon let out a

324

roar from high above the field. The Todani armies scrambled awake and again turtled up under their large shields. Swords and spears protruded from all angles. The Dragon chuckled.

Scoria's black scales were invisible in the darkness. He moved undetected by humans, high above the fray, landing in the middle of the field with a loud crash. He sniffed the area knowingly.

"Silly humans," the Dragon growled in Kepir's mind. "You can hide from my eyes, but ne'er my nose."

"Run!" Kepir shouted to his men, popping up in front of the Dragon.

The field exploded into life as specialists ran in all directions. The Dragon looked around him, spraying fire randomly, then turned to his front once more, but the leader of the hidden was gone.

"You cannot win, human," the Dragon taunted. "How can you expect to defeat something as powerful as I?"

"I do not have to defeat you. I only have to distract you," Kepir answered in a whisper.

"I will cook you and eat your bones, human!" Scoria growled, stomping forward to where he could smell men hiding. He let loose another blast of flame, immediately scorching the area and killing ten specialists in one breath.

"Kepir! Foolish one!" Henargya scolded. "Hodan are too brave for their own health!"

"Be careful, Dragon Mother. He is no ordinary Dragon!" Kepir warned.

"I fully understand my plight, young one! Flee!"

* * *

"Mages, up!" the Commander shouted to the rear of the formation.

Twenty souls in robes rushed to the front of the lines.

"Shield to the front, now!" the Commander ordered. "We are moving out on my order!"

Uilam's face was one of horror as he marched his unit out after Orus, who had galloped out onto the field when he saw his specialists in trouble. The King glowed slightly. His shield was covering half of his person, while he rode with a spear in his other hand. Uilam watched as Orus expertly guided his steed without hands toward the last known location of his brother-in-arms. Hodan was out in the open within seconds as a roaring battle cry filled the valley in front of them. Small fires had started in the woods and on the plains, as dead foliage and detritus burst into flame from Dragon fire.

"Ed, cover the flank! Keep those swine from maneuvering around our left!"

"Aye, Captain!" Ed said seriously, shouting orders to his lines to form up.

As Uilam was directing traffic, another booming roar reached the ears of everyone present. It was coming from inside the cave. It was Henargya, and she was livid. The Dragon in the field threatened her children and her friends. The mother had awakened and was on her way.

"Hold your ground! Mages, shield the units to the front! Elves, please use magic against that monster!" Uilam pleaded.

The Vynwrathian archmagi nodded, and lightning began falling from the skies. Fireballs launched toward the hulking black mass, crashing with little effect except to annoy the thunder lizard. Through his spyglass, Uilam saw the Hodan's static lines had formed on the battlefield. The Todani marched under the cover of the Dragon, as Orus reached his target. On the field near the obsidian death, a singed and beaten Master Kepir laid, crawling toward the shadows. Orus, having seen enough, dismounted within twenty yards of the beast as it turned to answer the pesky mages.

The Hodan King hurled his spear in anger, only to have it bounce off of the behemoth's shining scales. Grabbing Kepir, Orus threw him over his saddle and slapped the horse's hindquarters. The beast lit off toward friendly lines, arriving moments later. Orus, however, was still on the field.

Looking up at the towering creature before him, the Hodan King could not help but be awed. The amber light of burning refuse, forest, and bodies reflected gold off of the obsidian reptile's armored body. For a moment, the old Hodan warrior was gripped by a feeling he had not experienced in almost forty years—defeat. Closing his eyes, the King remembered the past. The beast roared, jetting flame at his Elfish mages, and the King snarled angrily at his fears. Taking one deep breath, the Hodan warrior reached down and grabbed a sword from a nearby specialist. The man lamented the sight of the lad, who was now no more than a cinder. Orus had no idea who he used to be or what race. The warrior was simply ash in the shape of a humanoid, but the metal of his weapon was barely scorched. Orus checked the blade, squinted with determination, and then turned to face his doom.

Likedelir watched with a grin. "This one IS no doubt a Champion!" he said with glee strengthening his man.

Orus stood tall with renewed confidence to the confusion of the Dragon, who turned to confront his new foolish foe.

Scoria taunted, "Are you mad, puny human!?"

"Perhaps, but I have lived as long as I care to without a nation, vile demon. What land would I have without my kindred? It would just be a lifeless potter's field, not a home!"

The army stood in awe as they witnessed one man stand before the now fully illuminated monstrosity that dwarfed him. Orus pulled his shield in front of him and prepared to die with this sword in his hand while standing his ground. He had never asked less from his own men. He would require the same of his own service.

* * *

Edmund's men had engaged the Todani. They held the high ground, but the Todani were relentless, being encouraged by the Dragon's presence. They knew that with this blessing from the Underlord, they had the upper hand. Uilam reinforced the defensive lines, and all seemed to be contained for the moment, when he turned to see the King standing alone before the demon in black.

"What are you doing, Orus!?" the young Captain cried out, calling for a unit to immediately reinforce the King. The Hodan Elites turned, as did a platoon of Elfish Rangers. They moved as quickly as possible, but everyone watching knew it would be for naught if the Dragon attacked. They could never arrive in time.

Uilam's hair stood up on the back of his neck as a strong breeze suddenly blew. A loud shrieking roar surprised the engaged armies as a slightly smaller copper Dragon crashed down in front of Orus, who had not budged one step from in front of Scoria, who openly mocked him.

"Oh, my gods, Uilam! What does His Majesty think he's doing out there!?" Edmund asked in disbelief of his eyes.

"I do not know, brother! Do not concern yourself with that! Watch the Toads! Keep them busy while we help His Majesty deal with this beast!"

"Yes, Sir! Luck in battle, brother!" Edmund said, saluting and charging to the front of the lines.

"We are going to need it, my brother," Uilam thought, shaking.

* * *

The Elves were also ancient comparative to the fleeting lives of humans and the slightly more durable Galdrissen. Time allowed them to practice, and with much study, the Elves were extremely skilled mages. The black Dragon was enraged that he could seemingly do nothing to the annoying pot-shotting Elves. Henargya used this folly against her foe, wasting no time in getting right to it. Immediately upon landing, she attacked the preoccupied opponent, removing a chunk of flesh from his side, while the Dragon continued in his attempts to set the Elfish archmagis afire. Scoria yelped out in pain and turned, burping out a blast of fire, but Henargya was already airborne.

High above the field and out of sight of those below, a battle raged in the sky. Two immense thunder lizards could be heard flapping their wings and snapping their enormous maws at one another. Occasionally, fire would erupt, illuminating the sky. No one knew where the sky would light up next.

"Sire," a voice called to Orus, "get out of there!"

Orus looked over, waking as if from a dream, realizing Uilam was frantically calling to him. The King walked to where his Captain called from. Uilam was frantic. Orus appeared as large as the legends made him out to be all those years ago when the Captain was but a brand-new recruit.

"Hurry, Sire! Before they land again!"

But the boy was too late. Henargya fell out of the sky with an unceremonious crash within yards of where Orus stood.

The Dragon was severely burned. The parts of her body that were not scorched were torn and bleeding. She was in great pain, stumbling to right herself as her attacker landed about one-hundred yards from her position. Scoria was looking much worse for wear also, but appeared to have the upper hand. The black Dragon limped, dragging a leg behind him. He tried to take flight, but could not manage to stay aloft for more than a second, before thumping hard on the ground. Both Dragons had taken the other to task. Henargya did not look as if she would be able to continue the fight for much longer.

"Protect my babies, human," the Dragon Mother pleaded. "You must protect them. I beg of you, great King of humankind."

"You have my word, my friend. I will do my best. They will survive, or we will not see the day without them."

Orus saluted and bowed. The Dragon Mother stood and faced her foe once more. A short battle ensued, but within a few moments, Henargya lay motionless on the ground.

Orus roared, "HODAN, ON ME! Attack that motherless serpent and send it to Haeldrun in pieces!"

His voice boomed, echoing off of the hills and trees. There was a chattering series of chirps off in the distance as Hodan turned to face the Underlord's minion.

329

Scoria responded with a chuckle. The battered foe had lost the use of one eye, but could still see out of the other well enough to light an entire legion ablaze in one breath. Screams filled the air, as did the smell of burning hair and flesh. The problem is, the thunder lizard, in his rush to inflict damage, had not seen with his injured eye that he had not only incinerated a Degran legion, but his fire also decimated the Todani army that was locked in battle with his enemy. Still, the remaining Hodan and Degran charged the demon at a run, shouting obscenities in many languages into the air.

The first lines met the impervious scales on the flanks of their foe, unable to inflict any damage. Searching feverishly for a solution, lest they all be eaten, Uilam noticed gaps in the armor due to the injuries inflicted during the battle with Henargya.

"Attack the bloodied spots on this bastard!" Uilam bellowed. "There is no armor where there are injuries! Spearmen, to the front!"

From the flanks, the surviving Hodan chopped feverishly at their foe, but it seemed they still were receiving the worst of the engagement.

* * *

"Mother!" the white Dragon called out into the darkness. He whimpered, questioning like a heartbroken child. "Mother?"

"She told us to stay with the whelps, young one!" his sister reminded, scolding.

"Not stay! MotheRRRRRRRR!" Smudge barked angrily.

"We must protect the youngers," the copper retorted.

"You stay! You protect! Smudge goes. Find Mother!" The younger Dragon spat fire randomly.

Smudge flailed angrily at his sister, baring his swordlike fangs when she sought to physically restrain him. Escaping her grasp, he flew out of a passage in the walls of the cave. Within seconds, the young Dragon had cleared the mountain and was halfway to battle. The air was filled with twenty of his sisters and brothers. They all looked at the angry adolescent Dragon for direction.

"MOTHER!" Smudge roared angrily, and the enraged brood echoed his call. Still, there was no response.

As Smudge approached the scene, all came into focus. There, on the field, was his mother. She was not moving, and the Hodan were swarming another, much like she was, but with a different aura. Smudge smelled his mother's blood in the air; it was mingled with the blood of many beings, but it was unmistakable. The rage in his heart overflowed. His eyes glowed amber.

"NOOOOOOOOO!" Smudge said, diving like a dart at the large black mass.

The colossal, jet-black head snapped up immediately at the sound of another Dragon's roar, but it was too late to react to the expanding plume of fire as it impacted his face, blinding the other eye.

Orus bellowed, and his Commanders echoed the call, "Back off! Back off! Back off! Fire! Fire! Fire! Regroup!"

Several more ranks of Hodan and Degran were either fatally burned by the airborne attack, or crushed to death by the elder Dragon's response. The obsidian lizard now thrashed wildly as it was utterly blinded, knowing that there was another of his kind coming in for the kill. Scoria did not realize that there were many more than Smudge to contend with.

The young Dragons took turns, sometimes one at a time, sometimes in groups, pounding the ancient into submission. Over an hour of continuous beating, they achieved the goal. Scoria was defeated, but not without additional cost. Ten more young Dragons perished in the attack. Orus looked at the scene with awe. He had seen this sort of thing once or twice before in his life, but only on the Arondayre was the action this close to his forces, and the losses on every side so extensive.

Smudge lay on the field beside Scoria. The Hodan King galloped over to the white Dragon, calling to his healers.

"Dryna! Dryna! Save this one! He is important to me. He has saved our skin more than once!"

Dryna acknowledged the King, looking up from the carnage she surveyed. Quickly, the Priestess gave brief instructions to her acolytes on how to tell who was going to live or die.

"Comfort those traveling to the other side. Spend your efforts on those who will be with us tomorrow." Dryna was weary of war. She ran to where Orus shouted.

"Dryna, please," Orus said, kneeling next to Smudge.

"Orus ... friend ...," the white Dragon wheezed in pain, unable to sit upright.

"Yes, I am," the King responded. He turned to the Priestess, begging, "Dryna ..."

The Priestess nodded. "I will do what can be done, Orus."

The Hodan King stood and watched as the Priestess bound the Dragon's wounds. She force-fed it a healing potion or two, as it protested, and then she kneeled to pray, as the young lizard slept quietly.

Orus looked over at Henargya's immense corpse. It was adjacent to where the demon Scoria's body lay. The stench of burned flesh and bodily waste filled the air. Orus frowned, grabbing a two-handed battle axe from the scattered weapons on the ground. Angrily, he walked over to the obsidian Dragon's body and spat on it. Swinging the axe in futility, he tried to cut the head of the Dragon off as a trophy, but the scales were still too strong for mere metal implements. As the sweaty King rested, he heard someone's steps approaching.

"Brother, what are you doing?" Kepir asked, chuckling. He was bandaged over most of his head and part of his torso. "You need a mage for that."

"I know." Orus said deadpanning, "but I was so angry, I thought perhaps my god would allow me superhuman strength just one time. What are you doing off of the healing mats!? Fool!"

"Fool? Me?" Kepir asked, limping over to his King and hugging him with one arm. "It seems another fool ran out in front of this monster to save one man."

"He is more than one man. He is worth fifty, no one-hundred!" Orus declared earnestly, then the brash King frowned. "And, he's the only friend from the old days who this old fool has left. You're not my servant. You are my brother. You would have come for me also."

Kepir nodded, smirking. "I love you also, brother. Thank you for saving this old wretch's life. Be well. I fear that I must rest now. On my way back to the cave, I will send a mage to finish this job for you."

Orus snorted. "Please do. This thing is not coming off of those shoulders any other way!"

* * *

The morning dawned a couple of hours later, revealing the true devastation of the battle during the night. Uilam tallied the dead and collected the names of those on the pyres. Among them, to his dismay, was Edmund, who had held the line against the Todani push. When the Scoria attacked, his fire burned both humans and Todani alike. Uilam retired to a corner of the cave and cried silently while drinking a skin of mead. A small green Dragon watched in curiosity, deciding to deter anyone in the area from disturbing his new friend.

"Human friend?" the green one asked like a little child.

"Yes, Dragon. Friend," Uilam said, sharing a piece of his rations to the lizard's delight.

* * *

Orus and Kepir were on the field with Dryna and her acolytes. They had conscripted a band of warriors to help with the collection of any of the bodies that were not already burnt to a crisp. The Priestess and her charges then proceeded to set the pyres of the dead—enemy and friend—while saying prayers for all of the deceased.

The Degran forces respectfully collected the young adult Dragons who fell in battle against Scoria, dragging the adolescent lizards into a circle around Henargya, their mother. The head of Scoria had been removed by the mages the night prior and now resided in a large logistics wagon, much to Dryna's displeasure. She was disgusted by its presence, but also understood what Orus meant to do with his new trophy. Fear was the only thing the Todani understood. Dryna smiled as she tried to imagine what would instill more fear within the fearless than an enemy warrior who showed up with the head of your deliverer, carried to you in a box?

The Todani would think twice about attacking Hodan after they saw that display, or at least that was the hope. If not, Orus still had friends of the scaly sort, but he hoped to keep them from the fray and fulfill his promise to their valiant mother.

Smudge was awake and as unpredictable as usual. He started the morning complaining about his injuries and then remembered the night's events. He looked over at his mother with a sense of great sadness in his eyes. Orus stood by the young Dragon as Smudge sat back and spread his wings. It was the first time Orus had seen the young one act so confident. The sister had arrived, Orus smiled. That was it.

"Mother has fallen, Smudge," the copper said tenderly. "I am sorry."

"Humans call you Aura now?" Smudge questioned.

"Yes, they have named me this," the copper responded.

"Aura. Mother—Avenged."

"I heard what you did, child," Aura smiled, nuzzling her younger sibling. "You are fearless, Smudge."

"Not fair," Smudge lamented.

"Nothing ever is, brother," Aura remarked. "Let us send them all to Aeternum, shall we?"

"Yes," Smudge responded, lighting off into the sky as if he felt better.

The Hodan, Degran, and Vyn all backed away to a safe distance from both felled Dragons. In a ring, the thirty remaining young Dragons, led by their new matron, a copper Dragon named Aura, lit Henargya and her fallen children afire in Dragon's fire. It was not long after that the bodies were consumed by the intensity of the flames. In contrast, the human pyres burned for the entire day.

* * *

"How many legions remain, Uilam?" Orus demanded.

"Ten Degran legions, two-hundred-fifty cavalry, five-hundred archers, a platoon of specialists, and a platoon of Vynwrathian Rangers, Sire," the newly-promoted Commander numbly responded, looking out at the pyres.

"Have them ready to march on Haeldrun Ir in two days, son," Orus said with a hint of apprehension.

"Yes, Sire. I will pass the word to the legion Captains and the Vyn," Uilam responded without emotion.

"I know, son. I know what you are feeling right now. Edmund was a good man. He will be missed. He will not be forgotten for his deeds," Orus said, placing his hand on Uilam's spaulder.

"He will never be forgotten. He was my best friend from the time we played in the gutters in Whaleford to the keeps in the mountains. He was my brother when we joined the Hodan at Redemption and fought not once, but twice against the Scourge. He died my brother last night, protecting my flank. You are correct, My King. He will never be forgotten."

Orus nodded and shook his new Commander's hand.

"Leave a rearguard in the caves with proper provisions to defend the Dragon den. I owe an old friend for her acts of bravery and sacrifice."

Uilam stood at attention and saluted his King. "It shall be done, Sire."

The Commander left to inform his Captains of their orders.

Chapter 20

The remaining Hodan and Vynwrathian armies marched four days westward, meeting very little resistance by either Dwarf or Todani. It seemed that both larger armies had retreated to their appropriate sides, waiting for the other shoe to drop. Sulfga and the Todani held their fortified positions, wondering what had become of their Dragon, Scoria. It had been quiet for almost five days now, and the Todani King wondered if the unthinkable had occurred. Still, he reasoned that he had not seen the vaunted human army, nor the Dwarfish war machine from the south. Their absence was encouraging.

"Maybe," the Todani thought, "they have retired from the field and will come to negotiate a peace?"

Hamrick II had more problems than he could handle on the home front. His armies were more than halved by combat with the northern kingdom. The populace of Dornat Al Fer, seeing the carnage and casualties of the open war with Haeldrun Ir, and now a Dragon, had soured on the proposition of continuing to support the war effort. Many mothers cried out for peace, having lost not one, but many sons on the field. Neither kingdom held an advantage after a long struggle, and now the fear of invasion from a new human threat had the people questioning what was going on with their new, young King. Many wondered if the young Dwarf had what it would take to right the ship, or if he'd continue making emotional decisions that the common Dwarf would be required to suffer for.

* * *

The Todani horns began to blow in every hamlet and village east of the walled city of Haeldrun Ir. Sulfga's sentries reported that a large army of humans and Elves were a day or two's march from the city walls. The villagers outside the gates were fleeing before the impressive display of hardened Degran warriors. The city courtyards were quickly becoming large, unorganized, and unsanitary refugee camps. The suffering was unbearable in every corner of the city. People began to wonder what their new King was up to. Things kept spiraling downward into chaos and despair, yet there was no address from their monarch-only silence.

Sulfga could hear the murmuring in the corners of the palace. He saw the unrest growing. Frustrated, the old warrior thought, *This will be the shortest reign ever, if I cannot get something done about this mess and soon!*

"Sire, they are visible from the gates," a squire reported.

"What are they doing?" Sulfga asked plainly.

"They have stopped marching and have set their lines. They have dug in and made field defenses. I am not sure if they are resting, or preparing for something more."

As the squire finished his report, another messenger bolted into the room with a spyglass in his hand. He was frantic.

"Sire! Sire! You must see this!" the young Todani unceremoniously blurted out.

"What is this all about, boy?" Sulfga grunted in aggravation.

"You must see it, Sire." The boy's face was sullen. It had paled with fear and confusion.

Sulfga took the spyglass and followed the boy to the tower. There, the messenger pointed to where Hodan was clearly visible. Sulfga calculated that they would reach the gates within day's march. He lifted the glass and looked at what the boy was squawking on about. He dropped the spyglass, wide-eyed and appalled at what he saw.

"Is that ..." The King trailed off, looking at the boy.

"We believe so, Sire. It is the head of Scoria, the savior sent by Haeldrun." The boy frowned. "They are going to kill us all, aren't they, Sire?"

"Pull yourself together, soldier," the King said, becoming the old General he had been just a short time ago. "We are never defeated, until we yield the field."

The boy stood up straight and responded loudly, "Yes, Sire!"

* * *

Orus could hear the horns and his few remaining specialists reported to him that the Todani fled when they saw the armies coming. The King was pleased, but did not look assured of his position on the field. He knew that the Todani would not just lay down and die. He had fought the tenacious little bastards too many times to be fooled by their retreat.

"Set the line, Kepir. We rest here." Orus watched his friend leave to do as he was ordered. He turned to Uilam. "Have the head brought out fifty yards in front of the main shield wall. Have braziers and standing torches set all around it. I want those savage little bastards to see the fate of their savior. I want them to know he is dead. They do not have to know that we didn't do it ourselves!"

Uilam snorted sarcastically. "I hope they soil their armor. As you command, Sire. It will be done."

* * *

In the bowels of the dungeon below the keep in Haeldrun Ir, Vyqua gathered her new converts. The new group began a community effort to help everyone within their circle survive. They shared their food and banded together to thwart intimidation by Todani adherents who sought to harm them, because they were considered traitors.

The new converts began wondering at the changes that had befallen them upon rejecting the Underlord. Not knowing who to pray to, the community begged the sky for an answer. Fear had begun to grip the remaining mob of Haeldrun followers in the cells. Many loyal to the Underlord skulked off to separate corners of the filthy cells. They did not wish to consort with the infidels and further anger their God. However, others wondered at the conversions of so many. When the whispers of the defeat of their Dragon savior, Scoria, began to circulate in the open rooms of the prison, many more of the followers of Haeldrun wondered if they were being forsaken. They questioned the silence of the Underlord, and became despondent by his lack of response to their cries.

As more days passed, the Galdrissen numbers continued to increase. The jailers were appalled by what they saw happening. The followers of Haeldrun were now outnumbered two to one by the traitors with golden runes. Every day, there were more.

* * *

"Bring that damned girl to me now," Sulfga fumed furiously.

"At once, Sire," a guard responded.

Sulfga sat at an elaborate table setting with two lavishly dressed Todani women. They ate their fills and drank until giddy. Sulfga smiled nefariously while staring at the two. He had plans for them later. A while later, after the King was well into his glasses of mead, the guard returned with a filthy prisoner from the dungeon. She stood silently, but defiantly. Her head was not bowed, and her eyes blazed a bright blue, as if they were ice from a glacier. Her runes stood out against her skin, luminescent as if there were molten gold poured into channels on her flesh. Sulfga sneered in disgust.

"Sire, the Princess," the guard responded, "as ordered."

"Shackle her to the post," Sulfga responded.

Vyqua was chained to a large wooden stanchion. It had several large iron rings on it where others could be secured to the post. It smelled of blood, sweat, and urine.

Vyqua stood silently, waiting to be spoken to.

"I can see by your markings that you have forsaken your people," Sulfga said with disgust.

"I have not forsaken my people, only their God," Vyqua responded calmly.

Sulfga nodded, and a guard struck the Princess in the face. She bled freely from a small gash below her left eye, and her upper lip began to swell.

"Well, know this, young lady," Sulfga stood up and walked to where the obstinate Galdrissen woman stared him in the eye. "I will not stand for you leading another rebellion. First, you seek to overthrow our government, and now, you even seek to sully our God's good name!"

"Good name?" Vyqua licked her lips, tasting blood. "He is nothing good at all."

Sulfga reached up to strike her again, but was disturbed by a voice from the table. It was one of the young Todani slave girls who addressed him. She was the one the General had been staring at for the longest time before Vyqua had arrived.

"You should not strike her, My Lord," she taunted, smiling. "The wolf is at your gates—or should I say the lion."

She stood defiantly.

"You will shut your mouth until I am ready to use it, whore," the Todani King responded angrily, readying to strike the Princess again.

"Oh, rest assured, *great one*, it is not a good idea to abuse the chosen of this new God. He does not take too kindly to it." She smiled mischievously.

"Guards! Tie that one up next to this one. She is next," the King demanded.

The young Todani woman, her eyes now aglow, said calmly, placing her hand on the guard who grabbed her, "Oh, I do not think so, wretch."

The guard fell to the ground unconscious.

"Who are you, witch!? Are you a Hodan mage come to assassinate me? I have many guards; they will have your head before the day is through,"

Sulfga stated with conviction.

"You mean like that one?" the girl responded, giggling. "And that one?" She pointed at the Todani near Sulfga, and he immediately fell to the ground, unconscious.

Sulfga backed away, fumbling for his sword. He had seen enough. This mage was one of considerable power.

The girl strutted up to the next guard. "How about this one, Sulfga?"

The guard looked at the girl with apprehension, and then fell where he stood.

"Who are you?" the King asked in fear. "What do you want?"

"I want my children, pig. Give them to me. Now."

The mage sat in a nearby chair without a care. She looked at the remaining guards with a challenge in her eyes, as if to say, "Do you wish to test me next?" None did. They held their ground.

Vyqua looked at the stunning beauty of the woman in the chair, wondering if this were Haya herself, in the pit of Haeldrun. She stared. The woman waved nonchalantly at the Princess and then turned back to Sulfga.

"I am sorry to ask this, but are you Haya, My Lady?" the Princess asked, averting her eyes.

"She's smarter than you are, King," the woman smirked and looked at her bowing convert.

"Answer her, intruder," Sulfga demanded, trying to maintain an air of control in his voice.

Angrily, the young woman stared at him. "And what if I was, fool? Would I be intimidated by a dolt such as yourself?" The woman stood defiantly. "You are a worm. You are just what father needs in his devoted. You are such a coward. You are as spineless as the rest of his Scourge."

"Father?" Vyqua asked, picking up on the word. "You said father? Is Haeldrun your father, My Lady?"

"Well, child, yes. Haeldrun, for all of his faults, is Father of all the Gods, save for Mother," the woman responded, walking within inches of the chained Princess. "So, if I'm not Mother or Father, who am I? That is your question?"

"Yes, My Lady. I am sorry that I do not know you," Vyqua said as she began to tremble with fear.

"Be still, child. My name is Likedelir, and I am your God. I am not a man or woman, but a God. I take the form of what I choose, for I am the center of all. I am known in hushed circles as the Conflict. I am the one who keeps the two sides at bay so all that is, remains. I am the response to your prayers—to all of your prayers. King Orus, who stands outside your gates, is my Champion, and with him is my High Priestess. Redemption is near for my people, or death awaits the Todani."

Vyqua's eyes were wide open as she looked at the woman's beautiful face. She was in awe of the presence of her god. It was a feeling of elation and unmitigated terror. The woman's smile welcomed the Princess and seemed to beg her to be calmed.

"Would this better suit you, Princess?" the God asked, turning into a twisted old, toothless man in rags. Sulfga gasped in horror that his love interest was now a wretch from the gutters.

"You!" Vyqua said, her mouth agape. "I ... I ... I ..."

"You were kind, child. Kinder than anyone I met in a month. I decided that you would be my Prophet to the Todani. Call them to me. No one shall harm a hair on your head, or I will show them what a real monster looks like."

Likedelir changed his form again, this time to a hooded traveler with a staff in hand and a bow hung over his shoulder. Reaching up, he released the Princess. He touched her face and healed all of her injuries. Then, he blessed her. Her clothing became bright white with golden runes on it. She was no longer filthy, but freshly groomed. Her silky, black hair was up with golden picks and ribbons. On top of her head was an elaborate headdress.

"Too much?" Likedelir asked, smiling at his new Prophetess.

The Princess saw her reflection in a nearby looking glass and was stunned. "My God, I am not worthy."

"You are as worthy as anyone else who treads upon the green, My Lady," Likedelir responded, lifting her chin. "No one is without sin. No one is without virtue. All who seek will find their place. Go find them in every

342

public place. I hear their voices, but they are afraid. Tell them there is room for them where you are now, if they will only listen to your words and ask to enter."

"But you cannot! My Lord will not allow this!" Sulfga bellowed.

"Silence, fool. He has not come to your aid, because you have failed to kill the light, yet again; foolish Todani failures. He is devising a new plan, I am sure. You are the old plan, and not a very original one, if I may say so. Mother's plan was quite entertaining. This one is of my design. Change or die, Sulfga. Your future is in your hands." Likedelir said another blessing on his Prophetess. Her runes actually lit the immediate area.

Vyqua looked down at her arms in disbelief. She cried, because she felt so unworthy, but to her dismay, her God just smiled at her patiently.

"Are you done with all of that now?" Likedelir asked, grinning widely.

Vyqua dabbed her eyes and sniffled, nodding like a schoolgirl who had just been scolded.

"Yesterday is a memory. This is now, girl. Go forth!"

Vyqua bowed. "As you command, my god."

Likedelir shook his head. "I see that bowing is not only for humans. So be it. Bowing it will be!" Turning to Sulfga and the many guards and ministers now in the royal feast hall, Likedelir declared in a loud voice, "Know this Todani! If anyone places their hand upon this child of Conflict with harm in their hearts, they will be struck down immediately. Try me on this at your own peril. I do not make idle threats. Let her glow be your reminder and warning."

Vyqua now stood alone, looking at her oppressor. "My God, where have you gone? Come back, please!"

"In the name of Haeldrun, seize that woman!" Sulfga demanded, but his guards all stood still in fear.

There was an awkward silence as everyone within the hall looked at the beautiful, white-robed, glowing maiden before them. No one wanted to touch her. Then one stepped forward, grabbing her arm forcefully. Vyqua stared at the face of the guard in fear.

The blood vessels in the guard's eyes immediately burst. The young

Todani cried out in pain, clutching his eyes, then falling to his knees as he gurgled loudly. He clutched at his throat, as if invisible hands choked him. Struggling, he gasped for breath as blood began to pour out of his now blackened eyes. Within seconds, the young man was lying motionless on his side.

The Princess frowned at the gore and looked up at the crowd of Todani before her.

"I should leave now. You should feed my people in the dungeons better. Please, move before more of *this* happens. I should not keep her—her, er, or him waiting," Vyqua said, slowly walking toward the exit.

Those who hadn't fled at the scene that had just occurred parted widely, staring at the Princess in horror.

As the Princess passed by the crowd of onlookers, several of the public cried out in pain, rising with golden runes upon their skin.

The Prophetess said calmly, motioning into the crowd, "Come, Redeemed, let us go out of this place!"

Twenty or so new Galdrissen meekly pushed through the crowd of stunned Todani. They joined the Princess and left the chamber unmolested by those who witnessed the scene.

* * *

Orus could see that no one was coming. He figured that the Todani were tucked safely inside their walls, so why would they venture out into an open field to meet the Degran and Hodan head-on. They had the defensive advantage, but Orus would starve them out if necessary. The King's only concern was that he was unsure of what the Dwarfish kingdom was up to. There was evidence of their decimation at the hands of Scoria. Orus wondered if they were still licking their wounds or regrouping for a counterattack? It had been some time since the old warrior had seen a hostile Dwarf.

"Kepir, how are your injuries healing?" the King asked his best friend.

"I am managing, brother," the scarred specialist responded.

Orus could see that Kepir now wore a patch on his left eye. The old warrior lamented the fact that his friend had endured so much pain. He wished that he had reacted sooner and spared his trusted ally the scars he now bore. Kepir picked up on his King's mood.

He responded, "Orus, my friend, no one could have done anything more than you did. No one dared to move. I am grateful to still see the sky above me and the green below. You have no reason to feel sorry for me! I will adapt to one eye. It's a bit different, but with time, I will figure things out. Besides, brother, this will be our final battle, if the Dwarves have decided to fold. Perhaps I will retire to a small ranch and raise chickens with some unfortunate maid who I beguile into marrying me."

Kepir's smile soothed his friend's guilt. Orus replied, "You shall have an estate wherever you choose, my friend—and any maid who chooses you, chooses wisely. Let us finish this once and for all. I think the Dwarves may be hunkered down under their mountain. That is the Dwarfish way when the going gets tough, it seems."

The remaining armies of Hodan, Degran, and Vynwratha marched with a purpose to a location just out of the reach of Todani siege weapons. Orus received reports from other specialists in the field that his navy was now just outside the ruined Port of Wargyrnim. The Todani on the shores hunkered down in makeshift defensive positions, as three warships opened their gun ports and began pounding the immediate shoreline and surrounding buildings within range of the guns. When the large guns were deployed, the ships were effective to over a mile inland. The Hodan ships began to spread terror within Haeldrun Ir. The Todani Navy sought to intervene, but as another ship splintered due to Thunder Ballista fire, the rest backed off, retreating westward and out of range. The bombardment was a staggered affair. The three ships' Captains ensured that explosive shot rained down on the port at a rate of one or two per minute. This lasted for hours, then two of the ships anchored, while one sailed conspicuously, patrolling the area and covering the wall of gunships from enemy advances.

Orus rolled the scroll and nodded to the saluting specialist. He handed the missive back to the young man.

"Take this down, boy, and run it to Commander Uilam. Set the shield wall lines and keep the cavalry back on the flanks for the time being. Archers to the rear, but ready. Do not advance until given the order, unless the enemy attacks directly. Do NOT move into siege weapons range."

Orus watched as the young man scrawled down his words. The King nodded, and the messenger sprinted off to where he knew the command tent was. Sighing, the old King watched as the boy disappeared from view and into the crowd of warriors, organizing into ranks to form a front.

"Send a message to the Todani, Kepir. Tell them to yield or face us. Threaten them with Dragons," Orus said gravely. "Tell them the ships will not stop pounding their shoreline until they surrender. Assure them that they will receive fair treatment, unlike what our men are subjected to."

"But, Sire, you do realize that they will never give up," Kepir said as a matter of fact.

"Be that as it may, my God requires that we give them an option. He will not tolerate us wiping them off of the Ert or Rynn. They will be allowed to remain as a part of Likedelir's notion of balance, but they won't do it here if I have anything to say about it!" Orus shrugged, shaking his head.

"It shall be done, Sire," Kepir said, bowing his head.

"Let's hope for a rational leader in Haeldrun Ir, my friend," Orus scoffed. "We can hope."

* * *

Sulfga was at his wit's end. The people were up in arms over the enemies at the gate. The common folk were terrified by fire from the seas. They cried out for someone to deliver them from the death that rained down from the black ships that appeared to be friendly vessels. On top of the already untenable conditions from refugees and the threats of invasion, rumors of Dragons circulated like wildfire through the already rattled Todani civilians. The fear, anger, and desperation of the masses were the perfect stage for Vyqua's message.

A shining white figure of stunning beauty walked among the chaos of violence, starvation, disease, and death. Calmly, the messenger passed through it all. Many thought her to be Haya in the flesh or her avatar, but it was quickly determined by closer examination that she was neither. She was simply a Todani woman, who had turned from the Underlord and accepted deliverance by a new, unknown deity, she called, Likedelir.

Many were outraged by her outward evangelizing to the suffering followers of Haeldrun. They charged to where the Princess stood, surrounded by hundreds of followers who behaved similarly as she. The acolytes tried to restrain the mobs of attackers, but some eventually broke through to their target, the new Prophetess. Things did not go as they planned. Each who laid their hands upon the iridescent figure, intending her harm, fell screaming where they stood. The glowing herald of the new god did not raise a hand to defend herself. This display of her power and the favor granted by this new God terrified the already frightened masses further.

Vyqua set up shop in the open plazas where the farmer's markets usually stood. She was surrounded by thousands of Todani looking for answers. She spoke to them with compassion and understanding, telling her story. She offered the suffering the same deal that she had been given by her God, just a couple of weeks prior. Many scoffed, cursed the former Princess, walking away to their homes in disbelief, but many more did not. Vyqua's following became a throng of thousands overnight.

Within a week, it seemed that the vast majority of the population had converted. Sulfga hunkered down, holding his head in his hands. He wondered how it had come to this. There was no escape from the issues that surrounded him.

A porter entered the chambers. "Sire," he said officially, "a messenger has arrived from Hodan. What shall we do with him?"

"Do not kill him, fools," Sulfga said emphatically. "Treat him with respect and bring him to me. I must weigh our options. To disrespect this communication from a worthy foe at this time would be unwise."

"Yes, Sire," the porter responded, bowing and leaving to fetch the Hodan emissary.

Chapter 21

Hamrick II finally rejoined the field, while Orus awaited the return of his courier. Orus pretended to ignore the Dwarves, as he watched a considerable force marching up to the edge of the area that Hodan occupied. The Hodan King wondered what his short adversaries were up to. He ordered the Degran, Hodan, and Vyn forces to the ready.

Despite the new threat to his left flank, the Hodan King was more concerned with the fact that the delivery of his demands to the Todani nation was taking too long. Orus wrung his hands as he waited. Shortly, there was movement at the main gate of the Todani city. He was relieved to see the lad returning on his steed as the courier departed the Todani walls at full gallop.

Kepir rode up, full trot, to his King.

"He returns. Find out what the Commander of the Toads has to say about my offer," Orus said, snorting.

Kepir smirked. "I am sure he was overjoyed with your generosity, my brother! By the way, the Dwarves have sent a delegation under a white flag out before their legion wall. My intelligence states that the wall is manned by young Dwarfish fools now. It seems the Todani and the Dragon, Scoria, took their measure of flesh from our overconfident former allies."

"It has come to that for Hamrick's boy, eh? Well, we are not that far behind, my friend," the Hodan responded.

"You speak the truth as always, My King. What shall we do about the Dwarves?"

"Fly a white flag for the moment to allay their fears of an engagement. Bring me that messenger and let me see what the Toads say. We will discuss our options with the Dwarves after we figure out what the Toads have decided to do."

Kepir nodded, and a white flag was raised and ridden to the Dwarfish front.

The messenger returned unharmed and reported to Kepir, who brought him to King Orus. The King read the response from Sulfga and thought over his options. The intentions of the Dwarves would weigh heavily on what would happen next.

* * *

Hamrick II was on the field. He had decided to accompany this unit into battle, because of public opinion, but also because it was his last chance to walk back the mayhem that he had created in his furor to avenge his father. The humans were of an honorable sort, the young King reasoned. He often lamented his father's choices when the old man had ruled. His father's ruthless ambitions had driven a wedge between Dornat Al Fer and the entirety of the Rynn. Where the Dwarves were once seen as the saviors of the light from the darkness, they were now reviled by all outside of their mountain.

The Kingdom of Dornat Al Fer was on the verge of failure. Violent protests had erupted over the past few weeks over the deaths of countless loved ones in a seemingly endless war. With the arrival of a black Dragon who single-handedly sent the remaining, seasoned legions on the front to their early graves, the young King knew the tipping point had been reached. Portions of the city were razed by angry mobs. Soldiers refused to engage their populace, sitting down where they were posted. Hamrick had lost control. The palace was threatened. It was surrounded by chanting mobs. He had to do something to right the ship. This was his last chance to end what he had started.

"They have flown a white flag, Sire," the Dwarfish lookout reported.

"Excellent. Thank you. Prepare my steed and notify my advisors to gather their things for the meeting. Alert my personal guard." Hamrick sighed.

"Yes, Sire!" the lookout responded. He left and passed the word.

Within half an hour, Hamrick II was on horseback in his finest armor. His guard was similarly attired. His scribes and advisors flanked the young Dwarfish King in the center of twenty heavily armed soldiers.

Now, they waited for the humans to arrive.

* * *

Orus watched Kepir with Dryna. The two had become very close over the past year. He visited her often, and she never seemed to be too busy to assist him with his ailments and minor injuries. Turning a blind eye, the King smiled.

"Good for you, Kepir," the King muttered.

Orus watched, eyebrows raised, as Dryna finally grabbed Kepir's face out of frustration, passionately kissing him in front of her entire clutch of acolytes. Some of the young girls twittered, while others gasped in shock. The older Galdrissen Priestess shooed them away, scolding them playfully for being too nosy for their own good. It was the first genuine laughter the King had seen in eons, and it came from the most unlikely of places. Shame welled up in his throat, as he remembered calling for the extinction of the Galdrissen on the Ert.

"I am sorry, My God. I am sorry, Puryn. I wish I could take it back, but that day is gone. I can only change what is now, not what used to be." Orus set his jaw. His face became stone. He had made his decision.

The Todani had surrendered, but with conditions. Orus did not know why they gave up without fighting. He only knew he had the papers in his hand. He was skeptical. He knew there was more to this than met the eye, and the Hodan King refused to give them an inch in reparations.

* * *

The Dwarfish King watched as the delegation slowly trotted in formation to where he waited. The scene was similar to his own. A square of formidable guards surrounded a man in blackened armor with a white lion's head on his chest. Although the young Dwarf had never met the man personally, saying that his reputation proceeded him was an understatement. Hamrick, the junior, knew that this was Orus, the Lion, King of Hodan. He was a human who hadn't existed on the Rynn in one-hundred years. Now, it was up to him to negotiate with this Champion and the renewed Degran nation, which had been forged in the crucible of the abuse over decades—abuse his own father refused to address outside of flowery speeches and empty promises. If the roles were reversed, Hamrick doubted he would listen to anything he had to say. Still, he hoped.

Horns announced the arrival of the Hodan. Hamrick smirked slightly at the annoyance shown by the human at the attempted pomp and circumstance. It was refreshing to see a man who was not impressed by shiny baubles and titles. He looked at the human and realized this was what a man of action looked like.

"Greetings, honorable King Orus, of Hodan," a scribe said politely.

"Greetings, honorable Hamrick, son of Hamrick, King of Dornat Al Fer," a Degran scribe replied in turn.

Hamrick began the parlay. "Thank you for coming, Sir."

Orus replied. "I only come to find out what Dornat Al Fer would ask of allies you turned your backs on in our time of need."

The words stung everyone in the Dwarfish delegation. Guards averted their eyes from Orus. This was not lost on the Hodan, who realized that this was not as a proud delegation as he had thought it was, but rather it was a group of shamed Dwarves looking to atone for the wrongs of the past.

Hamrick swallowed hard, but did not dispute the statement. "King Orus, it is true, my father betrayed your people and the Galdrissen at the fortress of Redemption. No one in power within our kingdom had a say in that decision. Father went about things secretly at times, and then justified it when our people were enriched by his treacherous actions."

Orus listened intently. His gaze never wavering from the face of the young Dwarf leader before him. The old Hodan tried to get a read on who the King of Dornat Al Fer truly was. The Hodan was getting a feeling that this leader was not malicious, but perhaps a bit too naïve and proud, leading to his poor decisions concerning the conflicts at hand.

The Dwarfish King paused, collecting his thoughts, and continued. "I formally apologize for the actions of my father and any hostilities between the Dwarfish nation and yours."

Orus was silent, thinking for a moment. The Dwarves had never aided him, except at Vynwratha, back in the beginning. He attributed that to Jaruz and his devotion to the Galdrissen mission. Everything else was done for show after Hamrick, the senior, had relieved the honorable Admiral and relegated him to a frontier fortress, which eventually became Redemption. Orus sipped a bit of mead from a tankard, wiping his beard.

"So, you apologize? That's it?" Orus asked plainly. "Hundreds of dead at Redemption, and you are sorry? Am I supposed to just smile and say it's all water under the bridge now?"

Hamrick bit his lip and breathed deeply, responding to the scathing response. "I was a child when this happened, Orus. My father did these things. Many who serve in my army were children when this happened. I do not wish to fight any longer. The Dwarves demand peace. I wish to give it to them. What say you? Shall it be peace, or shall we kill each other on this field for no other reason, but the pride of those who are already dead?"

Orus grunted. It was a rational response, but did not satisfy him. "What will it take, lad? I will tell you what I will take. I wish the lands from Whaleford inland to the ancient stones where the Degran claim ends. I want the lands that your people stole from the Degran after the last war. We will have the Kingdom of Degran, and all of its territories, in exchange for peace."

Hamrick thought about it, calling over his scribes, who muttered back and forth in Dwarfish while poring over old maps and scrolls. A consensus was quickly reached, and the Dwarfish King took a deep breath facing Orus.

"Orus, King of Hodan, I would capitulate to this demand, but I have one in response."

"Go on. What is it?" Orus goaded.

"The lands have long been in our possession, be it just or not, and now, many Dwarves reside in villages and hamlets within that frontier territory. Will you allow them to remain in your kingdom's territory, or demand that they uproot and leave?" Hamrick stopped speaking, awaiting a response from the Hodan King.

"I have no quarrel with the common Dwarf, King of Dornat Al Fer, and many came to Whaleford after the last debacle between our two kingdoms. I will assure you that no Dwarf will be harmed or displaced from the lands they occupy. All nobility, landed or not, will be required to relinquish their claims to the lands within Degran-Eras. They will be afforded the option to leave and return to Dornat Al Fer or to remain, but on a private farmstead like all the rest. They will not have servants who pay them taxes. That will be the domain of Degran-Eras. Anyone violating that trust will meet their end by the sword." Orus rested his demands there.

"Then it is settled, honorable King. Your territories are returned by royal decree of Dornat Al Fer, in exchange for peace between our peoples. I will send riders out into the lands to make the proclamations."

The scribes wrote up the documents, and the signatures were made. Orus rode close to the King of the Dwarves and looked him in the eye.

Extending his hand, he said, "I have trusted the Dwarves before and been sorely disappointed. I will trust you and expect more. If you betray me, the next step will not be as pleasant as a cordial conversation. Do I make myself clear?"

Hamrick nodded solemnly. "I hear your words, Orus, of Hodan, and I know that there is weight behind them. I am not my father. I am just a young fool with delusions of grandeur, brought on by inexperience and propaganda. We were the Dwarves; after all we had accomplished, how could we ever lose?"

"I have heard of other Kings in lands far away from this place who have said the same things and not lived to change their minds. Perhaps you are not as foolish as you think, son. Let us try to be better men, shall we?"

"We shall, friend, we shall," Hamrick responded.

"Well, what shall we do with our unwanted neighbors to the west, Hamrick?" Orus smiled deviously.

"What do you have in mind, Orus?" the Dwarf responded.

"Well, they are still holding out with one army on their gates, but what if you were to show up and bang your shields a bit on the left flank?"

Hamrick nodded. "I think that we can manage that, friend."

Orus and Hamrick II looked up at the gates of Haeldrun Ir with conviction.

* * *

The news of the unexpected alliance was not received well within the capitol of Haeldrun Ir. The population was already on edge, and outright panic had now ensued. Sulfga was barely holding onto control of the military, and that was the only reason the mobs had not rushed his throne room and thrown him out of the gates so the enemy could have him. Hodan, Degran-Eras, Vynwratha, and now the despised Dwarves stood on the field outside the gates. Siege engines began pounding the gates and the fortified positions outside of them. The ships that had been silent for several days again began bombarding the shoreline and nearby neighborhoods.

Vyqua and her new congregation had grown to critical mass. The vast majority of the common Todani nation had converted. Tens of thousands knelt where they were and prayed to their god in a cacophony of pleas for peace. The remaining adherents to the Underlord had dwindled to a few thousand souls, where before the war, their numbers were near a million. So many men, women, and children—warrior and civilian—had died in the conflict against four enemies that only a remnant remained. Men, women, and children cowered underground in the filthy tunnels that served as drainpipes for the city. The situation was dire, and every time a Galdrissen reached out to assist a Todani, more came to Likedelir.

Sulfga knew that all was lost. There were not enough Todani left to fight. There was no way to defend against this army. There was only one way for the Todani to survive. They needed to depart from the Rynn.

His conclusions were further solidified with the cries of another messenger. He screeched a new warning. The enemy was now surrounded by Dragons. Sulfga rubbed his eyes and looked around in disbelief.

"Scribe, pen this and send it to King Orus, of Hodan, immediately," Sulfga ordered.

The Todani nodded and took down everything his King spoke.

* * *

"Where did they come from!" Orus bellowed, gesturing toward the gaggle of young Dragons who flew in the skies above him. "I promised Henargya that I would protect her line, not get them all killed fighting Toads!"

Dryna was handing a pouch full of field rations to Kepir. She no longer hid her intentions. Kepir reciprocated.

The High Priestess responded, "Orus, have you ever tried to tell a Dragon what to do?"

"I tried, Dryna!" Orus said. "They do not care to listen to anyone!"

"Sire, the gates open!" Kepir declared, pointing at the city walls. "A rider approaches under a white flag!"

"Stand ready, gents. Here comes an adjusted proposal, I am sure," Orus gloated.

A leopard-spotted Dragon crashed unceremoniously beside the Hodan King. Smudge was changing color.

"Orus!" the young Dragon roared, "Friend! Todani ... NOT friend!"

Aura lighted down gingerly behind her brother. "Let's wait, brother. Do not be hasty."

* * *

The rider arrived at the Hodan lines and was immediately taken prisoner. He was searched and, once it was determined he was not a threat, released to address King Orus, who was now off of his horse. The King still towered over the more diminutive Todani warrior.

"What does Haeldrun Ir wish to say, messenger?" Orus demanded.

The messenger gulped as Smudge sniffed him furiously. Shaking, he handed a scroll case to the King. Kepir grabbed it quickly, giving it to a mage who inspected the case thoroughly. There were no magic traps or spells upon the device. Kepir then checked it for mechanical traps and poison needles, finding none.

"It is safe, Your Majesty. You can't be too careful with this demon spawn." Kepir stared menacingly at the Todani warrior, who looked as if he wanted to disappear.

Smudge leaned forward, sniffing the Todani even more fervently. The messenger could smell the breath of the lizard. It smelled of carrion and death.

Orus opened the scroll case. It read:

Great Warrior of the Degran,

I am Sulfga, former General of the glorious Kingdom of Haeldrun Ir. I have overthrown our treacherous former master, King Lyax, who led us to this folly with our neighbors to the south. We are unsure of who poisoned the King of the Dwarves, but be assured that it was not by my orders, nor by order of anyone who is alive to speak of it today. My kingdom suffers disease and famine, due to war with the entire continent. We only ask one thing in exchange for surrender—to live.

I, Sulfga, King of the Todani, wish to take my remnant and board our remaining ships, never to return to this place without consent. We only need water and provisions enough to get us out to sea. From there, we will find a new home, preferably where no one else resides.

It may not seem as if my words are truthful, great warrior of the Hodan hordes, but if I am unsuccessful in my negotiation, I fear that my people will cease to exist in the world. Our god has forsaken his people once again, and the traitors grow daily among my people.

With all humility, I ask that you consider my request.

Sincerely,

Sulfga, Rex

"Let's march in there with a delegation of Hodan and Degran to inspect the situation. We go in strong and show no mercy. We must ensure they do not perceive us as soft or compassionate, or they will use that to sway us." Orus rubbed his chin hair.

"Orus, I must go also!" Dryna demanded.

"No, that is out of the question, woman!" Orus chastised.

"There are more traitors daily?" Ma 'Dryna was not backing down. "Those traitors are MY people, Orus! This is not a request! I WILL be going."

Dryna ran off, grabbed her basic necessities and a couple of acolytes to assist her.

"Oh now, be reasonable, Dryna, them also?" Orus asked in exasperation, pointing at the girls.

"Yes, those two also."

"Orus, remember that she IS the High Priestess. It never went well for those who opposed the last High Priestess who I met back in Yslandeth. This one talks with Dragons, not trees!" Kepir smiled and then chuckled.

"Well, I just hope our god is watching over us, because a military mission is becoming a sight-seeing tour with security issues everywhere! You two," Orus pointed at Dryna's girls, "you will stay glued to your Mistress, understood?"

The two girls nodded meekly.

"And you, High Priestess, will stay with Master Kepir at all times. No arguments!" Orus demanded.

Dryna smiled. "Oh, how will I bear the strain of being accompanied by Kepir!?"

Orus squinted at Dryna with frustration and then shook his head, looking with concern at the young ones with her.

"Let's go. Let's get this over with. The Dwarves are staying put as a show of force. First legion, with Uilam in command. Let us make a show for our adversaries."

There was a screech from behind Orus. "Go!" Smudge roared. "Go see Todani!"

Orus looked up at the young Dragon, who had seemed to have grown three feet in a week.

"No eating them, Smudge!" Orus said like a father. "We must talk first. If they fight, then you can eat them!"

Smudge's eyes widened. He purred with excitement.

* * *

The Todani guards could see one thousand Hodan and Degran approaching the gates. There was no question about their intentions as the second rank of the legion all flew white linen napkins from their pikes. The shield wall moved as one. It moved as if it were a well-oiled, Dwarfish machine. Following closely from the rear of the procession was a small, well-dressed group, consisting of guards, scribes, clerics, and a few who appeared to be mages of some proficiency. In the center of it all was an imposing figure on a large white warhorse, wearing jet-black armor with a bright white lion's head in the center of the breastplate. All who witnessed the approach knew that this was Orus, of Hodan.

Bells were being rung and horns blown as the Todani army began to flee, abandoning their posts sporadically as the Dragons began to join the procession, flying high and perching atop the towers and palace spires. The Todani hid, cowering in the sewers, praying to the silent Haeldrun for deliverance, but awaiting death. Sulfga and his cohort were in the central courtyard out in front of the castle, awaiting the Hodan to arrive.

Sulfga saw the enemy procession entering the gates and sighed, wondering how he had failed so badly that his God had forsaken him. He bowed his head as a tear rolled down his cheeks from both eyes. He wiped them away angrily and took a deep breath, regaining his resolve.

Orus arrived. He dismounted, as did his adversary. The Todani General loosed his sword belt, removing the scabbard from his waist. He held his sword up horizontally, handing it to Orus. Orus looked on in disbelief, and then realized that it was true. Taking the sword from the Todani King, Orus gave it to Kepir.

"I relinquish my sword as a symbol of our surrender. I only hope you have found the mercy necessary to allow my people life." Sulfga bowed respectfully, which surprised the Hodan King.

"How will you remove all of the Todani from this city, when there were millions here once by accounts of my allies?" Orus asked, walking with the Todani to the open square.

Dryna screamed as they rounded the corner, her hands over her mouth at what she saw. There, around a captivating Galdrissen woman in white robes were tens of thousands of Galdrissen crammed into the commons.

"Orus—are there any Todani left to let escape?" the High Priestess asked in shock.

"I do not know," Orus said with a similar tone.

"When things became untenable, a god appeared to the one in the middle of the crowd. Her name is Vyqua. She is the daughter of Lyax. She had him killed and then, somewhere along the line, repented and found favor with a God named Likedelir. The downtrodden became disillusioned with Haeldrun's apparent disregard or disfavor. They turned to this new God.

He heard them. Here they are." Sulfga gestured all around him. The Galdrissen filled every corner of the city.

"Where are the Todani?" Orus asked, his eyes never leaving the one called Vyqua. Orus was stunned.

The white-robed woman's beauty was unmatched in all the world of the living. Dryna suspected that this was by her God's design. He had a purpose in everything. The Priestess giggled at the Hodan King's expression.

"They have hidden underground, King Orus, to avoid the bombardment from the sea," Sulfga responded.

The delegation of Todani and Degran traveled through the crowd of Galdrissen converts to where the culverts and drainpipes opened up. There, inside the filth and darkness, were men, women, and children, hiding. The faces of the young ones frowned. Tears streamed down their faces, as they clutched at hissing mothers who were armed with nothing more than stones. Orus was sickened as he remembered a time, many years ago, when he and his daughter lived in a muddy hole, not unlike the tunnel before him. They had eaten the grass of the field and whatever could be found until he killed his King, Jabir, of Hodan, in single combat. Then, as King, he too found peace with his enemy, Puryn, of Erynseere, the Champion of the Golden Queen. Orus knew that Puryn could have run over his people with his Draj, decimating that entire remaining beaten tribe without as much as breaking a sweat, but the Yslan warrior instead had compassion and made an ally that day.

Now, the Todani would never be allied with those of the light—if they tended to think that way, their runes changed, and they became something new! But Orus could not allow the slaughter of these young ones who begged for their lives over a war that none of them had any hand in causing. He looked over at Sulfga.

"How do you propose to get these people out of the city, Toad?" Orus asked gruffly.

"We have ships. We will load them and leave. To where? Only the Gods know. We shall find a home or die trying," Sulfga responded.

"There must be almost ten-thousand souls here, maybe more? My spies tell me that you have, but four or five ships total?" Orus said, scoffing in disbelief.

"Not true, Hodan," Sulfga replied. "We rotate them in and out from far to the north. We have fifteen ships left of fifty. We only showed you five in an attempt to rebuild our naval forces while your four ships terrorized the seas with that weapon of yours!" Sulfga was impressed by the Thunder Ballista and sounded envious.

"Hmm, so, you will just load up these people on your ships, with provisions and leave of your own free will?" Orus asked with suspicion.

"Truly, Orus, we have no choice at this point. We would choose to stay here in our homes, but that is impossible, given this current situation. At this point in our history, I would just choose for us to survive the ordeal and live to build another day." Sulfga stood awaiting a response.

"Bring in your ships. Get these people out of my lands. Tell them if they remain as hostiles, I will have them put to the sword without regret. If they leave, they will be allowed to live. Take the provisions you require. How long will it take for you to make the arrangements?"

"We can gather the supplies within a week while the ships come in from the north. We can be loaded within two or three days. Ten days, maybe twelve?" Sulfga offered hopefully.

"You have ten. Make it happen, Toad. Do not try my patience," Orus said, walking back to Kepir and passing the news.

Sulfga thanked the Gods silently and called to a nearby sentry. "Call the ships in. Have them moor as close to the shoreline as they can. Pass the word of safe passage to the remnant. Have them gather on the northern shores with only the essentials. We shall board them using the oar boats to transport the people and supplies. Have those who are able gather all the supplies that are available, for we know not how long the journey will be."

"Yes, Sire!" the young Todani replied, showing the first bit of hope that Sulfga had seen in months.

"Beware, Sulfga," Dryna chided. "You may find your runes the wrong color if you are not careful."

The King looked away and pretended not to hear.

* * *

High Priestess Ma 'Dryna made her way through the throngs of new converts. She was overwhelmed. She walked, unimpeded by those around her, who seemed by instinct to know who she was. Many bowed and recoiled from the Galdrissen healer in fear.

Calling out in a voice too large for her frame, Dryna declared, "Hear me now, my people! You have nothing to fear from me! We are a family now! We will work to better our station in this world! We will be blessed in our endeavors by Likedelir, if we keep our ways righteous in his sight!"

A loud cheer erupted in the square. The Todani looked at the mob of gold and silver-runed people. They shook at the roar of the people they had once persecuted and reviled, but their fears were for naught as the converts took to gathering the stores for the journey ahead of the Todani. Hundreds of Galdrissen carried supplies to where the Todani had gathered to board the ships to freedom.

Vyqua chuckled as the gesture increased her flock even more, with several hundred more becoming Redeemed as they watched the scene unfolding before them. Many of the Todani were afraid, thinking that Vyqua had some power to turn them into something else, and they hid from her gaze.

Returning to the commons after a day of loading supplies and Todani on ships, Vyqua and her inner circle sat and broke bread. Dryna watched with interest as she witnessed the Prophet of her god pray over the food and smile, eating with the rest of her brothers and sisters. They didn't have much, but what they had, they shared freely. Swallowing hard, Dryna remembered the Port of the Redeemed and her first love, Jaruz.

"He would be proud of us," Dryna said to no one.

The Priestess walked to where the beautiful young leader sat. The Prophet stood, bowing, and then knelt before the Priestess.

"Never kneel to me, young one," Dryna rebuked softly. "I am but a tool for his use as you are. We are partners, you and me. Look at what you have accomplished!"

Standing, Vyqua responded, "You all have endured such hardships. How is it that you have come this far?"

"It is because of our god and his Champion, Orus. The man on that horse, looking over here, in fact," Dryna said with amusement evident on her face. "It seems we have caught his attention, young lady. I should introduce you."

Vyqua seemed uncomfortable. Dryna picked up on it immediately. She smiled. "He does not bite. At least I do not think so, but he is Hodan, so there may be times when that is appropriate!"

Vyqua nodded nervously as the duo and many of the Prophet's inner circle approached the King, who sat in the saddle, looking away as if surveying the scene before him. Vyqua was self-consciously preening herself. It was not lost by Dryna, who could barely contain her snicker.

"Orus, I am here to report that we have over fifty-thousand Galdrissen living within these walls, and it's almost all this girl's fault." Dryna stifled a snort.

Orus looked over as if he hadn't noticed the exquisite young Galdrissen lass before him. The saddle-worn warrior cleared his throat and responded, "Is that so, Dryna? That's excellent news."

"Your Majesty," Dryna pretentiously said, "this is Vyqua, Prophetess of the god Likedelir."

"Your Majesty," the Princess said, curtseying nervously.

Orus stammered, which was new to Dryna, who now openly laughed. "Nice, er, wonderful, um, good to meet you, My Lady."

Dryna looked at the two, who were now locked in an awkward stare. Orus was flush, and the runes on the younger Galdrissen woman took on a distinct reddish hue.

Dryna fanned herself. "Is it warm in here?"

Dryna's chuckle broke the spell between Orus and Vyqua. Both turned away in embarrassment at the episode.

"You two should really talk and figure out what *that* just was," Dryna chided playfully.

"Mind yourself, woman," Orus said in embarrassment.

"Mind yourself, old man." Dryna spoke with levity. "Life is too short for games. You haven't taken your eyes off of her since we entered this hole, and she sees you and her runes turn a shade of rouge. It does not take a mage or a scribe to reveal what is going on here!"

The two were silent as the High Priestess merrily chastised them both.

"She likes you, Hodan. Do not be a fool. You do not know how many days you have left upon the green. You may as well smile for once! Come down from that horse and meet the lass."

Dryna was like a Hodan old-maid matchmaker. She would not be denied. Orus relented and stood a foot taller than the Princess. She looked up at the giant before in awe. Dryna snickered.

As the Priestess walked away to leave the two alone, she said, "Orus has that effect on people, Vyqua. Those who have just met him are awed, but if he lets you close, you soon see that he is a soft-heart—that is, once you peel away the layers of armor he has over his soul. I will depart and find my lord, Kepir." Dryna smiled, looking over her shoulder. "And Orus, you oaf, ask the lady what reddened runes mean on a Galdrissen or Todani maiden?"

Dryna looked directly at Vyqua, whose eyes were wide open in embarrassment. Her face was now as blushed as her runes.

"What does that mean, My Lady?" Orus asked without a clue.

Dryna laughed uncontrollably as she walked, hearing Vyqua stumbled with her words to explain.

"Orus, you oaf!" Dryna declared loudly between laughing fits. "It means she *REALLY* likes you."

Orus looked at the Princess with awe. She rivaled the beauty of a Goddess. She could have anyone she chose.

Vyqua sheepishly looked into Orus's eyes again. She swallowed hard and nodded with embarrassment.

Orus replied, "Oh ..."

Chapter 22

Peace was declared with the Todani. As agreed, the Scourge boarded fifteen ships, loaded with as much as they could carry. Sulfga kept his word, and the Todani sailed northward out of sight from land. The Hodan Navy escorted the armada of Todani ships for several days, finally turning away and back for home. The people of Haeldrun were gone from the Rynn and on the high seas, searching for a place to call home. The ordinary people were simply happy to be alive. Some attributed it to Haeldrun hearing their cries, some to Sulfga's shrewd deal-making. The reality of it was that Orus was listening to Likedelir and adhering to his one commandment of balance. Still, the Todani clung to their faith in their God and their King, and ultimately, their way of life.

The Dwarves withdrew from the border with Degran-Eras, focusing their efforts inward to heal the unrest in the Dwarfish Kingdom and to rebuild the infrastructure lost to riots. King Hamrick II honored his agreement with Orus. The lands of the southeast, including the territories that were now considered Ynus-Grag, where the Orcs had settled, were handed over to the Degran. Orus made a point of showing the Dwarfish declaration to his Orcish allies. Then the Hodan King directed his scribes to draft a new treaty on the spot. This newly written agreement officially gave the lands of Ynus-Grag to the people who already lived there. No longer did any kingdom have the right to claim the lands of the Orcs; it was officially theirs. The Orcs celebrated their new alliances and lived in peace within their marshes and sandy beaches. They traded with Whaleford and eventually with Dornat Al Fer and Vynwratha.

The Elves returned to their forests in Edhelseere and to their island of Vynwratha. Lourama reaffirmed the alliance between Elves and humans. The Vyn made peace with the Orcs, but both races were suspicious of the other. Elves and Orcs lived a long time, and memories were just as long. Still, for many years, the warrior Elves minded their own business and traded with anyone who had coin. Lourama visited Degran-Eras and her friends at every opportunity, fostering good relations with generations of Degran leaders, and eventually extending a hand in peace to the Dwarves.

Orus knighted Uilam with the sword of the great Degran hero Neirmynd, the brave. The Hodan King gave the sacred sword to his new baron and granted him the title of First Hero of Degran, because the man was the first to volunteer to fight against the Todani when the need arose. After fifteen years of fighting and killing, the King figured the man had earned his place in the lore of his people. Uilam eventually moved north to the city formerly known as Haeldrun Ir. Orus appointed him baron over the northern territory, charging him with clearing the harbor of sunken ships, as well as rebuilding the glorious infrastructure of the former capital of Degran-Eras. He eventually renamed the city New Hodan, in tribute to his King and the savior of his people. Ega, the mage and acolyte of Ma 'Dryna, joined Uilam on the baronial thrones as his wife. They would live in peace and direct the recovery of New Hodan for the rest of their lives. They lived in peace, and Uilam fathered three sons and one daughter, all of which looked just like their mother.

Kepir and Dryna married shortly after the war. They lived many years together near the Jackrabbit Canyon, north of Whaleford, where Kepir was made a baron of the entire territory. Dryna slowly relinquished her position to Vyqua, and eventually, Likedelir blessed her decision, freeing her to live in peace with her new husband. Pleased, the God blessed the couple with a son and a daughter. The couple lived in harmony for the rest of their lives and prospered in their lands.

Degran-Eras was in disarray. Orus now knew how it felt to stand on the stage in Empyr at the end of the Great War of the Ert. He remembered as Puryn was crowned King of Yslandeth, and his lady, Adasser, became his Queen. Both inherited circumstances worse than he. However, the magnitude of his rebuilding effort was not lost on the new King of Degran-Eras. The capitol was reborn in Whaleford. Orus reasoned that over the fifteen years or so of war, it was the least damaged. In fact, the seaport was fully functional, and the enormous Temple to the Goddess Haya was partially rebuilt. It was now a Temple to the God Likedelir, and it was being rebuilt by the thousands of his new devoted Galdrissen, who had gravitated to where the Prophet of their God had moved. Ironically, a majority of the populace of the barony of Whaleford was now comprised of Galdrissen, who revered Orus and his rule.

Vyqua had only moved to Whaleford for one purpose: Orus. She was smitten by this man. He was everything the Galdrissen in her revered—a powerful man, a renowned warrior, a person who commanded respect and fear, but even more than that, he was the chosen Champion of her God, Likedelir. There was an instant attraction to all he was, but when she saw him in the flesh, it was impossible to deny. She would have him as her mate. That was the Galdrissen way. Dryna explained to Orus that once a Galdrissen had made up her mind, there would be no other. Laughing, the Priestess said she knew Vyqua would have her prize that first awkward day in the conquered Todani capitol. Between the red runes of Vyqua and the stammering of the stolid warrior of Hodan, there was an immediate attraction that neither would be able to deny.

After shaking off the initial shock of the beauty he witnessed in Haeldrun Ir, Orus came to his senses. He smiled as he thought of his new interest. Vyqua was etched, indelibly, in his mind. The more he tried to put her out of his thoughts, the more she invaded them. Finally, admitting defeat, as Dryna had mocked, the King of Degran-Eras actively pursued the Prophetess of his God.

A short courtship ensued, resulting in the King asking her to marry him. From Dryna's account, the girl did not let him finish before she accepted his proposal. The two were married in private by Dryna, who doubled as the maid-of-honor and her husband, Kepir, was the best man. The announcement of the marriage of Vyqua and Orus was received by a kingdom-wide celebration that lasted for weeks. The Galdrissen were in awe that a person of their stock now held the hand of the supreme leader of their land. The downtrodden had been elevated from the gutters to the palace. No longer did the Galdrissen fear being driven from their homes in hate. They were finally accepted by their neighbors.

* * *

"So how are you, you old goat?" a man sitting on a chair asked, appearing out of thin air.

Orus smiled, genuinely happy for the first time in decades. "It is a wonderful day above the green, My Lord! How is it with you?"

Likedelir took a puff from a pipe he lit. "I can't complain, Champion. You have done a wonderful job of restoring the balance to this place."

"Thank you, My God. I am happy that you are pleased," Orus replied, toasting Likedelir and sipping his mead.

"I was wondering about Vyqua, though." Likedelir paused, toying with the Hodan. "You hesitated so much! I thought to myself, what more can I do to make him see?"

Orus chuckled and responded, "It has been said by many, not of Hodan, that we are not known to be philosophers or thinkers!"

"Well, my friend, love her and live long with her. She has proven herself worthy of you in my book, and you of her. Until we meet again, Champion." Likedelir faded away like a ghost.

"Be well, My God. Until we meet again."

* * *

After he was well-established, Orus decided that he needed to know of how the old world had fared without him. He called Captain Kren to his quarters for a discussion on how to make that happen.

"Kren, you have become an integral part of my kingdom, brother," Orus said thoughtfully. "I know that you have not set down roots here as of yet, and I would like to offer you one more mission, if you would take it." The King paused. "I will understand if you decide you do not want to accept."

Kren looked at his King smiling. "Of course, Sire. What is your need?"

"I need you to sail back home. To the Ert. To Hodan," Orus entreated. "I need you to return to Hodan. Find my daughter, Faylea, her husband Kairoth, and my grandson, Orus, the junior. Please, deliver these many missives that I have scratched down throughout all of these years. Let her know that I still live and that I love her very much. Tell her that I have married Vyqua. Tell her that my new wife is not a replacement, but a new chapter in my life. I will always treasure her mother's memory to the end of my days. Let her know that I am happy for the first time in forever. She needs to know, and I need to know that she lives happily also."

Orus seemed to be pleading with his man, and Kren felt uncomfortable with that.

"Sire," the Captain said, placing his hand on his King's shoulder. "I will go. She will know all these things, and I will tell the Ert of your exploits. You will be revered there, as much as you are here. They will know you live and prosper."

"Will you also take these missives north to Yslandeth? I have much to apologize for." Orus frowned, remembering how he had left the Ert and his brother, Puryn behind. "My brother needs to know that I understand what he was trying to tell me all those years ago. He was right. Tell him that I married a Galdrissen woman. He will not believe you, most likely."

"I will do these things as you command, Sire. If the Gods will it, I will return in time to report back to you with what I discover!" Kren seemed genuinely excited about this mission.

"Take a ship, a crew, and a security force. Get the charts from our scribes. Load with provisions for a long voyage—I know that you remember that trip as well as I do! Load the Thunder Ballista stores also. I will have my treasury load two tons of gold to pay the men with and to establish your life wherever you decide to live it, here or there. I remember when you saved my skin against the Todani all those years ago. Go, and make your preparations! I look forward to your return ... someday!?"

"I will return, My King. I will establish trade routes. We will trade with Suden! They like black ships!" Kren and Orus chuckled at the dark humor.

"Oh! That reminds me! Make sure you use my sails, Kren! If the shore defenses think you are a Todani ship, it will not be a good day for you!"

Orus smiled and shook Kren's hand. The Captain left and prepared to go home.

* * *

Kren returned to the Ert, narrowly avoiding a shooting incident off of the coast of Sudenyag. A Dwarfish survivor of the Great War saw the great black ship and panicked, calling for his Officer of the Day. Thankfully, the standard of Hodan was prominently displayed on the sails, and the call to stand down was passed by signal fires along the coast.

The Hodan ship docked at the Port of Valent. There, the local leadership greeted Captain Kren, and the Hodan sailor did as he had told his King he would. In every corner of the realm, the man told stories of the prowess of Hodan and specifically of Orus, informing the Ert that Orus was now King of a new land that the Hodan had conquered.

Stories in Sudenyag traveled like wildfire to every camp and village far and wide.

Hodan had conquered a new kingdom. Orus was King of a land called Degran-Eras. The most shocking to the average person was that Orus, of Hodan, had married a Galdrissen woman. After all of his protesting and hatred for the Redeemed, they were astonished at his change of heart.

Within a week, Kren's caravans, escorted by Hodan and Degran warriors, reached the border of Hodan. As they entered the nation, they were challenged by the local militia, and it was established that Kren was telling the truth when he claimed to be a Hodan Elite. Papers with the seal of Hodan and the signet of King Orus were produced to the magistrate, who cleared the caravan and allowed them to pass without incident.

Kren delivered a crate of missives to Queen Faylea and King Kairoth. The Prince was nearing his sixteenth birthday when the Captain arrived. Young Orus was in awe of his namesake. His grandfather was indeed a hero of old.

After Kren left, Faylea spent days reading all of the letters that her father had written her while he was away. She read of his adventures on the seas, some comical and others terrifying. The Hodan Queen read of the initial encounters with the Elves and Dwarves at the Port of the Redeemed and chuckled at the realization that all of the fighting parties eventually ended up as friends and allies. She marveled at the oil paintings and sketches done by artists. Her favorite image was one of Orus with Vyqua on their wedding day. She could feel the happiness in his face from the picture. It did her heart well to know that her father was finally not alone.

Many times, along the journey through the letters, the Queen could be heard, "Just like you, Da!" while sniffling and wiping tears.

When she finally finished reading all there was, she wrote back and had oil paintings of the family created by the finest Hodan artists. She cut a bit of her hair, her son's hair, and even Kairoth's, putting the samples in wax-sealed containers with their names upon the cases. She included a large clay pot full of Hodan soil so her father could touch his homeland once more. Packaging it all in a fine, water-tight box, the Queen had it delivered directly to Kren, who had returned to Suden, after dropping off his delivery in Yslandeth.

* * *

Puryn and Adasser marveled at Kren's reports. The King of Yslandeth smiled, genuinely happy to hear that his brother had survived his adventures and established his new kingdom in a foreign land. Adasser raised her eyebrows in disbelief at the news about his marriage to Vyqua, but then smiled at the Hodan's change of heart.

"Orus was gruff and could be stubborn, but he was always on the right side of the light," she reasoned with her husband.

Puryn pored over the correspondence and intelligence that Orus had sent him. He rolled out a table-sized map of the Rynn, with a detailed key that described the political landscape and potential trade partners as outlined by Kren.

After much contemplation, the King of Yslandeth decided he would commission ten ships to trade with this new faraway land. He wrote a missive in return to his brother on the Rynn.

It read:

Warm greetings from Yslan!

It is so good to know that you still tread upon the green, my dear brother, Orus! I am overjoyed to know of your station in your new lands. Your man, Kren, speaks of your legends. Your lore will rival that of Yslan, Torith, and Hodan combined!

As for your apology, my best friend, do not consider our disagreement as a reason to apologize. I understood your thinking and motivations, and had my misgivings also. I simply went with the faith in Haya's judgment and left it at that. I often worried that I had made an error, but the Galdruhn never gave me cause to doubt them. As with you, they grew on me, and soon they were dear friends.

I congratulate you on your marriage to your lovely new bride, Vyqua. It seems that our Gods and Goddesses have a sense of humor. They must wish to keep a close eye on us! They have paired us both with High Priestesses of our order! Even your daughter is married to a High Priest! This is a family tradition, and rest assured, my brother, you are still considered my family until my death—and even after.

I will send this missive and with a shipment of good old Hodan whisky to you when your man returns. I will also send you some Yslan whisky to wash that

Hodan dishwater out of your mouth.

If you want to come back to avenge the honor of your whisky, you know where I am. Our contest stands five fights to five! We have not decided who is the greatest warrior to date! Come look for me, if you ever decide to visit!

With all seriousness, my dear brother, may the Goddess bless you, your loved ones, your nation, your allies, and all that you hold dear. May your God do the same. May Hodan, Degran, and the Galdrissen prosper to the end of all things.

I love you, my brother, and if you need to hear it for some reason, I forgive you. If we do not meet again in this life, I will sit with you in Aeternum at the feast.

Until your next missive,

Puryn, your brother always.

* * *

Many months passed. Orus lived in peace with Vyqua. She bore him a son who he named Jux, after the third oldest brother of the Queen. Jux had stood between King Lyax and Princess Vyqua on many occasions, and ultimately paid for it with his life.

On one particular morning, a porter appeared at the King's door.

"Sire," the man deadpanned, "a Captain Kren comes bearing gifts, My King."

Orus jumped up from his seat and looked into the harbor. There was a black ship with his standard moored there.

Smiling like a boy at Winterfest, the King boomed, "Show him in, man!"

Kren entered the room and saluted his King, who abruptly hugged the man, almost tackling him. On a cart beside him, Kren had two waterproofed crates. Beside those was a small cask of Hodan whisky and a box with six bottles of the Yslan fare.

"Welcome home, my friend," Orus said, smiling widely.

"Good to be back, Sire. Have I got some things to show you!"

The Captain handed the two small crates marked private. One was sealed with the signet of Faylea, of Hodan, the other with the signet of Puryn of Yslandeth.

"I will afford you some privacy, Sire."

"Thank you for this, Kren."

Kren smiled and departed the throne room.

Orus cracked open the box sealed by Faylea first. Vyqua was introduced to her stepdaughter, one letter and painting at a time. The Queen held her King many times as he read the letters to her. Through every page and all of the tears, her man had never stopped smiling.

About the Author

Austin Belanger is married to his wife Karen and father to four excellent young men. He has also been blessed with ten beautiful grandchildren, two of whom have gone to heaven before him. Austin retired from the United States Marine Corps in 2005 and began a career in Information Technology.

Austin is a writer of many things. A published poet and member of several online writing communities, Austin published his first novel, "The Champion of the Golden Queen," in 2018 and followed it up with the sequel, "In the Shadow of the Great White Wall," in 2019.

His third novel, "The Long Run to Redemption," is the third in a series of medieval fantasy novels collectively called "The Tales of the Ert."

Also by Austin S. Belanger

The Champion of the Golden Queen

The Universe is void. Reality exists only in the perfect embrace of the light and the dark.

Haya and Haeldrun had the perfect arrangement. She was the goddess of light, and he, the god of darkness. Both were joined in an eternity of peace and bliss. How the chaos began is unknown to all that lives, but some wise men say that it was the egos of the first two gods, others blame blind chance.

Unexpectedly, the first couple was blessed with their three children. Their two sons, they named, Runnir and Gunnir, the sons of war and thunder, and their daughter they called Aluia, the goddess of peace and the waters. As their names portray them, the brothers warred with each other for the approval and attention of their parents. They were inseparable twins, but always at odds with each other. One of their many fights accidentally brought about the creation of the worlds of the Universe and the tears of their sister Aluia fertilized the first gardens when life began anew.

Haya was intrigued by this development and saw endless possibilities; Haeldrun was annoyed with his wife's distractions. Soon a rift began between the two original lovers that saw a goddess choose her new reality and a god skulk off to the darkness to create one of his own.

Now both sides strive to maintain the upper hand over the other. The goddess continues to try to reconcile with her love and preserve the light and life, but Haeldrun refuses to back down on his demands. He commands that his wife snuff out all of her other interests and return her attention to him alone to prove her love and fidelity.

So, Haya schemes to win back her betrothed while striving to maintain the life she loves, and The Underlord schemes to create a darkness so black that it will shut out all of her light and destroy all that lives.

Puryn, the newborn son of humble beginnings has no idea what his goddess has planned for him. The world known as the Ert has endured many dark, murderous days before his birth. Heroes of humankind and the elder races have defeated all challenges to the light before now, but never the Ert beheld a force of destruction such as the one that Haeldrun has conjured and planned over thousands of years.

This tome is the lore of Puryn, son of Durn and of those unsung heroes who stood together against the darkest moment in the history of a world known to all who live upon it as The Ert.

The Champion of the Golden Queen is the first book in a series entitled, "Tales of the Ert."

In the Shadow of the Great White Wall

The Goddess has won her battle, but her love, the Dark Lord, continues in his struggle for dominion. Puryn wrestles with gaining control of his ravaged and lawless lands. New smaller wars simmer in all locales around his borders as vile pretenders rise with claims of title and rights to foreign thrones. Civil war and strife threaten to derail the fragile peace of neighboring kingdoms. Evil seemingly survives and pushes to bring their Lord to the Ert to exact his revenge.

A new band of heroes is called to action as the new generation takes up the mantle of their elders. Theirs is the task of bringing the King's vision to pass. The teams are young, but they are the best that Yslan has to offer. A tenuous future rests in the hands of the unproven few.

"The Ert was a smoky, charred mess of disorder, chaos, and violence, and despite the gilded words of a victor's Scribes and Heralds, real people suffered in those first few years after the great reckoning of the Goddess. The official truth is always skewed, and seldom bears a resemblance to the reality of what happened. Humankind is known to tell a good tale when the drink is good, or the lady listening is fair, or when the truth is too ugly to remember. Many times, a scribe takes poetic license with the events of man, washing facts with cleansing waters of prose and legend. More often than not, fairy-tales are not written for the children of men, but instead for adults seeking comfort in better memories of their past deeds. These prettier versions of the truth soothe the guilt of many past indiscretions. This tale is not one of those stories. This account is of what happened next."
—The Ancient Tome of Lore